Angela lives in the heart of the Black Country with her partner, their bouncy Retriever and their potty-mouthed parrot. It has taken many novels to find that one character who just refused to go away. And so D.I. Kim Stone was born. The D.I. Kim Stone series has now sold over 4.5 million copies worldwide and been translated into twenty-eight different languages.

# ALSO BY ANGELA MARSONS

### DETECTIVE KIM STONE SERIES PREQUEL
*First Blood*

### DETECTIVE KIM STONE SERIES
*Silent Scream*
*Evil Games*
*Lost Girls*
*Play Dead*
*Blood Lines*
*Dead Souls*
*Broken Bones*
*Dying Truth*
*Fatal Promise*
*Dead Memories*
*Child's Play*
*Killing Mind*
*Deadly Cry*
*Twisted Lies*

### OTHER BOOKS
*Dear Mother* (previously published as *The Middle Child*)
*The Forgotten Woman* (previously published as *My Name Is*)

# Angela
# MARSONS

A D.I. Kim Stone NOVEL

# DYING
# TRUTH

sphere

SPHERE

First published in 2018 by Bookouture, an imprint of Storyfire Ltd.
This paperback edition published in 2021 by Sphere

1 3 5 7 9 10 8 6 4 2

A CIP catalogue record for this book
is available from the British Library.

ISBN 978-0-7515-7490-6

Printed and bound in Great Britain by
Clays Ltd, Elcograf S.p.A.

Papers used by Sphere are from well-managed forests
and other responsible sources.

MIX
Paper from
responsible sources
FSC® C104740

Sphere
An imprint of
Little, Brown Book Group
Carmelite House
50 Victoria Embankment
London EC4Y 0DZ

An Hachette UK Company

www.hachette.co.uk
www.littlebrown.co.uk

*This book is dedicated to all the victims of the Grenfell Tower tragedy. May this never be allowed to happen again.*

# PROLOGUE

## Saturday 7.52 p.m.

Kim knew that her left leg was broken.

She pulled herself along the path on her hands as the stone bit into her palms, shards of gravel embedding beneath her fingernails.

A cry escaped her lips as her ankle turned and pain shot around her body.

Sweat beads were forming on her forehead as the agony intensified.

Finally, she saw the light from the building as three familiar shapes hurtled out of the doorway.

All three of them headed towards the bell tower.

'Nooo…' she cried, as loudly as she could.

No one turned.

*Don't go up there*, she willed silently, trying to pull herself towards them.

'Stop,' she shouted out as they entered the metal doorway at the base of the tower.

Kim tried to still the panic as they disappeared from view.

'Damn it,' she screamed with frustration, unable to reach them in time.

She gathered all her strength and pushed herself up to a standing position, trying to drag her broken leg behind her as though it didn't exist.

Two steps forward and the pain radiated through her body like a tidal wave and brought her back down to the ground. She gagged as the nausea rose from her stomach and her head began to swim.

She shouted again but the figures had disappeared from view and were now in the belly of the tower, behind solid brick, mounting the stone steps to the top.

'Please, someone help,' she screamed, but there was no one to hear. She was a good eighty metres away from the school, and she had never felt so helpless in her life.

She glanced at her wrist and saw that it was three minutes to eight.

The bell was due to be rung bang on the hour.

The fear started in the pit of her stomach and grew like a cloud to fill her entire body.

She struggled forward another agonising step, dragging her useless leg behind her.

Torchlight illuminated the top of the tower.

*Damn it, they were already there.*

'Stop,' she cried again, praying that one of them would hear her even though she knew her voice wouldn't carry that distance.

The shafts of light moved furtively around the tower balcony ninety feet up in the air.

She saw a fourth figure amongst the three that were familiar to her.

The watch on her wrist vibrated the top of the hour. The bell didn't ring.

*Please God, let them get down.*

Her prayer was cut off as she heard a loud scream.

Two people were hanging from the bell rope, swinging back and forth, in and out of the torchlight that darted around the small space.

Kim squinted, trying to identify the two silhouettes, but they were too far away.

She tried to regulate her breathing in order to shout again, even though she knew no kind of warning would help them now.

Her worst fears had been realised.

'Please, please…' Kim whispered as she saw the bell rope swing back and forth once more.

One figure was snatched from the bell rope as the second continued to swing.

'No,' Kim screamed, trying to carry herself forward towards them.

The fear inside had turned ice cold, freezing her solid.

For a few seconds time stood still. The saliva in her mouth had gone leaving her unable to speak or shout.

Kim felt the ache that started in her heart when the remaining figure and the swinging bell rope disappeared from view.

Her ears suddenly filled with a blood-curdling, tortured scream.

But no one else was around.

The scream came from her.

# CHAPTER 1

## Six days earlier

Sadie Winters ducked around the side of the kitchen entrance, dropped her backpack to the ground and took the single cigarette from her jacket pocket. Once used as the servants' entrance it was a spot on the campus that she'd discovered two months ago. Not one school classroom faced the west side of the catering wing.

Just a minute, she thought, as she tried to straighten the slight curve of the cigarette that had bent in her pocket. A few moments of peace were all she wanted before she hurtled towards her next lesson apologising for her lateness. Just a rest from the chaos in her head.

She shielded the lighter from the late March wind and vowed it would be the last cigarette she smoked. She'd overheard one of the older girls in the dinner line saying she couldn't face the thought of maths class until she'd had a smoke. Said it relaxed her. So, a few days ago Sadie had pinched one from the girl's school bag and tried it for herself. She knew it didn't really relax her. She knew that she was inhaling carbon monoxide which decreased the amount of blood being delivered to her muscles. But for a brief time it felt like relaxation.

She drew heavily on the cigarette allowing the smoke to fill her thirteen-year-old lungs, remembering her first attempt and the coughing fit that had followed. She pictured it swirling around like fog in a clean jar. She didn't want to smoke. She didn't want to be dependent on cigarettes or anything, but the tablets were no longer having any effect. At first, they had numbed her, deadened her and quietened the destructive thoughts. The shards of anger had been softened as though covered in bubble wrap. Still there but less harmful. But not any more. The sharp edges were piercing the fog and the blackness had returned worse than ever.

And now being forced to sit in a room and talk to a bloody counsellor about her 'problems' because her parents thought that would be a good idea. They wanted to hope she didn't suddenly unburden herself to someone outside the family. She'd listened to his soft, sympathetic voice assuring her of his discretion. His repeated instruction that she could tell him anything. Like that was ever going to happen. Especially once he'd produced the piece of paper that had shown her she could trust no one.

Damn it, she thought, throwing the cigarette to the ground. She would not let them do this to her. It had been bottled up inside her for far too long.

She knew she wasn't supposed to know what had happened. She wasn't supposed to know anything. They thought they'd hidden it, but they hadn't. Another mile added to the distance that separated her from her family. Something else they all knew that she didn't. Another exhibit in the catalogue of proof that she didn't belong with the rest of them.

She had always felt it, known it. She was nothing like her sister; bright, adorable, pretty Saffie whose light shone into rooms like an angelic glow. She did not have her effortless grace or winning smile. And of course Saffie would always be perfect, always be the favourite, no matter what she did wrong.

Sadie swiped at the angry tears that had formed in her eyes. She would not cry. She would not give them the satisfaction. She would do what she always did. Retract her head into her hardened outer shell and pretend she didn't care.

They hadn't come to her aid. She had begged and pleaded with them to remove her from Heathcrest and allow her to attend a school closer to home. She hated the stuffy elitism and tradition that frowned upon individuality, stifled creativity and personal expression and promoted conformity. The place was a prison. But no, they had refused her request. No child of theirs would attend the local comprehensive. Heathcrest would build her character. She would form connections that would serve her for the rest of her life. Allies on whom she would be able to rely. But she didn't want connections and allies. She wanted friends. *Normal* friends.

The injustice of them both jumping to the aid of Saffie bit deeply into her soul. Her parents always managed to find new ways to make her feel inferior and oftentimes they didn't even know it.

Well, no more, she thought with determination. Tonight she would phone them, and she would make sure she was heard. And she had just the right weapon to use in her favour. Knowledge was power.

She stepped around the brick wall as a familiar shape appeared before her.

She frowned. 'What are you doing—?'

The words were cut off as a fist crashed into her left temple. Her vision blurred as she felt herself falling to the ground.

What was happening? What had she done?

There was no reason.

A second blow landed to the back of her head but this came from a foot. More blows continued to land along the left side of her body as she tried to shield herself. Her stunned brain tried to connect dots in her head as a blow to her kidney sent explosions of pain surging around her body. She tried to defend herself as her mind tried to hang on to a question. There had to be some kind of mistake, her brain screamed, as the blows continued to land.

She tried to turn on the ground but another kick to her left side brought a metallic taste into her mouth. She spat out the liquid that threatened to slide back down her throat. A small pool of red landed an inch away.

Her vision was beginning to fade on the left side.

Fear coursed through her as fists and feet continued to pummel at her flesh and the agony spread so that her entire body was on fire. All confusion had disappeared leaving only the terror and pain.

She cried out as the agony in her stomach turned into knives, hacking and slicing at her organs, white hot bolts of pain that took away her breath. The vision in her left eye had completely gone and darkness was coming at her from the right.

'Pl-please…' she begged, trying to hang on to the light.

A final blow to the head and the world disappeared from her view.

# CHAPTER 2

'Bryant, are you having a giraffe?' Kim asked, incredulously, as she turned to him in the driver's seat. They had just finished interviewing a woman who had changed her mind about testifying in court against her abusive husband. To Kim's dismay, no amount of cajoling could persuade her to change her mind back again.

They'd spent weeks reassuring her that she was doing the right thing; that her evidence would put the bastard away, but one visit from his mother had undone all their hard work.

Her husband would be returned to her within a few hours, and Kim was betting Mrs Worley would be counting new bruises before the night was out. Thankfully there were no children involved or Kim wouldn't have hesitated in contacting Child Services. As it was she could do nothing more than register as urgent any future calls of disturbances to the address.

She knew she had done everything within her power and yet still she wanted to drive back to the end terrace and try again. Damn, the ones that got away.

'I'm assuming you mean laugh, and no, I'm not.'

'We may be the closest but I'm not sure we're—'

'Look, guv, there's a thirteen-year-old girl on top of the school building threatening to jump. Pretty sure they just want someone on the scene as quickly as possible.'

'Yeah, but have they met me?' she asked, increasing her speed towards Hagley.

Heathcrest Academy was a co-ed private school responsible for shaping the hearts and minds of the wealthy, privileged kids from the Black Country and surrounding areas from the age of five right through to university.

Lodged between the dormitory village of West Hagley and the Clent Hills the school was placed at the picturesque edge of the urban conurbation of Stourbridge.

Kim had never met anyone schooled at the boarding facility. Graduates of Heathcrest didn't seem to filter into the police force.

If she took the dual carriageway along Manor Way and turned off Hagley Wood Lane she guessed that she could make it in just a few minutes. What exactly she'd say when she got there was another matter entirely. Not renowned for her tact, diplomacy or sensitivity she realised that dispatch really must be desperate.

On a scale of suitability for the task trained negotiators sat right at the top. Then there were people training to be negotiators. Below that were kids who aspired to the role. There were counsellors, there were normal people and somewhere way below that line was her.

'I'll hold your handbag while you go and talk to her,' she said, crossing the black and white sign into freedom of speed.

She crunched the gears into submission as she bullied the car up to sixty in three seconds.

'She'll probably be down by the time we get there,' Bryant observed. 'I'm sure that place has qualified people on site.'

Oh yeah, Kim thought, as she slowed for a bend followed by a small traffic island. She'd read an article a few months ago about a planned multimillion pound extension for a medical wing. It had sounded like the school had better facilities than most of the local town centres.

'Next left,' Bryant said, just as she hit the indicator stick.

The road turned into a single-track tarmac path that wound its way beneath arching willow trees with leafless branches that reached across the distance to intertwine.

At the end, the tarmac tapered into a gravel driveway that straightened. Kim ignored the sound of bricks hitting the side of Bryant's car as she sped along the track towards the Tudor-cum-Jacobean-style house.

'Time?' Kim asked.

'Four minutes,' he said, having timed from call to arrival.

An imposing bell tower stood to the right of the building.

'Bryant…' Kim said, as they neared the building.

'I can't see anyone up there, either,' he said, as she brought the car to a screeching halt, just yards away from a crowd of people, all looking down at the ground.

'Looks like you were right, Bryant,' she said, approaching the sea of horrified faces.

The girl had made it down after all.

# CHAPTER 3

'Police officer, move aside,' Kim commanded as she pushed her way through the circle of people formed of both adults and students.

Horrified gasps had been muted into silence, but the open mouths told Kim it hadn't been long. Damn, if she'd just broken the speed limit she might have been here in time.

'There's an ambulance on the way,' said a shaky female voice somewhere behind her.

Kim ignored it. An ambulance was no good to them now.

'Get everyone away from here,' she growled to a smartly dressed man leaning down towards the figure on the ground.

He hesitated for a second before springing into action.

She could hear Bryant's booming voice already moving students away.

Too late, probably, as they would never un-see the sight before them. It would play over and over in their minds and revisit them in their dreams. It never ceased to amaze Kim that people were so eager to give their minds something traumatic to grab and hold for ever.

'Damn it,' she said to herself, taking a closer look at the diminutive figure on the ground.

The girl was dressed in the school colours. Her yellow shirt was crumpled and falling out of the brown skirt that had curled over and exposed her bottom. Despite the dark tights covering her skin, Kim leaned down and gently folded it back.

She lay face down, her left cheek against the gravel, a pool of blood staining the white stones from the impact wound of her head hitting the ground. Her right eye stared along the path. Her left arm was flailed out as though reaching while her right lay close to her side. Both legs were straight and pointed to the metal grating that bordered a single row of daffodils close to the building. Her feet were encased in flat, black shoes. A grey smudge was visible on the sole of the right pump.

Kim guessed her to be early teens.

'What's her name?' she asked as the smartly dressed male reappeared beside her.

'Sadie Winters,' he replied, quietly. 'She's thirteen years old,' he added.

Jesus Christ, Kim thought.

He offered his hand across the body. 'Brendan Thorpe, Principal of Heathcrest.'

Kim ignored the hand and simply nodded.

'You saw her on the roof?' she asked.

He shook his head. 'I heard someone shouting in the corridor that a student was on the roof threatening to jump. I immediately called the police but by the time I got out here…'

'She'd already jumped?' Kim asked.

He nodded and swallowed.

Kim had to wonder what could have caused a thirteen-year-old to take her own life. How bad could her life have been?

'Just a child,' Brendan Thorpe whispered.

A child's problems were no less important or intense than the worries of an adult, she reasoned. It was all relative. A break-up with a boyfriend could mean the end of the world. Feelings of despair were not the sole property of adults.

The sound of tyres on gravel prompted her to turn towards the road. Two squad cars followed by an ambulance pulled to a stop behind Bryant's Astra.

She recognised Inspector Plant, a pleasant, permanently tanned officer with white hair and beard that contrasted with his skin tone.

He came towards her as Bryant reappeared.

'Apparent suicide,' she advised, beginning the handover. Although first on the scene they would not take the case. CID had no remit in a suicide, except to agree that was the cause of death with the pathologist, which they would do following the post-mortem.

In the meantime there were parents to inform, witnesses to be questioned, statements to be taken – but that would not be done by either herself or her team.

'Her name is Sadie Winters, thirteen-years-old,' she advised Plant.

A quiet shake of the head demonstrated his regret.

'Brendan Thorpe over there is the principal, who made the call to us, but she'd jumped by the time we got here.'

Inspector Plant nodded. 'Thanks, guys, we'll take it—'

His words were cut short by a female voice emanating towards them.

'Is it her?' cried the voice.

They all turned as a blonde girl dressed in the school uniform dodged the principal and barrelled towards them.

'Let me through,' she cried. 'I have to see if it's her.'

Kim lined herself up in front of the victim and tensed her body ready for the impact. This kid was hurtling towards her like a rugby player; stopping for no one.

'Got ya,' Kim said, planting her feet firmly and holding her so she couldn't pass.

The girl, only an inch shorter than Kim, strained to look beyond, but Bryant and Plant had moved into position and blocked her view.

'Please, let me past,' she shouted right into Kim's ear.

'I'm sorry,' Kim said, trying to hold her.

'I just want to make sure,' she cried.

'Who are—'

'Please, just let me past. My name is Saffron, and Sadie Winters is my sister.'

# CHAPTER 4

'Bloody hell, that was intense,' Bryant said as they headed back towards the car.

Oh yeah, her ribs were still smarting from the girl barging her to get past. Luckily the school counsellor had appeared and with the help of the principal had managed to drag the girl towards the bell tower.

They reached the car and turned. Inspector Plant and his team were scattered among the melee of students and adults as well as guarding the body for the arrival of Keats.

Sadie Winters's sister sat against the bell tower with her head down. The counsellor, a thin, wiry man with ginger hair and bushy beard sat beside her, while Principal Thorpe paced and talked to someone on his mobile phone.

And at the centre of it all was the body of a thirteen-year-old child.

Despite her limitations in the sympathy department Kim found herself wishing she'd at least had a chance to speak to the girl, understand what had been going through her head, reassure her that it wasn't all as bad as she thought. Emotional connection with other people did not lie at the top of her skill set but she couldn't have done any worse than this.

'Jesus, Bryant, maybe if we'd just…'

'Four minutes, guv,' he said, reminding her of how long it had taken them to get there.

'But she's so bloody young,' Kim said, opening the car door. She was sure that many teenagers had contemplated ending it all but that was a long way from actually doing it. How bad must things have been for her to actually jump to certain death?

She paused and turned, taking a good look at the building.

'What's up?' Bryant asked.

'Dunno,' she answered honestly, as her gaze travelled up from the location of the body to the roof.

Her brain was already sorting through the cases on her desk and the explanation to both Woody and the CPS about the collapsed case of Mrs Worley. Her mind had left this place and was already heading back to the office. It was only her gut that remained.

And something didn't feel right to her.

'Troubled, I heard the counsellor say to Inspector Plant,' Bryant prompted.

'Jeez, weren't we all at thirteen?' she said.

At that age she had just lost Keith and Erica, the only two adults that had ever loved her.

'Guv, you've got that *Ghostbuster* look on your face.'

'That what?' she asked as her eyes reached the top of the building.

'The expression that says you're looking for something that's just not there.'

'Hmm…' she said, absently.

Her eyes travelled over the grand three-storey building, taking in the high windows, the rounded arcade at the centre, the flat roof with stone balustrade that linked the two arched roofs that topped the ivy-covered wings standing proud of the recessed centre.

'Guv, time to go,' Bryant prompted. 'We've got plenty of our own cases back at the station.'

He was right, as usual. The major cases that landed on her desk did nothing to stem the flow of lesser cases. It wasn't a card game where a murder cancelled out sexual assault, robbery and gang-related violence. They were still playing catch-up from the

4

incidents that had mounted up during the recent murder of night workers on Tavistock Road.

And yet just because something looked like a duck and sounded like a duck. Didn't mean it really was a duck.

She slammed the car door shut.

'Guv…' her colleague warned.

'Yeah, in a minute, Bryant,' she said, walking back towards the building.

# CHAPTER 5

'Is this the only way up to the roof?' Kim asked, as they mounted stone steps from the third floor via a corridor that ran behind a row of bedrooms.

Brendan Thorpe shook his head. 'There's a fire escape in the West wing but that's been closed off to the roof for more than a year now,' he said, taking a set of keys from his pocket that hung lower than it would have done if his trouser belt had been working more effectively rather than sitting beneath the middle-aged paunch.

He tried the door first to find it locked.

'Could Sadie have got a spare key from anywhere?'

Thorpe looked puzzled. 'I don't see how,' he said, frowning.

'Well, she got up here somehow,' Kim observed, in case he'd forgotten there was a dead teenager on the ground. The girl's purloining of the key was about to be the least of his problems.

'I'm sorry, Inspector, you'll have to bear with me, I'm still in a little bit of shock,' he said, trying the wrong key.

'I understand that, Mr Thorpe, but it would be useful to know how many roof keys are in existence.'

'Of, course,' he said, as they stepped outside.

'There is one on my master set, the deputy principal has an identical set to mine. The janitor, the maintenance crew, each housemistress or master has a reduced set of keys, which includes a roof key.'

'So, that makes?' Kim prodded.

'A total of fourteen roof keys,' he answered.

Kim glanced at Bryant who took out his notebook.

She stepped outside onto the flat roof and looked around assessing the scale of the buildings joined together by walkways and ladders. From where she stood Kim could make out four clear wings, each the size of a couple of football pitches. Navigating the area from up here would be challenging enough, but downstairs, spread over three floors, she'd need a decent satnav to get her around the school.

She stepped over a roof light and around an air conditioning unit to head towards the area she thought was the side of the building.

Thorpe's phone began to ring. 'Please, excuse me,' he said, edging back towards the stairwell.

Bryant joined her on a patch of recently repaired bitumen.

'My apologies, Inspector. I have to go,' Thorpe said, gravely. 'Sadie's parents are at the police cordon.'

'Do they know?' Bryant asked.

He shook his head. 'Only that there's been an incident.'

Kim understood. Delivering such news over the phone was only done as a last resort. She did not envy him his next job.

'We'll let you know when we're done,' she advised as he re-entered the building.

Bryant shoved his hands into his trouser pockets as he stood beside her.

She narrowed her eyes at him when he started humming the *Ghostbusters* theme.

'Just look down there,' she said.

'Must I?' he asked, taking a tentative step forward.

Three storeys below lay the body of Sadie Winters, guarded by uniform officers while others worked to take details and clear the area. Keats had arrived, accompanied by his team of crime scene techs, who were changing into white protective suits.

'You think she jumped from here?' Kim asked, lining herself up with the body on the ground.

Bryant nodded and stepped back. 'Yeah, seems about right.'

'Hmm…' she said, taking five steps to the left.

'Was that the wrong answer?' he asked.

'How about here?' she asked, ignoring his question.

Again, he took a cautious step forward and shook his head. 'Too far away.'

She walked past him and headed to the right.

'How about here?' she asked.

'Guv, are you trying to make me throw up?'

'I haven't cooked for you in ages, now just look,' she urged.

He looked down and shook his head. 'Much too far away from where she landed,' he said.

She returned to her first position which was directly in line with the body. She frowned as she looked down.

'Who you gonna c— aah, I think I see what you're looking at,' he said.

'The railings,' she clarified.

A row of black wrought-iron spikes, about four feet high, surrounded a narrow-planted area she'd noticed on the ground. Four steps either way and there were no railings.

'It's obstructive,' Kim said. 'You look down and picture your body landing on those spikes.'

'Ugh,' Bryant said, looking away.

'Exactly,' Kim said. 'And you're a fully grown adult… allegedly.'

'But if I'm killing myself anyway I'm expecting a broken neck or a fractured skull?' he argued.

'But do you really want to picture yourself impaled on those spikes?' she asked.

'Not really but I'm not a troubled thirteen-year-old girl,' he offered.

'Yeah, but I was, and I can tell you that I would have noticed those spikes.'

People wanted to die painlessly and that was no different for suicides. Fast and painless. Logically, it didn't make sense to her. She recalled the grey mark on the bottom of Sadie's shoe as she took another look around the surface of the roof.

'Hmmm…' she said, not finding what she sought.

'What now?' he asked, wearily.

'The cigarette,' she answered. 'Sadie had recently ground out a smoke with her shoe but there's no cigarette butt here,' she observed.

'Guv, what exactly are you thinking?' he asked, with a note of fear in his voice.

'I'm thinking we might just have a chat with our good friend Keats before we leave.'

# CHAPTER 6

Kim stepped back outside into what appeared to be chaos.

Plant and his team had succeeded in clearing the area close to the body but were still trying to corral students and adults into some kind of order. Word had clearly travelled, and the number of spectators had increased tenfold. A third squad car had just pulled in and officers were trying to guide everyone back into the main building.

Kim ignored it all and focused her attention on the ground. 'There's one,' she said, pointing. 'And another…'

'Secret smoking spot,' Bryant said, looking around.

Kim frowned. 'That ash mark wouldn't still be on the sole of her shoe if she'd had her smoke all the way down here,' she observed.

'The butt could have blown anywhere up there, guv,' Bryant said, nodding towards the roof.

'Get 'em all collected,' Kim said, moving towards the focus of the forensic activity. She was pleased to see that a modesty blind had been placed around the victim.

'Can you not do something about all these people?' Keats asked, bypassing any form of greeting.

'Not really my case,' she answered, with a shrug.

'Then don't speak to me,' he said, pushing his glasses back on to the bridge of his nose.

'Bloody hell, Keats, who pissed on your chips so soon?' she asked. 'I've only just got here.'

'All these folks with smartphones trying to get a damn photo of this poor soul to plaster all over social media.'

Kim understood that just about the only person Keats cared about right now was the one that was no longer breathing. She gave him a moment of silence as he worked through his initial examination.

'Are you still here?' he asked, looking up.

'Time of death was between one fifteen and one thirty,' she offered.

He scowled at her and then pointed. 'And that guy standing over by the wall with the red hair is a potential serial killer.'

Kim confined her smile. 'I wasn't telling you how to do your job, Keats,' she said.

He stood up straight. 'No, really, why are you here?'

She raised an eyebrow. 'Just passing.'

'The word "passing" is indicative of continuous movement, so I'd suggest you carry on…'

'Anything suspicious?' she asked, ignoring his outburst.

'Do you mean other than the fact she's a thirteen-year-old girl that decided to end her own life?'

'Yeah, apart from that. Anything physical?'

He shook his head. 'Nothing yet but I'd like to take a better look at her first. And with that in mind, I'm not happy continuing here,' he said, glancing up towards the windows with faces crammed against the glass. 'I'll know more once I get her cleaned up.'

'You'll let me know?' she asked.

'Of course, Inspector, as I often have little else to do,' he said, turning to one of the techs. 'William, if you'd be so kind.'

William stood at the feet while Keats stood at her head.

They bent down in unison and gently turned her onto her back and onto the stretcher. Kim saw her whole face for the first time. She didn't look older than her years. There was no make-up, eye shadow or mascara.

She looked exactly what she was. A child.

'Come on, guv, we need to get back to the—'

'I know, Bryant, I'm coming,' she answered, beginning to turn away.

And then she turned back and took another look at her face. She noticed Keats doing the same thing with a puzzled expression.

She took a step closer and peered at the left cheek, where a red mark stretched up and over her temple. A gash around her ear had been responsible for the pooling of blood beneath her head. But there was something not quite right with what she was seeing. She would have expected to see a portion of the head caved in where the skull had met the ground and gravel embedded in the soft skin of her cheek.

Kim realised this did not look like a face that had just been smashed into the ground from three-storeys high.

# CHAPTER 7

Kim had not been surprised to see she had a missed call from Woody by the time she got back into the car.

Her conversation with Inspector Plant had been pleasant enough, and he'd been only too happy to accept her assessment of suspicious circumstances. He had graciously agreed to leave his team to continue taking witness statements which he promised would be on her desk by the following morning.

Her request to the coroner for a post-mortem on the body of Sadie Winters would not have gone unnoticed by her boss. Requests were made by police officers or doctors if the death was unexpected, violent, unnatural or suspicious. The main aim was to find out how someone had died and if an inquest was required.

The Winters family would probably not thank her but permission from the parents was not necessary regardless of Sadie's age. Her gut told her she was doing the right thing by looking more closely at the death of the young girl and yet she felt a moment of trepidation before she knocked on Woody's door. She guessed it was coming from the doubt she saw in the eyes of her colleague every time Sadie's name was mentioned.

'Sir?' she asked, popping in just her head and leaving her body on the other side of the door. She lived in hope that was enough of her and that the conversation would be short.

'Come in, Stone,' he said, taking his reading glasses from his head and placing them on the desk beside the photo of his granddaughter, Lissy.

Or not.

He pointed to the top right edge of his desk. 'Do you see that empty space there, Stone?' he asked.

She nodded, knowing what was coming next.

'It's been empty for the last two weeks. Around the time I asked for a copy of your staff appraisals, which I feel sure you have carried out, and copies of which you have simply forgotten to let me have,' he said, raising one eyebrow.

She held in the groan that was desperate to escape. Appraising the performance of her team members each year was not an activity that came naturally to her.

'The expression that you're trying to hide tells me that you have not yet completed them,' he observed. 'Please tell me that you've at least given them the forms to complete?' he asked.

'Absolutely, sir,' she said, nodding. About that she didn't need to find some imaginative way to hide the truth. And she'd had them back too. She just couldn't quite remember what she'd done with them. A fact she felt was unnecessary to share with her boss.

'You'll have them by the end of the week, sir,' she said, edging towards the door.

Now if she could just reach the handle before...

'The parents of Sadie Winters are not happy.'

'They know already?' she asked. It had been less than an hour since she'd left the site.

'Yes, they know.'

'Sir, who informed them?' she asked, frowning.

'That's not important right now. They have to face the thought of their daughter being butchered when it's going to do nothing to bring her back,' he said.

'Neither is ignoring the suspicious circumstances surrounding her death,' she countered. 'But I'm gonna do it anyway.'

'And you're sure the circumstances are suspicious, and this has nothing to do with the fact you didn't get to her in time?'

Kim frowned. 'Is that what you think?'

'More importantly, is it what you think?'

She shook her head. She couldn't have made it to the school any quicker, but she was stung by his words.

'Do you really think I would prolong the pain of the family to soothe my own guilt, sir?' she asked.

'Do I think that your failure to change Mrs Worley's mind in testifying against her husband was still on your mind when you got to the school? Do I think that you assume guilt for every victim you can't save and thereby bury yourself in responsibility and personal determination to right any wrong?' he asked, and then gave her no time to answer. 'Yes, on a personal level, I do. From a professional point of view there are going to be a great many influential people watching you closely on this one, Stone,' he said, meaningfully. 'They are also going to be hoping that you do find her death to be suicide.'

She nodded her understanding. Many rich and powerful people had been manufactured at Heathcrest Academy. The reputation of the facility was exemplary. And she was sure they wanted to keep it that way. Suicide as a manner of death was not the greatest recommendation for the school and was unlikely to appear on their marketing brochures, but it was better than other potential scenarios.

Influential people would be watching her every move and would not hesitate to take her down if she put a foot wrong. By following her instinct back to Heathcrest she could be risking her job, her career, the respect of her team and the good faith of her boss.

And none of these things bothered her one little bit when stacked against the death of a thirteen-year-old girl.

'So, I ask you again, Stone. Are you sure you know what you're doing?'

She met his gaze with stubborn determination.

'Yes, sir. I am.'

# CHAPTER 8

Kim carried her coffee through to the general office to begin the morning briefing.

'Okay folks,' she said, looking towards the empty board. 'Let's get started.'

Silence met her ears for a few seconds as her team glanced at each other but not at her.

'On what?' Bryant asked, finally, voicing the thoughts of the rest of her team.

'Not one of you thinks there's something here?' she asked, surprised.

Dawson shook his head. 'Poor little rich girl probably couldn't get her own way, tried to get some attention up on that roof and lost her balance,' he offered.

Stacey shrugged. 'Or her boyfriend finished with her and she was distraught.'

'Or she was pressured by the workload and it all got a bit much for her,' Bryant offered.

'So, we have three different theories but none of you think Sadie Winters belongs on our board? And of course this has nothing to do with the fact that she went to a private school?'

They looked from one to the other, and Dawson spoke first. 'Boss, I've got two serious assaults and a string of burglary offences.'

Stacey looked up. 'And I'm working on a list of armed robberies in Wolverhampton to see if there's any—'

'Hey, this isn't a bloody prove your worth competition,' she said, holding up her hands. 'But would someone like to show me where it says on their job description that we care less about suspicious circumstances surrounding the death of wealthy people?'

Dawson coloured. 'It's got nothing to do—'

'Of course it has,' she argued. 'You've already assumed she's a poor little rich girl who was seeking attention or that she had problems that you would class as inconsequential. What if this had happened at the school down the road from Hollytree, or the academy that's at the end of your road, Stacey? Would you still assume the same things?' she asked.

'Just doesn't look suspicious,' Dawson said.

'Looks like a suicide,' Bryant replied.

Yes, they were all right, she conceded and yet there were a few things she couldn't get out of her mind. Things that had accompanied her and Barney on their late-night walk and which had still been there when she'd opened her eyes that morning.

The first unnatural thing that churned her stomach was a thirteen-year-old girl taking her own life. Kim knew it happened but there had to be a big question why. You didn't just accept it and move on.

Physically she couldn't comprehend the spot Sadie had chosen to jump from. A quick look down and all she would have seen was those vicious black spikes staring up at her. She would have needed to leap forward to miss them instead of taking a few steps to the right or left where she would have had a clear fall.

The absence of a cigarette butt on the roof bothered her, too, but not as much as the lack of gravel marks on her skin. Individually these inconsistencies meant little, but together they mattered. Clearly less to her team than they did to her.

'What exactly do you think we're looking for, guv?' Bryant asked.

She shrugged. She really had no idea. She saw the collective sigh of relief as her team thought her admission signalled defeat.

Not one of them thought there was anything suspicious about this tragic situation.

So, it was a good job this was not a democracy and that she was the boss.

'Dawson, write Sadie's name on the board, now,' she said as her phone began to ring.

# CHAPTER 9

'So, why exactly does Keats want to see us?' Bryant asked, as he parked the car at Russells Hall Hospital.

'Sadie's parents have identified the body and are asking for a speedy resolution, which is understandable,' she acknowledged.

No parent wanted to think of their child being kept in cold storage in a morgue. They would want her body transferred to a funeral director where they could go and visit her and begin making plans for her burial.

'Just a formality then?' Bryant asked.

'Hmm…' she responded absently.

Once she and Keats had agreed it was suicide with no suspicious circumstances the body could then be released.

She was about to enter the hospital when something caught her eye. Just along the pavement on a wooden bench sat two figures huddled together. The man's arm was fixed tightly around the woman's shoulders as though holding her together.

Kim knew instinctively who they were. Their grief-laden shoulders and hunched backs told her she was looking at Sadie's parents. She stepped away from the doors and headed towards them.

'Mr and Mrs Winters?' she asked, standing before them.

They both looked up, startled.

She introduced herself and Bryant, who was now standing beside her.

Mr Winters made to stand but Kim shook her head.

'Please, stay seated. I'm sure what you've just seen has been quite a shock for you.'

This time yesterday they'd had two daughters and now they had one. On the face of it their youngest had chosen to end her own life. Their questions would never end. Their guilt would never end.

'She looked so peaceful,' Mrs Winters said, as the tears filled her reddened eyes. She turned back into the embrace of her husband, who pulled her tightly to him.

Both were dressed in casual but well-cut jeans. He wore a sweatshirt beneath a sports jacket, and she wore a chunky cable-knit cardigan over a pastel shirt.

'We are so sorry for your loss,' Bryant offered.

Mr Winters nodded and blinked his green eyes furiously to ward off his own threatening tears.

'Thank you,' he said, looking towards the door. 'I can't stomach the thought of her in there amongst…'

His words trailed away leaving Kim to wonder exactly what it was he feared. That she was amongst other dead bodies? No harm could come to her now.

'We were first on the scene, yesterday,' Kim said.

Mrs Winters's head snapped around.

'Did you see her? Was she alive? Did you speak to her?'

Kim shook her head. 'My understanding is that it all happened very quickly,' she said gently.

Mrs Winters nodded and cast her eyes down. 'That's what Principal Thorpe told us.'

Kim took a step away and then reconsidered. 'May I ask you a couple of questions?' She understood that they'd just identified Sadie's body, but they looked as though they could bear a question or two.

Mr Winters hesitated before nodding, and Kim understood that she needed to go easy.

'Had Sadie been having any problems you know of?' she asked.

There was no hesitation before Mr Winters nodded.

'Sadie has been troubled for a while now,' he admitted. 'She's been withdrawn, hostile at times. We've been struggling to reach her. We assumed it was a phase, but she must have been unhappier than we thought,' he said, looking away.

Kim wished she had some comfort to offer but she suspected it was considerably harder to monitor your child's psychological state closely when they were away at boarding school.

'We just want to make arrangements to take her home,' he said, quietly. 'Sorry, you know what I mean.'

Kim did know what he meant, and she would want the same thing.

He continued: 'That man in there, the pathologist, explained that he was waiting on the attendance of a detective.'

Thanks Keats, she thought, for throwing the responsibility and landing it firmly at her feet.

'So, you'll release her to us?'

'As soon as we can,' Kim said, making it clear that she could not answer him right now. 'We'll inform you as soon as we can but there are just a few formalities first.'

'But surely—'

'Mr Winters,' Bryant interjected. 'Don't concern yourself. Just take care of your wife,' he said, looking towards Mrs Winters who was sobbing quietly into his shoulder.

He nodded and stood, guiding his wife towards a Bentley parked on double yellow lines.

'I hope we can give them some peace soon,' Bryant said, as they headed towards the morgue.

Kim nodded her agreement as the automatic doors slid open.

'What you got, Keats?' she asked.

'More friends than you,' he responded without turning.

She shrugged. That was hardly an achievement.

'Just saw Sadie's parents outside. Cheers for throwing me under the bus,' she said.

'Is that really a viable option?' he asked, turning to Bryant, who shrugged in response.

Three responses curled around her tongue until she saw that his face was tighter than usual. The lines at the corner of his eyes appeared deeper, the dark circles duskier. He was unlikely to have slept well under the cloud of cutting open a child.

She watched Bryant's customary shudder whenever they entered the morgue. For some reason the cold, stark sterility of the surroundings unnerved him. Her, not so much. Kind of reminded her of her first studio flat.

'Obviously they want her back as soon as possible,' she said.

'They're hoping for a swift resolution,' he said, meeting her gaze.

Kim leaned back against a bed-sized metal dish. She thought about the distraught parents who were desperate to remove their child from this cold, sterile environment. She even considered the subtle urging she could feel coming from her colleague beside her. And then she thought about the railings and the ash mark on her shoe and the absence of gravel embedded in her skin.

'Shall we get started, then?' she asked.

'Already done,' he answered with a long sigh.

'You've done the post-mortem already?' she asked. Over the years she had begged, cajoled, attempted to bribe and used threats of violence but never had he performed a post-mortem so quickly.

'I have bosses too, Stone,' he said, meeting her gaze.

Bloody hell, this family did have friends in high places.

'Pressuring you for a suicide call?' she asked.

'Not pressuring exactly. Let's just say it would be preferable.'

'And?' she asked.

He reached for his clipboard. 'I can confirm that this girl did not take very good care of herself. All her major organs were healthy and apparently functioning fine; however neither her stomach, intestines or bowels held anything even remotely resembling a proper meal. Sadie Winters seemed to exist on a diet of energy drinks and breakfast bars, and as such was considerably underweight.'

Kim couldn't help wondering if the girl had harboured weight issues or if her intake of food and drink had been some form of control.

'Any evidence of an eating disorder?' she asked.

He shook his head. 'Nothing obvious but may have been too early to tell.'

Kim realised that the troubled expression she'd seen on the pathologist's face when she'd entered had not yet left it.

'Keats, despite the fact we're both under pressure to return this girl speedily to her parents, I'm guessing we're not going to be calling a suicide.'

The pathologist peered at her over his glasses. 'Very perceptive, Inspector. You are correct, and I'm now going to tell you the reasons why.'

# CHAPTER 10

She resisted the urge to turn to Bryant with her 'I told you so' expression. Instead she kept her focus on Keats.

'Go on,' she urged.

He lifted and rolled the sheet slowly from the tip of her toes, over her knees and stopped at her upper thighs. He gently pinched the skin between his thumb and forefinger and pulled it towards him.

'Bloody hell,' Bryant said, as her own eyes widened.

She was looking at twenty or more thin scars and scratches criss-crossing each other. Some were white and some red, healed by congealed blood and more recent than the others.

Bryant shook his head. 'What the hell is that?'

'Self-harming?' Kim asked, looking to Keats.

He nodded. 'There are a few on the right leg but she seemed to favour the left.'

Kim had encountered a few self-harmers during her childhood. Some chose places on the body more readily visible with the subconscious hope of the wounds being seen, a cry for help. The inner thigh was a common spot for the most serious self-harmers. So close to the intimate area was unlikely to be seen by anyone. Sadie had not been trying to get noticed.

'Jesus, this poor kid,' Kim said. Whatever had been going on it had been too much for a thirteen-year-old girl to deal with.

In life, there were younger thirteen-year-olds and older thirteen-year-olds. Some had discovered boys, make-up, sexuality and could pass for much older. Some had not. But in death, scrubbed clean, it made no difference. It was a thirteen-year-old kid lying here on the table.

'But, doesn't that just strengthen the suicide theory?' Bryant asked.

'Only if you ignore the anomalies,' Keats answered, reaching for a pile of X-rays. 'Do you recall the position of Sadie's body at the scene?'

'Of course,' she answered. The vision of the broken child was imprinted on her memory.

'Care to adopt the position for me, in the interests of my detailed explanation?' he asked.

She rolled her eyes as she began to lower herself to the ground.

'Not down there,' he snapped.

She looked to the metal workbench that was covered in X-rays.

'Just get on here,' Keats said, impatiently, pointing to the metal dish next to Sadie.

'Keats…' she warned.

'Oh, stop being such a baby,' he growled.

She shook her head before easing herself onto the side and then into the dish, trying hard not to think of the occupants that had filled the space before her. As she got into position she caught a glimpse of Sadie's left hand peeping out from beneath the sheet. She fought the instinct to reach out and hold it across the space that separated them.

'Okay, perfect, except your left leg needs to be a bit higher.'

She moved it as Bryant hid a chuckle behind a cough. She caught the wink that Keats sent his way.

'Err… guys,' she growled.

'Okay, imagine that's how you've landed.'

Kim closed her eyes and imagined that she had just thudded to the ground in this position. She felt the contact on the ground to her ankle, along the side of her lower leg, the edge of the knee and up to her hip, along the side of her ribcage and up through her shoulder.

'Areas of greatest impact?' Keats asked.

Kim didn't open her eyes as she answered.

'Ankle, knee, hip and shoulder.'

'All intact,' he said, causing her to open her eyes and sit up.

'But that makes no sense at—'

'Back down,' he instructed, as he put two X-rays onto the wall and switched on the light. He reached for a wand and came to stand beside her while pointing to the first X-ray. 'That broken bone is in her other knee, and it has snapped inwards as though being trod on.' He pointed to the spot on her own knee which wouldn't have made any contact with the ground. 'And the second broken bone is her right rib,' he said, again using the wand to show her exactly where.

The rib was nowhere near the ground.

'And lastly, how about right here?' he asked touching the top of her head.

She shook her head. 'Nothing.'

He moved to the X-rays and replaced the one on the first light board.

'Bloody hell,' Bryant said, as she sat up.

Kim found herself touching her own head at the point where Sadie's had quite clearly been injured.

The spot had been nowhere near the ground.

Kim climbed out of the tray and took a closer look.

'This makes absolutely no sense,' she said.

Keats nodded his agreement. 'I suspect that some of the broken bones were inflicted after death, but the cause of death was most definitely the blow to the top of the head.'

'Murder staged to look like a suicide,' Bryant said.

Keats sighed heavily. 'Indeed, Bryant. In my opinion, this poor girl was beaten to death.'

Kim's brain had already digested that fact and was now processing other anomalies.

It explained many things that had been nibbling at her gut. The absence of the cigarette butt up on the roof, the location of the jump point, the lack of gravel rash and the fact that they hadn't yet identified anyone who had seen Sadie Winters on the roof.

Because she'd never been up there in the first place.

# CHAPTER 11

## 6 January 2018

Hey Diary, Sadie here. Remember me?

Back at school and first day has gone much as expected. Endless chatter and showing off new tablets, smartphones, laptops, for school work, obvs!!! My dorm room sparkles like a mummy's tomb with new designer watches, bracelets, necklaces. The important stuff.

Christmas at home was perfect, as it always is.

Festivities straight out of a feel-good film. Midnight mass, early morning presents, Saffie having a strop because her new Gucci trousers were too tight. Christmas isn't Christmas without a Saffie strop, mother excused cheerfully. Christmas dinner was perfect, as was Saffie's piano playing after the Queen's Speech.

Later, Saffie disappeared to her room, no doubt to FaceTime Eric. My parents snuggled up on the sofa together to watch a Christmas film.

They glanced across and asked me if I was okay.

I lied.

I said yes.

How could I tell them how I really felt? How could I tell them that a piece of me dies every time I come home? How could I try and penetrate the perfect bubble around them? How could I reveal what I do to stay calm? How can I share the darkness that shadows every thought I have; the rage that heats my blood.

How could I tell them that I'm the broken child?

When it was Christmas and everything was so blindingly perfect?

Perfect, perfect, perfect. Not so fucking perfect now.

Perfection isn't real. It is only the top layer beneath which the ugliness lies.

> *Oh, Sadie, I felt nothing for you as you took your last breath, but now I get to know you through your own thoughts, recorded by your own hand in the privacy of your diary.*
>
> *You've suffered. I've suffered.*
>
> *You are at peace. I am not.*
>
> *Every blow and kick, every time my flesh met yours afforded me a release from the pain, the rage that thunders around me, trapped, growing, strengthening with hate and disgust.*
>
> *You repelled me. Your very existence an insult to my agony.*
>
> *I've been watching you, you see, knowing what I had to do.*
>
> *There was no choice.*
>
> *It had to be you.*
>
> *There was no other way. You had to die.*
>
> *You were the first. But you will not be the last.*

# CHAPTER 12

'That seemed to go a little too smoothly,' Bryant observed as she ended the call.

She nodded her agreement.

Upon leaving Keats she had immediately called Woody to give him the unwelcome news that Sadie Winters had been murdered. She had geared herself up to fight for her request to delay announcing the death as murder. She had been ready to tell him that what she needed was to speak to the staff and students at Heathcrest. That with more than a thousand potential witnesses she couldn't afford for people to turn silent for fear of getting into trouble. She'd been ready to argue a dozen points but hadn't needed to. Woody had agreed, readily, before telling her he wanted an update at the end of the day.

'I see he's here already,' Bryant observed as he idled into the gravel drive of Heathcrest.

Dawson waved from the cordon where he stood talking to Mitch.

Kim half smiled. Despite his earlier reticence at the nature of Sadie's death and his protest about his current desk load, Dawson couldn't resist the lure of a murder investigation. He would have been out of the office door before she'd even finished the call. She nodded at her colleague before turning to the head of the forensic team.

'Anything to note?' she asked.

He shook his head. 'Got all the fag ends, ground samples and a couple of stray hairs. No usable footprints, though,' he said, nodding towards his team. 'We'll be inspecting her clothes once we're finished here, which won't be long now. I'm gonna be honest though, Inspector, I'm not hopeful.'

She understood and appreciated his honesty. This case was not going to be solved by forensic evidence.

'Cheers, Mitch,' she said, walking away.

'So, you clear on what we're doing?' she asked Dawson as he fell into step beside her.

She had asked Stacey to start compiling background information on both the facility and the parents. Dawson was responsible for talking to Sadie's friends as she felt they were more likely to open up to a more youthful officer, and she and Bryant were taking the adults.

Kim could almost taste the exclusivity of Heathcrest as she stepped into the grand entrance hall. From the Persian rug that was almost big enough for a boxing match to the antique Grandfather clock in the top left-hand corner. Gilt-edged portraits lined the space beneath decorative coving. Marble pillars led the eye out of the hallway along a lit corridor towards the rear of the house. It narrowed away from her like a tunnel, giving her an idea of the scale of the building. There were few schools she'd visited where the contents of this hall would have remained intact and without damage.

Mr Thorpe was waiting for them with his hands linked in front of him. Gone was the frazzled, unkempt man operating on shock and adrenaline that she'd met yesterday. In its place was a calm, suited individual, complete with tiepin bearing the crest of the school. His dark suit was more flattering, and his belt appeared to be in the right place today.

'Good morning, officers,' he said, glancing across the three of them.

There was no offer of a handshake and Kim could feel the reticence behind the man. Principal Thorpe did not want them there.

He caught Bryant's gaze as it rested on the two busts either side of him.

'Lord and Lady Burdoch,' he said, turning to look at the sculptures. 'The founders of Heathcrest,' he said, proudly. Without prompting from either of them he continued. 'Elizabeth Burdoch inherited the estate from her parents whose only son died in the First World War. By the beginning of the Second World War, Elizabeth and her husband Charles were in their late forties and childless. They opened their home to children from the cities being bombed.'

'How did that develop into this?' Dawson asked.

'As the war continued Elizabeth became aware that the education of the children was suffering and began bringing teachers here. At first it was the basics, but once she saw the positive effect of learning in such an environment, she went on to employ science teachers, physical education teachers and eventually covered the whole curriculum.'

'Go on,' Dawson urged.

'The end of the war came but parents wanted their children to continue their education here. Unfortunately, the money was beginning to run out and Elizabeth could no longer afford to provide free education.'

'So, what happened?' asked Kim.

'Some children stayed, and some didn't.'

'The ones that couldn't pay were sent home?' Kim clarified.

'Yes,' he confirmed. 'Except for two. One girl and one boy were chosen each year to receive a scholarship to Heathcrest worth approximately thirty-five thousand pounds per year.'

'That's generous,' Kim said, before she could stop herself.

'Based on what, exactly?' Bryant asked.

'Normally some kind of exceptional sporting achievement or musical ability,' he answered.

Both very public careers that would reflect favourably on the school, she noted silently.

'So, who owns Heathcrest now?' Bryant asked, as two teenage boys crossed the hall giving Kim her first visual evidence of the purpose of the building.

'A board of trustees,' Thorpe answered, watching the boys' progress. Their chatter had stopped as they'd entered the great hall but began again once through the door on the other side.

'Before Elizabeth died she appointed five staff members as overseers, people she felt had been particularly loyal and invested to safeguard the running and reputation of the school. It's a lifelong commitment, and when a trustee dies the remaining four decide on a new trustee.'

'Couldn't they all just sell it?' Kim asked.

He shook his head. 'There is a no-sale clause in the trustee agreement. Although each trustee receives a dividend.'

'How much?' Kim asked out of interest.

'It's two hundred thousand pounds a year.'

Nice, Kim thought.

'Well, thank you for that, Mr Thorpe, but if you could direct us to the room we spoke about,' she said pointing at herself and Bryant. 'And Dawson will head off to have a closer look at Sadie's room.'

Kim saw the tightening of the jaw as he stepped out of salesman mode and remembered the reason for their presence.

'You will find the female dorm rooms in the East wing second level. Room thirty-six.'

Dawson thanked him and headed out of the grand hall.

'And I'll take you to the room we've made available,' Thorpe added.

She had asked Stacey to call ahead requesting space and an opportunity to speak to people who knew Sadie.

'May we?' he asked, touching her elbow and guiding her away from Bryant. She moved her arm away from his touch as Bryant fell into step behind them.

'Is this really normal practice for a teenage suicide?' he asked.

'I'm not sure there is anything normal about a teenage suicide,' she answered, evasively.

'It's just that we have many other students to consider and a police presence could be most distracting to their studies. Many of them are at delicate stages of—'

'Principal Thorpe,' she said, cutting him off. 'Let me be clear so that there is no misunderstanding between us. Right now I have concern for only one of your students, and I'm sure you can guess which one. Now, if our being here disrupts the studies of your students that would be unfortunate, but our presence will remain until we better understand the circumstances surrounding the death of Sadie Winters,' she said, as he came to a halt before a door bearing a brass plate marked 'office'.

'This space is spare since we moved Administration onto the first floor,' he said, opening the door.

A single antique desk was surrounded by modern office chairs. Three shelves, now empty, gathered dust along the longest wall. The windowless room felt dark and stuffy with only a 40 watt bulb to light the space.

Kim wondered idly if this was really the only place available in this vast property.

Principal Thorpe looked at his watch. 'I'll leave you to get settled, and Nancy, my assistant, will be down shortly. I'd assist you myself, but I have prospective parents due to arrive.'

'Please, don't let us hold you up,' Kim said, although Thorpe appeared to miss the sarcasm in her tone.

*Must try harder*, she told herself as he closed the door behind himself.

'Bloody hell, Bryant,' Kim said as the light from the hallway was extinguished. She had the sudden feeling of being trapped underground. The room was barely bigger than her bathroom.

'So, what do you think about him?' Bryant asked, removing his jacket.

'Guarded would be an understatement,' she said, choosing a chair and putting another one on the other side of the desk. 'And now he's gotta go sell the place the day after a child in his care died.'

'He'll have no trouble there,' Bryant said.

'I'd think twice, wouldn't you?'

Bryant considered for a second and then shook his head.

Kim sat. 'Why not?'

'Because as far as he's concerned it's a suicide,' he said. 'Suicide belongs only to the person that did it. It's a solitary choice for an individual's own reasons. No parent would think their child capable of the same thing. Murder or even accidental death indicate some kind of failing or neglect on behalf of the school but not suicide.'

'So, you'd still send your kid here?' Kim asked.

'Yeah, if I'd been on the four-year waiting list.'

She thought about the empty place at the school, vacated by thirteen-year-old Sadie Winters.

She supposed one family was about to get lucky.

# CHAPTER 13

Dawson knocked before entering the room number given to him by Thorpe. Silence met his ears and yet he still opened the door slowly and called out as he entered.

Walking into the private space of teenage girls made him feel uncomfortable. The room itself was bright and airy. One huge window looked out towards the courtyard at the centre of the property. Dawson understood that there were four wings that branched from the main house. The two front wings, facing the entrance to the site, housed all the school rooms and administration and the two rear wings were accommodation. East wing for girls, West wing for boys. All four wings backed onto a central courtyard the size of a village green.

He stood for a moment, assessing the space from the centre of the room. Each corner sported a single bed with a shared desk between the two pairs. Each bed had a bedside cabinet and a small wardrobe. Three areas had been personalised with posters on the wall and colourful bedding but one area in particular drew his attention. The spot at the top left, nearest the window, stood out as it was totally devoid of personality.

Dawson sensed he was looking at the space of Sadie Winters.

He took a step forward.

'Hey, who are you?' said a voice from behind.

He turned to find a ginger-haired freckled girl glaring at him. 'Detective Sergeant Dawson,' he answered. 'And you?'

'Err… I'd quite like to see your identification, please?' she said, without answering his question.

He took it from his pocket and held it forward.

She looked at it, closely. And nodded

'I'm Tilly,' she said, stepping past him and throwing her satchel on the bed. 'And I live over here.'

'You were friends with Sadie?' he asked, moving towards the bed opposite hers. He noted her posters were of world maps and horses.

'Umm… well…'

'You didn't get on?' he asked, in the face of her hesitation.

She scrunched up her face. 'Well, neither of the above, really,' she admitted, taking a textbook from her bedside cabinet.

'Sadie wasn't the easiest person to be friends with,' she said, and then frowned as though she'd said something wrong.

Dawson got it. 'It's okay to tell the truth,' he advised.

'Well, not really cos she's dead,' Tilly answered, tucking her red curls behind her ear.

Dawson wondered how the two girls could live in such close quarters and not be friends.

'Did you try to make friends with her?' he asked. Maybe Sadie had rebuffed her attempts.

She rolled her eyes dramatically. 'Jeez, look at me. I'm the ginger-haired kid with freckles. I look like a reject from the cast of *Annie*. I need all the friends I can get. Even the weirdos.'

'And was she one of those?' Dawson asked. 'A weirdo?'

'Not really, just closed off all the time. Serious, never hung with the rest of us. Mainly studied and sat there scribbling.'

'Did Sadie have a boyfriend?' he asked. He knew kids started young these days.

She shook her head. 'I don't think so, but she wouldn't have told us if she had.'

Dawson had a sudden thought.

'Was Sadie being bullied?'

Tilly actually laughed out loud. 'You're kidding. There's no one that would have bullied Sadie.'

'Why not?' he asked.

Tilly simply shrugged and headed for the door.

'They just wouldn't, and now I really gotta go.'

'Okay, thanks for the chat, Tilly,' he said as she bolted out of the door.

It had been a short conversation but one in which he felt he'd learned quite a lot about the young girl.

She had been withdrawn, unsociable and unhappy. He had been the first to question his boss's gut on this one. But now he felt his own instinct begin to react to something that Tilly had said.

She'd been so definite, resolute that Sadie Winters was not being bullied and now he wanted to know why.

# CHAPTER 14

'Well, that was helpful,' Kim said, as Jaqueline Harris left the room.

'Give the woman a break,' Bryant said. 'She's only been Sadie's housemistress for just over a month.'

'Oh yeah, she was very quick to tell us she's only been in the position for a short period of time and that she has ninety-six girls in her care. I think the word "troubled" is going to come up a lot,' she said, recalling the woman's brief understanding of Sadie Winters.

'That word seems to follow this kid around,' Bryant observed as the heavy oak door opened.

Nancy's permed head popped into view. 'May I offer you coffee or tea or—'

'Nancy, is there really no other room we can use?' Kim asked, looking around at the wood covered walls, stained and re-stained over the years to resemble the colour of melted chocolate. The heavy thick beams that ran the eight-foot length of the ceiling that seemed to be only inches from her head when she stood.

While Jacqueline Harris had been speaking Kim had realised why the room bothered her so much. Fairview, the children's home where she'd spent much of her childhood, had had a room just like it.

It had been called the quiet room. Allegedly, it had been a place of reflection for minor discretions, usually backchat, coming in late for curfew or another minor breach of the rules. And the quiet room had been quiet, indeed, and locked from the outside. Usually for eight to ten hours at a time.

She remembered she'd just turned seven years old and at the home for three months when she was first introduced to the quiet room for deliberately spilling another girl's drink at the dinner table. And she had.

Her open hand had knocked the plastic beaker from the new Jamaican girl's grip, and she had watched the cheap, thin orange cordial spread across the table as girls had squealed and backed away from the travelling puddle, raising their plates of limp cheese sandwiches out of the way.

Kim had refused to apologise and had been grabbed by Mrs Hunt and dragged to the quiet room.

She had been removed six hours later and ordered to apologise. Again she had refused, and her own stubbornness had prevented her explaining that she had knocked the drink away after seeing one of the older, meaner girls spit into it.

During her time at Fairview Kim had been no stranger to the quiet room. One carer had once joked about putting a nameplate on the door.

'Sorry, officer, but Principal Thorpe said this was the only room available,' Nancy said, bringing her back to the present.

*Oh, he did, did he?* Kim thought. If he thought trying to confine her to an office barely bigger than a jewellery box was going to speed up their investigation, he could think again.

'And I'm afraid Graham Steele, the school counsellor, won't be coming to see you next,' Nancy continued. 'He's had to leave site unexpectedly.'

'Okay, thank you,' Bryant offered, quickly, obviously seeing the scowl that was settling on her face.

She frowned as the door closed behind Thorpe's assistant.

Kim stood and opened it again before looking back into the room.

'Okay, Bryant, come on, give me a hand,' she said, lifting her side of the desk.

'You're kidding?' he said.

She shook her head and began dragging the desk along the floor.

'Jesus, hang on, you're gonna bloody hurt yourself,' he said, grabbing the other end.

'Yeah, well, I'm going to hurt someone else if I stay in here much longer,' she admitted. 'And the likelihood is that it's gonna be you.'

'Turn it sideways,' he said, as she reached the door.

Kim had quickly realised that the desk was a replica and nowhere near as heavy as the real thing would be.

'Where are we taking it?' he asked, once they were in the corridor.

'Just follow me,' she said, walking backwards.

Once she was back in the grand entrance hall she set her end down.

'This will do nicely,' she said, heading back for the chairs. She wheeled two out at the same time, one with each hand. Interviewees would have to pass them to get to the cupboard in which they'd originally been placed.

'Not sure Thorpe is going to be all tickety boo with this arrangement,' he said, as they sat down facing the entrance door.

'His problem, not mine,' she said, already feeling the cloying darkness evaporate from around her. She took a deep breath and began to relax.

'Okay, so seeing as our counsellor is MIA, who are we interviewing next?'

Bryant took the list from his pocket and appeared to do a double take before a slow smile spread across his face.

'The next one is a person I feel will need no introduction at all.'

# CHAPTER 15

Dawson sat on the bed and took a moment. How many times had Sadie Winters sat in this exact same spot and contemplated life, and even possibly death?

There was an alien feeling inside him at the thought of going through her possessions despite the fact he knew she wasn't going to barge in and accuse him of snooping. A teenage girl's bedroom was her safe place; somewhere she could express herself and evolve into someone that felt at ease with the world. A place she used while she found somewhere to fit and the person she was meant to be. And as this corner of the room was the place Sadie had spent most of her time, this was as good as it got.

He wondered why she had been so unhappy here and if she'd asked her parents if she could leave. He remembered pleading with his mother to take him out of school after Johnny Croke and his gang had forced him to eat ten cream crackers straight. The moisture in his mouth had been swallowed up by the second, leaving him coughing and choking as the dry flakes of each cracker tumbled down his throat. His discomfort had only made them laugh more. Only once the last bite had gone did Johnny Croke give him back his school bag.

He had been ten years old.

His mother had always offered him a goal. Kept him moving forward to the weekend, to a day out, a special event, a holiday. And it got him to the age of fifteen when he took things into his own hands and began to lose weight.

He hadn't left school with many friends and had failed to pick up many more along the way. His earlier experiences at school had left him suspicious of people's motives. Many times, kids had attempted to befriend him and always with the intention of ridiculing him.

He was aware that all those hours spent in the gym and running in the early morning when no one could see his rolls of fat jiggling along the pavement had instilled in him a selfishness and self-obsessed nature. But as the years since his school days increased he was able to take a breath and accept that he would never be forced into such a place of powerlessness again.

Time had also taught him to value the few friends he now had.

He wondered if he would find any evidence of the friendships in Sadie's life as he gingerly opened the top drawer of her bedside cabinet.

It contained a hairbrush, an array of dark nail varnishes, a few pieces of costume jewellery, marker pens and elastic bands. Dawson surmised this was her junk drawer. Everyone had one. It was the drawer that held everything you didn't know where to place.

The second drawer was full of textbooks, and the third held a few notebooks, two chocolate bars and a packet of crisps.

He looked around, ready to move on to the next space, wondering why there were no family photos: her parents, sister, even a dog.

He stood and opened the wardrobe door. The left-hand side was devoted to school wear and the right to casual wear, with a few smarter pieces shoved in at the end. The bottom of the wardrobe was filled with different coloured trainers and the top shelf with warm jumpers and a couple of jackets.

He felt along the shelves to see if anything had been placed there, but it was all clothes.

He stood at the foot of the bed and frowned. His search was complete.

He sat back on the bed and opened the top drawer of the bedside cabinet again. This was the space that bothered him. In addition to being the junk drawer, the bedside cabinet was also normally used for quick access. The place you kept the most important stuff.

There was nothing of any importance in this drawer, which could only mean one thing.

Someone had been here first.

# CHAPTER 16

Kim's expression gave nothing away as the familiar figure sauntered across the great hall towards her.

'Cheers, mate,' she said, under her breath to her colleague who really could have warned her.

The expression of Joanna Wade was amused as she took a seat on the other side of the reproduction desk.

'We meet again, Miz Wade,' Kim said, meeting her gaze and recalling her insistence on the title the last time they'd met.

'As I knew we would, Inspector,' the woman offered, sitting back and crossing her long legs.

'Death unites us once more,' Kim observed. 'But what brings you here?'

Kim had first met Joanna Wade a couple of years earlier while investigating the murder of school principal Teresa Wyatt, a woman linked to the discovery of bones at the site of a derelict children's home. After interviewing most of the woman's colleagues and receiving the exact same 'saintly' description, this woman had been the only one to tell them the truth, while flirting outrageously with Kim.

She had changed very little, Kim noted. Her long blonde hair was tied back in a ponytail revealing a strong, square jaw and piercing blue eyes. Her plain black trousers were well cut, emphasising her long legs, and a plain white silk shirt showed a St Christopher around her neck.

'Buy me a drink and I'll tell you,' she said, smiling.

Kim ignored the response and continued. 'You taught Sadie Winters?' she asked.

All amusement disappeared from Joanna's eyes and was replaced by sadness.

'I did, indeed, Inspector,' she said.

'For how long?'

'Since I joined the team last September.'

'So, just over six months?'

'Six months is a long time here,' she replied.

The response took Kim by surprise. Not so much the words as the tone. It was covered with a quick smile, the type one uses to convince the other person it was a joke, but Kim had not missed the regret. She really found herself wondering why Joanna Wade had made the move but guessed that she was not going to find out.

'Different to your last school?' Kim asked. If she recalled correctly Joanna's teaching methods had sometimes been unconventional and derided by her boss despite getting and keeping the attention of her students.

Joanna simply nodded, and Kim understood she was getting no more.

'So, what was she like, Sadie?' Kim asked. 'And please don't say troubled,' she added.

Joanna shook her head. 'I wasn't going to. I'd describe her as introspective, reflective and far more talented than she gave herself credit for.'

'In what way?'

'Poetry,' Joanna answered. 'She saw her writings as pointless ramblings. They were expressive and occasionally a little self-indulgent, but she was thirteen. I think we were all captivated by our own emotions at that age. Her poems reflected much of what was going on in her mind.'

Kim saw Bryant make a note. She guessed it was to ask Dawson about such writings amongst her personal possessions.

'Like what?' Kim asked, wanting to understand the girl better.

'Her place in the world, fear, often loneliness, just stuff,' Joanna said, glancing away.

Kim waited for her gaze to return. '"Stuff"?'

There was something that Joanna was keeping to herself.

'As I said, Inspector, she was thirteen years of age.'

The set expression was back, and Kim felt the woman's resolve to say nothing more on the subject. She had a feeling that Joanna's stubbornness mirrored her own.

'Did you ever have any trouble with her in lessons?' Kim asked.

Joanna shook her head. 'I didn't.'

'Indicating that someone else did?' she pushed.

Joanna opened her hands expressively. 'Sadie loved English, so she was never any bother to me.'

Kim opened her mouth to speak as Principal Thorpe entered the grand hall and stopped dead. The young couple chatting excitedly behind almost walked into him.

The woman's right hand instinctively covered her extended stomach.

These folks were getting in early.

The principal's face turned thunderous before he remembered prospective customers were right behind him.

'May I ask…'

'My apologies for relocating,' Kim said, pleasantly. 'But the office allocated for questioning and taking statements was not particularly suitable.'

She wanted to ensure that the young couple were under no illusion as to who they were.

They both frowned towards the principal whose face was colouring with rage. The woman's hand had remained against her stomach.

'Alternative facilities will be found, Inspector,' he said, with a slight flare of the nostrils.

He offered her a look as he guided the young couple past, leaving Kim in no doubt they'd be rehoused at the earliest opportunity.

Joanna Wade smiled at her ruefully. 'Does Inspector Kim Stone normally get everything she wants?'

'Most times,' Bryant answered for her.

'So, Miz Wade, what more can you tell us about Sadie's accident?' Kim asked.

'Not much,' she admitted. 'I wasn't there.'

'How did you come to know about it?'

'I was in my classroom preparing for a lesson when I heard a commotion in the hallway. I heard her name and the word roof. I can add two and two like any other person.'

'And where is your classroom?' Kim asked, wondering how far away from the action she'd been.

'I'm at the front of the house facing the second row of elm trees.'

'To the left of the metal grate in front of the daffodils?' Kim asked.

Joanna thought for a moment and then nodded. 'Pretty much,' she answered.

Kim realised that if Sadie had jumped she would have sailed right past the teacher's window.

'Okay, thank you, Miz Wade.'

'Finished with me so soon?' Joanna asked, allowing her voice to drip with disappointment.

Kim hid her smile. Different case, different location but Joanna Wade had not changed one bit.

'If we need anything further we know where to find you.'

'At the Waggon and Horses on a Thursday night playing darts, as I already told you.'

'Thank you,' Kim said, holding the woman's intense gaze.

Joanna offered her a smile as she stood, turned and walked away.

Kim took out her phone as a thought occurred to her.

'Yeah, boss,' Stacey answered on the second ring.

'Stace, you got the witness reports there from Plant yet?'

'Yep. He dropped 'em in about an hour ago.'

'How many?' Kim asked.

'Around forty, fifty or so,' she answered.

'Drop the background checks for now and go through them all, Stace. In detail.'

'Okay, boss, what exactly am I looking for?'

'We now know that Sadie was never on the roof, but everyone heard that she was. It had to have started somewhere. I want to know who was the first to say they actually saw Sadie Winters up on that roof.'

# CHAPTER 17

Dawson was sure he'd traversed this corridor once already. For the second time, he was passing the mahogany bookshelves holding all the leather-bound Heathcrest yearbooks. He decided that this damn place was fine for people who already knew their way around it. Plenty of signs on the outside of the building but not so much inside.

If he was honest, he couldn't wait to get out of the place. The air of privilege was as oppressive to him as the dark wooden beams that bore down on him from every wrong turn he took while trying to get back to the great hall.

Places like this didn't sit well with him.

His own school experience had been in overcrowded classrooms with harassed teachers trying to get through a tight curriculum. He recalled a parents' evening when he was fourteen years old. His mother had been ten minutes into the conversation with his form teacher before realising they were discussing the wrong kid.

His worst gripe with private education was the weight of aspiration. In schools like Heathcrest it was assumed that you would amount to something. In his school, it had been assumed that you would not.

At his school, the focus had been on getting a kid through the basics so they'd be equipped to get a job. Here it was preparing them for a career.

His career choices had been woodwork, metalwork, mechanic, or bus driver – at a push. Here, he was looking at future doctors, surgeons, athletes, and politicians.

He thought of his own child, Charlotte, two years old and into everything. He already felt, as her father, that she could be anything she wanted to be. And he would do everything within his power to make her dreams come true. But how the hell could he ever compete with this?

A movement through an open door caught his attention. He stepped back and took a look. Approximately fifteen lads, aged around twelve, were jogging from one end of the gym hall to the other.

'Come on, Piggott, keep up,' called the teacher from the sidelines.

Dawson spied the kid who was half a room length behind the others. The perspiration had stained his blue tee shirt, and his white fleshy legs wobbled as his shorts rode up between his legs. Dawson guessed him to be a couple of stone overweight.

'May I help you?' asked the teacher, who had spotted him at the doorway within seconds.

He swiftly produced his identification and introduced himself. 'Here regarding the incident with Sadie Winters. Did you know her?'

The man offered his hand, while shaking his head. Dawson tried not to envy the thigh muscles that strained at the navy shorts or the size of his biceps that looked like the man was hiding a football in each arm. He didn't need to lift his tee shirt to know there would be an impressive six-pack under there.

Dawson guessed him to be early- to mid-forties and was struck with the sudden vision of this man strolling into the pub in twenty years' time still wearing clothes that would show off his physique.

He really should get to the gym more, he berated himself.

'Philip Havers, boys' physical education and sports coach; and honestly, I didn't know the young girl at all. I have enough trouble keeping track of my boys,' he said, glancing at the small group still trotting backwards and forwards.

Dawson wondered if he'd ever worked at a real school, classrooms stuffed full with thirty or more kids. Having them all running up and down in one room would have been like a herd of stampeding bulls.

'Bloody hell, Piggott, you're losing ground. Step it up,' he called out.

Even Dawson could see the fat kid had lost another half metre.

'Come on, pig, catch up,' called one of the other kids over his shoulder.

Fate could not have been crueller in allowing pig to form part of the fat kid's name. Dawson waited for Philip Havers to remonstrate the child who had turned and called out.

He did not.

Instead he rolled his eyes in Dawson's direction. 'The kid's all in and this is only the warm-up session.'

Dawson remembered it well. He recalled pushing his muscles to the limit to try and keep up. He could feel the burn in his legs as though it was happening right now.

'Three more lengths, and will someone give Piggott some encouragement?' Havers called out.

The kid who had called out began chanting: 'Pig, Pig, Pig.' By the third call, all of the kids were chanting his name.

Dawson felt the tension crawl into his jaw. Not the encouragement he would have liked to have heard.

'Peer pressure works every time,' Havers said above the collective chanting. 'He's clawed back half a metre already.'

*Yeah, humiliation and embarrassment will do that for you*, Kev thought, viewing the scene before him differently to the teacher. The poor kid looked exhausted. His face was red from exertion, and the sweat beads were now lines of moisture trickling down his temples. His mouth was permanently open as he tried to send more air to his lungs.

'A bit harsh?' Dawson observed, which didn't even come close to how he really felt.

'Not if it makes him think twice about eating the next cream cake, or two.'

'So, would any of these kids have known Sadie Winters?' Dawson asked, guiding himself to solid ground. Punching the PE teacher in the face was unlikely to do the case, or his career, any favours.

The teacher looked around as the boys began their final length of the hall. Piggott's earlier exertion had caught up with him and he was now paying the price, lagging almost half a length behind.

'Can I talk to any of them?'

Havers thought for a minute. 'Yeah, take Piggott, he's pretty useless at basketball anyway.'

Before Dawson could respond Havers blew a whistle and began issuing instructions to the boys to bring in the equipment from the edge of the hall.

'Not you, Piggott, over here,' he called, as the lad hit the wall for the last time.

The boy looked both confused and relieved as he half walked and half staggered towards them.

'Police officer here wants a word,' he said, squeezing him on the shoulder.

The boy's breathing was hard and laboured as he nodded.

Dawson looked around 'Where can...'

'There's a bench outside the door,' he said, pointing to the corridor.

Dawson nodded his thanks and headed outside.


'Here,' he said, handing the kid a handkerchief from his pocket. The activity had stopped but the sweating had not.

'Thank you,' he said, mopping his head, face and around the back of his neck before offering it back.

'Keep it,' Dawson said.

The kid mopped his brow again.

'So, what's your name?' he asked.

'Piggott, sir,' he answered.

'Your first name,' he clarified.

'Geoffrey, sir,' he replied politely.

'Did you know Sadie Winters?' he asked.

Geoffrey shrugged. 'A bit. She wasn't like the other girls here.'

'In what way?'

'She wasn't stuck-up or mean. She didn't care all that much about girls' stuff like hair or make-up or jewellery. She was on her own a lot. She didn't need to be in a group, pointing and making fun.'

Dawson could hear his disdain for the female species. He had felt the same way when he was twelve and had thought he'd always feel the same way. Boy, did this kid have a shock coming.

'Do some of the girls make fun of you, Geoffrey?' he asked.

Geoffrey hesitated before nodding. 'But not as much when Sadie was around,' he admitted.

'Did Sadie stick up for you?'

He nodded and dabbed at his forehead once more.

'Were the other girls scared of her?' Dawson asked. That wasn't the impression he'd got from Tilly.

He shook his head. 'Not scared of her but she defended me one time when some girls kept pushing me to the end of the dinner line, telling me to miss a meal.'

'What did she do?' Dawson asked, fighting off his own similar memories.

'She grabbed my hand and took me back to my place in the line and stood there, glowering at them, until I had my food. And once I'd been served she just disappeared.'

Dawson suspected he would have liked this girl.

'Did you see much of her around the school?'

'Sometimes I'd see her just sitting in some strange place, on the floor, up against the wall, reading or scribbling in a book.'

Another mention of the scribbling in a book he'd been unable to find.

'I'd sometimes try and catch her eye, but it was like she was always somewhere else.'

'Was she being bullied?' he asked, as he'd asked Tilly.

Geoffrey shook his head, immediately. 'No, no one would bully Sadie.'

Dawson was confused. By all accounts Sadie Winters was different to the other girls. She didn't mix, and she didn't conform. A definite recipe for being targeted. But this was the exact same response he'd received from the girl with whom she'd shared a room.

'Why not?' he asked, as Mr Havers appeared in the corridor.

'May I have my student back, officer?'

Geoffrey stood but Dawson put a steadying hand on his arm.

'Just one more minute,' he said to the teacher, who disappeared back into the hall wearing a look of irritation.

'I really must go,' Geoffrey said, glancing at the teacher's disappearing back.

'Okay, Geoffrey, but can you just explain why the other girls left Sadie alone?'

He was already edging away.

'They left her alone because of her connections to The Card Suits.'

'Connections? Suits?' Dawson queried.

He nodded as he turned to leave.

'Yes, her sister is the Queen of Hearts.'

Dawson frowned as the kid slipped back into the gym hall.

What the hell was the Queen of Hearts?

# CHAPTER 18

'So what's the plan now?' Bryant asked, glancing at his watch. It was almost five o'clock and they were taking a breather outside.

True to his word Mitch had packed up forensics a few hours earlier. The bloodied gravel had been removed and a patch of brand new pristine stones dropped in its place. But even without the marker she would have been able to pick out the exact spot of the young girl's bloodied head.

So far, they'd spoken to fifteen teachers and not one of them had been able to offer anything useful. In fact, all they'd managed to establish was that Sadie had left one lesson completely intact and had never turned up for the next and no one had seen her in between.

'I want to speak to Sadie's sister,' Kim said. 'We're getting nowhere with the adults. I want to know more about Sadie, but I don't want to mention the self-harming to her parents yet. Saffron might have known,' she said.

'We could always do my appraisal,' he said, taking her by surprise.

She hadn't given it a thought, despite Woody's prompting.

'Err... not right now,' she said.

'Why not, we're clearly not going to see any more teachers and I'm sure getting the address for Saffron Winters can wait for ten minutes.'

'You think that's how long it will take?' she asked, raising an eyebrow.

'If you conduct them the way you do everything else, we'll probably have it nailed in five and still have time for a cuppa.'

'It's just not the right—'

'Guv, is something wrong?' he asked.

'No, it's just—' she stopped speaking as her phone began to ring.

'Ah, just the person,' she said to Bryant, seeing Principal Thorpe's name on the display.

'Stone,' she answered.

'Inspector, it's Principal Thorpe,' he offered, formally.

She waited for him to continue.

'I'm calling to confirm that alternative arrangements for questioning have been made should you require them,' he offered, tightly.

Kim fought back the smile.

'That's very kind of you, Principal Thorpe,' she said. 'And while I have you would it be possible to take down the address for Mr and Mrs Winters?'

'Of course, I have their main address in Droitwich and their holiday home in Snowdonia. Which would you prefer?'

'Whichever address I can find their other daughter, Saffron.'

'Oh,' he said, surprised. 'In that case you'll be needing neither. Saffron Winters is still here, at school, with us.'

# CHAPTER 19

'Well, this is a bit more acceptable, don't you think, Bryant?' Kim asked, as they looked around the room.

Principal Thorpe had kindly guided them to a spacious reading room adjacent to the library. Despite the falling dusk she could still make out the view of the hockey pitch and tennis courts.

Bryant whistled appreciatively. 'Good result even if your methods are somewhat—'

'Imaginative,' she answered for him.

'Not the word I was going to use but we'll stick with it for now,' he replied, taking his seat beside her.

'So, why do you reckon she hasn't gone home?' Bryant asked, voicing the question on both their minds.

'I have no clue, Bryant. I'd have thought the family would have wanted to be together. Surely the best place for her is with them at home.'

'Definitely where I'd want to be if my sister had just died,' he answered.

'Unless this feels like home,' Kim pondered. 'The kids spend so long here it may be more familiar to them than their own homes.'

'Could be, but I'd still want to be where my parents were,' he said. 'Surely no school can replicate that security and safety.'

'Hmm…' she said thoughtfully, as a confident knock sounded on the door.

'Come in,' Bryant called.

Kim offered a smile to the girl that had barrelled towards her the day before. 'Please sit down, Saffron.'

The girl nodded and walked towards them. 'Call me Saffie, please,' she said, taking a seat.

Two words struck Kim immediately. Elegant and confident. From the top of her corn-coloured blonde hair to the tips of her black Lanvin chain-embellished leather boots there was an assured grace to Saffron Winters not present in most sixteen-year-old girls she'd met.

Kim tore her gaze away from the footwear over which she'd hankered herself but at more than one thousand pounds were well beyond her level of disposable income. Even dressed in a plain cold shoulder tee shirt and light blue jeans there was something about Saffie Winters that demanded attention.

Her blue eyes were piercing and set in a face moulded by the gods.

Kim remembered who her parents were and realised this girl had inherited the best of both of them. And clearly Sadie had not.

Bryant introduced them both before turning genuinely sympathetic eyes on the girl. 'Saffie, we're very sorry for the loss of your sister,' he said.

'Thank you,' she said, with politeness but little emotion.

Kim wondered if it had all sunk in yet. It had barely been twenty-four hours.

'You didn't want to go home?' Kim asked, gently

She shook her head. 'I'm busier here,' she said simply.

Kim would have liked to explore the reasons for that further but decided to push on. She had some tough questions to ask.

'Were the two of you close, Saffie?'

She gave the question serious consideration, before shaking her head. 'We were once but not so close any more.'

'So, you didn't spend much time together?' Kim continued.

Saffie shook her head.

Kim tried to understand an environment where the sisters boarded and schooled together but spent little time in each other's company.

'We're hearing the word troubled a lot in relation to your sister. Would you agree?'

There was no hesitation. 'Yes, officer, I would agree. I don't think she had any friends.'

*And yet you still spent no time together*, Kim thought.

'She preferred her own company,' Saffie said, as though reading her thoughts.

'She liked to write, apparently,' Kim said. 'Poetry,' she added.

Saffie looked surprised. 'Did she? I didn't know that.'

'Her English teacher thought she had a talent for it.'

Saffie nodded but Kim detected an air of impatience or disinterest in her expression; all too soon it was gone.

'Saffie, where were you when Sadie was on the ground outside?' Bryant asked.

'I was in the music room,' she said.

Exactly where Principal Thorpe had said he was going to fetch her from half an hour ago. She seemed to spend a lot of time there.

Kim had the uneasy feeling there was something lacking from this exchange. She'd felt more genuine emotion radiating from Joanna Wade than she was detecting right now from a blood relation.

'Saffie, were you surprised when you heard that Sadie had jumped from the roof?'

Saffie shook her head. 'My parents had been trying to reach her for months without success. The more they tried the more she retreated.'

Kim had the feeling that Saffie could have been talking about anyone.

'Did you know that your sister was a self-harmer?'

This time, genuine surprise shaped her face, telling Kim the shock at the poetry admission had been false. She caught the flash of annoyance that followed the shock.

'She cut herself,' Kim added.

'I probably shouldn't be surprised,' she said.

'Why's that?'

'Sometimes she did like to grab all the attention,' Saffie said.

Except she hadn't done it anywhere that someone could see, Kim thought to herself, so she wasn't grabbing anyone's attention, or even trying to.

'Did she ever talk to you about it?'

'No, Inspector, she didn't,' Saffie said impatiently.

'But you're her—'

'Officer, I think you should know that my sister didn't like me very much.'

Kim found herself taken aback by the frank admission.

'Any particular reason?' she asked.

'I got bored of asking, to be honest with you. Just like my parents, I couldn't reach her either.'

So, had everyone just given up? Kim wondered. Had no one tried to find a way to reach her?

'I've asked about friends and you say she had very few—'

'No, I said she had none,' Saffie clarified.

'So, what about enemies?' Kim asked.

'I'm not sure why you're asking that, but I would assume not. Just as she failed to interact positively I'm reasonably sure she failed to interact negatively.'

Kim sat back in her chair. 'I'm starting to get a picture here of a young teenage girl largely ignored by everyone to the point of invisibility.'

Kim thought about the pile of ironing in her spare room at home. She had ignored it for so long she didn't even see it any more.

'If that's how it was then that's exactly how she wanted it,' Saffie answered, glancing at her watch.

Kim really had little else to ask her at this point.

'Okay, Saffie, thank you for your time, and if we need anything further we'll come and find you.'

'I'll be here,' she answered.

Kim tipped her head. 'You don't plan on going home to spend time with your parents?'

'No, Inspector. They'll be fine. They have each other.'

Again, there was no emotion. Just statement of fact.

Saffie nodded at them both and then left the room.

Kim heard voices on the other side of the door before Principal Thorpe's head appeared. He dangled his set of keys.

'Are you finished for the evening, only we lock this room…'

'Of course,' Kim said, standing. It was almost six.

'Strange, don't you think, that she hasn't chosen to go home at a time like this, Principal Thorpe?'

He smiled with sadness and a hint of pride.

'We tried to insist but she wouldn't hear of it. She didn't want to let us down.'

Kim was confused. 'How would going home and grieving for her sister in any way be letting you or the school down?'

'Saturday night, Inspector, is our annual gala night, and Saffron Winters is the star of the show.'

# CHAPTER 20

Despite having little to report Kim found herself knocking on Woody's door at ten minutes to seven, as instructed.

The day had been frustrating and had not proven as fruitful as she'd hoped. And now she had to admit that she'd been wrong to ask for the murder announcement to be delayed. It had earned her nothing.

'Sir, I don't have a great deal to tell you,' she said, taking the seat he pointed to.

He nodded for her to continue.

'We've spoken to Sadie's friends, teachers, her sister and the picture that's emerging is of a lonely, emotional young girl who appeared to have retreated from everyone around her. She was not a mean kid and had no issues with anyone.'

'Well, clearly she did judging by those injuries,' he said, nodding towards his computer screen. Obviously he had studied the post-mortem report.

'Nothing that stands out,' she clarified.

'No suspects at all?' he asked, frowning.

A picture of Saffie floated into her head but she shook it away. 'No, sir.'

'You hesitated,' he said, narrowing his gaze.

'Her sister is a bit strange is all. They didn't get on, which is nothing unusual. I'd be stretching to call her a person of interest.'

'So, what next?' he asked, picking up his pen and rolling it between his fingers.

'We'll regroup in the morning before the press conference and then I'll announce Sadie's death as murder,' she said.

Woody shook his head. 'No, you won't.'

She made no effort to hide her surprise. Normally Woody pushed her to deal more with the press.

'Won't what?' she queried. 'Announce it as murder or take the press conference.'

'Neither,' he answered.

'Sir, we need to announce it. We've found no clear motive for the murder of Sadie Winters. No forensics to try and match. How do we know other kids are not at risk? I appreciate you giving me the day to find out, but we really now have to be fair to the parents who may want to remove their children from the school.'

'Murder is not to be mentioned by us, do you understand, Stone?'

'No, sir, I don't,' she replied. 'Please explain why we are going to risk the lives of more children by not being honest about Sadie's death.'

'I will not explain my decisions to you,' he roared.

'But are they yours?' she asked, unable to stop the words shooting out of her mouth.

He stared at her for a long minute. 'That'll be all, Stone,' he said, shortly.

'Sir, I really must protest. We cannot put more children—'

'I said, that'll be all. Now get out.'

She headed for the door and even though she knew she had already said too much she turned back for one last attempt to voice her argument.

But her boss had already picked up the phone.

# CHAPTER 21

The cards filed into the candle room one by one, their shoes shuffling along the bare concrete. Casual dress but no trainers. Always shoes.

The dark space beneath the bell tower had been the meeting room of the Spades since 1949 and now had a single light bulb in the centre of the fifteen foot square space. It wasn't switched on. Instead the room was lit by a tall candelabra in each corner, casting willowy shadows around the room. It was tradition.

The Joker waited until all the cards stood behind their chairs at the round table, the King to his right and the Jack to his left. His own chair stood before the framed black Spade sewn together from pieces of the graduation gowns of the first twelve cards back in the early fifties.

He sat, and the others followed.

This was an unscheduled late-night meeting. There was an empty chair. One card was missing and that was the reason they were there.

But that would wait for a short while.

'You all know that Sadie Winters is dead?' asked the Joker, gravely.

He watched as they all nodded in turn. As was customary, a card did not speak unless spoken to directly.

'Is there anyone here who knows anything about the incident?' he asked, looking around the circle.

Heads shook in the negative.

The Joker held the gaze of the King for a second longer. A couple of cards had clashed with Sadie Winters, but the King had been closer than most.

The King shook his head.

'Spades don't take the law into their own hands,' said the Joker, to ensure they all understood. 'Punishments are discussed and agreed,' he said, nodding towards the empty chair.

'There is one amongst us that does not adhere to the rules.'

They all nodded and understood the reason for the empty chair.

Six had not been invited.

'Which one of you explained the rules?'

Every head turned towards Seven.

'And did you tell him about Lewis Millward?' the Joker asked.

Seven nodded.

'Speak,' he instructed. It had been a direct question.

'Yes,' Seven answered.

Lewis Millward's experience served as a cautionary tale that had been handed down for the last twelve years. Lewis had been fourteen years old when offered the Ace of Spades at roughly the same time one of his buddies had been invited into the Clubs.

Lewis had felt he could choose which rules he would follow and which rules he would not and continued to spend time with his former friend. Despite warnings from the Joker and all other cards he had continued to flout the rules.

One night he had been removed from his bed and taken to the shower block and placed beneath a stream of freezing cold water to recite the rules until he fully understood them. Only once his lips had begun turning blue was he allowed to get out and dry off.

Finally, he got it.

Spades and Clubs didn't mix.

The importance of the rules was made clear to every card from the moment they were invited to join.

'Recite them to me, Seven,' the Joker instructed.

Seven shifted uncomfortably. His humiliation would ensure that he drummed the rules into the next new recruit.

The Joker said the words in his head as Seven recited them.

> *'Respect the suit and its cards beyond all others.*
> *Keep the secrets of the suit and all its cards.*
> *Once a Spade, always a Spade.*
> *Always be ready to help a fellow card.*
> *Never aid a Club suit card.'*

And that was the one they would discuss today.

'Six helped a Club with his chemistry homework.'

A low murmur travelled around the table.

As was tradition, the person who had explained the rules was responsible for the punishment.

The responsible card raised his head. He understood.

'Okay, Seven, you know what you have to do.'

# CHAPTER 22

'So, who's up first?' Kim asked, stepping into the squad room.

'I'll start, boss,' Stacey said. 'Went through the witness statements as you asked.' She shook her head. 'Cor find anyone who actually saw her on the roof.'

Kim frowned. How the hell was that even possible?

'Did you track all the statements?' she asked.

'Yes, boss,' Stacey said standing up and moving over to the spare desk.

The statements had been laid out in vertical lines overlapping each other, like playing cards in the game of patience.

'First and longest line are the people who state who actually told them either by phone or in person. The second line are the ones that heard about it from shouting in the hallway, and the third line are people who cor remember how they found out.'

'Damn it,' Kim said, unable to comprehend that they could not track it to the original source. She was sure that had been the work of the murderer.

'Anything else?' she asked.

'Just started getting some background on the adults. Sadie's parents are obviously well-heeled.'

'Two girls at a private school for thirty-five grand a year. I'd have thought so,' Dawson observed.

The detective constable slid back into her seat and tapped a few keys.

'Laurence Winters was born into the illustrious Winters family that specialise in manufacturing medical equipment. There's been a Winters child at Heathcrest since Laurence's great-grandfather was sent there during the War.

'And Hannah Winters?'

'A bit more colourful. Hannah Winters descends from the Sheldon line, a blue blood family who can be traced back to the 1400s. Lots of titles but not a pot to piss in. Made their money from horse breeding and racing, until Hannah's grandfather lost a coveted race and in a fit of madness shot every horse and then himself.

'Left with crippling debts, Hannah's father sold off every property they owned and managed to keep enough back for Hannah to go to Heathcrest with the single directive of—'

'Finding a rich husband,' Kim finished.

*And she'd certainly done that*, she thought.

'Anything else?' Kim asked.

'Not yet,' Stacey said with a look of glee. 'But give me chance. There's some real saucy stuff goes on behind these rich and powerful doors.'

Kim raised one eyebrow at her colleague.

She wondered idly if Stacey felt she'd been backtracked slightly. On their last major case, she'd been paired up with Dawson and both had done an outstanding job of uncovering a network of slave labour. Kim been allowed additional manpower and had seconded Austin Penn, from Travis's team; but she knew that Woody wouldn't sanction that again, and anyway, Kim needed someone with Stacey's data skills on this one.

From the look on her face, Kim was reassured that Stacey wasn't taking it too badly at all.

'Kev, anything from Sadie's friends?'

'Not a lot. The girl doesn't seem to have had many friends, to be honest. She certainly was a loner.'

'What did you turn up from her room?' Kim asked.

He shook his head. 'A big fat nothing, boss. No writings, no doodles, no backpack; in fact, nothing personal at all. The drawers were pretty much emptied.'

'Someone got there first?' she asked.

'I'd say so. Something there that someone didn't want us to find.'

'Hmm…' Kim said thoughtfully, wondering who would want to hide Sadie's personal effects from them.

'Any boyfriend?' she asked.

'Nothing so far. Seems like a decent enough kid but not what you'd call outgoing.'

'Okay, Kev. Doesn't seem like we're going to find out much more there, so if you move over to—'

'Boss, do you mind if I keep at it for a bit? There're just a couple of things I want to tie up. I heard something about secret societies at Heathcrest yesterday. Packs of cards or something. Not sure exactly what that means but it might be connected.'

It was on the tip of Kim's tongue to refuse his request and put him on data mining and background checking with Stacey, but if she trusted anything about Dawson it was his instinct.

'Okay, one more day and if you get nothing…'

'Got it, boss,' he said.

'Okay, so we found out pretty much the same as Kev about Sadie's social interaction or lack of it. We also discovered from Keats that Sadie had a history of self-harming, and that her older sister Saffie knew nothing about it.'

'Sister didn't seem to know anything about anything to do with her younger sister,' Bryant offered.

'Not really unusual though, is it?' Dawson asked. 'Looks like they were complete opposites, and who wants their awkward younger sister around them when they're sixteen years old?'

Kim agreed that he had a point, but it had seemed as though they were speaking to Saffie about a complete stranger.

'Any reason why she hasn't gone home?' Stacey asked.

'Practising for a gala at the end of the week. Star of the show with a piano solo.'

'Stiff upper lip and all that,' Stacey said.

Something like that, Kim thought as she glanced around the room and chose her first victim. She had twenty minutes until Woody's press conference.

'Okay, Dawson, you're up. Step into my office,' she said, nodding towards the bowl.

He looked at his two colleagues for a clue.

'Who did I piss off this time?' he asked.

'Me, if you don't get moving,' she said, standing in the doorway. He stepped in and she closed the door behind him.

# CHAPTER 23

'Jesus, Dawson, lighten up,' Kim said, placing his appraisal form between the two of them.

Seeing what it was they were about to discuss seemed to do little to reduce his trepidation.

She had quickly glanced over it once she'd found it underneath a bike magazine in her second drawer down.

'So, I see you've marked yourself five out of five on ability, attendance, work quality and… just about every subject, really?' she said, perusing the whole form.

He grinned. 'Gotta aim high, boss,' he said.

She took a moment to read through the criteria in detail.

'Yeah, nice try but no banana, Kev. You're not gonna get a five for leadership, meeting deadlines or teamwork, and you can rethink the organisational skills score. Getting Stacey to do it for you doesn't count.'

She crossed out the fives and entered a score of four in each box. She turned the page over and back again as though looking for something.

'Hmmm… not sure where to put this,' she said, frowning.

'What's that, boss?'

'Your refusal to listen to my instruction regarding press appeals. I'm looking for the appropriate box.'

He raised his eyes to the ceiling. 'It was one time, boss, and I learned from it.'

Oh yes, he'd learned from it all right. When he'd watched the rest of the team, herself included, stay late into the night ringing back every pointless lead they'd received after she'd told him that was exactly what she knew would happen.

'You took the bullet on that one, eh, boss?' he acknowledged.

Yes, she had told Woody that it was her that had made the press appeal instead of letting on that Dawson had been tricked by a junior reporter. Which she was sure would come up in her next appraisal. Woody hadn't bought it for a minute.

'Which brings us on to areas of improvement,' she said. 'And I see you've left that box blank.'

'I think I'm doing good, boss,' he said, refusing to give an inch.

Kim opened her hands expressively. 'Well, how about we swap seats then and you—'

'I ain't doing that good,' he said, fighting a smile.

'Damn right,' she agreed and then thought for a moment. 'Rash, Kev,' she said, honestly. 'Not the skin kind but the acting sometimes without full consideration for the consequences kind.'

He narrowed his eyes. 'Boss, I'm not sure I'd agree…'

'And bloody argumentative,' she said, pretending to write it down. 'The second doesn't bother me so much. Your umm… challenging nature while intensely annoying, irritating and frustrating does give me pause for thought, now and again. However, your impetuousness will ultimately get you into trouble.'

He thought for a second and then nodded. 'But the thing is, I have this boss who—'

'Isn't being appraised right now,' she interrupted, making a note in the empty box. 'Curb it, before someone gets hurt.'

He opened his mouth against her expression which actively discouraged a debate on the subject.

'Got it, boss.'

She read the entry in the last box on the form marked 'Future Goals'.

'Really?' she asked.

He took a breath. 'I think I'm ready for that next step, boss. I'm not on probation,' he said and then glanced at the appraisal form. 'I think I've demonstrated competence. I have no live warnings or improvement notices and…'

'You trying to convince me, Kev?'

Kim knew that any requested registration form would result in a line manager endorsement form being forwarded to her.

'I've got a family, boss. I wanna provide for Alison, give Charlotte a decent education, you know, give them both a good life.'

Kim understood but it was not a fast or easy process. He would need to sit a legal knowledge exam, be assessed against rank-specific competencies and endure a temporary promotion and work-based assessment before he could even sniff the permanent promotion.

'And, to be honest your opinion means as much to me as—'

'It won't be me making the final decision on—'

'I know, but I'd like to know what you think,' he said, honestly as a polite tapping sounded on the already opening door.

'It's coming on, guv,' Bryant said from the doorway.

She nodded in his direction and stood.

'Boss?' Dawson said, waiting for an answer to his question. Did she think he was ready?

'When we find Sadie's killer I'll be sure to let you know.'

He smiled and followed her out of the door.

\*

They all gathered around Stacey's computer; she had loaded the news channel onto her screen. There stood her boss in front of the north side of the building, not visible from their window.

He was flanked by press liaison officers with lanyards hanging around their necks but no other police officer was present. His authoritative demeanour in his smart black uniform commanded all the attention.

'Turn it up, Stace,' Dawson said from the back.

'…*incident at Heathcrest Academy that has resulted in the death of a thirteen-year-old girl. Our condolences and thoughts are with the family at this time and officers are working*—'

'*Are the circumstances suspicious?*' shouted one female voice from the front.

Kim groaned. She knew that voice well.

Woody ignored the question. '*Officers are currently determining*—'

'*Was it suicide or accidental?*' Frost shouted again, getting the attention of the *Sky News* camera, which now flitted back and forth between the reporter and her boss.

Woody stared straight ahead. '*Our enquiries are ongoing at this time*—'

'*Chief Inspector, was it murder?*' Frost shouted.

The camera whipped right back to Woody, who hesitated before speaking again.

'*We will update you as soon as we have more information,*' he said, before turning away and heading back into the building.

'Bloody Frost,' Kim said, shaking her head. This was exactly what her boss hadn't wanted.

The only thing that would be taken away from this press conference was that one word and his refusal to deny it. *Murder* would be screamed from every headline.

'I'm thinking that Jack is definitely out of the box now, boss,' Dawson observed.

'I think you're right,' Kim said, as her phone began to ring.

She recognised the number as Lloyd House. West Midlands Police headquarters in Birmingham.

*

'Stone,' she answered, heading back into the bowl.

'Detective Inspector Stone, this is Chief Superintendent Briggs.'

Kim had the urge to laugh out loud. She'd heard the name, had even seen his photo, but this man wasn't Woody's boss. He was Woody's boss's boss.

'Sir?'

'Whatever you were doing next, please cancel it. The Winters have requested your presence at their home. They have something they'd like you to see. Immediately,' he said before the line went dead.

She stared at the phone for a full twenty seconds as a feeling of unease stroked the hairs on the back of her neck.

She had the impression that someone was trying to put this Jack back into the box.

# CHAPTER 24

'So, how'd it go, Kev?' Stacey asked as soon as the boss and Bryant had left the room.

He shrugged. 'You know, she confirmed what I already knew. I'm fucking awesome.'

'So, she day mark you down at all?' Stacey asked, knowingly.

'Well, maybe in one or two areas…'

'And she day mention you being tricked into going against her express instructions and doing that public appeal?'

He narrowed his gaze at her. 'It might have come up.'

'And she didn't suggest that sometimes you're—'

'Stace, it's supposed to be confidential,' he snapped. 'But I suppose you've scored yourself modestly?'

Stacey nodded. 'You know, when I was a kid my mum told me never seat yourself at the head of the table, because it's a longer walk if you're asked to step down.'

'Whatever, Stace,' he said, moving around some papers on his desk.

He knew what Stacey meant but he also knew his boss liked confidence. Yeah, there were times he appeared arrogant and cocky, but the boss knew him, and she'd been pretty fair with her scoring. He would have preferred a nice tidy row of top scores, but he'd take what she'd given, and he'd been honest with her too. Yes, he wanted promotion. One day he wanted a team of his own, too, but what he really craved was her endorsement.

He realised his colleague was still looking at him.

'So, what you up to, Kev?'

'What do you mean?' he asked, innocently.

'Look, I know you hate fact-checking but you really gonna avoid spending time with me by making up a line of enquiry to follow?'

He chuckled at her playful tone.

'Hey, who blew who off?' he asked, good-naturedly.

He'd asked if she fancied a drink after work the night before. That Geoffrey kid had stayed on his mind and he hadn't wanted to take it home with him. His own childhood had been thrust right back into his present and he was having trouble shaking it off.

'Sorry, mate, but I'd made plans,' she said, staring at her computer screen.

'Devon, again?' he asked.

Stacey nodded

'Bloody hell, Stace. I make that three dates in a week. You two getting serious?' he asked.

She raised her eyes above the screen edge.

'Well, we have talked about making a commitment—'

'A what?' he gasped.

'To a weekend away somewhere,' she laughed at his expression.

He smiled, enjoying her excitement. From what he knew his colleague had been seeing the immigration officer for a few weeks now, and the change in her was noticeable. He sometimes saw the slow, secret smile on her face when she glanced at her phone when she thought no one was watching. He saw the way she carried herself differently, more confidently than he'd ever seen before. He saw the flash of concern when a case caused them to work late. But what he really saw was the light behind her eyes, that warm glow that came from starting to fall in love.

He wasn't sure if she even knew it herself yet.

'So, ain't that commitment thing enough to get you running for the hills yet?' he asked, playfully.

It was no secret that the drop-dead gorgeous Devon had been interested in Stacey for some time. It was only Stacey who had lacked the confidence or self-worth to give it a go.

'You know, there's only one thing that bothers me more,' she said, seriously.

'What's that?'

'Why you're still sitting here when the boss has green-lighted your line of enquiry.' She narrowed her eyes. 'Now, as much as I'd like to think you're that interested in my personal life, I suspect it's cos you want something from me, so come on, cough.'

He smirked. Jesus, she knew him well.

'Need some background on a couple of kids from Heathcrest. Young lad named Geoffrey Piggott and a girl named Tilly Tromans.'

'Why?' she asked, simply. 'There are hundreds of kids there, why these two?

He shrugged. 'The only two I've found so far who seem to have known Sadie at all.'

'Okay, but you'll have to get in line. Boss's work comes first,' she said matter-of-factly.

'Thanks, Stace,' he said, with a wink.

'So, what did you find out that you didn't share with the boss, Kev?' she asked shrewdly.

He smiled but said nothing. Her antenna was too well tuned this morning.

He wanted to find out a little bit more about this Queen of Hearts.

# CHAPTER 25

'So, what you thinking the grieving parents want to show us, guv?' Bryant asked, as he drove through pools of water from an earlier storm.

The town of Droitwich sat on the River Salwarpe and was the only Midlands area to be in Halifax 'Quality of Life Survey' of 2011.

The satnav deposited them at a tarmac drive flanked by bare, gnarled trees with branches like witches' fingers beckoning them to enter. The trees gave way to natural parkland with a dwelling a half mile in the distance.

'Their own lake?' Bryant observed, glancing to his right.

Kim said nothing. Whatever their material trappings and possessions they had just lost their thirteen-year-old daughter. How much of this would they be prepared to give to get Sadie back? Every bit of it, she suspected.

Although she couldn't help the stab of disappointment at the house as they neared it. The flat white frontage of the monstrous property screamed Regency incarnation but without the age or history behind it. Any 'original features' inside the house would be the total opposite. Manufactured to appear authentic.

Bryant parked the car between two identical Range Rover models. One in black and one in white.

'Nice,' Kim observed.

'Queen of understatement there, guv,' Bryant said.

She shrugged. Give her a bike, any bike and she could tell you its history but fascination with cars was a bit of a mystery to her.

'If I was a fifteen-year-old boy this is the car that would be on my wall,' he continued, looking in the window as he passed. 'It's the new SVAutobiography, 5 litre V8 engine and 539 break horse power.'

Kim remained unimpressed.

'That's the equivalent of five Ford Fiestas, and they come in at around one hundred and fifty grand each,' he explained.

So, if cars of that value are parked outside, exposed to the elements, what on earth is being stored in the three-car garage on the west side of the courtyard? she wondered.

'Not guessing, Bryant, so don't even ask me,' Kim said as they strode across the pristine white gravel towards the pillared portico entrance.

Secretly she would have guessed the house value at around six million, but she was more fascinated with the cleanliness of the tiny white stones on the ground.

The door opened before they had chance to knock. Mrs Winters stood before them, pale faced with a tremulous smile and a proffered hand.

'Thank you for coming so promptly, officers,' she said.

Briggs hadn't really made it sound like a choice, but Kim acknowledged the words.

'Please, come in,' she said, standing aside.

The hallway was blindingly white, from the floor to the walls and the doors leading from the space. A round marble table stood at the centre beneath a circular opening to the upper level.

They followed Hannah Winters to the right of the staircase and into a room furnished in pastel colours. The cream, plush carpet instantly made Kim wonder if there was anything on the bottom of her shoes.

'Please, sit,' she said, fingering a heart-shaped diamond necklace that nestled at the base of her throat.

Kim noted that her nails were painted a soft pink colour to match the cashmere sweater she was wearing over cream slacks. With her straw-coloured hair down and sitting on her shoulders Kim could see the definite resemblance to her eldest daughter, Saffie.

'My husband will be through, shortly, he's just on a call,' she said, offering a polite smile.

Kim detected a recent dose of Botox was responsible for the lack of movement to her features and the absence of lines around her eyes or on her forehead.

'Mrs Winters, may I ask what it is that you—?'

'A letter,' she said. 'It's a letter we found in Sadie's things.'

'From the school?' Kim clarified, recalling Dawson's words.

Hannah hesitated before nodding.

'You took her possessions before we had chance to take a look?' Kim asked, working hard to keep the edge from her voice.

'We did, Inspector,' said Mr Winters as he entered the room with a clear plastic tub. 'And this is everything that was in there,' he said, handing it to her as though they'd done nothing wrong and it was the most natural thing imaginable that he should have access to her belongings first.

She took it from him and placed it on the floor. There was no way she could be sure it was everything or if it was only the items the family were prepared to let her have.

'Mr Winters, it would have been better to have left Sadie's belongings in place so that we could assess the importance of the evidence before—'

'What evidence?' he asked, frowning. 'She took her own life. Why would you need to see her things?'

She had avoided the word 'tampering' only because they were grieving parents.

'Mr Winters, did you see the press conference an hour ago?' she asked.

'Of course and I think that reporter should be taken to task for her behaviour. How dare she try and insinuate that anyone could have any reason to murder our child.' He shook his head with disgust. 'As hard as it is for us to accept that Sadie took her own life, we do not need hacks trying to make a headline out of our misery. The sooner we put this investigation behind us the better. Feel free to take a look,' he said, nodding towards the box.

She removed the lid and took a quick peek inside. She saw hair brushes, a couple of pairs of shoes, a phone, iPad and a few books. She moved a couple of items around until she could see the bottom of the box.

'No diary?' she queried.

'She didn't keep one as far as I know,' Laurence offered, sitting down.

Kim found that unusual even though she'd never kept one herself. But Sadie appeared to love words and exploring her feelings. Definite reasons for keeping a diary.

She knew Sadie had kept something.

'No exercise books?'

The couple looked at each other and shook their heads. 'No, Inspector,' they said together.

'May I ask who collected Sadie's belongings from her room?'

'Saffie,' Hannah answered.

'Sadie liked to write,' Kim explained. 'Her English teacher said she spent many hours recording her feelings. Had quite a talent, apparently,' she offered kindly.

It appeared to be something about their youngest daughter they didn't know. They both regarded her blankly.

'We met Saffron yesterday,' Kim said. She knew there was something these people wanted her to see and she would. All in good time.

'We were surprised that she was still at school, considering—'

Hannah shook her head. 'She's always been a headstrong girl, very determined. We begged her to come home with us, but she insisted that she won't let the school down for the gala. It's her way of coping, I think,' Hannah said.

'Were they close?' Kim asked.

'Not really,' Laurence replied. 'Not even as children. The three years between them seemed so much more. Saffie has always had an older head on her shoulders. She was never interested in the childish games Sadie wanted to play. She chose to spend most of her time at the piano,' he said.

Hannah nodded. 'Eventually, Sadie stopped trying to get her sister's attention, and the two of them kind of drifted apart.'

Kim could hear the sadness in the woman's tone.

'Neither of us had siblings and wanted our girls to grow up close. We always hoped that once they were…'

Kim saw her eyes redden at the realisation that any hopes they'd had of those bonds forming later in life had been lost for ever.

She thought about the photo on her own fireplace at home. The bond she'd had with her own sibling, her twin brother, had been only six years long but it was a bond she had treasured.

'So, what was it that you wanted to show us?' Kim asked.

Laurence stepped over to the mantelpiece and retrieved a single piece of plain paper.

'We did find this in her things?' he said, nodding towards the paltry box of possessions.

Kim had lost interest in the box. It had been filtered through too many hands already. Stacey might find something on the phone or tablet, but Kim suspected not, or it would have been held back.

She took the piece of paper.

The handwriting began tidy, neat and small. The words measured. It was a letter of two halves.

Bryant scooted closer to read with her.

*Dear Mummy and Daddy*

*I can't find the words to explain how I feel. Every day my mind is like a tropical jungle overgrown with foliage, dense plantation. A mist rises every now and again and blocks out the sunlight. I try to wade through it. I try to reach you but the jungle gets in my way.*

*I try so hard to meet expectation but I drop through the cracks of reality because I also want to be me. I don't know who that is yet. I don't know how much longer I can stay in this foggy existence waiting to see what I become. It's too hard. I can't bear it any more. I have to make it stop.*

Kim went back to the top of the letter and read it again.

She felt Bryant sigh beside her.

It was tough to read the muddled, sincere, lost thoughts of a thirteen-year-old girl that was now lying in the morgue. However she had spent her last days or hours, she had not been happy or at peace. Especially with herself.

Kim raised her gaze to find that Laurence had moved to stand behind his wife. His hands rested on her shoulders. Hannah had turned her face into her husband's forearm as though the truth was just too much to bear.

'And how do you see this letter, Mr Winters?' Kim asked, gently.

He swallowed back the tears.

'I think this letter leaves no doubt whatsoever that our daughter wanted to end her life.'

Kim felt torn between revealing the nature of Sadie's injuries and waiting until they had something more substantial to share. The word 'murder' had been shouted from the rooftops by Tracy Frost, but this couple were choosing not to hear it.

She stood. 'Thank you for sharing this letter with us, Mr Winters. I'm sure it will help us with our enquiries.'

Laurence nodded and walked them to the door.

Kim promised they'd be in touch soon.


For a minute she stood against the car.

'The answer is no before you even think about it,' Bryant said, opening the car door.

'You don't even know what I'm thinking,' she countered.

'Oh yes I do,' he said as she got in beside him. 'Clearly the Winters have friends in high places. Now, those friends have already prompted a call from the top of the food chain. For whatever reason they're determined to believe their daughter killed herself. If you go back in there and try to force them to believe she was murdered, what then? You don't think we're being watched closely enough as it is? Their well-placed friends are gonna want this thing wrapped up within the hour, and right now we have nothing.'

'So, you're saying we should just continue to allow them to believe a lie?' she asked.

'I'm saying we take the opportunity to find out who killed her so we can give them some real answers.'

'Damn it, Bryant. I know you're right, but I know I'm right too,' she said, exasperated.

He started the car and turned it towards the drive.

'Great, I can't even have one right on my own.'

She sighed as they crunched across the gravel. 'Bryant, you think Sadie would have written a letter to Mummy and Daddy?'

'Not a bloody chance,' he said, reaching the road.

No, strangely enough, neither did she.

# CHAPTER 26

Dawson checked his watch as he approached the recreation area; at his school it had been called the playground. The area was the size of a small housing estate and appeared to be shared by the whole school.

He heard a bell in the distance before the sound of voices and chatter filled his ears. Kids streamed from the doorways as though a tap had been turned on. Immediately the groups formed: girl groups, boy groups, a few mixed but the majority were gender-specific. A group of eight lads headed for the centre of the space and threw down their jumpers to be used as goalposts.

Some things were universal, Dawson thought, regardless of the school you attended. And young boys playing football between classes was one of them.

He searched the crowd for Geoffrey, and when he couldn't see him, he took a second to recall his own experience. Where does the fat kid go when they're forced outside for fresh air in between lessons but doesn't really want to be noticed?

He started walking the periphery of the recreation area. A few benches hid beneath a row of elm trees, shielded from the emerging sun. Most had groups sitting on the bench, on the wooden arms and on the backrest with their feet on the seats. All except one.

On the bench at the furthest point away from the school building, barely noticeable behind hanging branches of elm, was a kid chomping on a packet of crisps.

Oh how he understood the cycle. He'd been a bit weighty, been picked on, made miserable, eaten, been picked on, made miserable... Well just stop eating crisps and cakes onlookers might think. And if only it was as easy as that.

'Hey,' Geoffrey said, looking at Dawson and then guiltily at his packet of crisps.

Dawson understood. He too had felt the shame every time he was seen eating anything that wasn't an apple or stick of carrot. Average-sized kids could eat whatever they wanted without judgement or attention. The fat kid received stares and head shakes as though they were doing something wrong.

'Mmm... chicken flavour, my favourite,' Dawson said.

Geoffrey proffered the packet, and Dawson took one.

Geoffrey left the packet hanging between them.

'Got a minute for a chat?' Dawson asked.

He nodded towards the group playing football.

'Best be quick. They'll be wanting me back any minute.'

Dawson saw the ironic look on his face and laughed out loud.

Geoffrey smiled in response. Apparently pleased that he had made someone laugh.

'You mentioned something about the Queen of Hearts, yesterday. What's that all about?' Dawson asked, taking another crisp. He'd forgotten just how tasty they were.

'I shouldn't have said anything,' he said, looking around.

'Why not?' Dawson asked, looking around too, even though no one was anywhere near them.

Geoffrey lowered his voice. 'We're not supposed to talk about them. They're a secret.'

'From who?' Dawson asked, feeling slightly ridiculous.

'Principal Thorpe. He doesn't like them. They're banned.'

Dawson couldn't help being intrigued. 'I won't say anything to anyone, I promise,' he said, leaning in closer.

Geoffrey seemed reassured.

'Okay, there are four clubs here at Heathcrest, strictly by invitation only. Two boys' clubs and two girls' clubs. The girls are Hearts and Diamonds and the boys are Clubs and Spades.'

'Like those fraternities they have in America?' Dawson asked.

Geoffrey thought. 'I suppose so, but they don't live together or hang out or anything. They're all different ages. There are twelve members in each club.'

'Why only twelve?' Dawson asked.

'The girls have no King and the boys have no Queen.'

Dawson frowned, trying to get it straight, as he took another crisp.

Geoffrey looked down at the packet and handed it to him, wiping his own hands on his trousers.

'So, there's a hierarchy in the clubs?' Dawson asked.

Oh, how he detested exclusive clubs and groups. Just another way of making the average kid feel inadequate.

'Oh yeah, it rises in number. Newest member is the Ace and then it rises to the King or Queen of the suit of that club. Each suit is run by a Joker – an adult, could be a teacher or an ex-card.'

'And how does one get into these exclusive groups?'

'Chosen by the other members, I think,' he said.

'And you move up over time?'

Geoffrey nodded. 'If a person leaves—'

'Leaves the club?'

Geoffrey shook his head. 'No, leaves the school, then everyone automatically moves up a place leaving space for a new Ace to join.'

The bell suddenly sounded the end of break. Geoffrey looked longingly at his sandwich box before returning it to his backpack.

'So, is it all good-natured fun, the interaction between these four clubs?' he asked, as Geoffrey hauled his pack onto his shoulder.

'The girls are not so bad,' he said. 'But the Spades and Clubs hate each other's guts.'

# CHAPTER 27

Thorpe was not surprised at the knock on the door. He'd been waiting for over half an hour for Graham Steele.

'What took you?' he asked, sharply. He'd asked Nancy to make the call to the counsellor half an hour earlier, and he'd been waiting for the oaf ever since.

'My aunt is fine, thank you for asking,' Graham said, tightly. 'And if you must know I'm late because I'm still prioritising the order of callbacks for the students.'

'"Callbacks"?'

'I've had forty-three requests for counselling since Sadie died. Obviously, the kids are concerned.'

'Of course, of course,' Thorpe said, trying to hide the fact that he should have realised. They were all concerned. Not least because every phone call he'd taken had been from a parent threatening to take their child out of the school, especially since the disastrous press conference.

'Just how troubled was Sadie Winters?' he asked.

'You didn't know her well?' Graham asked.

'Of course not,' he snapped, sensing rather than hearing the accusation in the tone of his colleague. There were far too many students in the school for him to know them all personally, but he hated that in just a few words this man could make it sound like a catastrophic failing on his part. 'Just answer the question. Was Sadie in need of specialist care?'

Graham thought for a full two minutes before answering. 'I feel that Sadie has been quietly withdrawing for quite a while now. I think that her lack of social interaction and academic application began to wane as the star of her sister, Saffron, began to—'

'Will you please answer the question?' Thorpe pushed. He was not interested in the counsellor's extensive theories on the history of the girl's mental state. One of his biggest concerns right now was duty of care.

Graham's face grew dark. 'I will if you ask it.'

Did he really have to spell out everything? 'Should we have known?' he asked, through gritted teeth.

Again the counsellor seemed to weigh his response carefully, and Thorpe realised that was one of the reasons he found conversation with the man so infuriating. Every single word was dissected and measured before it left his mouth.

'There was no indication of suicidal thoughts or I would have spoken to you about—'

'That is not what I wanted to hear,' Thorpe said. That admission was only going to add fuel to the detective's suspicions.

'Brendan, she barely spoke,' Graham exploded, using his first name uncharacteristically. 'During the three sessions we had she hardly said good morning or goodbye. Despite my constant questioning she sat in front of me and picked at her fingernails, so how the hell do you expect me to deduce suicidal thoughts from that?'

The air sizzled between them.

Thorpe understood that for Graham to admit that Sadie had been suicidal would be to bring his own ability and performance into question. But the detectives would never go away if they perceived any doubt that the girl had ended her own life.

'You'll be meeting with the police later today?'

'I would imagine so. I haven't yet had chance to speak with them. Why?'

Thorpe met his gaze and held it. 'I want to make sure we're in agreement,' he said.

Graham looked at him blankly.

'I want you to give the police officers everything they need.'

Graham frowned at him. 'Why would you suspect I'd give them anything less than—'

'I mean everything they need,' he said meaningfully.

'Are you asking me to lie to the police to speed up their investigation?' he asked.

'For God's sake, Graham, catch up, will you? Jesus, you've always been a bit…' he stopped himself from saying any more. He wanted this boor of a man on his side and revealing what he thought about him, had always thought about him, would not help him achieve his goal.

'Why stop what you were going to say? You think I don't know how you viewed me when I came to this school?' he asked, shrewdly.

Thorpe could feel the heat entering his cheeks. Yes, he had tried and failed in his capacity as deputy principal to sway the principal and to reject him for the vacancy. Had he been in his current position when Graham applied he would have refused the man an interview. He didn't fit at Heathcrest. But right now he needed him onside.

'Don't be ridiculous. You'd earned your degree and studied—'

'The first time,' Graham clarified.

Thorpe coughed into his hand. 'I don't recall…' he sidestepped, even though the memory of Graham's first day was clear in his mind for many reasons. Although not sporting the beard at the age of thirteen, Graham's reedy appearance and unruly red hair had not helped matters for the new boy at all.

'There were two of us, if I recall.'

Thorpe shook his head. 'I really don't remember the girl, Graham. It was so long ago.'

Graham narrowed his eyes. 'Her name was Lorraine. We were both scholarship students chosen for our sporting—'

'As is still the practice, today,' Thorpe said, shifting uncomfortably. Graham had been chosen for his ability to jump a long way into a sandpit. He'd been close to championship distances before hitting his teens, but an injury to his right heel had failed to mend properly, ending his athletic career at the ripe old age of fifteen.

Graham caught his gaze and held it. 'Not easy being a scholarship kid in a place like this.'

'You seemed to manage okay,' Thorpe snapped. The fact that Graham had been a member of the Spades instead of him still didn't sit easy with Thorpe. Even after twenty-five years. Graham's father had been an assembly line worker at the Range Rover plant in Longbridge. Thorpe's father had been a respected novelist and his mother a judge. He should have been offered the Ace of Spades instead of this buffoon.

But he was in charge now.

'What I'm asking you to do, Graham, is help the police officers reach the natural conclusion that Sadie's death was suicide in a timely manner. Basically I want you to get them out of my school.'

# CHAPTER 28

Kim could still feel the weight of Sadie's letter against her breast as they walked into Heathcrest.

'Follow me,' she said, striding through the grand hall to the corridor that ran behind the rooms that looked on to the front of the building.

She stopped at the third one along and tapped lightly. By her reckoning they had around fifteen minutes until lunchtime was over.

Kim pushed the door open and was not surprised to see Joanna Wade sitting at her desk with a half-eaten tub of homemade salad beside the book she was reading.

'No staff room?' she asked.

Joanna smiled in response. 'I'm fine here, thanks.'

Again, Kim wondered what had prompted the move for this woman. Something about her didn't fit in this environment.

'Joanna, do you have any of Sadie's writings that we can take a look at?' she asked, unsure when it had become comfortable to call this woman by her first name. She wanted to compare something Sadie had written to the note in her pocket.

'You don't have enough?' she frowned.

Kim shrugged. Even Joanna assumed her personal possessions would be stuffed with poems and musings.

She turned and opened a sliding door.

'Guv,' Bryant said, 'I'm just gonna round up some coffee from somewhere.'

She smiled at him gratefully. Her coffee reserves had not been replenished since leaving the station.

Joanna took down a lever arch file and opened it. Kim pulled up a seat beside her as she began to leaf through the contents.

'There was a poem she wrote just a few days ago that stuck in my mind.' She continued to turn over single pieces of paper with different names in the top right-hand corner.

'Why are you here?' Kim asked, suddenly, surprising herself.

The Joanna Wade she'd met a couple of years ago had seemed more vibrant, more animated. There was something missing. It was like she'd been through the washer a couple of times and had faded just a little bit.

Joanna's hand stilled for a second as she picked up the next sheet.

'One game of darts and I might tell you,' she said.

Kim laughed at the comment which was both opportunistic and distracting.

'Ah, here's one she wrote just last week,' she said taking a sheet from the box and placing it before Kim. 'Not the one I'm after but this'll give you some idea of her talent.'

The poem filled the whole page but with only one word on each line.

Kim read it twice and shook her head.

'I don't get it,' she said, honestly.

'The theme was isolation,' Joanna said. 'Now take another look.'

Kim read it again. 'Okay, so every word is linked to loneliness, which could have been done from any thesaurus.'

Joanna rolled her eyes despairingly. 'Look beyond the words, Inspector. See the whole thing.'

Kim looked again and ignored the words.

'Single words on a line, surrounded by space. Other words are around but not close by,' Kim said.

'Exactly,' Joanna replied. 'She captured the theme in much more than the words. She made the actual page stark to paint the picture of loneliness. Not bad for a thirteen-year-old girl, eh?'

Kim nodded her agreement as Joanna frowned.

'Ah, I remember now, I gave that other poem to her counsellor. I'll get it back so you can take a look.'

Kim took Sadie's letter from her pocket.

'What do you think of this?' Kim asked. 'Knowing her writings as you did.'

Kim knew Sadie had not committed suicide, so why was there a suicide note?

Joanna read the letter, paused and then read it again. She nodded, despite the frown that touched her features.

'Definitely something Sadie would have written.'

'But?'

'I don't know. There's something not quite right about that letter.' She looked at Kim. 'But I honestly don't know what.'

Kim had felt the same way when she'd read it at the Winters' home and when she'd read it again in the car.

Joanna continued to study it as Bryant appeared bearing two mugs of coffee.

Joanna's frown deepened, as she placed her hand across the top of the page, covering the words 'Dear Mummy and Daddy' that Kim had found jarring.

'Read it now,' Joanna suggested.

Kim read the words aloud.

'"I can't find the words to explain how I feel. Every day my mind is like a tropical jungle overgrown with foliage, dense plantation. A mist rises every now and again and blocks out the sunlight. I try to wade through it. I try to reach you, but the jungle gets in my way.

'"I try so hard to meet expectation, but I drop through the cracks of reality because I also want to be me. I don't know who that is yet. I don't know how much longer I can stay in this foggy existence waiting to see what I become. It's too hard. I can't bear it any more. I have to make it stop."'

'See what I mean?' Joanna asked.

Kim nodded her understanding.

'You're gonna have to enlighten me,' Bryant said.

'It's not a suicide letter at all,' she explained, to her colleague. 'Remove the salutation at the top and this is nothing more than a cry for help made to look like a suicide letter.'

# CHAPTER 29

Shaun Coffee-Todd realised he was last to leave the locker room again. He folded his towel and placed it into the plastic bag before putting it back into his sports bag. Although the bell had gone to signal the start of the next lesson he didn't want to rush and just wedge his damp towel against his school books. He'd done that once before and had been forced to try and read out his essay on King Henry VIII that had become an ink-run, damp mess in his exercise book. His mistake in reading out a word that should have been 'hunt' had reduced the class of his fourteen-year-old peers to hysterics for the remainder of the lesson. Miss Wade wouldn't thank him if he did it again.

He lifted his bag and threw it over his shoulder. The momentum almost threw him off balance. He often forgot just how much he was carrying around. He rolled his eyes and turned back to the bench, allowing the bag to slip from his shoulder on to the wooden slats.

He unzipped the side pocket and felt inside. His fingers curled reassuringly around the EpiPen. He always checked after his bag had been left unattended in his locker. Fourteen-year-old boys didn't always think and, since a close call where he'd used a knife that hadn't been cleaned of nut oil properly, he intended never to be without it again.

As he lifted the bag back onto his shoulder he stumbled forward as the force of something hit him between the shoulder blades. The fixed bench went nowhere, so he found himself doubled over the slatted seat.

His head was swimming at the force of the blow. He tried to throw himself backwards to get back to a standing position, when he felt a presence behind him. He tried to turn, but a line of fabric was being tied around his head, covering his eyes. He recognised the woolly texture of a scarf of some type.

'Knock it off, lads,' he called out, trying to call back over his shoulder.

There was no response.

'Guys?' he said, feeling the uncertainty settle in his stomach.

A few of his classmates had bundled him into the shower one time, fully clothed, and soaked him on his birthday. There'd been no ill will or malice. It had just been a bit of fun. He'd heard them baying and laughing in the background as they'd gathered behind him and pushed him towards the shower. They had been guffawing and nudging each other as they marched him across the tiles and into the cubicle.

But there was no noise now.

'Wh-who is this?' he asked, trying to stay calm as he was lifted up by his blazer.

There was no response.

'What are you…'

His words trailed away as he was turned and turned and turned in a circle silently until he thought he was going to throw up. Again he wondered if this was some kind of prank. His friends trying to make him vomit but, other than the sound of his own rubber soles on the white tiles, he was surrounded by silence.

The anxiety began to build in his stomach as he felt his head spinning with motion sickness. Who was doing this to him, and why?

'Please stop,' he pleaded as the nausea began to rise over the anxiety.

And suddenly he was lowered to the ground.

'What… Why…'

Two fingers pinched at his nose, forcing his mouth to fall open. Even though he knew his body was still, his head appeared to be moving as though watching a slow motion washing machine.

Something landed on his tongue. Instantly he recoiled and stuck out his tongue at the smooth saltiness that tanged. More alien objects landed in his mouth. The saliva in his mouth tried to do its job and encouraged him to chew.

*But what??*

He suddenly realised what was floating around in his mouth, touching his tongue, his gums, resting behind his teeth.

Nuts. Salted peanuts.

He felt the heat enter his body as the fear engulfed him.

He tried to spit them out, but a hand on his head and one beneath his chin had clamped his mouth closed.

'Please…' he tried so say. He had to make them understand what could happen if he didn't get these nuts out of his mouth immediately.

His unfettered hands reached around him for his gym bag. If he could just get his pen. He heard the bag move along the floor as though being kicked out of reach.

More nuts were forced into his mouth as he tried to writhe away from his captor.

He could feel the nuts bobbing around in his mouth. His saliva was catching them like a tidal wave and trying to take them down his throat. His teeth switched to autopilot and began to chew automatically so that he didn't choke. Smaller pieces of nut were being washed down his throat and into his intestines.

Shaun had been lectured repeatedly about the sudden release of chemicals that could send his body into shock. He pictured the histamine being unleashed to get him.

The facial swelling was immediate. He could feel the flesh on his lips and eyelids expand and stretch with each passing second.

The panic was growing within him. He needed his pen. Without it he was going to die.

He could feel his throat beginning to narrow, breathing was becoming harder. His breath rasped in his chest as he fought for each gulp of air, but someone had built a brick wall across his windpipe. He could no longer swallow, and the drool began to leak from his mouth.

He lurched forward as the pain ripped through his abdomen. The nausea followed, and he prayed he would not vomit. The scarf covering his eyes had slipped and was now resting around his mouth, but he was blinded by the tears that had formed.

There was no doubt in his mind.

He knew he was going to die.

As he fought to take just one breath into his lungs he saw a shadow cross the doorway. Someone was there. Someone had heard, and they had come to help.

He reached out towards them, but they were gone.

His arm fell back to the ground as he took his final breath.

# CHAPTER 30

Dawson was hoping to find Tilly in the dorm room.

Her head was bent studiously over a pile of books.

'Hey,' he said, quietly, from the doorway, so as not to startle her. It didn't work as she jumped out of her skin anyway.

'No lesson?' he asked. The end-of-lunch-break bell had sounded fifteen minutes ago. He stepped into the room, careful to leave the door open.

'Free period, which I decided to spend with Mr Pythagoras here,' she said, slapping the top book.

'And, how is he?' Dawson asked, sitting on Sadie's bed.

'Let's just say our relationship is complicated' she replied, seriously.

Dawson smiled at her earnest expression.

'Got a minute?' he asked.

She glanced at the books and then turned to face him.

'Shoot.'

'I've been learning a bit about these groups here. The Hearts and Spades and all that. Can you explain a bit more about how they work?'

He'd run out of time with Geoffrey, who had seemed to grow in discomfort talking about them. He suspected Tilly would have no such problem.

She nodded. 'You know they're supposed to be secret, right?'

Dawson nodded.

'The playing cards are almost as old as the school. They are elite societies within an elite society,' she said.

'Do people aspire to be a member of these clubs?'

She rolled her eyes. 'Err… yeah. There's no higher honour than being a playing card. It means you were chosen to join the most important club you'll ever belong to.'

Dawson smiled. 'That's a bit of an exaggeration, surely?'

'It's not just while you're here. You're a member of that club for life. The other members of your club are closer than family. Other cards know all of your secrets.

'Cards go on to become politicians, bankers, barristers, doctors and stuff. The last deputy prime minister used to be the Nine of Clubs,' she said. 'Cards are influential in the outside world. Cards help each other throughout life.'

'As long as it's the same suit?' he asked.

'Of course,' she said, as though that was obvious.

'And how are new cards chosen?' he asked. 'What's the criteria for becoming a card?' he asked, feeling ridiculous.

She shrugged and wrinkled her nose. 'Could be the kid excels in some academic subject or sport or something like that…' She hesitated. 'That's it really.'

'What is it, Tilly? You were going to say something more but stopped yourself.'

She coloured, and he recalled what she'd been saying.

'Is there another way to get chosen?' he asked.

'Not officially,' she said.

'How about unofficially?' he asked.

'I think you can get a calling card because of family.'

'"Family"?' he asked.

'Like, if your parents hit the rich list or they get a huge promotion or become famous for something.'

'So, the kids themselves don't have to be gifted as long as their parents are influential?'

She shrugged. 'I'm just saying. It happens.'

The more Dawson learned about these exclusive clubs the more he grew uncomfortable with their existence.

'What if you refuse the invitation?' he asked. 'Say you don't want to be in one of these clubs?'

'No one refuses an invitation to be a card,' she guffawed as though he'd lost his mind. 'Unless you've got a couple of screws loose.'

'Tilly, did Sadie receive a calling card?' he asked.

She reddened slightly before shrugging.

'I wouldn't know. It's secret.'

'Could Sadie have refused the invitation to join one of the girls' exclusive clubs?'

The idea of the Sadie he'd come to know gleefully receiving and accepting a red ace on her bed was not a picture that would form in his mind.

'I'm sorry, officer,' she said, turning back to her books. 'But I really must get on with my work.'

Dawson knew that the girl hadn't answered his question either way.

# CHAPTER 31

'So, who do you think tampered with the letter?' Bryant asked, as they awaited the arrival of their next interviewee.

'Could have been anyone,' she said. 'In all the chaos the murderer could have gone to Sadie's dorm room, rifled through her things and changed the letter. It could have been Saffie. It could have been the parents who are convinced Sadie took her own life.'

'Do you think they've held the diary back from us?' Bryant asked.

Kim thought for a minute and shook her head. 'I've got a feeling that anything in a diary of Sadie's would support the suicide they're so desperate to believe. I think the diary was in her missing backpack. Where else would you keep something that held your most intimate thoughts?'

'Jesus, guv, you think the killer has her diary?'

Kim was prevented from answering by a knock on the door.

*

Bryant called out for their interviewee to enter.

Kim recognised the man that came into view as the one who had been sitting on the ground beside Saffie two days before. Kim guessed him to be around six feet tall, with a skinny frame. His smart black trousers were topped with a plain white shirt and red tie.

'Mr Steele,' Bryant said, standing to greet the psychologist who worked as a counsellor for the school.

'Please call me Graham,' he said, pleasantly.

'Graham, please take a seat,' Bryant said, pointing to the other side of the desk.

'And thank you for making time to see us today,' Kim said, pointedly. 'I hope your personal business was not too harrowing.'

He smiled politely. 'My aunt was taken into hospital with a suspected heart attack.'

Bryant leaned forward. 'Sorry to hear—'

'It was a bad case of indigestion, officer. Tomato seeds do not agree with her.'

Bryant nodded his understanding.

Kim sat forward. 'As you know we're here investigating the circumstances of Sadie's—'

'Suicide,' Graham offered.

'Death,' she clarified. 'And I see here you've been at Heathcrest for seven years now,' she asked.

'I have indeed, officer.'

'And as the school counsellor you've probably dealt with all kinds of minor grievances from the pupils?'

'And major ones too,' he defended.

'And what about Sadie Winters?' Bryant asked. 'Was she a minor or a major problem?'

'Aah, poor Sadie. She was a troubled young lady,' he said, shaking his head.

Kim felt that if she heard that word used one more time to describe the child she might scream. It was as though a memo had been circulated listing key words and phrases.

'When did you first meet with her?' she asked.

'It was just a few weeks ago. I met with her a total of three times.'

'Why?' she asked, directly.

'I'm sorry, what...'

'There are almost a thousand students here and you can't chat with them all, so what was the reason for the sessions with Sadie?'

He thought for a moment. 'If I recall correctly, it was Mr Campbell, her physics teacher. She'd become withdrawn and sometimes obstructive in science lessons.'

'Do you remember why?'

He shook his head. 'I met with her only a few times. She was not the most communicative pupil I've spoken to.'

'So, she didn't open up to you?'

'No, but I have my own theory, which I tried to discuss with her.'

'Which was?'

'I think that she felt inadequate beside her sibling and began to rebel to get attention for herself. I think she tries to meet her parents' expectations for greatness and falls short.'

The picture was becoming a little clearer for Kim. After reading that letter from the girl it seemed she was searching for her own identity. The kid had probably had Saffie rammed down her throat. No wonder she hadn't opened up to him. He had laid his own opinion at her feet and even he had wanted to talk about her sister.

'But hasn't Saffie been a musical star for years?' Kim asked. 'Why would she suddenly begin acting up about that now?'

He shrugged. 'Add a few teenage hormones into the mix and it becomes a bit more likely that—'

'You don't think it's something more recent than that?' Kim asked. 'Something that happened just in the last few weeks that caused her to rebel?'

Although her behaviour was hardly what Kim would call rebellious. Quiet, morose, withdrawn and obstructive was how she herself spent most days of her life.

'Were you surprised when you heard the news of her… death?' Bryant asked.

He hesitated and then shook his head.

'No, not really. She was an unhappy child.'

'Did she ever speak to you of enemies? Was there someone she was having any trouble with?'

He looked surprised. 'Not at all.'

'So, you logged and recorded your concerns with…' Bryant asked.

Kim hid her satisfaction. Like her, Bryant was feeling that this kid had been let down on just about every level.

'Well, no, I didn't actually log…' his words trailed away as he seemed to realise his own contradiction.

'Sir, I'd like you to—'

'What the hell is going on out there?' Kim asked as the sound of footsteps and raised voices increased outside the door. She was sure they'd have heard a fire alarm.

Steele stood and opened the door as Dawson's flushed face appeared in the doorway.

'Fourteen-year-old boy, boss,' he gasped. 'Suddenly collapsed and is being rushed to hospital.'

All three of them ran for the door.

# CHAPTER 32

Dawson arrived at the A&E department of Russells Hall Hospital two minutes after the ambulance. The boss had told him to go, and he had driven in the slipstream of the ambulance until two motorcycles had got in his way.

He hurried through the waiting area, filled to overflowing with sick and injured, to stand behind a woman holding a coughing child complaining about the wait.

The receptionist checked and told her there were just a couple more people in front of her. Appeased the woman turned and looked around for her seat, which had been taken.

Dawson approached the window. 'A teenage boy, Shaun Coffee-Todd, has been rushed in. Can you tell me…'

'And you are?' she asked, glancing at the screen.

He held up his identification.

She appeared unimpressed. 'So, you're not a relative or guardian?'

'No,' he answered.

She folded her hands and shook her head. 'Then I'm sorry but I can't give you any information.'

He opened his mouth to argue, but realised he had no information or leverage that would persuade this woman to allow an unrelated male to attend the bedside of a minor. He accepted her judgement and moved to the side of the room, pleased to see the woman and coughing child had been offered a seat from someone.

He took some change from his pocket and chose a black coffee from the vending machine, which spat the steaming liquid into a flimsy brown cup and stood with his back against the wall.

He'd been leaving Sadie's dorm room when he'd heard a commotion at the end of the hall. As he'd headed towards it, two paramedics had shoved past him followed by Principal Thorpe.

He hadn't been able to get close enough to see the kid, but the actions of the medics had been quick, and the boy had been placed on a stretcher and rushed to the ambulance.

Principal Thorpe had hurried away, already on his mobile phone. He had stood for a moment listening to the astounded whispers of classmates and gathered that it was a fourteen-year-old boy who had been found unconscious in the shower block.

His eyes went to the door as a couple entered wearing expressions of panic.

Dawson recognised the man that entered as Anthony Coffee-Todd, a local newsreader and celebrity, who looked considerably older than his young wife without the studio make-up.

They hurried towards the window and offered a few words. The receptionist picked up the phone. The woman tapped anxiously on the reception desk as Dawson began to head towards them.

A nurse appeared at the swing doors and immediately ushered them both through.

Dawson didn't like the feeling of dread that was beginning to grip his stomach, but for now, he just had to stand back. And wait.

# CHAPTER 33

Kim stood at the back of the hall as Saffie Winters took her place at the piano.

With lessons over for the day students and teachers were milling around the space, carrying boxes and bringing in chair stacks and placing them at the edge of the room. Kim tried to imagine the galas and balls that had taken place amongst the priceless tapestries that adorned the walls.

She had sent Bryant off to find out what he could about the boy who had collapsed. There had been no word from Dawson, which she hoped was good news.

Saffie stood behind the stool as though composing herself for this practice piece. Her gaze made a quick sweep of the room, ending at the doorway. She took a breath, sat, and flexed her fingers. The second her fingers hit the keys the room silenced. Discussions ended mid-sentence and activity stopped as all attention channelled towards the single figure on the stage.

Four notes in and Kim could understand why.

She recognised the piece as 'Hammerklavier', by Beethoven, a notoriously hard piano piece that required extreme dexterity and concentration, declared unplayable by some musicians. It was a piece she had listened to many times as she worked in her garage, and most times she found herself pausing in her task to simply close her eyes and listen.

As Saffie played her head occasionally lifted from the keys to glance at the door. A secret smile rested on her delicate mouth, and Kim turned to see why.

Along the back wall Kim saw a dark-haired youth leaning against it. His hands were resting in his pockets. His school tie had been abandoned, and his top button opened casually.

A couple of people turned and waved in his direction, but he saw nothing as his gaze was locked on the girl performing on the stage.

Her glances were less often now but occasionally their eyes met across the distance, and Kim could feel the intensity. It was like a power line was stretching between the two of them. Kim was sure that if she stepped between them she would be frazzled to a crisp.

She could not shift her gaze from the silent interaction between them. Saffie's eyes seemed to hold a tentative question. His face offered no response. She sought something from this boy, and his rigid expression was giving her nothing in return.

Bryant came to stand beside her but said nothing until the piece had finished.

The room responded with enthusiastic applause.

Kim knew that the entire sonata lasted forty-five to fifty minutes, which required a great deal of stamina to complete. Saffie acknowledged their appreciation and instantly looked to the doorway, but the lad had already gone.

'She's good,' her colleague said.

'She's more than that, Bryant,' Kim said. 'That girl is world class,' she added, as she watched Saffie leave the stage without a glance at anyone.

'I'll be back in a sec,' Kim said, rushing for the door.

*

She turned left and caught up with the male captivated by Saffie's performance.

'Excuse me,' she said, touching him on the shoulder.

'Yes?' he said with a look of distaste.

It suddenly occurred to her that Thorpe seemed to feel that Heathcrest was a place where they produced superior people.

She was coming to realise that Heathcrest just made people feel superior.

'DI Stone,' she said, without producing her identification.

He said nothing but continued to look at her derisively.

'Firstly, drop the attitude, fella, I just want to ask you a couple of questions.'

His expression warmed a couple of levels to impatience as he offered his hand and a modicum of good manners. 'My apologies, officer, I was just in a rush. My name is Eric Monroe.'

She ignored his outstretched hand and enjoyed his discomfort when it dropped back to his side.

Yes, she had attitude and she'd bloody well earned it.

'You seemed particularly captivated by the performance of Sadie's sister in there a moment ago?'

'I was appreciating Saffie's musical ability,' he replied.

It was more than that and Kim knew it.

'Are you two a couple?' she asked. If this boy knew Saffie well, then he might also have known Sadie.

'Not any more. We broke up,' he said, without emotion.

'Recently?' she asked, surprised, recalling the level of intensity between them.

He frowned and although his face was not puckering up into the disdainful look he'd sported earlier, it was getting there. 'Yesterday, actually, but I'm not sure what that has to do with your inv—'

'Did you know Sadie at all?' she asked.

'I saw her a few times,' he said. 'They weren't close, but she was an angry little thing.'

'About what?'

He shrugged. 'Don't know what her problem was but she barged into Saffie's room one night saying they had to talk.'

'Did she say about what?'

He shook his head. 'Saffie told her to get out and not come back. That was the only time…'

'Why did the two of you break up?' Kim asked, directly.

And the derision was back in full force. 'My reason for ending our relationship is definitely none of your business, officer and now I must—'

'Couldn't you have waited to finish with her?' Kim asked, struck by the callousness in his tone. 'She has just lost her sister.'

His lips pursed into an unpleasant sneer. 'I can assure you, officer, that she's lost a lot more than that.'

He turned and walked away from her. She saw little point in following him. He'd said all that he was going to say.

*

As she headed back into the hall Kim considered what she'd learned. Saffie wanted something from Eric, Eric was angry with Saffie, and Sadie had been angry with just about everyone.

'What do we know?' she asked her colleague, who took out his notebook.

'So, the kid is fourteen-year-old Shaun Coffee-Todd, son of the newsreader and a former studio runner. He seemed fine in the previous class but never reached his next lesson. Apparently suffers with an allergy to nuts.'

'Jesus,' Kim said. She'd seen an anaphylactic shock reaction before and it wasn't good.

The ringing of her phone stopped her thoughts.

She took a breath before answering.

'Dawson,' she said.

'Kid didn't make it, boss. Pronounced dead ten minutes ago.'

Kim ended the call and closed her eyes for a second before turning to Bryant.

'This school has now given us two dead kids this week and it's only Wednesday. What the fuck is going on?'

# CHAPTER 34

The cards filed into the candle room one by one.

Again, one chair was empty. The same chair.

A few glanced towards it but more did not.

'Thank you all for coming,' said the Joker, pulling out his chair.

The sound of wooden chair legs scraping on the concrete followed.

'You all know that Six is dead?' the Joker asked once everyone was seated.

There was a rumble that travelled around the circle.

The Joker turned to Seven. 'Did you do it?'

Seven shook his head.

'Answer, damn it,' the Joker growled.

'No, I didn't get to him soon enough to…'

'You didn't make him eat a nut or something as a punishment for breaking the rules?' the Joker asked, wondering if Seven had done so without realising the consequences.

Seven shook his head, vehemently. 'No, no, I was going to push some tacks up through the soles of his shoes, but I hadn't found the right moment.'

Yes, a popular punishment. Just three or four tacks and the wearer didn't realise until their own body weight had pushed the flesh down onto the sharp points. It would have done the trick and taught him a valuable lesson.

The Joker sighed heavily. 'If you did this, you can tell us. If this was your punishment for his rule break, which went wrong and you didn't understand the consequences, tell us now. You know that the secret will be safe here. Remember Noah?'

Seven nodded.

Noah Gless had been the Four of Spades in the mid-sixties. He had gone on to become the head teacher of an exclusive all-boys school in Kent. For fifteen years his sexual abuse of young boys had remained secret. Until an eight-year-old had told a nurse while being treated for a broken arm. His admission had brought forward a flood of complaints. All correct and horrific.

Noah Gless was charged with thirty-four counts of sexual assault. The Spades had formed a wall of protection around him. His barrister pleaded diminished responsibility based on the sworn testimony of an eminent psychiatrist. Noah was sentenced to five years in a mental health facility, which was appealed down to three, and he walked free within a year.

'I didn't do it, I swear,' Seven reiterated.

The Joker searched his face. And believed him.

'Okay, cards, reach for your glasses,' the Joker instructed.

All cards took the shot glass placed in front of their chair. A small measure of whisky had been poured into each one, as was the custom if a card died. It was barely a mouthful and reserved only for a death in the family.

'To Six,' the Joker said, raising his glass and drinking the shot.

The cards all followed suit and placed their glasses on the table.

The Joker nodded to the King on his right, who collected up the glasses.

'And now to congratulate Five, Four, Three, Two and Ace who all move up a card. Well done to you all.'

The Joker waited for a few seconds before continuing.

'We have two small matters to deal with before the process of choosing a new Ace. First, Nine has an important basketball game in two weeks' time. He needs to practise. Who volunteers to take his homework?'

The hands were slow to rise but eventually three cards offered their services.

'Seven,' said the Joker. 'That one is yours.'

Seven nodded.

'Secondly, Eight is being bullied by his biology classmates for passing out when dissecting a frog.'

The King's hand was first in the air, and the Joker nodded in his direction. 'I'll trust you to suitably advise the boys concerned.'

The Joker hesitated for a moment, reaching to the side of the chair. 'Okay, our next order of business is to choose a new Ace.'

He lifted a pinboard that held two A4 photographs.

'Take out your pins,' he instructed.

Each card reached into their pocket and produced a black Spade tiepin that had once been worn with pride. But now remained hidden in trouser pockets.

Tradition dictated that the Joker would propose two possibilities to join the suit and give the reasons why.

Right now the room contained two potential world class athletes, a musician, a boy already on his way to medical school, an artist, a boy who had joined Mensa before he reached the age of six, the son of a cabinet minister, a banker, and the sons of two international businessmen.

The Joker pointed to the first photograph. 'I have proposed subject one as his father has recently been awarded an MBE for setting up a charitable education initiative in Uganda.'

The cards nodded in response.

The Joker pointed to the second photograph. 'I have proposed subject two because both of his parents are successful barristers.'

The proposal needed no further explanation. Just as many children followed their parents through the education system, they followed their careers too. There was a good possibility that subject two would also choose to enter the legal profession and be useful in the future.

The Joker sat back. 'Okay, cards, you know what to do.'

The King thrust his left hand forward and used the Spade pin to prick his thumb. He waited for the bubble of blood to form before smudging it onto the face of the photo of his choice.

The process continued around the table, ending with the Jack.

The Joker looked down at the ten droplets of blood ground into the pudgy little face.

The choice had to be unanimous.

It was.

# CHAPTER 35

'Okay, boy, what'll we listen to tonight?' Kim asked Barney as she scrolled through her music library.

He offered no response as he waited for key words he understood, despite the fact he'd eaten his evening meal, crunched away on a carrot and had been for a two-mile walk. Still, he lived in hope of something more.

After listening to Saffie earlier her ear now craved a burst of Beethoven. Kim scrolled to the playlist, found 'Hammerklavier' – the piece played by Saffie earlier – turned up the volume on the speaker and hit play. Immediately the piano notes seeped into her ear and travelled right to her nerve endings, massaging away the stress of the day.

She stood back and observed her current project. Two months earlier she had tasked an ex-criminal named Len to find her a bike frame for less than five hundred quid. He had taken the challenge and three weeks later presented her with the bare bones of the 1968 Norton Commando she'd asked for.

She had offered him the money, and he had refused, saying that in man-hours he had spent no more than a day searching and the frame itself he'd managed to get for less than a hundred. Kim had insisted that he take it. To her a deal was a deal. Reluctantly he'd agreed.

The following morning she'd stepped out of her front door to see his pushbike leaning against her fence and him on his knees with a pile of weeds to his right.

When she'd asked him what he was doing, he'd said following her advice and providing value for money. He was a man desperately trying to put his criminal past of burglary behind him and provide for his young family.

Seeing the job he'd done on her garden, Charlie – her neighbour – had given him some odd jobs to do. Len's girlfriend, Wendy, had secured a part-time early morning cleaning job, and the small family were now off benefits and trying to make their own way.

The whole journey of this bike caused her a smile every time she looked at it. The Commando was in production for ten years from 1968 and won Machine of the Year for five years running up to 1972, which came as a surprise, not least to the company's owner, as the production of the bike was filled with problems. Early clutches couldn't hold the engine torque and two small internal pins would shear off leading to severe slippage. The side stand on the bike often broke off if the rider was too forceful when kicking off.

But those were the reasons she loved the MK1 750cc model. It wasn't perfect. It had fought back.

And although she was enjoying every minute of working on the bike she couldn't help her mind wandering back to the events at Heathcrest. Two children dead in a few days; one murder and one accidental. The full post-mortem on Shaun Coffee-Todd was due to take place in the morning. The press hadn't got their hands on the story yet, but she was sure by the morning it would be out there.

The piece that she'd heard earlier that day continued to fill her ears. She felt the joy enter her heart as her eyes closed to savour the notes. She pictured the intensity of emotion passing between Saffie and Eric Monroe as the girl had played the piece. Whatever lay between them was still raw like an open cut.

The music ended, and Kim opened her eyes as a sudden thought occurred to her.

Saffie Winters had played that exact piece earlier that day and it had elicited no emotion in Kim at all. Although technically accurate it had been lacking a vital ingredient.

The performance had had no soul.

# CHAPTER 36

'There's little in this scoring I'd change,' Kim said, glancing up at Stacey above her appraisal form. Before the death of Shaun Coffee-Todd, she had asked Stacey to meet half an hour before the morning briefing. They were all eager to get on with the murder of Sadie Winters, but Woody had left her in no doubt that the damned appraisals had to land on his desk before the end of the week.

They had been through the individual criteria together, and Kim had found Stacey's account of her own performance both accurate and honest. She signed the bottom of the form and put it on top of Dawson's sheet.

She saw the look of relief that passed over the constable's face.

The official appraisal was over, but Kim had more to say. Things that had no place on an official document that would live on her personnel file for ever. Despite her integral role in the team Kim always felt that Stacey was trying to prove something.

She recognised it because she had been exactly the same when she'd joined the police force. But it had been a different animal back then. Most female police officers had felt the need to work harder and stay later than their male counterparts. She hated the thought that Stacey had felt the need to act in the same way, especially under her direction.

Kim sat back in her chair. 'Stace, why do you still feel you have so much to prove?'

Stacey shifted uncomfortably.

Kim continued. 'You stay later than anyone else, you carry on working when you get home. Your mind is always on the job…' Kim hesitated before going on. 'You have to make a life too,' she said.

She was not the kind of boss that got involved in the personal lives of her team. It was something that made both her and them feel uncomfortable; but from what she could gather Stacey had other priorities now, a budding relationship. Something to divert her constant focus from her work.

Stacey looked down at her hands.

'Look, Stace, don't let opportunities pass you by because you're trying to prove yourself to people who already know—'

'I'm not,' Stacey said, simply.

Kim tipped her head and waited for her colleague to continue.

'I heard what you said almost three years ago,' Stacey said, biting her bottom lip. 'Just two words.'

Kim shook her head, no idea what Stacey was referring to.

'I'd just joined the team. It was my first week and I had no clue what I was doing. I thought I'd made a huge mistake in joining CID. You all seemed to be working around me, doing your jobs, while I sat dumbly on the side like a spectator. I made coffee, I fetched lunch and generally tried not to get in the way.'

Kim nodded. 'You were just finding your—'

'Woody came down and spoke to you in the office. He thought I couldn't hear and offered to have me transferred to another team.'

Kim had almost forgotten. Yes, she remembered it now.

'Two words, you said to him. When he offered to have me removed from the team you said to him "try it". I've never forgotten.'

Kim did remember but she'd never thought for a minute that Stacey had overheard.

Stacey had found her own niche within the team as Kim had known she would. She had identified a gap in their skills spectrum and had filled it with her superior knowledge of data mining.

Stacey stood. 'So, you see, boss, I'm not trying to prove anything to anyone. I'm just trying to make you proud.'

Kim opened her mouth to speak but Stacey was already out of the door.

She found herself relieved as she had no clue what she would have said.

# CHAPTER 37

'Okay, folks,' Kim said, glancing around at her team. 'Following the performance of Tracy Frost at the press conference yesterday, and the death of Shaun Coffee-Todd, an official statement has been issued from Lloyds House declaring that Sadie Winters was murdered. Her parents were notified last night and understandably are in shock at the news. I suspect we'll be seeing them later at Heathcrest.'

'By whom?' Bryant asked.

'Sorry?' Kim asked.

'Who informed her parents? It wasn't us.'

'I suspect it was the same person who was trying to insist it was suicide but that's not our concern right now.'

Woody's phone call last night had been terse and cool.

'So, what are you thinking about Shaun Coffee-Todd?' Dawson asked.

Kim held up her hand. 'Slow down, Kev. One kid at a time,' she said. 'Sadie first.' She looked to the detective constable. 'Stace?'

'Okay, Principal Thorpe left Heathcrest in 1993 and attended Oxford, where he studied social sciences and economics.'

'Bloody hell,' Dawson said. 'He was a busy boy, wasn't he?'

'And did well in all subjects,' she said. 'So, he left the education system in 1997, spent five years teaching at a private boys' school in Kent before returning to Heathcrest in '02 as a maths teacher, before being promoted to deputy principal in '09, and principal three years ago when Principal Richmond retired. He has a long-term girlfriend named Catherine.'

'Christ, Stace, where did you get all that from?' Bryant asked, impressed.

'Tinder,' she joked.

'Okay,' Kim said, mentally filing the information away. 'Next.'

'Graham Steele left Heathcrest a year after Thorpe and attended Cambridge. He trained as a doctor and then chose to specialise in psychiatry. Volunteers as a counsellor at the QE hospital for child bereavement couples and came back to Heathcrest seven years ago. No wife, kids, boyfriend or girlfriend.'

'Don't tell me, Facebook?' Dawson quipped.

'Instagram and Twitter,' Stacey offered with a wink.

Dawson turned to Kim. 'Boss, I'd like a job where I get to spend all day on social media too,' he said.

'Then you should have worked harder at school,' she replied. 'Anything else, Stace?'

'Looking at more of the parents next, so I'll keep you updated.'

Kim nodded her thanks. 'Kev?'

'We got an awful lot of cloak and dagger stuff at this place,' he said, shaking his head. 'Exclusive clubs, calling cards, selection process...'

'And?' Kim asked, impatiently. Was this really what he'd been investigating?

'Oh yeah, and our victim's sister is right at the top of the pile.'

Kim hesitated. 'Go on,' she said. There was something about Saffie Winters that caused the hair on the back of her neck to stand up.

'There are four groups, all named after card suits. The red ones are girls and the boys black. Twelve members in each suit, the head of the group being either the King or the Queen.'

He paused and, receiving no comments, he continued.

'Cards are chosen based upon the power and influence they may have in later life. Of course it doesn't hurt if your parents are powerful too. A new card is chosen by the rest of the suit, and an ace is left on the bed of the new card.'

'Why an ace?' Bryant asked.

'Each new card has to start at the bottom and work their way up. They accept the card and then have to do some kind of task, and their place in that suit is secure. For life.'

Stacey mock yawned. 'Really, Kev? We're investigating the murder of a young girl and you're spending your time on playing cards?'

Dawson shook his head. 'You're not getting it, Stace. Once you're in these clubs, you don't leave. It's like a bond for life. You're tied to these people for good.'

'And Saffie Winters?' Kim asked.

'Is the Queen of Hearts,' Dawson replied. 'The highest she can be. Probably due to her future as a pianist as well as her family connections.'

'And Sadie?' Kim asked.

Dawson shrugged. 'No evidence she was in a suit, but she may have been invited and refused. Apparently, you don't refuse,' he said.

'Jesus, Kev,' Stacey said, rolling her eyes.

'But why would she have been invited in the first place?' Kim queried. 'By all accounts Sadie wasn't gifted or special in any way, so why would they have wanted her?'

'Nepotism,' Dawson offered. 'Maybe her sister wanted her in the group.'

'Or maybe she didn't,' Kim said, changing her earlier opinion of his wasted time. 'Stay on it, Kev. I want to know a bit more about what goes on in these groups, and while you're at it I want you to do your best in tracking Sadie's last movements.'

'Will do, boss,' he said.

Right now she had no clues, leads, suspicions or facts that would aid her in finding Sadie's killer but what she did know was that in this environment the kids outnumbered the adults by fifteen to one. In a murder investigation they were not odds that she was comfortable with.

'Okay, guys, we're two whole days clear of Sadie's death and we have absolutely nothing. We need to be considering every option right now. We have to look more closely at the kids.'

'Guv, seriously…'

'Whether we like it or not, kids kill kids, Bryant, and it's a line of enquiry we have to explore.'

They all nodded and began their prescribed tasks.

She turned to Bryant.

'Carry on to Shaun's post-mortem. There's somewhere I need to go.'

# CHAPTER 38

'So, how'd it go, Stace?' Dawson asked her as soon as the boss and Bryant had left.

'Is it your business?' she asked without looking up. 'I don't recall you sharing all that much.'

'Come on, show me yours and I'll show you mine,' he said, winking across the desk.

'I'm showing yer nothing and there is nothing of yours I wish to see,' she offered with a smile.

'Did the boss tell you off for working late all the time?' he asked.

'I'd hazard a guess the boss didn't tell you off for that,' she replied.

'Aww… come on, Stace. What were your areas of improvement?' he pushed.

She met his gaze. 'Chatting with my colleagues too much,' she said, pointedly.

Stacey had no wish to share the details of her appraisal with him. She hadn't meant to reveal to the boss the real reason behind her motivation and work ethic, but she'd hated the fact that the boss thought she was having to prove herself. She had never been made to feel that she had to outperform her male colleagues to be taken seriously. The boss would never have allowed that.

'All right then, did you find out anything for me?'

She tutted. 'Yeah I was all over it while you were off talking about bloody playing cards.'

'Did you or not?'

She stared at him. 'See that thing in front of you, it's called a computer. You can do all kinds of wonderful things on it like search…'

'Stace…'

She rolled her eyes in despair. Sometimes he frustrated the life out of her.

'Okay, just a few facts. Tilly Tromans's parents are new money. Father won EuroMillions jackpot two years into the marriage. Spent the first few million on yachts, houses and holidays and a huge divorce settlement after a string of affairs. Tilly had already been registered at Heathcrest and about the only thing her parents do agree on is the education of their child.

'Completely different for Geoffrey Piggott, whose family dates back about seven centuries. Both parents are barristers, and his mother has just won a landmark Human Rights case.'

'Right to stay?' he asked.

She nodded. 'And if you want any more than that you can flipping well search yourself,' she said, huffily.

'Didn't see Devon last night, eh?' he asked, smartly.

Stacey opened her mouth to answer but Dawson had already turned his attention back to the screen.

And by the look on his face there was something he was desperate to find.

# CHAPTER 39

Kim knocked on the door that she had known from when she was six years old.

She heard the humming before Ted Morgan answered the door.

His surprise turned to delight. 'Kim, what a surprise. Come on in,' he said, stepping aside.

She entered the two bedroom terrace into the lingering smell of bacon and eggs, a smell that was as familiar to her in this house as the man himself. She continued through to the kitchen and sat down as he passed her and reached for the kettle. He filled it and turned.

'How are you, my dear?' he asked.

'I'm well, Ted,' she answered.

'And Barney?'

'Is well, too,' she said.

'I'll make coffee and then you can tell me what's troubling you.'

Kim felt a stab of guilt that she only visited the man when she needed something from him. She had first sought him out when dealing with the sociopathic Alexandra Thorne and had continued to bring him difficult questions since.

'Don't feel guilt, on my account,' he said, knowing her better than anyone else on earth. 'I am honoured that you trust me with your troubles.'

Kim instantly relaxed. Ted had been a part of her life for as long as she could recall.

At various stages of her childhood she'd been sent to him for counselling. Never had she opened up to him about her feelings and she doubted that she ever would. Ted knew every bad thing that had ever happened to her, from her file. And despite her resolute silence throughout their sessions, he had never given up trying.

'Nasty business a few months ago with that girl of yours,' he observed.

Kim guessed he was talking about Stacey's abduction.

'And I suppose the reports were true?' he asked, turning to look at her.

'About what?' she hedged.

'That you entered the property unarmed even though there were guns involved?'

Kim didn't answer. The question was rhetorical.

'She must be quite a detective,' he observed. 'For you to risk your own life. One might even say she's important to you, don't you think?'

Kim opened her mouth to speak and changed her mind. There was nothing innocent about anything Ted said to her. Every word was designed for a response that he could read, analyse and probe further.

'Ted, I need you to talk to me about something.'

'Of course, dear,' he said, placing a mug before her. 'What do you need to know?'

She took a breath. 'I need to know about children who kill.'

# CHAPTER 40

'Jesus Christ,' Dawson said, sitting back in his chair.

Stacey ignored him and continued tapping.

'I said, Jesus Christ,' he repeated.

'I heard yer the first time, Kev,' she said. 'As well as all the loud sighs that were designed to get my attention in the last half an hour.' She pushed away her keyboard. 'And now you have it, so what's up?'

He shook his head with disbelief. 'You have any clue what goes on in some of these places?'

'What places?' she asked.

'Schools, private schools. All the secret clubs and societies?'

She shook her head.

'Even Yale has a super-elite secret undergrad society called Skull and Bones which meets in bloody tombs of all places. They're called Bonesmen, and former members include presidents, supreme court justices, cabinet members and industry leaders.'

Stacey shrugged. 'So?'

'They use a certain number as a code for something important in their lives. Says here that the bonds between Bonesmen often supersede all others.'

'Kev, what are...'

'Don't you find it all a little bit creepy?'

Stacey shook her head. 'People like to belong to groups and shit like that. Didn't you ever want to be part of a certain group or gang at school?' she asked.

He shook his head. It would have been enough for him not to have been shamed and humiliated on a daily basis.

'Oh, I did,' Stacey admitted. 'Year seven I was ten years old. Poppy Meadows,' she rolled her eyes. 'Great name, eh? Well, she was the most popular girl in school. Great family, great clothes, great friends, great at everything and I so wanted to be in her gang.'

Dawson's interest was piqued by the smile on her face. Maybe Stacey could help him understand the things he'd just read.

'So, what did you do?'

Stacey pursed her lips at the memory.

'She was the school's best gymnast and her group consisted of other great athletes. So, I thought if I could impress her with my own acrobatic abilities she'd let me into the group.'

'Go on,' he urged.

'Practised my cartwheel all night in the back garden. My wrists were sore by the time I went to bed, but I was convinced I had it perfect.'

'And?' Dawson asked, sensing this was no happy ending.

'I waited until they were all standing outside in a group. I counted to three and performed the perfect cartwheel in front of them.'

'Really?'

Stacey shook her head. 'Nah, that was what happened in my head. In truth, I didn't look before my hands landed on the ground right on top of a dying bee that stung me in the palm. I screamed and just kind of crumbled into a mass of arms and legs.'

Dawson laughed out loud. 'Did they notice you?'

'Oh, they noticed me all right. And laughed at me for the next two years.'

He sobered. Stacey had recounted that story not with fondness but an objectivity and ruefulness for others to see the normality of her experience. It was a fact of life.

'But what drove you to do it?' he asked, wondering why she'd been so eager to humiliate herself.

She shrugged. 'For validation, I suppose. I wanted to be as cool as they were; liked, respected, adored. They were special, and I wanted to be special too.'

'What would you have done to be accepted into that group?' he asked.

'Jeez, Kev, why so serious?'

'Go on,' he urged. 'What would you have done if they'd asked you?'

She thought for a minute. 'I honestly don't know. Why do you ask?'

He pointed to the screen. 'Do you have any clue how many people have died from hazing incidents due to their desperation to get into these clubs?'

'" Hazing"?' she questioned.

'Initiation rites to gain entry. It goes right back. Stuart Pierson in Igos, Cincinnati, was taken into the forest and was found hit by a train. No one was ever charged. A kid named Michael Davis in 1994 was beaten, kicked and punched repeatedly, taken back to his student apartment and died from massive internal injuries. A kid named Jack Ivey was involved in a drinking contest, stripped to his underwear, tied to the back of a truck, driven around and left for dead. The perpetrators got bloody community service,' he snarled.

'But what...'

'There are hundreds of 'em, Stace. Hundreds of pointless deaths because of these exclusive clubs that people are desperate to join, and most of the time no one gets punished. It seems that what happens at school stays at school,' he said with disgust. 'There's a code of silence that fucks me right off.'

'And this involved Sadie Winters how?' she asked, bringing him back, subtly, to the case at hand.

'I don't even know that it does,' he said, honestly. 'But there's something going on at that school, and I want to know what it is.'

Stacey sighed. 'When you're like this, Kev, there's no reasoning with you, and this is as good a chance as you're gonna get.'

'Meaning?'

'The boss told you to follow your nose for today, so it had better lead you somewhere good,' she said, pulling the keyboard towards her, signalling the end of the conversation.

Stacey had a point and he already knew where he wanted to go.

Over the course of the last two years there were three student names not repeated on the term list. Meaning they had left the school, quickly, mid-term.

And he wanted to know why.

# CHAPTER 41

Ted placed the mugs of coffee on the table that separated the two wooden seats of the companion set that overlooked the fish pond. Ted had insisted that such a conversation required caffeine.

'Moby died,' she observed, as he slowly took his seat beside her. She noted that his joints appeared to be giving him trouble and pushed away the pang of sadness.

'Yes, my dear. Just a couple of weeks ago.'

She said nothing but felt the loss of the gold carp she'd named many years earlier.

'So, you think a child could be responsible for a murder you're investigating?'

'I don't know,' she answered honestly. 'But I can't rule it out. Someone has to consider it.'

'Your colleagues are less open to the possibility?'

She nodded. 'And yet somehow it seems easier for me. Why is that, Ted?' she asked, quietly.

Her dark mind always seemed able to explore a depth of depravity that was deeper than most normal people could go; her brain more able to accept the heinous level that humanity could produce.

'Because the very idea of a child being able to kill, especially *another* child, challenges our belief in innate innocence, which is not something you have extensive experience of, my dear.'

He sipped his coffee and continued. 'Your eyes were opened to the evil that exists around us at a very early age. You never had that blissful ignorance of the horrors that should be a God-given right. There is no preconceived notion that needs to be destroyed before you can consider the possibilities, all possibilities, however dark or misguided they may be.'

'And are they, misguided?' she asked, hoping he would quote some kind of statistic that would assure her that they couldn't possibly be.

'Not necessarily, I'm afraid,' he said, flexing fingers that were showing signs of arthritis. 'Children do kill, and they do kill other children. Experts have categorised them into three types. You have the ones that kill for the thrill. They enjoy the hands-on kill, torture beforehand and sometimes mutilation afterwards. Our very own Jon Venables and Robert Thompson fell into that category when they abducted two-year-old Jamie Bulger from that shopping centre.'

He shook his head and closed his eyes. 'Those boys did unspeakable things to that child. There were forty-two injuries.'

Kim held up her hand to stop him from continuing, she'd read the accounts of the torture and had been unable to remove the images from her mind for months.

'Although before your time, I'm sure you've heard of Mary Bell. In 1968 she killed a four-year-old and a three-year-old when she was only eleven herself. Her own mother had tried to kill her on numerous occasions and forced her to perform sexual acts from the age of four.'

'I know the case,' Kim said. She'd researched it after the woman's lifelong anonymity and that of her daughter had been threatened by the release of a new book.

Ted continued. 'There was a thirteen-year-old kid named Eric Smith who abducted a four-year-old boy. He strangled him, dropped rocks on his head and then used a tree branch to—'

'Thanks, Ted. I get the picture. So are these kids evil, the ones that get a thrill from killing?'

Ted's eyes widened. 'Oh, my dear, that is a very big question and I'll attempt to answer it as best I can.'

He took another sip of coffee, and so did she.

'It is generally felt that it is possible for kids to grow out of the behaviours that led them to kill in the first place, and there is evidence on both sides of this argument. The court-appointed psychiatrist for Mary Bell said she displayed classic signs of psychopathy but has never re-offended, and Eric Smith still has no ability to express emotion after twenty-four years, leading the courts to believe he will never be rehabilitated.'

'You said there were three types,' Kim said.

He nodded. 'The second type targets their prey for innocuous reasons – annoyance or anger.

'Also before your time was Brenda Ann Spencer, a sixteen-year-old girl who used a rifle to shoot eight children in San Diego. The school was right opposite her house. When asked why she'd done it she claimed that she just didn't like Mondays. She showed a complete lack of remorse and no serious explanation. She was annoyed. For her it was that simple.'

Kim found it difficult to comprehend that eight children had lost their lives because a kid had got out of the wrong side of bed.

'And the last group?' she asked.

'These are the ones that kill specific targets out of anger, hurt or wounded pride. Just in 2014 there were two girls, not named, who were dubbed the 'Snapchat Killers'. They tortured and murdered a girl named Angela Wrightson and took photos while they were doing it. They even took selfies from inside the police van.'

'Bloody hell,' Kim said.

'So, how many victims do you have?' Ted asked.

'I have two children dead, in a few days. One definitely murdered and made to look like a suicide and the other I'm not sure yet.'

'Are the two of them linked?' he asked.

'Not obviously,' she said, as her thoughts returned to something he'd said.

'You mentioned Mary Bell being potentially labelled psychopathic or showing tendencies. Even as a child?'

'Oh, we're getting into dodgy ground now, my dear,' he said, draining his mug. 'No mental health professional will be bold enough in this day and age to fix such a label to a child while there is still the possibility they will grow out of psychopathic behaviours.'

'So, does it exist, Ted?' she asked, pinning him for a straight answer.

'It's not something I can—'

'Ted, can a child be a psychopath, sociopath or whatever it is you want to call them?'

'Kim, it's not as cut and dried as that.'

'Come on, Ted. You've treated enough kids in your time. Did any of them fulfil these criteria? Were any of these children evil?'

'I've never treated an evil child,' he said.

'But they do exist?'

Ted looked at her long and hard. 'Kim, I'm really not qualified to say.'

Kim knew there was no point pushing him any further.

On the subject of evil in children he might not be qualified to say.

But she certainly knew someone who was.

# CHAPTER 42

Dawson sat outside the address of Carrie Phifer and wondered if he'd made some kind of mistake.

Heathcrest Academy charged more than thirty thousand a year. Not a fee that seemed accessible for the three-bed semi with a box porch in Hasbury. He checked the details he'd logged into his phone. Yep, he was in the right place.

He walked around a Skoda Fabia before knocking on the door.

A tidy woman dressed in jeans and a shirt opened the inner door. A casual smile on her lips turned to a frown. She did not open the porch door before asking who he was.

*Finally, a woman with the sense to keep a closed door between her and a stranger.*

He held up his identification while saying his name.

Her expression turned to alarm as she reached for the key and opened the door.

'Is anything... has something...'

'There's nothing wrong,' he assured her quickly. 'Mrs Phifer?' he added, as a question.

She nodded and although some of the anxiety had left her face it was still etched with concern.

'May I come in?' he asked, although he was beginning to suspect he knew the answer to his question.

'Is your daughter home, Mrs Phifer?'

She shook her head, as she guided him into a tastefully furnished lounge.

'No officer, she's at school,' she answered. 'Has something happened?'

'Your daughter is fine, I'm sure,' he reassured.

'So what…'

'Carrie attended Heathcrest Academy until a couple of years ago,' he said.

The tension that filled her jaw was immediate.

'Yes, that's right,' she said, warily, as she took a seat and motioned for him to do the same.

'She left mid-year?' he asked.

Mrs Phifer simply nodded.

'May I ask why?' he urged, although the answer was pretty obvious. If the family had been able to afford the fees once they certainly couldn't now.

'I removed her from the school,' she said.

'Would you mind telling me why?' he asked. He didn't wish to humiliate the woman by pressing her to discuss finances, but he just had to be sure.

'Of course, if you'll tell me why you want to know.'

He smiled. 'I'm sorry but I can't really—'

'You're here for a reason, officer. What is it?' she asked.

'I can't help but wonder why your daughter was removed part way through the year,' he admitted. He looked around and then stood. 'I think I understand,' he said. 'And it must have been very difficult for you.'

He had no wish to force this woman into an uncomfortable position of admitting she had been unable to continue her daughter's education at Heathcrest because she couldn't afford it.

'Oh, you're wrong, officer,' she said. 'Removing Carrie from Heathcrest was the easy part. Losing my beautiful home and lifestyle, along with my marriage not so much, but I don't regret it for a minute.'

Dawson faltered. He'd read the situation and he'd read it wrong. He sat back down.

'My husband tried to insist that Carrie return to Heathcrest, but I wouldn't budge and that was the end of my marriage.'

'Your marriage broke up because of your daughter's education?' he asked, incredulously. Surely there could have been a compromise?

'No, our marriage failed because only one of us cared about the safety of our daughter.'

Dawson sat forward. 'Please go on, Mrs Phifer.'

'Carrie did not wish to return to the school, but Douglas was insistent. It was his old school and he believed heartily in their ability to educate. I hated boarding schools but went along with it as long as Carrie was happy, but she didn't want to return. She was terrified, and Douglas was unused to not getting his way. His lawyer was much better than mine,' she said, looking around the room. 'What broke our marriage was his insistence she go back even though she became hysterical at the very mention of it.'

'Mrs Phifer, what happened at Heathcrest to make your daughter so frightened?'

'She received a card. The ace of diamonds. They have exclusive clubs there that—'

'I know about the clubs,' he said.

'Then you'll know that most kids will do anything to join these groups?'

He nodded, remembering his conversation with Stacey.

'She was tasked to perform an initiation rite of doing continual star jumps until she was told to stop.' Mrs Phifer closed her eyes. 'Nine minutes she managed. When she slowed down her calves were hit with a garden cane. She tried to explain, she tried to tell them, but they wouldn't listen. They wouldn't let her stop.'

'Tell them what, Mrs Phifer?' he asked.

'That she was asthmatic, officer. Eventually she collapsed and almost died. She was on a ventilator for two and a half weeks.'

Damn it, Dawson thought. This was exactly what he'd been afraid of.

'And the school's response?' he asked, fearing the worst.

A look of total disgust shaped her attractive features.

'As far as they were concerned the incident never happened.'

# CHAPTER 43

An overwhelming sadness stole over Kim as her eyes rested on the sheet that smothered the small form on the metal tray.

She glanced at the back of Keats who fiddled with something over at his desk. Yeah, he gave her shit, and plenty of it. But this week his career of choice had dictated that he cut open and dissect the bodies of two children.

She had the sudden urge to tell him that she understood. That she knew that neither the job description nor the training could ever prepare you for the reality. That they had both signed up to represent the dead and neither of them got to choose. She wanted him to know that she got it.

She opened her mouth to speak.

'There is no doubt this boy died of anaphylactic shock,' Keats said, beating her to it.

*Yes, probably better that way.*

He peeled back the sheet to reveal Shaun Coffee-Todd's face, and pointed to the mouth.

'His lips and tongue are blue, indicating respiratory collapse. As he couldn't get air into the lungs the blood couldn't be oxygenated. The heart muscle needs oxygen to pump the blood around the body.

'Once one major organ of the body starts to falter, in turn others become strained until they are unable to function. Death is the result of such a catastrophic systems failure. Low blood pressure occurs then eventual circulatory collapse are the final events.'

'How long did it take him to die?' Kim asked, quietly.

'If the shock only affects the respiratory system it may cause respiratory depression and later brain damage in three minutes and death a few minutes later; but death comes quicker if the shock leads to arrhythmia, which it did in this case.'

'So, how long?' she asked again.

'No more than a couple of minutes,' he said, staring down at the body. 'But they would have been the most horrific and frightening couple of minutes you could imagine.'

And Keats had lived every second of them with this poor child, she thought, as the tip of her fingers found the boy's soft cheek. There was an instinct inside her that wanted to offer this child comfort for the fear and pain he had suffered.

During her last major case, she had been held down and choked almost to unconsciousness. She swallowed, still able to recall the feeling of panic that had screamed throughout her body and mind as she'd struggled to get air into her lungs.

And this was a fourteen-year-old boy.

She shook away the memory.

'Keats, how long would this have happened after ingesting the nuts?'

Keats shrugged. 'Most food-related symptoms occur within two hours of ingestion, but severe cases start within minutes. Given this boy's history and the circumstances the onset would have been almost immediate.'

Kim frowned. 'What circumstances? This happened at the end of his gym lesson. It would have been at least an hour before that he could have accidentally eaten—'

'Sorry to interrupt you, Inspector, but this was no accidental ingestion from a trace of nut products.'

'But the kid knew of his condition. His epinephrine was in his gym bag.'

'Exactly my point,' Keats said, placing an X-ray on the light board.

'This is the boy's throat,' he said, pointing. 'And those two objects are whole peanuts.'

Kim glanced at Bryant as she made sense of the pathologist's words.

Someone had force-fed nuts into this poor kid's mouth.

# CHAPTER 44

## 28 February 2018

Hey Diary,

I got back to school just two hours ago and half of that time I've spent hidden in the toilets.

Always the same cubicle. The one furthest away from the door. I'm silent when I'm in there despite the tears that fall from my eyes.

My hand trembled as I used the razor blade to make the first cut. It's simple, perfect beauty sliced through the skin. The calmness hit me instantly. I wondered if it was how a heroin addict felt when taking a hit. The relief, the release. The feeling of inner peace.

I sat back against the cistern with my eyes closed, my mind blank and calm, my breathing deep and even, totally relaxed.

Two more and I was ready to face the world.

As I walked back to my dorm, I could feel the fresh cuts rubbing deliciously against the skin of my inner thigh despite the sterile plaster.

But the peace inside was fleeting.

All too soon the memories of home returned; the hushed conversations that stopped completely when I walked into the room. The three of them looking away unable to face me. My feelings of being a stranger in my own home. My mother spending hours in Saffie's room. My father making secret phone calls that he claimed were for work.

I tried to talk to my mother. I tried to explain.

'Not now, Sadie,' she said. 'Don't bother me with this right now.'

So I slunk back into the shadows and watched until it was time to come back. Just waiting for the chance to get into my cubicle at the end of the row.

But the hungry demons have not been quieted. The feelings are worse than ever.

I don't know how to shut them up and then I remember what I've been told and I pop the pill right into my mouth.

*Oh Sadie, I see now that I did you a favour. You were too unhappy to live.*

*I know you so much better now from reading your innermost thoughts. I understand your pain, and I know that you thank me for setting you free.*

*And now you're not alone. You have your good friend Shaun to keep you company.*

*It wasn't the same, though, Sadie. You were the first and you were special. Very special.*

*Shaun fought so much harder than you. He made it so bloody hard. My sense of satisfaction and righteousness, enjoyed and relished after your death, was nowhere to be found. He didn't follow my script.*

*If he'd just stayed calm and eaten the fucking nuts – but he clamped his mouth shut. If he'd just chewed them I wouldn't have had to get rough, but his teeth were welded together because he understood that he was about to die.*

*He tried to run past me, back into the hall, but I blocked his way and threw him to the ground. I lay across him using my weight to pin him down. I forced a handful of peanuts into his mouth and held it closed, one hand on his head and one beneath his chin.*

*He chewed and whimpered as the nuts began to go down and he realised the horror that was to come.*

*And horrific it was. I stood aside as he writhed and shook and dribbled and trembled and tried to crawl towards me, his face contorted with pain and fear. But eventually he stilled.*

*And as his small body fell against the tiled floor I heard the sound of the gym hall door close.*

*Someone must have heard us, and I need to find out who.*

# CHAPTER 45

Kim parked outside St Paul's Chambers on Caroline Street in the Jewellery Quarter.

'I remember it in the old days,' Bryant moaned as they got out of the car.

She understood what he meant. The area was moving towards urban chic with apartment blocks, cafés and bistros where there had once been craftsmen and artists.

The building they were here for was a new development a stone's throw from the leafy oasis of St Paul's Square, the last remaining Georgian square in Birmingham. It housed eight high specification apartments, with the penthouse being a cool 3,300 square feet worth more than a million pounds. And that was the one they were here to visit.

'How the hell are we going to tell them how their son died, guv?' Bryant asked as she hit the button on the intercom.

'All we've got is the truth,' she replied before introducing herself and Bryant to the male voice on the other end. The electronic buzzing signalled their acceptance into a hallway that boasted a very different kind of art to what they were used to seeing in apartment buildings. No crudely drawn genitalia and swastika motifs here.

Kim spotted the camera in the elevator as she stepped in and pressed the button market 'P'. No number, no floor, just a 'P'. Kim only knew the elevator was moving once it landed silently on the top floor and the doors opened with little more than a welcoming whoosh.

'Just like Hollytree,' Bryant observed, sarcastically.

The lift deposited them in a small hallway with one apartment door and a fire exit escape to the right.

Before she had chance to knock, the door was opened by a man she recognised from the local television news.

Anthony Coffee-Todd struck her immediately as a man fighting his mid-forties. The depth of brown of his hair contradicted the smattering of grey in his stubble. The slightly receding hairline was not fooled by the forward combing of the hair.

She understood that being in the public eye added pressure to maintaining youthful good looks when your face was being broadcast to millions of viewers, but in the stark daylight in his own home without the assistance of clever lighting and a professional make-up person, his age was staring him in the face.

Unlike Louise Coffee-Todd, whose youthful skin matched her thirty-four years.

She understood that this was Anthony's second family. His other son had moved to Australia with his mother when the family had broken up fifteen years earlier. Right around the time Louise had started at the television studios as a runner.

'Please, come in,' he said, standing back for them to enter.

She stepped right into a vast open space with stark white walls holding a selection of black and white art. The furniture was placed at the centre of the room on the largest rug she had ever seen. Three sets of double doors stretched across the space that led out onto the roof terrace. Somewhere in the distance Kim spotted an arch that led into a kitchen.

She tried to stop her biker boots from sounding on the wooden floor as she approached the island of carpet in the middle where Mrs Coffee-Todd stood waiting for them.

'Please sit,' she said, pointing to one of the four sofas.

Kim did so, and Bryant followed.

'We are so sorry for your loss,' Bryant said, as Mr Coffee-Todd joined them.

The couple sat on separate sofas.

'We understand this is a difficult time,' Kim said. 'But we need to ask you some questions about Shaun.'

'Of course but surely it was just some kind of accident…'

'This was no accident, sir,' she said.

'What are you talking about?' he asked, frowning. 'We've been told it was a reaction to something he ate. He has a nut allergy,' he said, as though this explained everything.

'We're aware of that, but there are other—'

'But Principal Thorpe said—'

'Principal Thorpe is not a pathologist, sir, and has not carried out the post-mortem on your child.' Kim hadn't meant to sound so brutal, but she could only indulge them for so long.

A penny dropped somewhere behind Louise's eyes.

'Sadie Winters too?' she asked.

'It's fair to say we are investigating the deaths of both children,' she offered.

'So, you're saying that both of our children were murdered?' Anthony asked, with disbelief.

Kim nodded, understanding they would be suitably shocked.

The horror shone from Louise's eyes. 'But why? I mean… who would want to hurt our…'

'I don't believe you,' Anthony said. 'It's some kind of accident. They both are. No one would want to hurt Sadie either. She was a lovely girl. I'm sure there's some kind of—'

'You know Sadie well?' Kim asked.

'Of course. Our families have been friends for years. Saffie and Sadie are like cousins to our…' His words trailed away as he realised that two of the three children he'd just mentioned were now dead.

'I'm sorry but I think you've made a mistake…'

'Mr Coffee-Todd,' she said, firmly, having wished to spare them the details. 'Your son had two peanuts wedged in his throat.'

Louise's head whipped around. 'Shaun would never have—'

'Precisely,' Kim said. 'We understand he managed his condition very well and would never have chosen to eat nuts.'

'But murder?' Anthony asked, running his fingers through his hair. 'Surely an accident or some kind of prank that went—'

'"A prank"?' Kim asked, interrupting him and remembering some of the things Dawson had talked about. 'Did Shaun belong to any of those secret clubs?'

There was not a second's hesitation as Mr Coffee-Todd nodded his head proudly. 'Yes, officer, Shaun was Six of Spades.'

# CHAPTER 46

Geoffrey Piggott hurtled into his dorm room and aimed for his bed in the corner. Beads of sweat had formed on his forehead from the sprint from his history class as well as the knowledge that he could have sworn his essay on the French Revolution had been folded inside the pocket of his backpack.

When called to produce it he had searched and searched, feeling his face redden and his armpits grow moist as the attention of the whole classroom had been focused on him. He'd found himself wishing that nice policeman would walk in and rescue him from humiliation as he had the other day. But he hadn't, and Mrs Tennison had ordered him to go and find it. He had ignored the sighs and jeering and the missile that had caught the back of his head as he'd left the classroom.

As he rushed back he tried to remember the events of the night before.

His three roommates had returned from social time and taken residency on the bed opposite his own. He'd heard them chuckling at something on one of their mobile phones. His own phone had dinged a notification. With his back to the three figures on the bed he had checked his Facebook page, to see he'd been tagged in a video by one of his roommates.

The video was a near-naked overweight woman dancing around a silver pole, her cellulite-covered skin wobbling and jiggling all over the place. Roddy had commented with:

'*Piggott's future wife.*'

He had placed the phone back on the desk and offered no response. He had learned years ago that any reaction at all fed their amusement.

He had continued to work on his essay but had been aware of their presence the whole time. In many ways he had hardened himself to the insults. Although the names still hurt him, they were not at the root of his fear. His anxieties came from the constant thought of what was to come. How would they torture him next? When the lights went out would something come flying across the room and land on his head?

Only when he heard the sound of their deep rhythmic breathing would he allow himself to fully relax.

His watch alarm was set for five thirty each morning so he could be awake before they were. Alert and ready.

He stopped to think – when he'd woken he'd been thinking about his lessons.

'Aah,' he said aloud as he reached across his bed to the small bookcase.

He opened his biology book, and the essay fell out.

Relieved that it had not been taken this time he reached for it and headed towards the door but paused before he got there. A sick feeling began to build in his stomach as his brain caught up with something his eyes had already noted. Maybe he was wrong, he thought, hopefully, as he turned back towards the bed.

The sweat beads increased as he realised he wasn't wrong at all.

The stripes on his pillowcase were not perfectly in line with the stripes on his bed cover.

It was a checking mechanism he had devised after his room-mates had poured a whole box of Coco Pops and a pint of milk into his bed.

He approached the bed with caution as his heart began to hammer in his chest. As ever, his anxiety was fuelled by the trepidation of whatever they'd done to him now. He had a vision of his mattress crawling with maggots or some kind of insect. Damn the fact that he'd been so eager to get down to breakfast. He should have known better than to leave the three of them alone.

He touched the corner of the quilt tentatively and began to peel it back, looking through squinted eyes. His breath seemed to stop in his chest as he saw the plain white cloth of his bedsheet. He almost collapsed with relief as he tore the quilt off completely.

And then he saw it.

Right in the middle of his bed lay a single playing card.

He stared down at the ace of spades.

# CHAPTER 47

'Sorry, sir, do you want to run that by me again? I don't think Bryant heard you right,' Kim asked incredulously, looking first at Woody and then to her partner who appeared equally dumbstruck.

'The school is not being closed down,' he repeated as a muscle jumped in his cheek. She was unsure if that was linked to her attitude or what was actually coming out of his mouth.

She had called him the second they'd left the morgue and had been surprised at his instruction to come in as they were leaving the Coffee-Todd home. His revelation that the school was not closing down following a second murder would not land in any sensible, processing part of her brain.

One murder in one house and the whole street got closed down.

'But surely Ofsted will be all over—'

'Stone, you know as well as I do that independent schools don't have a single umbrella organisation and—'

'But they have to be registered with the government,' she protested. 'Surely someone can close them down?'

'Stone, Heathcrest is registered with the Independent Schools Council and is assessed regularly by their inspectorate. They have to satisfy criteria across five main areas, which are moral and social development, premises and accommodation, complaints procedures, quality of education and safeguarding which—'

'Well, there you are, then. Safeguarding covers health and safety, which Thorpe can't contest and keep his face straight at the same time, surely?'

'If you interrupt me one more time you will be removed from this case, do you understand?'

Kim seethed inwardly but nodded.

He continued. 'Heathcrest's infringement notices are in the single figures and notices of improvement aren't much higher.'

Kim understood the difference. Infringements were normally recommendations and improvements were instructions.

'Surely having no more kids murdered could be classed as a definite improvement?' she asked, sourly.

'There are schools ordered to close by Ofsted years ago that have simply ignored the instruction and are awaiting court action. So, even if Ofsted rolled up there this very minute there are protocols to be followed.'

'Surely we can close the school down?' she asked. They were the police, for God's sake.

Woody took a deep breath. 'We're not closing it, Stone.'

'Sir, we have two murdered kids, two,' she repeated for clarity. 'How the hell can we properly conduct an investigation in these conditions?'

Bryant coughed beside her. His way of telling her she was close to crossing the line. She didn't need to be told that: she was standing right on top of it.

'You'd do well to listen to your partner's warning,' Woody said, raising one eyebrow in Bryant's direction. 'The school is instructing a private security company to come in and patrol the grounds.'

'Sir, the fact that I almost blew a raspberry at you there indicates my feelings of the level of effectiveness that will have. Whoever is doing this is not running on and off the premises. They're right bloody there.'

'I'm sure a uniformed presence will make the parents feel better.'

'Surely being forced to take their kids home would help them a lot more?'

Woody's expression was steely, and Kim ached to ask him for the origin of the directive for keeping the school open. *Who the hell had made the compromise of a private security company?*

She knew it wasn't Woody. As detective chief inspector a decision of this magnitude would go much higher.

'Sir, may I ask if Chief Superintendent Briggs is steering elements of this investigation?'

'No, Stone. You may not.'

And there was her answer. From the moment Sadie Winters's body had been discovered efforts had been made to divert and disrupt the investigation. She didn't feel as though her hands were tied but more that they'd been cut off at the wrists. For the sake of her own deep respect for the man before her she would have liked to know whether he agreed with it.

'Is there anything else, sir?' she asked, conceding defeat.

'No, that's all, Stone. And I do understand that this is a difficult investigation but do feel free to make a nuisance of yourself,' he said, giving her the answer.

Oh yes, she fully intended to.

# CHAPTER 48

'Jesus,' Kim said, as the external gates of Heathcrest came into view.

The image of the press pack reminded her of the old migrant jungle in Calais. Two police officers and four private security guards, all in high visibility coats, stood in front of cones that blocked the entrance.

Bryant was forced to slow and show his identification.

A familiar face appeared right next to her window.

Bloody Frost.

Kim wound down her window.

'Care to comment on the double murder of—'

'What do you think?' Kim asked. 'And nice trick you pulled the other day, Frost. You should be proud of yourself,' she said, as the car crawled past.

Kim hadn't forgotten the woman's attempts to claim all the attention at Woody's press conference, probably still hoping to be noticed by the national press.

The reporter's initial surprise was quickly covered by a rueful look. 'Even now, that's what you think,' she said, stepping back into the crowd.

'Bloody woman,' Bryant said. 'Could be a decent reporter if she'd just stop trying to grab headlines.'

'Yeah,' Kim agreed, although the expression on Frost's face stayed with her until Bryant parked the car at the front of the school.

Another two security guards flanked the entrance.

Again, Bryant showed his identification.

'You might want to staple that to your forehead,' Kim said, wondering if they were going to have to do this all day.

She entered the building and turned left.

'Heading for the English teacher's classroom again, guv?' Bryant asked.

'Spotted anyone else speaking to us quite so openly, Bryant?' she snapped.

'Nope, she seems very open to you, I mean us, guv.'

She cast him a look.

'Amenable,' he said. 'That's the word I was looking for.'

Kim knew Bryant was being deliberately smart to ease the tension that had been building since they'd left the morgue. Bad enough that Keats's findings had marked indelibly on their brains a graphic picture of the young boy's terrifying, horrific death but add in the obstacle of investigating two murders around a functioning school and their day so far had not been a positive one.

They arrived at Joanna's classroom as the bell signalled the end of the second lesson.

The two of them stood aside as a stream of younger children filed out, chatting and laughing.

Joanna's eyes lit up when she saw them.

'Inspector, nice to see you again,' she smiled.

Kim nodded her acknowledgment.

'You taught Shaun Coffee-Todd?'

She nodded as a shadow fell across her face and her eyes instantly reddened. 'Of course,' she said, wiping away the words on a blackboard.

'Can you tell us what he was like?' Kim asked, gently, giving Joanna a moment to collect herself.

'Very pleasant lad. Well-mannered. Keen to learn. Not that keen to be called upon. He was intelligent and—'

'Did he have any enemies that you know of?' Kim asked, feeling ridiculous that she was asking that about a fourteen-year-old boy.

Joanna shook her head as she turned towards them. 'Not that I know of. I never saw any particular issue with anyone, and why would you even ask that?'

'We have to,' Kim said, realising that word of his murder had not yet reached her.

'What I'm surprised about is that he didn't have his pen. Shaun was well aware of his condition, as were we all, and he managed it excellently, only ever eating the foods prepared for him or sent in by his parents and checked—'

'Joanna, it wasn't an accident,' Kim said.

'Wh-what?' she asked, dropping to the chair.

'It was deliberate. We know that it wasn't accidental.'

'You're sure?' she asked, clearly praying for some kind of mistake.

Kim decided to spare Joanna the details of the nuts being forced into his system.

'We're sure,' she said and left it at that.

Joanna shook her head as though unable to accept the facts.

'First Sadie and now Shaun. It's just not—'

'Was there any tie to Sadie at all?' Kim asked.

Joanna shook her head. 'Not that I know of.'

'What do you know about these secret clubs, the cards?' Kim asked.

After Anthony Coffee-Todd's admission that his son had been a Spade she had to consider there was some kind of link, even though Sadie's only tie to the groups was her sister. A quick call to Dawson had confirmed that he was following that lead right now.

'I know that Thorpe, sorry, Principal Thorpe hates them and has tried his best to stamp them out but…'

'You don't agree with him?' Kim asked, surprised. 'You approve of these clubs?'

'Not even for a minute,' she replied, quickly. 'But trying to ban them has just sent them underground. It was once a badge of pride, worn by everyone involved, and so you knew who they were, kids, teachers, parents but now they have to hide.'

'Shaun was a member,' Kim said.

Joanna smiled sadly. 'Exactly my point. I would never have known.'

'So, was he a sociable kid?' Kim asked, recalling how withdrawn Sadie had been.

Joanna frowned. 'Not so much one of the popular crowd. He was one of those kids that existed somewhere in the middle. Not with the cool kids but not unpopular either.'

'One of the invisibles?' Bryant asked.

'Probably,' Joanna agreed. 'He got a bit of good-natured ribbing about being late to lessons but he—'

'Late to your lessons?' Kim asked.

'Sometimes,' she said, with a fond smile. 'My understanding is that he used to hang back in the showers until most of the other boys were done.'

Kim frowned. 'He comes to you after gym on…'

'Monday morning and Wednesday afternoon.'

'And was he late yesterday?' Kim asked.

Joanna nodded.

'So, what did you do?'

'Sent Christian off to get him.'

Kim felt a seed of dread form in her stomach.

'You sent one of the other children to hurry him up?'

Joanna nodded and frowned. 'Of course, bloody hell, I've already been through this once with Thorpe and Steele,' she said, exasperated at having to repeat herself.

'And what did—'

'Christian Fellows,' Joanna offered.

'What did Christian say when he returned?'

Joanna thought for a moment and then tipped her head. 'He didn't return. Not before all the noise sounded in the corridor when Shaun had been discovered.'

Kim felt the dread turn into a wave. 'So, we don't know if Christian actually saw something when he went to chivvy up Shaun?'

Joanna shook her head. 'I certainly haven't asked him. To my knowledge Shaun had accidentally ingested a nut product.'

Kim glanced at Bryant. The alarm was reflected on his face as they both realised what they'd just learned.

Christian and Shaun had been out of the classroom at the same time. There were two possibilities. Either Christian had murdered Shaun or, if not, he might have seen who had.

Whichever scenario was accurate they needed to speak to the boy right now.

# CHAPTER 49

Christian Fellows now understood that he had never felt real fear in his thirteen years.

Not when he'd climbed the ancient elm tree in the garden and realised that he didn't like heights. Or when he'd fallen and broken his left arm. Not even when his parents had sat him down for the 'chat' five years ago when he was eight years old. They had talked to him of not getting along, of separate houses and they would both still love him whether they were together or not. He now knew that had not been fear.

This was fear running around his body as though it was attached to his blood cells.

Because right now he was on his own.

He had made sure he'd been amongst people since he'd been sent to find Shaun the previous day.

He had heard Shaun's cries for help, had seen him crawling across the floor, with a scarf covering his eyes, fighting for breath. He'd known that his classmate was dying, and he'd also known someone else was in the room.

He hadn't seen the person. He didn't know who it was. But the person didn't know that. He wanted to put a sign on both his back and front stating 'I didn't see you' so that whoever it was knew they were in no danger from him. He couldn't tell anyone, in case he was telling the person who had done it.

He still didn't understand why anyone would want to hurt Shaun. Shaun didn't upset anyone. He wasn't the worst at anything or even the best. He was just Shaun.

From the moment he'd run away and hid in the library, trying to form his thoughts, trying to get his own breathing under control, he'd made sure that he was with someone every single minute.

All day he'd attached himself to any group so that whoever had hurt Shaun couldn't get to him.

But he was alone now.

Mrs Atkinson had instructed him to leave the biology lesson and report to the headmaster's office.

The hallways were deserted.

One more corridor to go and he'd be outside Mrs Lawson's office and he'd feel safe again. Just down three stairs and then past the janitor's room. Just ten more steps and he'd be safe.

He didn't know why the headmaster wanted to see him. Did he know his secret? Did he know he'd seen Shaun and he'd done nothing but run away in fear? The heat of his shame flushed his cheeks.

If only Miss Wade had sent someone else. Maybe they'd have known what to do. Maybe they wouldn't have run away, terrified. Maybe Shaun would still be alive.

*Please just let me get to the office*, he prayed, as a hand grabbed the back of his neck.

# CHAPTER 50

Kim stepped into the gym hall to either prove or disprove the fear that was growing within her after speaking to Joanna Wade. The room was empty except for an athletic male dragging blue plastic mats to a pile at the side of the room. A pommel horse was the only item of equipment left to move. A line of blue tape was stretched across the doorway to the locker rooms where forensics were searching for clues to help them identify Shaun's killer.

His face formed an instant frown at the intrusion of strangers into his work area. It faded as he realised who they were.

'Police officers?' he said, to make sure.

Both she and Bryant reached into their pockets for their identification.

He raised his hand. 'It's fine. I believe you. If you want to talk to my boys they've been sent to the pool block to shower.'

Kim said nothing. It took him two seconds to realise she was waiting for him to introduce himself.

'Philip Havers, sports coach, PE teacher and general fitness expert,' he said, offering his hand.

Bryant took it and shook it.

'You found Shaun?' she asked.

'Yes, but not quickly enough to save his life,' he said, swallowing and looking away.

'Was he gone when you found him?' Bryant asked.

Havers nodded, touching his lips. 'They were blue, and his eyes were just staring. It's like he was looking straight at me. I'll never forget it.' He turned towards her. 'And yet the picture in my head is of him looking peaceful.'

She could understand that. After what Keats had described ravaging his young body, eventual death must have come as a kind of relief.

'Could you give us the timeline?' she asked.

Havers nodded. 'The gym lesson was a good one. The kids love a basketball session. Guys went to shower up. Coffee-Todd hung back, as usual, putting away the equipment and being the last into the locker room.

'I don't supervise their shower time, officer, but I do stay close by in case I hear any issues arise in there,' he explained.

'Is that a safeguard for the children?' she asked.

'No, Inspector – it's a safeguard for me,' he explained.

She could imagine that false accusations could occur as well as genuine ones. And both could destroy a career.

'I was tidying the girls' locker room when the bell went and the boys all tumbled out and headed for their next lesson. After the rabble left I headed to the staff room for a coffee…' He paused. 'If only I hadn't gone to the—'

'Wasn't he known for hanging back?' Kim asked, to be sure.

Havers pulled himself out of his regret. 'Yes, he was often the last to leave but the truth of it is that I never gave the kid a thought.'

The guilt of his honesty flashed across his face.

Kim was beginning to suspect that happened a lot with this child. By all accounts he was average. He wasn't memorable academically or physically and was no troublemaker either.

'So, you came back around—?'

'Roughly ten past three. I got talking—'

Kim held up her hand. 'I don't want to know.'

She didn't need him to explain himself to her. If she allowed it, he would then expect some kind of understanding or empathy from her, which she wasn't prepared to give. He had forgotten a child and she didn't make excuses for that.

Shaun Coffee-Todd had been left alone for fifteen minutes and was now dead, and she wasn't about to start offering guilt pardons.

Mr Havers looked as though he wanted to say more. To explain himself, excuse himself but that wasn't why she was here.

'And could you show us exactly where you found Shaun?' Kim asked.

'I've already shown the crime scene guys.'

'It would be most helpful,' she said, lifting the crime scene tape for him to pass through.

They followed him along a tiled corridor that opened up into a locker room. Full-sized cabinets all had keys dangling from their locks. Long wooden benches separated the row of lockers. Beyond was a wall that wound around to a row of six showers.

'Just point,' she said, ignoring the crime scene techs that looked her way. She wasn't committing any sins. Havers's DNA would be all over the place.

'Mr Havers, did you see a child named Christian Fellows at any time?'

Havers frowned as though trying to recall. He began to shake his head. 'All the others had gone to—'

'Christian Fellows was sent back to get him,' Kim clarified.

'No, I never saw him, Inspector.'

'Okay, thank you for your time, Mr Havers, and if you could just give us a minute.'

Philip Havers nodded and walked away as Kim headed back to the shower.

*

The journey from the nearest shower to Shaun's final position was roughly thirty feet, which the poor kid had crawled on his knees, desperately trying to reach the only thing that could save him.

'What could this kid possibly have done to upset anyone?' her colleague asked.

'Absolutely nothing, Bryant,' she agreed. 'He wasn't significant enough for that,' she said, not unkindly. She suspected his place in the suit of Spades was likely due to his famous father.

'He hadn't done anything wrong. He wasn't troubled like Sadie. He wasn't a bad kid or a bully. He had no enemies and yet someone wanted him dead. He had no links to Sadie, and they were completely different kinds of kids,' she said, walking back to the entrance to the shower block where it divided for boys and girls. She walked it again, slowly.

As she turned the first corner she saw herself in the full-length mirror. But that wasn't all she could see. The mirror offered her a view of the exact spot where Shaun had taken his last breath.

'So, what are you thinking?' Bryant asked, appearing beside her.

'He saw something, Bryant,' she said, walking back towards the gym hall just as Havers disappeared into the main corridor.

'Christian Fellows definitely saw something, and we need to find out where he is.'

Dawson parked the car beside a Range Rover Discovery that sat in front of a spacious barn conversion. This was nearer to the picture in his mind for the registered address of a Heathcrest Academy pupil.

The door was answered by a woman he guessed to be in her early sixties. Her hair was a short shock of white atop a naturally tanned skin tone. Simple stud earrings adorned her lobes, and a silver chain around her neck accentuated skin that had spent time outdoors.

But this woman was too old to be the mother of the boy he was seeking.

'May I help you?' she asked, pleasantly.

'I'm sorry, I'm looking for Tristan Rock,' he said. The family must have moved in the nine months since he'd attended Heathcrest.

'You know Tristan?' she asked, stepping aside.

Dawson shook his head as he entered the property. 'Is Tristan here?'

The woman nodded and offered her hand. 'Louisa Rock,' she said. 'Tristan's paternal grandmother.'

Dawson shook her hand and introduced himself.

She looked puzzled but invited him to sit.

'What business do you have with my grandson?' she asked, reaching for a small china cup on the coffee table.

'I'd just like a moment with either your grandson or his parents, if I may,' Dawson replied, assuming she was living here in her son's house. If Tristan was home, he guessed he must be home-schooled now.

'I'm afraid Tristan's parents don't live here. This is my home, and Tristan lives here with me,' she said, protectively.

'I didn't realise that. Are you his legal guardian?' he asked, trying to keep the open challenge from his voice.

There was something sinister going on at that school that may or may not be linked to the death of two children, and he had a feeling that Tristan Rock could offer him some help.

'Tristan has lived with me since he was four years old because of my proximity to the school. And the fact that his parents are very rarely in the country,' she said, unable to keep the disapproval from her voice. 'My son lives off his inheritance from his father, who gave him too much money and not enough sense, I'm afraid.'

Dawson was forming a picture in his mind.

'They didn't want Tristan?' he asked, lowering his voice.

'There's no need to whisper. He can't hear you. They wanted him at first but not when he became an inconvenience to their lifestyle. I'm afraid to say my son is very spoiled and has never worked a day in his life. He chose an equally fickle wife, and they have much in common. The main thing being that they both love themselves more than anything else in the world.'

Dawson couldn't help the smile that touched his lips. 'Mrs Rock, your candour is refreshing.'

'I blame myself, of course, and my late husband. No one wants to see their child struggle but having the financial means to remove all adversity isn't always the kindest thing to do for one's children.'

'Does Tristan see his parents?' Dawson asked. Her honesty made him feel he could ask her anything.

'Not for a few months now,' she admitted.

Dawson realised that so far he'd found nothing to envy among these privileged kids at Heathcrest. The only thing that had kept him going through the misery of his school days had been the closeness of his family.

'You still haven't explained why you'd like to meet my grandson,' she said. 'Or offered me any reason to allow it.'

Well, Tristan might not have the love of his parents, but Dawson wouldn't want to take this woman on. Thank goodness the kid had someone in his corner.

Her own honesty prompted the exact same response from him. 'Mrs Rock, there have been incidents at the school that are currently being investigated. In the course of that investigation we've stumbled across what appear to be episodes of bullying, hazing, intimidation, and I wondered if your grandson could help me better understand exactly what is going on.'

She shook her head. 'I'm afraid Tristan can't help you.'

'But, if I could just speak to him for a moment. Or if you could explain why he left the school in the middle of the year…'

'He can't explain anything to you, officer,' she said, resolutely.

Dawson tried to hide his frustration. 'Mrs Rock, there are children being intimidated into silence, forced to join elite clubs and compete for popularity and acceptance. It is sickening and cruel and I really need—'

'Follow me,' she said, standing.

He fell into step behind her as she returned to the hallway and entered a door on the right.

'Officer, I'd like you to meet my grandson, Tristan.'

Dawson felt his eyes opening wide as he stepped into the room.

# CHAPTER 52

Kim barged past a security guard and into Thorpe's office without knocking.

'Where is Christian Fellows?' she asked, ignoring the secretary who sat on this side of the desk and viewed her with disdain.

'I'm sorry, Inspector, but what—'

'I need to know what lesson Christian Fellows is in, now,' she said.

He looked to his secretary.

'Physics,' she said. 'Block A,' she clarified.

Kim thought she knew where that was and opened her mouth to ask.

'But he's on his way here right now,' she said.

So that was how the woman had been able to pluck the information from nowhere.

'For what?' Bryant asked.

'A welfare check,' Thorpe answered. 'All of the boys in Shaun's class are being checked on. It's traumatic for all the boys.'

'How long ago did you send for him?' Kim asked.

'About five or ten minutes,' the woman answered.

'Which is it, five or ten? How long should it take for him to get here?'

She shrugged. 'Not very long but I don't understand—'

'Come on, Bryant,' Kim said, sprinting out of the office.

*

'I know where the physics class is,' Bryant said, leading the way. 'You have to pass it to get coffee.'

They sprinted along the corridors for a full two minutes before Bryant stopped and pointed across the hallway.

'That's it,' he said.

Kim thrust open the door to the surprise of a middle-aged woman who turned to her and frowned at the sudden intrusion.

'Christian Fellows?' she asked.

The woman shook her head. 'He's with the principal right—'

'Damn it,' Kim said, closing the door. They had just taken the route he would have followed, and they hadn't met him on the way.

'Okay, back we go,' Kim said. 'Sweeping every room.'

The kid had to be somewhere.

Bryant's eyes widened. 'Do you know how many rooms there are between—'

The door she'd just closed suddenly opened. 'May I help you with something, officer?'

'Christian isn't with the principal, and we need to speak to him urgently,' Kim said, trying to keep the panic out of her voice.

'Well, he can't have gone far,' she replied. 'I'm sure he's just been dawdling along somewhere.'

Kim prayed to God she was right.

'Boys,' she called, and twenty young bodies appeared in the hallway. 'Teams of two, full search of all areas between here and the admin block. Go.'

The boys began running in all directions.

'Thank you. We'll head back to the office to see if he's turned up there yet,' Kim said.

'I'll alert the next classroom and get more children searching.'

Kim thanked her before she and Bryant began the sprint back to the principal's office.

'Damn it, Bryant, where the hell is…'

Her words trailed away as a scream filled the corridor.

'Shit,' she said, launching past Bryant towards the blood-curdling noise.

She found a woman, a member of the housekeeping team, standing in the doorway of a room with her hands covering her mouth.

Kim pushed past her and also came to a stop.

Dangling from the ceiling beam was the body of Christian Fellows.

# CHAPTER 53

Kim's stunned gaze travelled from the upturned stool beneath the child's feet right up to his closed eyes and then to the sheet that was knotted around his neck. She had the sudden vision of them hurrying past the door to this room while the kid was hanging there.

The sensation of Bryant behind her prompted her into action.

Kim moved into the janitor's room and turned the stool back upright and jumped up onto it. She grabbed the boy's legs and lifted him up to take the pressure from the sheet around his neck. With one arm around his waist she reached up and untied the crude knot around the beam.

The boy's body slid down her own. She threw the sheet aside and used both arms to hold him tight. She didn't want to let him go.

A familiar feeling began to wash over her. His body was still warm. Minutes. They had been just minutes too late for Sadie and now minutes too late for Christian, who had been murdered for something he might or might not have seen.

'Fuck it,' she said, holding the boy tightly to her chest, his head lolled against her cheek.

'Guv,' Bryant said. 'Let me—'

'Hang on, shush,' Kim commanded, listening and feeling beyond her heart beating loudly in her ears.

No way. She was imagining things. It was what she wanted to feel. It was wishful thinking.

But no, it wasn't her imagination.

She had just felt his warm breath against her cheek.

'Hurry, Bryant,' she shouted. 'Give me a hand. This child is still alive.'

# CHAPTER 54

Dawson could not remove his gaze from the inert figure lying in the hospital bed.

Tristan's possessions were placed around the room as though he'd left them moments before to take a nap. A pair of dirty trainers sat beside his bedside cabinet, a grey hoody hung from the wardrobe door handle. A skateboard propped up against the wall. Posters of gothic art lined the walls and a pile of magazines was stacked in the corner. Dawson suspected that his grandmother was making sure his things were ready for when he came back.

Louisa Rock had taken a seat beside her grandson after asking the nurse to leave them alone for a moment. The woman checked the ventilator, nodded and left the room.

'He is more than what you see here,' she said, following his gaze around the room, and Dawson understood. She would not allow his personality to be packed away, out of sight.

Her hand touched his temple and gently pushed a lock of dark hair to the side.

'Every day I pray for signs of improvement,' she said, sadly. The doctors insisted he was brain dead and could feel nothing, but I still feel that Tristan is in there fighting to come out.'

Dawson knew the boy to be seventeen years old, but he looked much younger. His dark hair framed a smooth and youthful face with thick, dark eyelashes and strong, handsome features despite the paleness of his complexion.

His arms were laid at his side, long and athletic but not thin and wasted. His pyjama-clad chest rose and fell rhythmically in time with the machine that had not only taken on the function of his breathing but the sound as well.

Dawson wondered if it had been some kind of accident or an illness.

'His parents wanted to give up on him, but they don't know him the way I do. The best way to get Tristan to succeed at something is to tell him he can't do it,' she said, taking his hand. 'Which is ironic, considering—'

'How did this happen, Mrs Rock?' he asked, gently, already forming an exit strategy. As tragic as it was, Tristan Rock's condition was not going to help him prove his theory.

'It's not something we talk about, officer. Agreements were signed.'

'Agreements?'

'Non-disclosure agreements. Between Tristan's parents and the school.'

Dawson balked. 'This happened to Tristan at Heathcrest?'

She nodded. 'My son accepted a financial settlement to help compensate for the inconvenience of the accident.'

'"Accident"?' he asked, aware that he was repeating her words.

Louisa Rock pursed her lips and nodded.

'Mrs Rock, what is the nature of your grandson's condition?'

She sighed heavily.

'It's called Hyponatremia. Otherwise known as water intoxication. Excessive water intake creates a sodium imbalance causing cells to swell. He drank himself into unconsciousness.'

'How do you know?'

'He filmed himself doing it, officer. He used his phone to capture the whole event as he drank pint after pint of water and, in effect, eventually drowned himself. The phone caught his eventual collapse and the entrance of his room-mate an hour later, by which time it was too late.'

Dawson pictured the phone positioned, filming as his condition worsened, an eye on him that could not communicate to anyone.

'The doctors did all they could, but he was already brain dead.'

Dawson felt the rage building within him that the school had so easily been able to avoid yet another scandal by handing over a fistful of money.

'But why did he do it in the first place?' Dawson asked.

'It was his initiation task. It was a dare from the King of Spades.'

# CHAPTER 55

Kim watched the ambulance race away with its blue lights flashing before turning to the surprisingly athletic man beside her.

'Thank you,' she said.

He nodded as the colour began to return to his face.

Bodies had converged on them from every direction in response to Bryant's call for help. She had held the boy tight, watching his breathing, ready to perform CPR if his chest failed to rise.

The second she'd thought she heard sirens Graham Steele had gently taken Christian from her arms as though he were no heavier than a feather and charged through the crowds to get him to the front of the building as quickly as possible. No one had stood in his way.

While holding him Kim had wondered how he was still alive and her mind recalled the placement of the sheet around his neck. The knot had rested beneath his chin and not pressing on his windpipe.

'He was a friend of Shaun's,' Graham said, as though that explained everything. It did not. 'He was actually on his way for a welfare check. If only I'd seen him.'

'It's not attempted suicide,' she said, as the ambulance disappeared from view. Bryant was in the building somewhere right now talking to Woody and explaining that fact.

'What do you—'

'The chair,' she said. 'I stood on it and could barely reach the beam, so Christian wouldn't have had a chance. The chair was staged to look like he'd kicked it away, but he couldn't have.

Someone tried to kill this kid,' she said, meeting his doubtful gaze. 'The third in a week,' she observed.

'But they're just children,' he said, shaking his head. 'What possible motive could anyone…'

'You speak to many of the students here, Graham,' she observed. 'Is there anyone you think is capable of committing—'

'You think a student could have done this?'

'Don't you?' she asked.

He shook his head. 'I'm sorry but I'm not going to even consider such a hypothesis,' he said, walking away.

Kim chewed on her own frustration. First Ted and now the school counsellor. Was there no one prepared to have this conversation with her?

She headed back into the school, forcing her way through groups chattering and whispering, dissecting the latest events.

Crime scene tape had been stretched across the doorway to the janitor's room and two techies dispatched from the shower block were assessing the scene from within.

Bryant headed towards her carrying two coffees. As he got closer he shook his head.

'No go,' he said.

'What the hell is it going to take to close this bloody place down?' she growled. How many kids had to die? She wondered, relieving Bryant of one cup.

'Oh no, brace yourself,' he said, looking behind her.

She turned to see Thorpe attempting to bypass the crime scene tape and enter the janitor's room.

She stepped towards the doorway and held up her hand. 'Sorry, Principal Thorpe, but I can't allow you to enter.'

His face reddened to full ripeness.

'You can't keep me out of—'

'Oh yes I can,' she said, stepping away and sipping coffee. 'Tell him, Bryant.'

Her colleague's lips twitched as he approached the doorway.

'Sir, we cannot allow any further contamination of the crime scene,' Bryant said, as she leaned against the wall and took a sip of her coffee. 'We are following all necessary protocols for a double murder and an attempted murder, and I'm sure you're equally keen that we uncover the perpetrator at the earliest opportunity.'

'Of course, officer. I have parents calling and turning up to remove their children. I'd like you to speak to them and offer them your reassurance that their children are safe here.'

Kim almost spat her coffee right in his face. 'That's not gonna happen, I'm afraid. Unfortunately, the word is out now, making everyone's job a whole lot harder, but we will not offer reassurance that we cannot guarantee. Now, I'm thinking that closing down the site and sending the kids home might be a reasonable guarantee of their safety.'

'The board and I discussed the possibility while exploring alternative options.'

'And decided to employ a private security company,' she said, looking behind him. 'And they are, err… where exactly?'

'We can't hold them responsible for this,' he argued.

'But their presence didn't exactly prevent it either, did it, Principal Thorpe?'

'It's a reassuring presence,' he said. 'It will make everyone feel better.'

'Do you really believe that?' she asked, incredulously. 'Or is it so that you can use it to convince quivering parents to keep their children here while trying to keep the reputation of the school intact, because if you take a look at the press community camped at the school gates that ship has pretty much sailed.'

He bit his lower lip before answering. 'Inspector, the reputation of this and other independent schools is what our clients pay for.

Our students must learn to face adversity to prepare them for life after Heathcrest.'

Kim looked to Bryant to see if he was smelling the same level of bullshit.

His expression told her he was.

She stepped closer, despising his priority of reputation. 'I am so pleased that current events have served the school in the name of character building for the remaining students, but might I remind you that there is a killer on these premises, Principal Thorpe, and two of your charges are already dead. I suggest that becomes your pressing priority, and the fact that parents are arriving to remove their children restores my faith in the power of their judgement. Now, please leave us alone to do our job.'

His eyes widened and his teeth ground together as his gaze bore into hers.

She did not look away. Four seconds later she was watching his back as he stormed along the corridor.

'Feel better there, guv?' Bryant asked.

'Oh yeah. I needed that.'

'Good to see you adhering to Woody's instruction, guv?'

'Which one?' she asked.

'Making a nuisance of yourself.'

'I like to do what I'm told,' she said deadpan.

Bryant sputtered his coffee as her phone began to ring.

'Keats,' she said into the handset.

He didn't beat around the bush as he gave her the results of the toxicology report he'd received for Sadie Winters.

She listened silently as he explained in layman's terms what had been found.

She ended the call and turned to Bryant.

'Locate Saffron Winters. I want to talk to that girl right now.'

# CHAPTER 56

Kim tapped her fingers on the desk impatiently.

'So, what exactly are we talking to Saffie Winters about?' Bryant asked as a gentle tapping sounded at the door.

'You're about to find out,' she said, before calling out for Saffie to enter.

The girl appeared in the doorway and Kim beckoned her forward.

She glanced sideways at Bryant.

This interview was hers.

'Please sit down, Saffie,' Kim said, keeping her voice cool and even. Not at all reflective of how she was feeling.

'How are you?' Kim asked.

Saffron shrugged and then nodded. 'As well as can be expected under the circumstances.'

'You do know that another child died, and we had a third incident less than an hour—'

'But that's not anything to do with Sadie, is it?' she asked, looking from one to the other.

'We can't rule out a link between all three incidents.'

The girl swallowed deeply but said nothing.

'Saffie, I have to ask if you can think of anyone who would want to murder your younger sister, or what link she might have to Shaun Coffee-Todd?' Kim didn't include Christian's name, as she remained convinced that he'd been targeted because he'd accidentally stumbled into the shower block during Shaun's murder.

Kim was choosing her words carefully. She had points to make and harder questions to ask but she had to remind herself that she was not dealing with a fully cooked adult, but neither was she dealing with a child.

This sixteen-year-old was somewhere in between.

Saffie shook her head vehemently. 'There is no one that would want to hurt her,' she said.

'And yet she is dead, Saffron,' Kim pushed. 'Beaten around the head and made to look like suicide.'

'Please, stop,' Saffie said, as the colour began to drain from her face.

'You've already admitted the two of you weren't that close, haven't you?' Kim asked.

Saffie nodded.

'But you didn't tell us she was angry with you. Why did she storm into your room the other night and demand to talk?' Kim asked.

Saffie's initial surprise turned to anger as she put two and two together and realised how Kim knew that.

'Yes, I spoke to Eric yesterday after your concert practice. I gather the two of you split up recently, but he definitely recalls Sadie being unhappy with you. What was that about?'

'I'm sorry, I don't recall,' she said as a blotch of heat appeared beneath the heart-shaped pendant.

'It wasn't so long ago,' Kim pushed.

Saffie's chin raised an inch or two. 'I really don't remember. She probably felt as though I'd slighted her or something like that. She could kick off for no reason, officer,' she said, gaining her composure.

Kim knew she was not going to divulge the reason for Sadie's anger.

'I suppose she was a bit of an embarrassment, wasn't she?'

The colour returned to her face in the form of a blush, and although she shook her head the truth was spreading an ugly red stain across her cheeks.

'Really, the two of you couldn't have been more different. You must have sometimes wished she would disappear.'

'I didn't do anything to Sadie,' she said, horrified.

'I'm not saying you did but you didn't like her very much, did you?'

'She was my sister. I loved her, but I just didn't understand her.'

'So, why try so hard to protect her, Saffie?' Kim asked, sitting back in her chair.

'How so?'

'By removing all of her personal possessions from her dorm room.'

The colour in her face deepened. 'I just thought—'

'What did you think? That it was okay to tamper with evidence. You thought it was all right to remove anything you felt was incriminating?'

Saffron fiddled with her hands and looked to the ground.

Suddenly, this was not the assured, confident girl they had spoken to the other day. Part of her wanted to tell the kid everything would be okay, but another part knew that there were too many secrets in the space between them.

'I can't help wondering if it was you that chose to tamper with your sister's suicide letter that wasn't a suicide letter at all,' Kim said.

Saffie shook her head but didn't look up.

'Saffron, is there any chance that Sadie was involved in these secret clubs. Was she ever asked to be a Heart or Dia—'

'Don't be ridiculous,' Saffie said, raising her head. 'Why would she have been chosen?'

'But how can you be sure?' Kim challenged. 'You seem to know very little about your sister.'

'I can be sure of that,' Saffie said. 'I know every member of both Hearts and Diamonds and I can assure you—'

'Okay, I believe you but there's something else I need to ask you about, Saffie.' Kim took a breath. 'The toxicology report detected traces of Fluoxetine and Clonazepam in Sadie's blood.'

There was no reaction, which indicated no surprise.

'Why did you remove her antidepressants?' Kim asked, pointedly.

Saffron seemed to open her mouth as if to refute her words and then changed her mind. She simply shook her head.

'Were you trying to avoid the stigma of having a sister with problems? Is your image that important to you?' Kim asked.

'No, it's not that.'

'So what is it, Saffron, why did you do it?'

'I was told to.'

'By whom?'

'My parents,' she whispered.

Kim was confused. 'I really don't understand the problem if your sister had been prescribed…'

Her words trailed away as Saffie met her gaze for the first time in about five minutes.

Kim followed the breadcrumbs that the girl had dropped.

'They weren't Sadie's tablets, were they?' she asked.

Saffron didn't argue, and Kim finally, fully understood.

The Winters had been medicating their thirteen-year-old daughter.

# CHAPTER 57

Dawson pulled up at what must have been the grandest house yet.

He knocked the front door of the home of Harrison Forbes; the last name on his list. Harrison's name had appeared on the roster eleven months ago and had simply disappeared for the beginning of the spring term.

Dawson paced a few steps before knocking again. He heard the sound echo around the hall.

He stepped back and took a look around. There were no vehicles parked around the property, and there was an air of silence.

He strode to the three-car garage block and tried the handle. Locked.

He walked back to the house and knocked again.

He wasn't expecting anyone to answer. There was clearly no one home but it was best to check before he began peering in windows. He had no wish to frighten the living daylights out of anyone.

He stood on tiptoe and glanced in through the bottom left corner of the kitchen window. At first glance, it appeared tidy and organised. Until he took a second look. The kitchen wasn't uncluttered, it was empty.

He moved along to the next window, which revealed a grand, spacious lounge area, without one item of furniture.

Damn it, the Forbes family had evidently moved out, and he had no other address.

*

He got into the car and headed back down the drive. He entered the traffic to the main road and then took the next left, leading him up the drive of the next available neighbour.

Oh, to have your nearest neighbour about a quarter mile away, he thought. But a bugger if you just needed a cup of sugar.

The blaring lights and three parked cars told him he could at least speak to someone.

The door was open before he'd even parked the car. Of course, a house like this would have cameras and a security system.

The man that came towards him was holding a bull mastiff who was slobbering at him disturbingly on a short, tight leash.

'May I help you?'

The politeness of the question was at odds with the hungry-looking dog.

The man was dressed in a white shirt and black suit trousers. He guessed he had just come back from work.

'Sorry to disturb you,' Dawson offered, half talking to the dog. 'I was just at the Forbes' property next door and—'

'You want to buy it?' the man asked doubtfully, eyeing his Renault Megane.

Oh, how he hated judgemental people.

'No, I'm a police officer and I need to speak to the family. Do you have a forwarding address?'

The man shook his head as the dog lunged uncomfortably close to his genitalia. His owner tugged him back to his side.

'They didn't leave an address, and may I know your interest?'

'I'm afraid not. It's a matter I can only discuss with the family.'

'Then I'm sorry, but we can't help you. They didn't tell us where they were moving to, and we just keep a check on the house now and again.'

'So, you have a telephone number for them?' he asked, hopefully.

The man shook his head. 'There is a managing agent and a solicitor, and everything goes through them.'

'All sounds a bit mysterious,' Dawson said, trying to lighten the mood.

The man did not respond in kind.

'Not surprising, after what happened,'

'And what was that?' he asked.

The man's face closed completely. 'Not for me to say, officer.'

Too late, Dawson realised that he had not played that very well. If he'd been thinking clearly, he would have used the old trick of pretending to know what had happened to at least elicit some detail. He blamed the fact it had been a long day and he was tired.

He reached into his pocket, and the dog snarled and growled in his direction.

'Easy, boy,' the man said, tugging him again.

'It's just this,' Dawson said, holding out a card. 'Could you pass along my details through the communication channel. Just tell them I could really do with talking to them.'

The man took the card and turned to move away.

'Please, tell them it's about Heathcrest.'

The man nodded and stepped away, muttering something as he went.

Dawson couldn't be sure, but it had sounded like 'I wouldn't hold your breath.'

He sat back in the car and rubbed at his forehead. He really should call the boss and head home.

He took out his mobile phone and called up a search engine. Something had happened to Harrison Forbes, and he wanted to know what.

He typed in the kid's name and got precisely no matching results. Hundreds of hits for his father who owned valuable rental property in London but not one item for his son. No Facebook account, Twitter, Instagram, Snapchat. Absolutely nothing and not one news report of any kind to corroborate what the neighbour had said.

And why all the secrecy surrounding the family moving away. Who or what were they afraid of?

# CHAPTER 58

Kim had done everything she could to distract herself from the nagging thought in her head.

It was a half thought that had been growing in her mind all day. Ever since her conversation with Ted, which seemed like a lifetime ago.

She'd made coffee, walked Barney, eaten, and then plonked herself on the floor amongst approximately one hundred parts of Norton Commando. She viewed these components as a chef might view basic ingredients. Alone and separate they didn't amount to much but bring them all together and the result was pure magic.

And even that hadn't distracted her.

Killing a child was a heinous act in itself but the deaths occurring in a place where students outnumbered adults by fifteen to one she had no choice but to consider the unthinkable, and yet no one would discuss the possibility with her. No one wanted to consider the validity of what was in her head.

That the murders might have been carried out by another child.

So, did that mean she was dealing with evil in a person who wasn't yet fully grown? Was there such a thing as an evil child and would they ever be capable of such a thing?

Many of the examples Ted had offered had involved children from broken homes or complicated backgrounds. Heathcrest was a place of wealth, privilege and achievement.

Yes, she supposed the flip side of that was ambition, ruthlessness and power but what the hell had Sadie Winters done wrong? She hadn't been a threat to anyone.

And yet there seemed to be an insidiousness surrounding the adults linked to Heathcrest. Many of the staff had been students and had gravitated back to the facility. The majority of the parents had once been students at Heathcrest. Both students and adults were involved with the secret societies that some people were trying to abolish and yet were still going strong.

She sighed as the thoughts continued to chase their own tails around her mind. She could avoid it no longer. The notion that had been with her all day propelled her to her feet.

Right now she had no clue who had killed Sadie and Shaun or why, but she needed a better understanding of evil and all its forms.

She needed someone who wouldn't shy away from a difficult conversation.

And for that, there was only once place she could go.

# CHAPTER 59

Kim dismounted the Ninja and removed her helmet.

The entrance to Drake Hall Prison had changed very little since her last visit. The grey metal gate adjoined the tall grid fencing designed to contain the prisoners within. But Kim knew evil managed to seep through the gaps.

The courtesy call she'd placed before leaving home had been met with cooperation at her unorthodox request. An unscheduled visit with an inmate outside normal visiting hours and without their permission had depleted her favours reserve at the prison, and she just hoped it was worth it.

Warden Edwards greeted her at the door with an outstretched hand.

'Detective Inspector Stone, good to see you again,' he said, warmly.

She returned the handshake.

This man had offered her the courtesy of believing her accusations against Alexandra Thorne when no one else would. Her claims of Alex's power beyond the confines of the walls and barbed wire had sounded fanciful even to her own ears. That she could concoct a plan for murder and implement it without getting even a speck of dirt on her own hands had not surprised Kim in the least. Warden Edwards had listened, and it had saved lives.

Twice now Kim had crossed paths with the sociopathic psychiatrist and both times the woman had tried to penetrate her psyche and break her down. And both times she had failed. Just. Seeing her again was a risk Kim had to take, because no one knew evil like Alexandra Thorne.

'Did you do as I asked?' Kim said as he escorted her to the front desk and handed her a pass.

He nodded. 'She's in the visitor's room but doesn't know you're coming.'

Kim wanted the element of surprise on her side. Giving Alex the time to plan for a conversation would have been foolhardy.

'And how's she been?' Kim asked as Officer Katie Parkes appeared behind the desk.

'Inspector Stone,' she greeted, warmly. 'Nice to see you again.'

Yes, the warden had kept her visit very secret indeed. Even from the staff.

'Officer Parkes will fill you in,' he said, checking his watch. 'But, I really have to get on.'

'Thank you,' she said, nodding her understanding.

Parkes came from behind the desk, and Kim noted that she'd lost a few pounds. Her uniform no longer strained in all the wrong places, and her hair was tidily pulled back to reveal clear skin and fresh eyes.

'You're looking well,' she observed.

Katie Parkes had been the recipient of Alex's manipulation, resulting in trouble for herself. Alex had used the guard's recent pregnancy to gain sympathy and a mobile phone. Tired and emotional from the challenges of being a new, single mum Parkes hadn't stood a chance and had found herself trapped and blackmailed for trying to be sympathetic and helpful. Typical traits of Alexandra Thorne were to turn someone's humanity against them.

'I'm very well, thank you,' she said, brightly, leading the way along the familiar route.

'And how's our prisoner been behaving?'

Parkes shook her head. 'You know Alex. Always trying to get a rise out of someone. Got her own little bunch of cronies led by her cellmate, a kid called Emma Mitchell, who hangs off her every word.'

'Is there anything in particular that—' Kim began to ask and then stopped herself. She'd been in the prison less than ten minutes and was already becoming embroiled in Alex's world, fearing for the safety of everyone she came into contact with.

'We keep a close eye,' Parkes said, knowingly.

Kim wished that she felt reassured, and she didn't doubt the diligence of the staff, but she knew Alex. And much as she would love to keep a permanent eye on the woman there were others that needed her attention more.

Hence the reason for her visit.

Kim felt her heart rate quicken as she approached the entrance to the visitor's room. She almost faltered as she heard Alex's familiar voice.

'Officer Parkes, is that you? Are you bringing me my surp—' Alex's words trailed away as Kim stepped into view.

In a nanosecond Alex's irritation turned to confusion followed by a slow smile of pleasure that spread across her face.

'Mitchell, out you come,' Parkes said to the girl sitting on the tabletop next to Alex.

'Up yours, Parkes,' she said, looking to Alex for guidance.

Alex didn't even glance in her direction.

'Get lost, Emma,' she said.

The girl waited for a couple of seconds as though she'd misheard, but Alex's gaze didn't falter as she appraised Kim.

The girl huffed and offered Kim a murderous expression.

Kim wondered if this was the girl's first experience of being dismissed by her idol. She was sure it wouldn't be the last.

'Kim, how lovely to see you,' Alex said pleasantly, as though they'd met for coffee only last week.

The woman looked exactly as she had the last time they'd met. Her blonde hair was tied back in a loose ponytail exposing a face that was stunning despite the absence of expensive cosmetics. The icy blue eyes were fixed on her, and Kim offered her a smile as she sat.

'Those additional ten years look good on you, Alex,' Kim said. It had been almost two years since her initial sentence and the additional time deemed it unlikely she'd see freedom before her fiftieth birthday. And that was the price you paid for attempting to murder the people that stood in the way of your appeal.

Kim had learned long ago that the best form of defence with Alex was attack.

'Were you missing me?' Alex asked, ignoring her jibe. 'I could always send you a weekly visiting—'

'That won't be necessary,' Kim said. 'This is a one-off visit, I can assure you.' Kim raised her eyebrows. 'There will be no questions, no games and no attempts at manipulation.'

'So, basically there's no fun in this meeting for me at all?' Alex asked, tipping her head.

'Nothing at all,' Kim confirmed, feeling a little uncomfortable at the ease with which they had both slipped into their battle positions and the feeling of familiarity that surrounded them both.

Already Kim knew she had to be cautious. This woman could read her better than anyone. Even the slightest deviation from her script or demonstration of emotion would give Alex every bit of ammunition she would need. Alex had once taken her to the edge of sanity and dangled her over the edge. Kim had to make sure she never got that chance again.

'So, what brings you here to see me, Detective Inspector Stone?' Alex asked, lacing her fingers.

'I want to know more about the traits of evil,' she admitted. 'Especially when it comes to kids.'

A slow smile spread across Alex's face. 'Well then, it looks like you've come to the right place.'

# CHAPTER 60

Alex took a deep breath. 'So, do you want the official version or mine?'

'The official version,' Kim answered.

'There is no such thing, clinically, as an evil child or a child sociopath. It is felt that a child has not matured sufficiently to be labelled. Specialists will admit to sociopathic behaviour but that's all. They are more likely to be diagnosed with conduct disorder which can be a precursor to sociopathy.'

'"Conduct disorder"?' Kim asked.

'Starts in early adolescence, more common in boys. Typically selfish, don't relate well to others, lack guilt, often aggressive. They'll likely be bullies, cruel to animals, deceitful and rule breakers.'

'Charming,' Kim observed.

'But a child won't be diagnosed with conduct disorder unless they've first been diagnosed with oppositional defiant order which is a precursor for conduct disorder.'

Kim frowned as a vision of Russian dolls sprang into her mind. 'Hang on, so, you're saying it's like an escalation process throughout a child's formative years. All of these criteria have to be met? Oppositional defiant disorder leads to conduct disorder leads to antisocial personality disorder?'

Alex nodded. 'And for a child to be diagnosed with antisocial personality disorder they require a conduct disorder diagnosis before the age of fifteen.'

'Treatment?' Kim asked, hopefully.

Alex rolled her eyes. 'There's no cure or medication, Kim. You know that. Behavioural approaches don't work as they target specific acts and minimise the bigger picture.

'The diagnostic criteria ties itself up in knots. A child needs to have experienced three or more of the following in the last twelve months: bullying, fighting, use of a weapon, physical cruelty, mugging, extortion, armed robbery, forced sexual activity—'

'Jesus,' Kim interrupted.

'There are more: fire starting, destruction of property, lying to obtain goods, shoplifting, staying out, running away or playing truant. And one of these must have occurred in the last six months.'

'Sounds like passing the buck to me,' Kim observed. 'Everyone pushing the problem in another direction so they don't have to make a difficult judgement.'

A slow, lazy smile spread across Alex's face. 'Inspector, for once we agree.'

'Enjoy it, Alex. It's unlikely to happen again,' she said. 'Okay, talk to me about causes.'

Perhaps if she at least understood that she could begin to narrow down the potential suspects.

'Problems occur more in children of adults who exhibited problems. There may be deficits processing social information or they were rejected by peers as young children; eighty per cent of children outgrow it by adulthood.'

Kim was relieved. She'd been after a number and that seemed like a good one to her. 'That's a reasonable—'

'It's rubbish,' Alex said, cutting her off. 'That's an impossibly high figure of achievement, which doesn't take into account a statistic that no one will ever be able to estimate.'

'Which is?'

'The ones who have learned to hide it.'

'Like you?' Kim asked.

Alex smiled but there was no warmth. 'Yes, Kim. Exactly like me.'

'So, what are you saying?' Kim asked, unsure she wanted to hear this answer. She suspected they were now wandering into Alex's version of the truth.

'What I'm saying, Kim, is that chickenpox doesn't turn into measles once you reach the age of eighteen. The person I am now is the person I've always been since I was capable of a conscious thought. I have never loved anything in my life. I have never felt even a second of guilt for any of my actions, only disappointment at what went wrong. I care about no one and nothing. I have no bonds to anyone and every person I meet exists only to give me what I want.'

The intensity of Alex's expression held Kim in its thrall. She could not look away from the honesty she saw there.

'Now, what you have to understand is that this didn't happen on my eighteenth birthday when I could be diagnosed as a sociopath, psychopath or whatever else they call me. I was always this way. Even when I was a cute little toddler learning to walk or a sweet little girl starting at nursery, opening presents in a pretty dress on my fifth birthday. I was always a sociopath except no one had the courage to call it.'

'Would it have made any difference?' Kim asked, trying to fight the intrigue she felt.

'Not to me,' she said, honestly. 'I am what I am, and a label wouldn't have made me act any differently, but it might have persuaded my parents that the last thing I needed was more hugs, love and understanding. These were just more tools for my manipulation toolbox.'

Kim was grateful for the woman's honesty, despite how uncomfortable it made her. It was a side of Alex she'd never seen.

The woman's eyes suddenly fixed on a spot above her head.

'Self-knowledge is a wonderful thing,' Alex said wearily, as she travelled somewhere Kim couldn't follow. Alex swallowed deeply. 'But it doesn't help when your parents gaze at your sister with uncomplicated adoration and view you with suspicious wariness. Do you have any idea what that does to a child?' she asked, with a catch in her voice.

Kim shook her head. Her own mother had hated both her and her twin equally. But it was only Mikey in which she had seen the devil.

'Sweet little Sarah got it all,' Alex continued, as a tear formed in her reddening eyes.

Kim raised an eyebrow doubtfully, but Alex wasn't even talking to her any more.

'I knew as soon as Sarah was born that she was going to be the favourite. I could see it in my parents' eyes. She was warm and sweet and loving: everything that I wasn't.'

She wiped away the tear and another formed instantly.

'From that point on I was excluded from everything. My parents had their perfect little daughter, the one they'd always dreamed of, and the imperfect one, the broken one, was cast off and ignored, classed as weird, strange. Maybe if they'd just tried a little bit...' her words trailed away as she stared down at the table.

'Would that have made any difference?' Kim asked.

Alex raised her head. Her eyes were amused and clear of all emotion. 'Of course not but look how quickly you were willing to believe it could have done.' Alex appeared frustrated, as though Kim was a pupil that had not paid attention. 'With all that you know of me and what I've done your own feeble emotions fail you and influence your logical mind. I don't have that failing. You want to believe that there's a part of me that can be reached. Even you, as emotionless and remote as you are, have the exploitable weakness of hope.'

Kim shook her head. 'You are unbelievable.'

Alex smiled as though she'd just been complimented. 'I learned very young that if I stared at a spot for long enough without blinking my eyes would water.'

Kim felt frustrated at her own willingness to believe there was an ounce of humanity or regret in the woman.

'The trouble is that you want to believe there is a part of me, however small, that craves normality. I didn't want family bonds. I didn't want to be part of a family. You got that and look at the good it did you,' she said, pointedly. 'You carry around guilt and hurt that has shaped every decision you've—'

'Alex,' Kim warned.

Alex pulled a face. 'Jesus, you really meant it when you said there was nothing in this for me, didn't you?'

Kim raised an eyebrow.

'Okay, but do you get it? You've got to stop thinking that everyone can be saved. It's what gives people like me even more power to manipulate you.'

'So, what should I be looking for?' Kim asked.

'A child that is disengaged, withdrawn from relationships with parents, family, peers, teachers. They may be socially isolated by choice. Little attachment and impervious to punishments.'

Kim began to think of the people she'd met over the last few days.

'But bear in mind, that if they have come to terms with who and what they are, some of these traits might be hidden.'

Kim opened her mouth to respond when her phone vibrated the receipt of a message.

She took out her phone and read it.

She put the phone back and met Alex's quizzical gaze.

'Someone special?' Alex asked.

'No one you know,' Kim said, pushing herself backwards from the table. 'And I now find that I can stomach you no more. You truly are as deplorable as I thought.'

'But now you understand that it's not my fault.'

Kim thought for a minute before answering.

'What you are doesn't let you off the hook, Alex. You're here for the things you've done. As you just explained to me, all your decisions have been conscious choices. They have been your actions. You understand the difference between right and wrong and still do it anyway. So, it is your fault, Alex,' she said, walking away.

'You're not ready, you know,' Alex shouted after her.

'For what?' Kim asked, turning.

'Whoever sent you that text message. I saw the smile on your face that you didn't even feel forming. I don't know who it was from, but I can tell you now that you're nowhere near ready.'

'Fuck off, Alex,' Kim said, not bothering to explain that the text message had been nothing like that.

It had been a request to meet at the Waggon and Horses for some urgent information.

And the text had come from Joanna Wade.

# CHAPTER 61

Kim turned into Cradley Heath High Street and headed towards the Waggon and Horses.

She would give Joanna five minutes before heading back home. Alex had given her a lot to think about.

The sound of a siren reached her ears. She checked her rear-view mirror but saw no lights. She motored through the traffic lights at the four ways intersection, onto Reddal Hill Road. Despite the darkness she could see a huddle of people in the middle of the road and a woman waving at her to stop. Right outside the pub she was heading for.

Kim screeched to a halt and kicked the stand out to park the bike. She was off, and her helmet removed in a second.

'Police officer, what's happened here?' she demanded as she pushed through the crowd.

'An accident,' someone said.

'Hit-and-run,' another voice offered.

'Let me through,' Kim cried as the siren of an ambulance grew closer. The feeling of dread in her stomach jumped into her throat as she reached the centre of the circle and her worst fears were realised.

The person on the ground was Joanna Wade.

'Get away from her,' Kim shouted, as she bent down and appraised Joanna, who was lying on her back.

The woman's left leg was bent at an impossible angle, and Kim suspected at least two fractures. The left arm appeared to have been dislocated from the shoulder, and a couple of fingers were broken too.

Kim's immediate concern was that Joanna was far too quiet.
*No, no, no*, her mind screamed.

None of the injuries she could see were life-threatening, but they were all agonisingly painful. She should have been screaming the place down.

'Joanna,' Kim said, gently, touching the unbroken arm. She fought to keep the emotion from her voice.

The eyes fluttered open and a slow smile spread across her face.

She swallowed, and her voice was barely more than a whisper. 'You came.'

And that's when Kim saw what she'd been missing. The blood from underneath Joanna's head was pooling at her left ear like an oil stain.

She wasn't crying out with pain because she was beyond it.

Kim swallowed down the building emotion in her throat as she took Joanna's hand in her own.

'Of course, I came,' she said, gently rubbing her thumb across Joanna's wrist.

Their eyes met, and Kim prayed that Joanna could not see the truth there.

Joanna licked her lips before speaking again.

'Kim, look in…'

Her words trailed away as her head lolled to the side and her eyes stared unseeing into the crowd.

Kim allowed the paramedics to extricate her from the woman and move her away.

There was nothing more that she could do.

Joanna Wade was dead.

# CHAPTER 62

Kim took a deep breath before she started speaking.

'Okay, so you all know that Joanna Wade was killed in a hit-and-run accident last night.'

The room silently acknowledged her words with solemn nods.

'But what you don't know is that she was probably waiting outside for someone to arrive. And that someone was me.'

She felt the surprise as they all looked at each other.

'Joanna had sent me a text message earlier saying she had something to tell me, but I got there too late.' She neglected to say where she'd been when she'd received the message. Knowing the effect the woman had on Kim, the rest of her team would not have been thrilled to know she'd visited Alex.

'Was she still alive when you got there, guv?' Bryant asked.

'Briefly,' she said, pushing the picture from her mind. She could still feel the sensation of Joanna's warm skin on her palm.

'Did she manage to…'

'No,' Kim said. 'Traffic are still investigating, and it's been categorised as a hit-and-run random attack.'

'Surely they have to see it's linked to our investigation?' Dawson asked.

'They'll see nothing until they've completed their investigation,' she replied. 'In the meantime, Stace, I want you checking CCTV in the area, just in case Traffic don't end up seeing it our way.'

Stacey made a note.

Kim pushed the image of Joanna's face out of her mind. The only way she could help her now was to find the bastard who had done it. Her guilt at being the reason Joanna was outside would be dealt with another day.

'Okay, updates from yesterday. We found out that Shaun Coffee-Todd's death was not accidental, although we have uncovered no motive as yet. We have forensics on site but nothing from them so far.

'Called the hospital first thing to check on Christian Fellows, who is conscious and stable but remembers nothing and didn't see who attacked him. He doesn't want to speak to us, and his parents are not going to force him to right now.'

'He saw nothing?' Bryant asked, disbelievingly. 'Or recognise a voice?'

Kim shook her head. 'Apparently not and it's too early to push. I'm guessing the kid is terrified. We'll see how we go and may consider trying to talk to him later.

'Also found out that Sadie was being fed her mother's antidepressants, and that Saffie removed them from Sadie's room.'

'The mother's own tablets?' Stacey asked.

Kim nodded. Bad enough that a thirteen-year-old girl was being medicated, but not even by a doctor.

'We'll be asking them about it later today,' she said, turning to the detective sergeant.

'Kev?'

'Found a lot of shit connected with the school yesterday. Just not sure any of it's connected to Sadie's death,' he said, honestly.

'Share, anyway,' Kim said. It was only just after 7 a.m. and still a bit early to be knocking on doors. 'We know that Shaun was a member of the Spades, so I'd like to know what you found.'

'There've been a lot of incidents there over the last few years that the school has worked hard to keep quiet and most of them seem to have some kind of link to these bloody secret clubs,' he said, glancing across the desk expecting a smart remark from Stacey. None came.

'So, I got the names of three kids that had quietly left mid-year. No fanfare, no drama, no scandal, just disappeared from view. First kid I went to was removed by her mother after an initiation landed her in hospital fighting for her life. The girl was forced to do star jumps until she collapsed in a heap from an asthma attack.'

Kim frowned. 'To be honest, Kev—'

'I know, I know,' he said cutting her off. 'Could have been nothing more than a prank gone wrong.'

Yes, that was exactly what she'd been thinking.

'I was on that thought train myself until I visited the second kid; a sixteen-year-old lad who lives with his grandmother. Except living isn't really a word I'd use for Tristan Rock.

'He was dared by the top card to drink four gallons of water in one hour. Kid videoed the whole thing on his phone and pretty much drank himself to death.'

'He's dead?' Stacey asked.

'Might as well be,' he said. 'Apparently drinking too much water in a short period of time means the kidneys can't flush it out fast enough and the blood becomes waterlogged. Cells expand and well… it's not pleasant. Tristan is completely brain dead. Only being kept alive by machines while his grandmother prays for a miracle.'

'Jesus,' Bryant said. 'His parents?'

'Accepted an undisclosed settlement and a gag order. No one was punished.'

'Go on, Kev,' Kim said.

'There seems to be a culture at Heathcrest; a complete lack of accountability. No one even got a detention for the things I've mentioned never mind any kind of charges. That school is more terrified of scandal than anything else at all. And I don't even know about the third family.'

'Why not?' Stacey asked.

'They've moved in the few months since the kid left school. No forwarding address and contact with the neighbours through a third party only. The man next door with a scary dog spoke of an incident but wouldn't elaborate.'

Kim frowned. That sounded to her like the actions of a family in fear.

'Stay on it, Kev,' she instructed. 'Stace?' she asked.

'Okay, spent a lot of time in people's financial affairs yesterday, and one thing I can say is that not all parents pay the exact same fee for the education of their kids at Heathcrest.'

'I thought it was a fixed price per year,' Kim said.

'You'd think, wouldn't you?' she said. 'There are some families paying as little as twenty-six grand a year and some as much as thirty-nine, with the majority around thirty-four per year.'

Kim's only hope was that such vast amounts of money were producing doctors, physicians, physicists, economists and peacemakers. Nobel prize winners. People who would have the opportunity to do some good. Although Dawson's findings were taking a good swift kick at that ideology.

'Hang on,' she said, as her phone began to ring.

'Keats,' she answered, seeing his name on the screen.

'Am I to expect your presence at the post-mortem of Joanna Wade this morning?' he asked.

'Not my case,' she answered, ignoring the fact that she had no wish to see Joanne's body being violated regardless of Keats's sensitivity. 'Traffic are holding it as a hit-and-run.'

Force Traffic were based at Chelmsley Wood and Wednesbury and were responsible for all roads except motorways. Supported by the Collision Investigation Team they took the lead on accidents involving fatalities or life-changing injuries.

'Oh, so, she's not a teacher at the school where you're investigating the deaths of two children?' he asked, sarcastically.

She rolled her eyes. 'You know she is but it's not my case and I'm under strict, very strict instructions, to behave myself on—'

'Then I suggest you happen along for coffee,' he snapped, ending the call.

Keats inviting her along for a social call.

What the hell was going on?

# CHAPTER 63

'Okay, Keats, where's the coffee?' she asked, walking into the morgue.

She looked above the figure in the metal dish that she guessed to be Joanna Wade. The image of the last breath leaving her body was bad enough. She didn't need to replace it with a picture of her naked flesh cold and scarred.

'There's no coffee,' he answered. 'But there is this,' he said, passing her a piece of paper.

'What's this?' she asked, before looking at it.

'The contents of Joanna Wade's back jeans pocket.'

Still Kim didn't open it. 'But Traffic will want any evidence—'

'It's a copy,' he said. 'The original has been bagged for their err... eventual arrival.'

Much as she had wanted to unfold the piece of paper immediately she was conscious of contaminating evidence that the Collision Investigation Unit would pass on to the forensic scene investigators.

'Have you done it yet?' she asked, nodding towards the tray.

He followed her gaze. 'That's not Joanna Wade,' he answered.

Kim couldn't explain the wave of relief that went through her.

'That's an urgent case from Hollytree. Stabbing, potentially gang-related.'

Kim understood that this case took precedence. Murder over RTA. Had Joanna been her case she would have already called her death murder and she'd be arguing priority with Keats right now.

'You gonna read it?' Bryant asked, looking to the sheet of paper in her hand.

She moved to the side of the room beside Keats's desk and opened it up.

The paper was lined with faint pencil writing. The words appeared tentative; some were crossed out and overwritten on the top half of the page. Kim frowned as she recognised Sadie's writing. It was the poem that Joanna had mentioned. The one that had bothered her.

She squinted and tried to read.

*About life*
*Broken life*
*Obstructed life*
*Ruined life*
*Tentative life*
*Everlasting life*
*Destroyed life*
*Life*
*Life*
*Life*
*Life*

'I don't get it,' Kim said, looking up from the page.

'What, the poem?' Bryant asked, taking it from her hand.

'That, and what it was that troubled Joanna. Seems like more of Sadie's emotional outpourings.'

'Why's "life" repeated so many times?'

Kim shrugged as her eyes landed on the desk. 'Keats, what's that?' she asked.

'Joanna Wade's phone. Also found in the back pocket of her jeans.'

'Not bagged yet?' she asked, suspiciously.

'Getting round to it, Stone,' he snapped.

'Bloody hell, Keats, getting a bit lax in your old age, eh?'

'Children are dying, Stone,' he raged. 'And I have to cut them open to find out how.' He glanced at the desk and more directly at the phone and then back at her. 'And now I'm going to fetch the coffee.'

Kim looked at Bryant as the doors closed behind the pathologist.

'You're not going to touch it?' he asked, reading her thoughts.

There was barely a second of hesitation before she reached across the table for a pair of blue latex gloves.

'Bryant, we both know that Traffic is not gonna put these pieces together. Even Keats knows it,' she said, aware that this was exactly what he'd been hoping she'd do.

He sighed. 'You can't tamper—'

'If you're worried, go help Keats bring the coffee,' she said, picking up the phone. A single crack travelled diagonally from corner to corner. She pressed the home button, which brought up the passcode screen.

'Damn it,' she said, putting it down and reaching for her own phone.

Stacey picked up the phone on the second ring.

'Hey Stace, hypothetically, if I wanted to bypass the screen password on a smartphone that I shouldn't really have in my possession, how would I go about it?'

Stacey hesitated and then began calling out instructions.

'Hang on, Stace, let me put you on loudspeaker so I can hypothetically do it while you talk.'

Stacey started from the beginning and spoke slowly.

Four instructions later and the screen burst into life.

'Stace, that was worryingly easy,' Kim observed.

'Only if you know what you're doing,' Stacey said. 'Hypothetically, of course.'

Kim smiled and ended the call.

'Nice to see,' Bryant observed.

'What?'

'A smile on your face. First one today.'

'Yeah, it was wind,' she said.

'Ha, it was because you're doing something you shouldn't be.'

She had to concede he had a point.

Kim wasn't surprised that Joanna's wallpaper was a gorgeous woman in a bathing suit. She went straight for the internet search engine, which clearly Joanna didn't clear out very often.

'She was on Tinder,' Kim observed.

'Who isn't?' Bryant asked.

'Me,' she said.

'Or me,' he answered

She continued to scroll and spoke as she went. 'Darts tournaments, Airbnb in Fife, how to cook a perfect beef Wellington and—' she stopped speaking.

She turned to Keats as he entered the room with three cups.

'Keats, could Joanna have been pregnant?' she asked, unlikely as it might be.

He frowned. 'I can't say for sure, but my initial examination didn't offer any indication. No noticeable bulge of the tummy.'

Kim shook her head. 'Not her then,' she said, handing Bryant the phone.

His eyes widened. 'She searched seven different sites about illegal terminations. But why...'

Kim shook her head as she looked from the phone to the piece of paper. There was something here that she was missing.

Why had Sadie written this poem? What exactly had she been trying to say?

# CHAPTER 64

'You know, guv, this might be a good time,' Bryant said as they got back in the car. 'Just while we've got a spare minute.'

'For what?' she asked.

She had put the copy of Sadie's poem in her pocket. She had read the words so many times she was no longer even seeing them.

He rolled his eyes and shook his head all at the same time. 'You know what, and why are you putting it off anyway?'

She sighed. 'Because I read your appraisal form, and I have to change some of your scores,' she said, uneasily.

He shrugged. 'Okay, I just put what I thought was fair and accurate but if you disagree and have to deduct—'

'That's not the problem, Bryant,' she said, glancing out of the window. 'As ever you've undervalued yourself and your contribution to the team. I have to mark you up.'

She caught his brief smile out of the corner of her eye.

'And that's a bad thing?'

'Are you never going to seek promotion?' she asked, thinking about the section detailing career prospects.

He shook his head. 'Once was enough, thanks.'

A few months earlier, when she'd been working alongside Travis and the West Mercia team, Bryant had been handed the temporary rank of detective inspector in her absence. Once the case was over he'd thrown it back like he'd got the business end of a branding poker in his palm.

'But you would make a great DI,' Kim said, honestly.

'You know, guv, I don't think I ever told you about one of Laura's parents' evenings a few years ago. We sat for a long time with lots of her teachers and even longer with her science teacher who insisted that Laura had the makings of a doctor, possibly even a surgeon. We were thrilled. We'd always known she was a bright, hard-working kid – but a surgeon? Our daughter a surgeon? We were beside ourselves in the car driving home. Laura not so much.

'I asked her why she wasn't elated about what the teachers had said, and it was simple. It was what they wanted for her more than what she wanted for herself. She'd decided when she was eleven that she wanted to be a midwife and she had never faltered from that goal.'

Kim nodded her understanding.

The girl was now at college studying midwifery.

He continued. 'I always wanted to be a police officer, not manage a team of police officers. It's your ambition for me, not mine for myself.'

She nodded, conceding his point. 'Well, I have to find some area for bloody improvement,' she said. 'Otherwise it's just gonna look like favouritism.'

He shrugged. 'I'm sure we could come up with something.'

She looked at him. 'Not sure that's how it's supposed to work.'

But she honestly could not think of an area of his performance that he could improve. Not one she could put on the form, anyway.

'Occasionally, you're a bit overprotective,' she said, truthfully. 'You try and shield me from the shit and the crap like back there with Keats. Instantly you wanted to stop me accessing that phone even though you knew it could give us a clue.'

'And land you on suspension,' he countered.

'It's my risk to take. Sometimes you gotta let me get my hands dirty.'

'I'd level that same accusation about protection at you,' he offered. 'I know you're exploring possibilities with this case that lie outside my comfort zone but I'm a big boy. I can take it.'

Yes, she had explored the possibility that a child could be behind the murders, and she also knew the very notion would make him sick to his stomach.

She smiled. 'Okay, I'll stop protecting you if you let me deal with my own crap and shit now and again. Deal?' she asked.

'Deal,' he agreed. 'So, are we done then?' Bryant asked. 'Is that my appraisal completed?'

She knew his attitude to performance appraisals was much like her own. He assumed he was doing a good job until he heard otherwise and not the other way around.

'Yep, we're done,' she said, taking the single piece of paper from her pocket.

'Hang on one second,' Kim said, seeing it with fresh eyes. She narrowed her gaze and remembered what Joanna had told her. See the whole picture, read the words, read the page.

'Fuck,' she said, looking at Bryant. 'It's here. It's right here.'

'What is it that I'm not seeing?' he asked, taking another look at Sadie's poem.

Kim pointed. 'Look closer. Ignore the words for a second and just look.'

He shook his head. 'If I'm not supposed to look at the words…'

'Here,' she said, stabbing at the page. 'Each word that starts the sentence. About. Broken. Obstructed…'

'Aborted,' he said. 'If you read those capital letters from the top it spells aborted.'

'Someone has done something they shouldn't have done, and Sadie knew all about it,' Kim said. Finally, they were heading towards a possible motive for the young girl's death.

'You think one of the students at Heathcrest had an illegal abortion?'

'Could be,' she said. 'And with how everyone feels about scandal…'

'But there are over five hundred girls at that school. How the hell are we going to find out who?'

Her excitement took a kick in the head. He was right. She suspected the girl was not suddenly going to come forward and reveal herself.

'Hang on,' she said, turning the problem on its head. 'Bryant, remember everything Dawson has told us about those clubs at Heathcrest? That they were filled with powerful people, and you were a member for life?'

'Yeah,' he said, not yet catching up with her thoughts.

'Where would you go if you found yourself in a spot of trouble?' Kim asked, already dialling Stacey's number.

'Dawson still with you?' Kim asked when she heard her colleague's voice.

'Yep,' she answered.

'I want you both to drop whatever you're working on. There's something I need you to do.'

# CHAPTER 65

'Every doctor that was previously at Heathcrest?' Dawson asked, incredulously.

'Yeah, Kev, because twenty years of Heathcrest graduates multiplied by one hundred and ten students per year that graduate means two thousand students to check,' she said, sarcastically.

'But the boss said…'

'Jesus, Kev. Put your thinking head on. The boss expects us to work out how to do this on our own, you know. We're probably talking private clinics within a radius of say ten to twenty miles. So, we do it backwards. We look at the clinics and hospitals and see how many doctors came from Heathcrest.'

'But that might still—'

'And then we look at the year they graduated. If it's someone the parents of a child knew it's not gonna be someone who left seven years ago, is it?'

'Why seven?' he asked.

'Medical training,' she said, widening her eyes. 'Jesus, it's like you just hatched or something.'

Dawson shook his head as Stacey began typing, amazed at the speed and logic that lived inside her head.

'Did she say why we're doing this?'

Stacey offered him a murderous glance. 'Seems Joanna Wade was interested in illegal terminations, twenty-four weeks and over if you want that explained for you too. And after all your yapping about secret clubs and lifelong societies she wants us to look in that direction.'

'Got it,' he said.

'Any more questions?' she asked.

'Just one, Stace. Do you still love me even though I'm thick?' he asked, with a grin.

'Bloody hell, Kev, just crack on, will yer and get looking?'

Following her instruction, he put his head down and began to search. Except he'd had a different idea of where to look.

# CHAPTER 66

Kim followed Mrs Winters through to the informal lounge. Mr Winters placed his laptop beside him on the sofa.

Her stomach was still reacting to what they'd found on Joanna's phone, but for now, she had to let Stacey and Dawson do their job. She needed answers right here.

Mrs Winters moved the laptop and took a seat beside her husband, reaching for his hand.

Kim sat opposite in a chair next to an ornate fireplace filled with cards of condolence, best wishes at this time and sorry for your loss. The wall to the left was filled with family photos displayed in a descending chronology.

'Mr Winters, Mrs Winters, we need to ask you a couple of questions about Sadie and the medication she was taking,' Kim said, gently but firmly.

Mrs Winters coloured and looked to the floor.

A few seconds passed before Mr Winters answered.

'She needed help,' he said, simply.

'With what?' Kim asked.

They were not going to get off that lightly.

'Mood swings, feelings of depression, anxiety.'

'So, you gave her your own medication?' Kim asked, looking to Mrs Winters.

She did not raise her head, letting her husband do all the talking.

'Did you try to get her any help?' Kim asked. 'Like an appointment with her GP or a counsellor?'

'There's no better counsellor than the one at Heathcrest but she wouldn't talk to anyone. She just clammed up, and I suppose we just wanted to help make her feel better.'

It seemed clear they'd made no effort to get to the bottom of her withdrawal. Had it not occurred to them that Sadie's problems had started when her sister had become the superstar of the family?

'That's why we weren't surprised at the news of her—'

'Murder,' Kim interrupted. This couple seemed determined to believe that their child had taken her own life.

'And you asked Saffron to hide the pills from us?' Kim asked.

Mr Winters nodded. 'We didn't want anyone to know,' he said, honestly.

'I understand that, Mr Winters, but with all due respect you have done little to aid the investigation into the death of your daughter. You have removed evidence and withheld important information. I understand that reputation and appearances are important but is there anything else you're not sharing with us?'

Despite her neutral tone it was clear by his face that he did not appreciate the chastisement but, grieving parents or not, it was not their prerogative to judge what was relevant and what was not.

'There is nothing more,' he said, glancing away. 'And you're right. We shouldn't ever have asked Saffie to touch her things.'

Slightly mollified that he at least understood the gravity of what they'd done she continued. 'And how is Saffron coping?' Kim asked. 'She's still not come home?'

Mr Winters shook his head. 'She's busy at school. It helps to keep her mind off it. Too many reminders here,' he said, glancing at the photo wall.

Kim wondered if these parents could see the irony in the display. The photos at the top of the wall were portraits of them all. Below were photos of the two girls together. One so dark and one so light but laughing and close. And then two lines, one of each girl vertically travelling down the wall, separate.

'And you don't think it's a good idea to insist that she come home, given the death of a second child at—'

'Oh God, poor Anthony and Louise,' Mrs Winters said, shaking her head.

Mr Winters squeezed her hand. 'We met the Coffee-Todds a few times, at social functions at the school.'

'Do you know the parents of Christian Fellows, the boy left hanging in the janitor's room yesterday?' Kim asked.

Mr Winters shook his head. 'I don't think we've ever met.'

'And you know that a teacher was killed last night?' she asked.

'Road accident, Principal Thorpe said.'

'She was run down by a vehicle, Mr Winters,' Kim corrected. 'Which is currently being investigated.'

'Clearly unrelated,' he said.

Kim looked to Bryant, wondering if any words were actually coming out of her mouth.

'And you still don't think that your other daughter should be safely home here with you?' she asked, incredulously.

Bryant sat forward. 'Three separate deaths in one week is probably nudging above the national average, Mr Winters, so if my daughter—'

'Saffie is very independent, officers. She is sixteen years of age and rarely obeys her parents.'

Except when they were urging her to hide her sister's possessions and obstruct the investigation of the police, Kim thought. Right now she was unsure just how many laws they had broken by medicating their own child, but she knew CPS wouldn't touch prosecution of grieving parents.

Kim stood. 'Well, thank you both for your time. We'll be in touch.'

Bryant followed her out of the front door.

*

Kim sat in the car staring back at the house. There was a knot in her stomach that only came when she felt she was being led in the wrong direction.

She replayed the conversation in her mind.

'Damn, damn, damn,' Kim said, reaching for her phone.

'Bryant, we need to speak to Stacey and Dawson now.'

She had the overwhelming feeling that she'd been looking the wrong way.

# CHAPTER 67

## 21 March 2018

Hey Diary,

The feeling is still there but I don't know if it's real. My senses are telling me that there is someone behind me, watching me but when I look there's no one there.

Is it real??????????

Or is it the pills????????

But it can't be the tablets. My parents would never have given them to me if they could make me feel like this; a shadowy half person trudging through fog every minute of the day.

The dark thoughts are still there but the sharp, angry icicles are wrapped in soft, fluffy snow. They're there but they don't pierce me any more.

But these pills don't just take the bad thoughts. They're not homing beacons attaching themselves only to the crap. I can't think straight. Everything has a furry edge. I have a vision of the pill exploding inside my brain, releasing a gas that seeps into every part of me. Only yesterday I found myself at the wrong classroom.

I am reminded of episodes of *Star Trek* that my dad used to watch. Whenever they needed to save power the captain would order 'life support systems only' and all non-essential power would be closed down. That's how I feel. All the unnecessary services have been switched off and I'm left just able to function.

Tonight I went to her room, to confront her. I barged in as Eric stormed out.

I wanted to ask her how she could do it, how she could be so cruel, so cold, so unfeeling.

And then I saw the redness around her eyes, the telltale blotching of the skin on her forehead that comes out whenever she's upset. I wanted to ask who she was crying for but then I saw the hard, cold veil drop over her face. That faint look of distaste that shapes no particular feature but is present all the same.

She screamed at me to get out and I knew. I knew there was no way back for us. We would never be like sisters again.

> *And that is why you are special to me, Sadie. You knew and you're up there watching and you approve. You know that secrets and lies have a consequence. A price. You condone everything I've done and everything I must do. We are bonded, you and I, more than you will ever know. But how I wish I could have let you live, you troubled little soul.*
>
> *I wonder how you would have felt about Christian. I think you would have understood and you would have forgiven me.*
>
> *But how the hell did the little fucker not die?*
>
> *Thank God I approached him from behind. It wasn't difficult to push him into the janitor's room. It wasn't a challenge to close my hands around his scrawny little neck, my thumbs digging into the back as my fingers pressed hard against his Adam's apple. He spluttered and choked and then went still against me.*
>
> *I tied a clean sheet around his neck and winched his limp body up over the light fitting. He dangled like a piece of meat in the butcher's shop. I closed the door and waited for a cleaner to happen upon his hanging, lifeless body.*

*There was no satisfaction. He was a means to an end. He was a mistake to be cleared away like the flour on the tabletop. He was just mess that occurred from baking the cake. He was nothing to me. Not like you, Sadie.*

*And now he's awake and has not named me. He doesn't know who tried to throttle the life from his body.*

*I should have checked he was dead. Another mistake.*

*But I am learning. There will be no more errors.*

*Keep watching, my little Sadie, because the best is yet to come.*

# CHAPTER 68

Kim put the phone onto speaker and held it between herself and Bryant.

'So we can find no motive for the murders of either Sadie Winters or Shaun Coffee-Todd?'

Everyone answered in the negative.

'And we agree that Christian Fellows was attacked because he might have seen something, even though his parents insist he saw nothing and won't let us near him?'

'Looks that way, guv,' Bryant offered.

'And we all know is that we're dealing with an environment that doesn't seem to operate like the real world.'

'Oh yeah,' Dawson agreed.

'So, are we looking in the wrong direction?' she asked, remembering the conversation at the Winters' home.

She continued. 'Mrs Winters referred to the parents of Shaun by their first names, Anthony and Louise, but Mr Winters was very quick to state that they'd only met at a few school functions. Why would he do that when Anthony made it clear that the families were very close?' she asked. 'Almost like cousins, he said about the children,' she added.

'You think Winters would hide something to do with his own daughter's murder?' Bryant asked.

As a father to a twenty-year-old girl she could understand her colleague's disbelief. But that was okay. Suspicion of everyone they came into contact with was her job.

'He's already hidden the fact Sadie was on antidepressants, and someone changed that note to a suicide note,' she reminded him. 'Now, let me ask, who believes that the events of this week are unrelated?'

No one spoke.

'And yet the children have not done anything to anyone that we can find, so where does that leave us?'

'Parents,' Stacey said.

Kim nodded. 'Stace, I want you to carry on looking for doctors. We have to sign that one off. Kev, I want you to see if you can find any link at all between Sadie's parents and Shaun's parents. For all we know they weren't even at Heathcrest at the same time, but we need to rule it out.'

'And what about us, guv?' Bryant asked, as she ended the call. 'Are we gonna just sit here and watch?'

'Ha, you wish, Bryant. There's someone I want to see, so you and I are going back to the school.'

The possibility that she'd been looking the wrong way still hung heavily around her neck as they approached the press pack at the entrance to Heathcrest. Woody sometimes said that there were times that she couldn't see the wood for the trees.

The thought of Woody coincided with her gaze landing on Tracy Frost standing away from the crowd, her five-inch heels sunk into the patchy grass. Her hands shoved deep into her pockets.

'Awww... shit,' Kim said, as something occurred to her. 'Stop the car, Bryant.'

He did so, and she lowered her window.

Frost narrowed her eyes but approached anyway.

'Wanna be shitty again, Stone?' she asked.

'He fed you the line, didn't he?' she asked. 'Woody put you front and centre and told you what to say.'

Frost shrugged.

She should have seen it. Woody would never have let pressure from above stop him doing everything he could to protect the children at that school and alert the parents to the danger. He had asked Frost to shout murder knowing it would be out there in seconds. *He* hadn't said it. *She* had.

'Look, I'm sorry—'

'Save it, Stone,' Frost said, shaking her head. 'Keep your apology but maybe next time have a bit more faith in people. Both him and me,' she said, returning to the press pack.

'Well, that told you,' Bryant said, driving through the cordon.

'Yeah, and I deserved it,' she admitted. Frost she was still on the fence about but Woody she should have known better.

*

She sighed heavily as she got out of the car.

'How is this even possible?'

Three deaths and a fourth attempt in a few days and students were walking to class as though nothing had happened. Should Joanna have been taking a lesson this afternoon, she wondered sadly, glancing at the window of what was once her classroom.

She headed along the second corridor towards the end of the wing. She passed Principal Thorpe's office and knocked on the door of the office next to it.

'Come in,' called the counsellor.

'Mr Steele…'

'Graham,' he said, waving them in.

He stood as she sat, and she nodded her appreciation of his good manners. There was a gentleness about this man that reminded her of Ted; a softness around the eyes, a note of compassion in his voice.

'May we ask you about Shaun Coffee-Todd?'

'Of course,' he said, colouring.

Kim remembered comments about the boy not being the most memorable child. 'You didn't know him well?'

He hesitated and then shook his head. 'If I'm honest, I'm afraid not. In my position it's often the kids that cause the most trouble that come to my attention.'

She could understand that. Teenage problems and angst often presented as loud, troublesome and disruptive behaviour.

'Did you have any reason to see him at all?' Kim asked, wondering if there was some kind of link there.

He shook his head. 'I've checked my records in case my memory had failed me, and he never asked to see me, nor did I have cause to seek him out.'

'You know he was in one of those secret clubs?' Kim asked.

'Damn groups,' he said, angrily.

'You don't approve?' she asked.

'I fully support Principal Thorpe's efforts to stamp them out. They offer nothing positive to the majority of the students and a sense of imperialism to the few. Any group that insists on initiation pranks to join is not a good place to be,' he said, lacing his fingers. 'Now, is there anything else I can help you with?'

Kim got the feeling he wanted to move on.

'Joanna Wade gave you a poem of Sadie's?' she asked.

He nodded. 'She did and then asked for it back.'

'Did you read it?' she asked.

He hesitated. 'I did, but I didn't really understand it,' he said, looking sheepish.

She didn't hold that against him. She wouldn't have got it had it not been for Joanna.

'Did you speak to her about it?'

He nodded. 'I tried to ask her about it. I know Joanna was concerned about something in the poem, but she didn't say what. She knew I was meeting with Sadie, so asked me to raise it and see if she opened up at all.'

'Were you hopeful?'

He shrugged and then shook his head. 'She hadn't opened up so far in our sessions, but I gave it a try. Sometimes it just takes something small, a catalyst if you like, to take the first brick out of the wall.'

Kim took the poem from her back pocket.

Graham looked surprised and then smiled. 'I won't ask.'

'It's a copy,' she explained. 'But I'd like you to take another look at it and tell me what you think.'

He took the sheet from her and reached for a pair of John Lennon-style glasses that looked totally lost on his face. He read and frowned at the same time. 'I'm afraid I still don't get the content, but it does seem as though she's angry about something.'

Kim leaned across and pointed at the capital letters at the beginning of each line spelling out the word ABORTED.

'Oh, Oh, I see,' he said, colouring slightly. He stared at it for a full minute. 'I should have spotted that,' he said, shaking his head. 'Seems so obvious now.'

'Don't feel too bad,' Kim said. 'We're detectives and didn't see it at first.'

His face filled with horror. 'You don't think Sadie—?'

'No,' Kim said, shaking her head, quickly. 'Definitely not Sadie but would you have any idea who she might have meant. Have any of the girls—?'

Graham held up his hand and stopped her. 'If they had I wouldn't be able to divulge it as you well know, Inspector.'

She accepted his point.

'Has anyone required additional or urgent counselling?' she asked, going for the same answer in a roundabout way.

He smiled. 'It's safe to say I've been busy, and I really wish I hadn't been.'

'Anything out of the ordinary?' she asked.

'What I can say is that all I have seen are normal reactions to a sudden and unexplained death or three,' he said.

'Has Saffie Winters been to see you?' she asked.

He considered and then shook his head. 'No, but I really wish she would. I did seek her out yesterday to see if she wanted to talk. Her refusal to return home to her parents has us all concerned, but it would be unwise to force her,' he said.

Kim agreed. 'And would you categorise her response as normal?'

Graham shook his head. 'People react differently to traumatic events, Inspector,' he offered, evasively.

'And now would you answer the question I asked,' Kim responded.

He smiled. 'Probably not but…'

'Graham, may I ask you a question that you may feel uncomfortable answering?' she asked, recalling his reaction the previous day.

His gaze narrowed. 'Of course.'

'Are there any students here that you've met with that you consider capable of violence?' It was not a theory she was yet ready to abandon until she had something more substantial pointing towards an adult. 'Someone physically able to haul Christian up over that beam?'

He shook his head. 'I'm sorry, officer, but that's not a possibility I'm prepared to consider.'

'But it's one that we have to,' Kim said. 'Is there anyone with a history of fire starting or animal cruelty?' she asked, recalling Alex's insight.

Again, he began to shake his head but paused.

'There's something, isn't there?'

'It's probably nothing. I mean…'

'Please, let us be the judge of that,' she advised.

'Alistair Minton, sixteen years old. I had to speak to him a couple of months ago, but I can't imagine that he—'

'What about?' Kim asked.

'Animal cruelty,' he said, as a look of distaste clung to his mouth. 'There was a stray cat that used to hang around the kitchen, just taking the odd scrap. He caught it, glued its—'

Kim felt the tension seeping into her bottom jaw. 'Is this an image I really need in my head?' she asked.

'Probably not,' he agreed.

'And his explanation?' she asked.

The counsellor shook his head. 'That he thought it would be a laugh. There was no remorse or empathy for the animal's suffering.'

'So, what did you do?' Kim asked.

'Informed his parents and voiced my concerns.'

'And?'

'They cancelled his half-term skiing trip.'

'Devastating,' Bryant said, mirroring her thoughts.

'I still don't think he's capable of—'

'Thank you for your help,' Kim said, standing.

Bryant was ahead of her and opened the door as the counsellor spoke again.

'Officer, it's probably no more than a coincidence but there's probably something else you should know about Alistair Minton.'

'Go on.'

'He's the ex-boyfriend of Saffron Winters.'

'Okay, let's see what Alistair Minton has to say,' Kim said, tapping on the door to the physics lab. A quick call to Thorpe's assistant, Nancy, had revealed his location.

Stepping into the room, Kim was again struck by the privileged surroundings. Less than twenty students were in the class and each had their own workstation, which reminded her of the layout of *Masterchef*. It was a far cry from the ten kids she'd been among all huddled around one Bunsen burner at her old school.

The white-coated teacher moved towards them, a questioning smile on her face.

'Alistair Minton,' Bryant asked as Kim looked around the room.

Her eyes fixed on a kid whose goggles were perched on his head like an aviator rather than covering his eyes. Kim was not surprised when he began walking towards them.

He removed the goggles, offered a smile and a hand.

Kim turned away and headed towards the corridor. No way was she shaking a hand that had tortured an animal that way.

Bryant closed the classroom door behind them.

*

Alistair ran a hand through his straw-blonde hair and leaned against the wall. She didn't miss his quick up and down appraisal of her. He smiled lazily, revealing white, even teeth. There was a cockiness emanating from him that tickled the hairs on the back of her neck. The fact that police officers wanted to speak to him appeared to be a bit of a lark.

'Alistair, we'd like to talk to you about the murder of Sadie Winters, do you know anything about it?'

'I know she's dead and that other little twerp too, what of it?'

'You sound incredibly sorry about that,' she observed.

'Why would I be?' he asked, simply.

'We were wondering if there was anything you'd like to share with us?' Kim asked.

He shook his head. 'Not really kids I hang around with,' he answered.

'I'm not asking if you were in the same social circle,' she snapped. 'But you do like to hurt things, don't you?'

Understanding shaped his features and then a smile. 'Oh, this is about the cat, isn't it? Straight out of the *Psychology for Dummies* book. Animal cruelty equals serial killer. Bloody hell, officer, give me a chance to finish school. Even I don't know what I want to be yet.'

Kim resisted the urge to slap him.

He reminded her of her overfilled laundry basket at home, so full of items that it was misshapen, bulging. It was like he'd been stuffed to overflowing with good looks, a lean athletic body, excessive charm and charisma bursting out of his sixteen-year-old body. Once he emptied the basket and learned moderation, he'd be a dangerous individual.

'Look, it was a mangy cat and I don't get the fuss over it, but I've got no reason to hurt kids that mean nothing—'

'It wasn't a prank that went wrong that you then had to cover up…'

'You can save that shit for the morons in the not-so-secret groups, officer. Not my bag.'

'But you knew Sadie's sister?' Kim pushed.

He shrugged. 'Not as well as I'd have liked but hey ho, you can't win 'em all, eh?' he said with a wink.

Kim simply stared at him for a few seconds.

'Your charm didn't work on her then?' Bryant asked.

He smirked. 'Would've done with a bit more time but the golden couple cock-blocked me.'

'Sadie's parents?' Kim clarified. It wasn't the first time she'd heard them referred to as such.

'Yeah, well, Queen of Hearts and all that. They wanted their precious daughter spending time with someone more appropriate.'

'Eric?' Kim asked.

He rolled his eyes. 'Yep, the good old King of Spades. Power couple.'

'So, Laurence Winters managed to get rid of you before you got what you wanted?' Kim asked, thinking it had been impeccably good judgement on the man's behalf.

'I was warned off, all right, but not by him. He's a wimp. It was Hannah who did the deed. Now if you want to talk ruthless—'

He stopped speaking as her phone rang.

Eager to get away from this kid, Kim headed to the end of the corridor to take the call.

'Hey Stace,' she said, giving Bryant a nod to let him go back to class.

'You're not gonna believe what we've found,' Stacey said, excitedly.

'Go on.'

'Not only were Laurence Winters and Anthony Coffee-Todd at Heathcrest at the same time. They were in the same year.'

Kim frowned. So why had Laurence Winters played down their acquaintance?

'But even more interesting is that another of their classmates, Gordon Cordell, works at the Oakland Hospital in Stourport-on-Severn.'

'Stace, don't tell me…'

'Oh yeah,' she said animatedly. 'The man is a gynaecologist.'

'Jesus,' Kim said as her head spun.

'Hang on, Kev wants a word,' Stacey said, passing the phone.

'Boss, I know it might not mean anything, but all three of them were in the Spades.'

'How the hell did they find all that out?' Bryant asked as they drove over the Stourport road bridge that straddled the River Severn.

'Apparently, Dawson let Stacey do it the hard way before guessing that the annual yearbooks that grace the halls of Heathcrest would probably have been uploaded electronically too. Each yearbook has a section on the achievement of previous students, and Cordell's graduation from medical school was right there.'

'What about the Spades thing?'

'Right there in the book under their graduation photos. Remember the clubs weren't secret back then.'

'Trust Dawson to find a shortcut,' Bryant observed as he took a left into a wide tree-lined street.

Kim knew that Oakland Hospital was a private healthcare facility that had opened on the outskirts of Stourport-on-Severn in the mid-seventies. Ten years later it was absorbed into a larger chain when private healthcare boomed. In the years since, the minor operations had developed into life-saving transplants along with cosmetic procedures. And just about everything in between.

If the entrance to Russells Hall Hospital sometimes resembled a Black Friday electronics sale, then Oakland was more like a leisurely stroll around Harvey Nichols.

Kim took a moment to assess her surroundings as Bryant introduced them both and asked to see Doctor Cordell.

Soft music replaced the din of agitated voices. Plush, pastel furnishings took the place of plastic, functional seating. Warm and friendly reception staff sat in the place of terse, stressed administrators. Framed prints of old movie posters replaced noticeboards screaming information on health issues.

Oakland did not resemble any hospital that Kim had ever visited, and Gordon Cordell did not resemble any nimble-fingered surgeon she had ever met, she thought, as a chubby, clean hand reached across the desk towards them.

Gordon Cordell was a short, rotund man with a chin that was fighting to remain separate from the neck.

Kim didn't try to ignore the immediate sensation of mistrust for the man in front of her. There was a guardedness that seemed to be emanating from him and they hadn't yet opened their mouths.

'Mr Cordell, thank you for seeing us at such short notice,' Bryant said, pleasantly. If her colleague was feeling the same wariness as she was he was hiding it well.

'I'm afraid I only have a few minutes.'

'Of course, doctor. We'll try not to take up too much of your time. We're here in connection with Heathcrest Academy. We understand you were a student there?'

Cordell nodded uncertainly, which did nothing to quiet the growing suspicion in Kim's stomach. It was a simple enough question and required no hesitation. He either was or he wasn't. The cynical part of her felt he was deliberating over every question for fear of revealing something.

'And you graduated?'

'In 1992,' he answered.

'Good school?' Bryant asked.

He nodded.

It appeared the man barely trusted himself to speak.

'You kept in contact with some of your old school friends?'

'Some,' he answered.

Kim had learned that there were two kinds of nervousness when being questioned by the police. Over-talkers and under-talkers. For some the nervousness went straight to the vocal chords and they said more than they needed to, filled every silence in an effort to reinforce their truth, often repeating a phrase over and over. Others clammed up completely and offered as few words as possible, not even trusting their own tongue.

'And you were part of a group there, Clubs, I think—'

'Spades,' he corrected, promptly.

'Maybe you could tell us about that?' Bryant asked, clearly hoping an open-ended question would elicit more than one-word answers.

'For what reason?' he asked, rubbing at the skin on the side of his nose.

*Or not*, she thought.

'Because it may help with our enquiries, Doctor Cordell,' Bryant said, pleasantly.

Cordell glanced at the phone on his desk, either praying it would ring or it was an unconscious movement of the eyes.

'We're just here for background,' Bryant assured him.

'It's just a club,' he said, rubbing that same area of skin again. 'It's just some harmless fun when you're at school, like a gang of friends. You must have had a set group of friends, officer?' he asked.

'Of course,' Bryant said, pleasantly. 'Kind of lost touch after we left school though. Is that the same at Heathcrest?' he asked.

Kim could feel Cordell's growing discomfort.

'I'm sorry. I'm not sure what you mean,' he said, buying time for a simple question for an intelligent, educated man.

'Well, do all you little Spades stay in contact once you're out in the big wide world?' Bryant asked the question with just the right amount of dismissive amusement to get a jaw clench from the man. This was Bryant's baiting at its best. Subtle but effective and a joy to watch.

'I don't think you quite understand how—'

'Oh no, I get it,' Bryant said, now cutting the man off when he wanted to speak, which was just going to add to Cordell's annoyance. 'When I was a kid, one of my mates took some money from his mum's purse, and we went and bought as much pick 'n' mix from Woolworths as we could carry. We swore it would be our secret. Pricked our thumbs, exchanged blood and everything.'

'That's not exactly—' Cordell said, trying to interrupt but Bryant was on a roll.

'Thing is, by the time I got home I felt sick as a dog. Not just cos I'd swallowed enough sugar to fell a wildebeest but because I knew I'd done something wrong,' he said.

The tension on Cordell's face was very telling. She marvelled at how her colleague had an anecdote for every occasion.

'I couldn't eat my tea, and by bedtime I was convinced the police were going to be knocking on my door. And suddenly the promise I'd made earlier to keep my mouth shut was no longer as important. Not compared to bringing shame upon my family.' He paused and then lowered his voice. 'Do you have family, Doctor Cordell?'

The doctor met Bryant's intense gaze, and Kim knew what was coming next, as did her colleague.

'I'm sorry, officers but I have nothing that will aid your investigation and I really must get on with my work.'

Bryant stood and offered his hand.

'Thank you for your time and I hope we can speak more fully the next time we meet, probably best at the station when you're less busy.'

*Yeah, leave that threat hanging there*, Kim thought. Bryant mentioning the next time assured Cordell that their business was unfinished and the idea of attending the station had prompted three deep swallows.

*

Kim closed the door behind them and Bryant leaned down to re-tie his shoelace.

'Nice story about the sweets,' she observed.

'No story,' he admitted. 'And I haven't been able to look at a Jelly Baby ever since,' he said, straightening. He looked at her. 'You ready?'

'Oh yeah.'

Bryant stood close to the door and listened. She saw his mouth count to three before pushing down on the door handle

He hesitated for just a couple of seconds before speaking but it was long enough.

Cordell stood at the window already speaking on his mobile phone.

'Sorry, doctor, but… oh never mind, it can wait,' Bryant said, holding up his hand in apology and backing out of the room.

'Works every bloody time,' Kim said, as they headed along the corridor towards the front of the building.

By silent agreement they had acknowledged that they were going to get nothing from Doctor Cordell, so Bryant had focused his questioning on simply rattling the doctor, knowing full well that if he were guilty of something he'd be on the phone to someone as soon as they'd left the room. And he hadn't disappointed them.

'So, what did you hear?' she asked.

'Three words distinctly,' he said. 'I heard "know about Lorraine".'

Yes, that was exactly what she'd heard too.

# CHAPTER 72

'Just about to call you, boss,' Stacey said, answering the phone.

'Okay, but stop what you're doing and search the list of current students at Heathcrest for the name Lorraine, and get Dawson over to the school to start asking in person.'

'You think she's the girl that had an illegal abortion?' Stacey asked.

'At the minute, yes. Doctor Cordell was as nervous as a turkey in December and was definitely hiding something. I have a real feeling he's been doing something he shouldn't have.'

'Okay, will do and I have something for you, boss. Traffic have been on. They want you to meet them at the entrance to Hollytree estate.'

'For what?' she asked, frowning. Right now, Hollytree seemed a million miles away from their current investigation.

'The hit-and-run on Joanna Wade, boss. They think they've found the car.'

# CHAPTER 73

It had been a few weeks since Kim had set foot on Hollytree and nothing had changed since. The sprawling estate of maisonette buildings still guarded the three tower blocks at its core.

Kim was reminded of Dante's nine circles of hell. The circles were concentric, representing a gradual increase in wickedness and culminating at the centre of the earth, where Satan is held in bondage.

Kai Lord had once lived at the very centre of Hollytree; although not Satan he had been close enough.

Her last major investigation had removed the kingpin of the organised crime gang that ruled the estate. But as she had cut off one head another had simply grown in its place.

'Jesus, is that it?' Bryant said, pulling onto the car park.

Five uniforms and two detectives huddled around a grey Nissan Micra.

Kim understood his question. For the damage that had been done to Joanna, she too would have expected a bigger vehicle.

'Inspector Adams,' Kim acknowledged, heading towards the front of the car.

'Inspector,' he nodded in response.

Kim fell silent as she appraised the damage to the car. The dent in the bonnet measured two feet across and ended an inch away from the windscreen wipers. The radiator grille was indented, and the passenger side headlight was smashed.

Kim tried to ignore the image of Joanna being tossed into the air as the car struck her.

'How'd you find it?' she asked, tearing her eyes away.

'Collation of witness reports, CCTV and some observant police officers,' said Adams. 'You know, good old-fashioned police work.'

Kim wondered if he knew of her derogatory comments the previous day. If he did, there was egg on her face right now. She doubted her team could have got this result any quicker.

'Why here?' she said, looking around. She couldn't help but feel that no one living on Hollytree was connected to the staff or students at Heathcrest.

Adams pointed to the left-hand tower block. 'I'd say because the owner lives over there on the ninth floor.'

That information served to convince her this had been an untimely accident and had no connection to the death of Sadie Winters.

'All right, Inspector, thanks for—'

'Not so fast,' he said, raising one eyebrow. 'You're missing the most important part,' he said, moving to stand beside her.

'Take a closer look at the passenger side front wheel.'

She took a step back. The rubber of the tyre was bulged, and the wheel trim buckled. She got it.

'He hit and mounted the kerb?' she asked.

Adams nodded.

This was no accident. The bastard had aimed right for her.

# CHAPTER 74

'He couldn't just see me for a minute?' Dawson asked, as Nancy put through another call to Principal Thorpe's office. He had headed to the school on the boss's instructions to ask around about Lorraine Peters.

Following her call after meeting with Doctor Cordell he had returned to the yearbooks and searched for any student named Lorraine, and he had found one. Her photo had been included in the spring intake of 1990 as a scholarship student and then nothing. No graduation photo, no record of achievement. It was as though she had disappeared somewhere among the pages. Thorpe had been a student around that time and Dawson wondered if he remembered her.

The principal's secretary shook her head. 'I have five calls on hold, another seventeen messages from concerned parents seeking reassurance, and three mothers and fathers making their way here right now to speak to him directly.'

He ignored the look in her eyes as she said the words 'concerned parents' as though it was his fault. He'd been waiting half an hour.

'But if I could just squeeze a minute in between—'

'And get me fired?' she asked. 'We each have our priorities in our work, officer. And mine is assisting Principal Thorpe in limiting the damage of recent events.'

He would have liked her priority to be in catching a murderer or making sure no one else got hurt, just like him, but he managed to keep that thought to himself.

He began to wonder if he was going about this the wrong way. He sighed and ran a hand through his hair. He loosened his tie for good measure.

'Yeah, I've got a boss just like it,' he admitted with a wry smile. 'Maybe you can help me,' he said. 'In fact, you're probably the best person I could speak to,' he added.

She tipped her head and smiled. 'Go on,' she said.

'I wanted to ask him about Lorraine Peters,' he said.

'Lorraine who?' she asked, licking her lower lip.

'An ex-student here,' he clarified. 'I wondered if you could tell me a little more about her.'

She stared at him blankly.

He offered her his best smile. 'Maybe if you could just look up her records?'

She regarded him coolly. 'Well, officer, you've tried flattery, trickery and good old-fashioned charm in the space of three minutes, so I'm giving you ten out of ten for effort,' she said putting through another call.

This time his smile was genuine.

'Give me her name again,' she said, tapping a few keys.

'Lorraine Peters,' he said, gratefully.

She typed in the name and shook her head. Nothing.

'She enrolled early nineties on a swimming scholarship,' he said, offering the total sum of his knowledge.

She tried again and shook her head once more.

'No records,' she said. 'And long before my time, so I can't help you.'

Dawson frowned.

'There has to be something, please try again,' he asked.

She didn't hide her irritation at his insistence as her external phone line began to ring again.

'Sorry, officer, there is no education or attendance record for a girl named Lorraine Peters.'

Dawson stepped away from the desk. It appeared that the girl really had just disappeared.

# CHAPTER 75

Kim knocked on the door of flat 47a, the home of Monty Johnson.

The name of the occupant and the abode did not sit well together.

Two chains slid back to reveal a dark-haired man in a red-patterned dressing gown over shorts and a tee shirt. A freshly lit cigarette dangled from his fingertips.

'Mr Johnson?' she asked, doubtfully.

He huffed and rolled his eyes dramatically.

'Well you clearly have no news for me if you're asking me that,' he said, and flounced back along the hallway to the living room. The open door indicated he wanted them to follow.

Kim had been in these flats before and usually a dark, narrow hallway led to a spacious light lounge with big windows.

The man stood next to the window, ignoring a smoking ashtray. He was clearly lighting one after the other.

Bryant reached towards the ashtray, and Kim offered him a warning glance. His abstinence was more than three years old, but still. He ground the offending cigarette against the ceramic edge, extinguishing it.

'Why all the interest in Monty's car?' he asked, without turning.

His response told them he was not the man they were looking for.

'Is Mr Johnson here?' Bryant asked.

'Obviously not,' he answered shortly. 'Now why are all those police—'

'And you are?' Kim asked, directly.

He turned, lips pursed at her tone.

'I'm Monty's significant other,' he said, using his fingers to form speech marks around the phrase.

'Name?' Kim asked.

'Rupert Downing,' he answered. 'Or Miss Kitty if you come to Nexus three nights a week.'

'Thanks for that,' Kim said. 'Now about Mr Johnson. Can you—'

'What the hell are they doing now?' he squealed.

Kim glanced out of the window to see a tow truck parked behind the car.

'The car is being removed for further examination, Mr Downing; now if you could just sit down I'll—'

'Examined for what?' he asked, with his arms folded.

'If you sit down I'll explain,' Kim said, as her limited well of patience began to run dry.

He sat, like a berated schoolboy, his hands folded neatly in his lap.

Kim sat opposite.

'Sir, do you have any idea where Mr Johnson is? We really do need to speak to him.'

The man shook his head. 'Is he in trouble?'

'Yes, I think he might be. When was the last time you saw him?'

'Last night,' he answered. 'Monty dropped me off at the club and then came home.' He frowned and glanced outside. 'At least I think he came home but now that you mention it…'

'What?'

'No cereal bowl,' he said, nodding towards the kitchen. 'Every morning he leaves his used bowl in the sink with cold water in, as though it's going to clean itself. A standing joke between us, but there wasn't one there this morning.'

'But the car is outside,' Kim queried.

'Which is why I thought he'd come home.'

'You haven't tried to call him?'

'Not until those people started to mess around his car.'

'Why not?' Kim asked, suspiciously. 'How did you get home?'

'I always take a taxi home from the club at around 1 a.m.'

'And you didn't wonder why the car was here and he was not?' Kim queried.

He reached for the pack of cigarettes. 'We'd had a row,' he admitted. 'I told him to drop dead and got out of the car.'

'About what?' Bryant asked.

'Cheating, officer. I'm pretty sure Monty was cheating on me. Constantly on his phone, texting and stuff.'

'And did he answer when you called?' Kim asked.

Rupert shook his head. 'No, it went straight to voicemail. I thought it was just him playing the drama queen but there's something wrong, isn't there?'

'Is there any chance he could have gone somewhere for a drink to calm down, maybe had one too many?'

Rupert shook his head. 'Absolutely not. He was wearing trackie bottoms with a rip at the knee. Monty would never have been seen out in such a state.' He shook his head. 'I really don't understand what this is all about.'

Kim could feel the panic rising within him.

'Mr Downing, we have reason to believe that Monty was involved in a road traffic incident last night. A very serious incident, I'm afraid.'

'No, that can't be right,' he said. 'Monty is a very careful driver. Sometimes feels like *Driving Miss Daisy*, to be honest. I can't believe…'

His words trailed away as he glanced towards the window. The car was being winched onto the back of the truck, and the front end damage was obvious.

'Mr Downing, we believe he hit someone,' she explained.

His hand shook as he brought the cigarette to his mouth.

'How serious?' he asked.

'The woman died,' Kim said, pushing away the image of Joanna lying on the ground.

Rupert stood and began to pace.

'No, no, no,' he repeated, shaking his head. 'It's not possible. He always drives so carefully. It can't be true. He's never even had a minor accident.'

Her gaze met Bryant's and she nodded.

Bryant coughed. 'Mr Downing, we don't believe it was an accident.'

'What are you saying?' he asked, as his hand went to his throat in horror.

'We think Monty hit the victim deliberately.'

'You are out of your minds, officers,' he said, looking from one to the other. 'Monty wouldn't hurt a soul.'

'Does the name Joanna Wade mean anything to you?'

He shook his head, still reeling from their words.

'I don't know that name. Is that the lady that was... that...'

'Yes,' Kim confirmed. 'That's the woman that Monty hit. She died at the scene.'

'I honestly don't recognise the name.'

'She is... was an English teacher at a place called Heathcrest which is...'

'I know exactly what it is,' he whispered, reaching out to the sofa for support. All colour had drained from his face.

'Mr Downing, what is it?' Kim asked.

'Dear God,' he said to himself. 'Will that infernal place never let us go?'

# CHAPTER 76

Kim and Bryant had waited patiently while Rupert poured himself a generous measure of whisky. He sipped, scowled at the burning in his throat and then sipped again.

'Monty and I met at Heathcrest when we were fourteen years old. I was the new boy having moved into the area.'

'There was room for you?' Kim asked, remembering the pregnant couple being shown around, planning years in advance.

'My father is Lord Rumsey. If your parents are wealthy and powerful enough, they'll make room,' he said, taking another sip.

Kim wasn't sure who Lord Rumsey was, but clearly, he'd been known to the people at Heathcrest.

'On my second day, I received the ace of spades in my bed.'

Kim frowned.

'The calling card to join one of the most influential clubs on site,' he said. 'Completely expected, of course. I'd been a member of a similar club at my previous school. I accepted, obviously, thinking it would be similar to my old place.'

'And it wasn't?' Kim asked.

'Good gracious, no,' he said. 'Far more rules and regulations that were dressed up as guidelines. But Monty and I soon found out they were not merely guidelines.'

'Go on,' Kim said, sitting forward, remembering how they had all been amused at Dawson paying so much attention to these secret societies. She wasn't laughing now.

'A very important guideline was no fraternising with members of the other male group. You see, Monty was a Club at that time. The Four of Clubs.

'We both thought it was a silly rule and ignored it. We were found out and suitably advised, verbally, by our Kings. We ignored the warning and continued to see each other in secret. Of course, we were found out again and the second warning was a little rougher.'

'You were hurt?'

He nodded. 'We both were. My punishment was a broken ankle on the hockey pitch, and Monty a dislocated shoulder due to falling down some stairs.'

'And did the warning work?' she asked, wondering how far these groups went in enforcing the rules.

He sighed heavily. 'Not for me but it did for Monty. He was threatened with excommunication from the group. A thought he couldn't bear. Being part of the elite was more important to Monty than it was to me.'

'But you're together now, so…'

'Oh, it gets worse, officer,' he said, lighting a cigarette. 'We went our separate ways. I built my own business trading textiles, which grew into a success over twenty years.'

Looking at their location on Hollytree, Kim found that hard to believe.

Rupert caught her look. 'And I had a very nice home in Romsley,' he said. 'And in that time Monty had achieved career success as a chartered accountant.

'We met again five years ago, quite by accident, and realised our feelings hadn't changed. We both had disastrous, failed relationships behind us and suddenly we knew why. Because we'd never been with the right person. We realised that we were meant to be together.'

This should have been the point at which he told her they lived happily ever after, and there was a part of her that wished he was.

It was like watching a film for the second time and hoping for a different ending.

'So, we got together and for a couple of years our life was idyllic, perfect. We set up home together in a wonderful old chapel in Shipley and finally began to enjoy life.'

'Until?' Kim asked.

'Three years ago, after we appeared together in a newspaper article for our charity work with an AIDS foundation. From that moment everything changed. Suddenly every one of my business loans was called in. I lost three major clients who collectively represented seventy per cent of my business. A few months later Monty was audited, and irregularities were found in VAT submissions made to HMRC on behalf of some global, influential customers. His reputation was destroyed overnight, along with his career.'

'What happened next?' Bryant asked.

'We limped along for a few months, selling our possessions to pay bills. Sold our lovely home with negative equity because we couldn't find the monthly mortgage payment but were forced to declare bankruptcy eighteen months ago anyway. We can't get a mortgage, credit card, anything.'

'And you think someone was behind all this?' Kim asked.

'No, officer, I think *someones* were behind all this.' He shook his head. 'You really have no idea how deep these bonds and rivalries go. The rules didn't just apply when we were at school. These ties are for life.'

'But you were just kids?' Bryant said.

'But we swore an oath, sergeant, for life.'

'And how did Monty react to this treatment?' Kim asked.

'It's destroyed him,' he said, sadly, extinguishing the cigarette. 'The club always meant more to him than to me. He still tried to make contact with them, to beg forgiveness, to be allowed back in but they wouldn't even take his calls.'

'And who exactly are "they", Rupert?' Kim asked.

'Very important and powerful people, Inspector,' he said, standing. 'And I think I've said enough, so if you don't mind I need to try and find Monty before—'

'Mr Downing, are you still so afraid of these people that you won't offer us any names at all?'

'Officer, I am far more terrified of their power than I am of yours. I have lost my business, my career, my home and possibly the man I love because of an oath I made over twenty-five years ago. Now I'd like you to leave.'

Kim stood and followed him along the hallway. 'But we have crimes that are happening now, Mr Downing, children are being hurt at that bloody school,' Kim said, frustrated.

This man had names and he wasn't prepared to give them up.

'You could help us if you chose to stop living in the past.'

He smiled wearily as he opened the front door.

'You should remember, Inspector. That the past never stays in the past.'

'So, you think he's being a bit overdramatic or what?' Bryant asked, as they reached the car.

Kim gave it a little thought. 'Not sure. Could be coincidence that everything went wrong at the same time but then again...'

'You don't care much for coincidences, do you?' he asked as they got into the car.

She took out her phone and held out her hand for the photograph they'd asked Rupert for before he'd pretty much thrown them out.

She studied it. 'Don't you think there's a sadness to this man?' she asked.

Bryant glanced at it before putting the key in the ignition.

'I think you're projecting,' he said. 'After what Rupert just said about him.'

'Maybe,' she said, and yet she detected an air of hopelessness around his eyes. There was a smile on his lips that didn't touch any other part of his face.

'What is this need to belong to some kind of group?' Bryant asked.

She shrugged. 'Human nature. The need to belong is among the most fundamental of all personality processes. It spans all cultures. There are many psychological theories and even an evolutionary opinion.'

'Our ancestors?' Bryant asked.

'Back in the day belonging to a group was essential to survival. People hunted and cooked in groups so it's kind of ingrained in our DNA,' she said. 'If you consider that we all belong to some kind of group whether it's family, friends, co-workers, religion. There's a need to be part of something greater than ourselves.'

She paused for a minute before continuing. 'And for the kids at Heathcrest it's probably even more important. They're away from friends, family and every group they've known. The instinct to re-form must be quite overwhelming.'

'A bit too deep for me,' Bryant said. 'Just not sure our guy was as deeply affected by excommunication as his partner would have us believe.'

Kim glanced at the photo and silently disagreed. If the need to belong wasn't so fundamental to psychological well-being people wouldn't feel severe consequences of not belonging.

She took a photo of the photo with her phone and sent it to Stacey. And then followed up with a call.

'Got it, Stace?' she asked, when the detective constable answered the phone.

Stacey hesitated, and Kim heard her hit a few keys.

'Yep, got it. That's our driver, Monty Johnson?'

'It would appear so. And you'll never guess where he went to school.'

'No way,' Stacey replied.

'Find out what you can about him from the records but first circulate this photo as widely as you can. We need to speak to this guy and find his connection to Joanna Wade.'

Silence was the response.

'Stace, you listening to me?'

'Sorry, boss. No, I was just listening to the radio. Just heard a transmission. A patrol car has already found Monty Johnson and—'

'Fantastic. Tell me where and we'll get right over.'

'And Keats is already on his way.'

'Shit,' Kim said, closing her eyes.

If Keats was on his way, that could only mean one thing.

Monty Johnson was already dead.

# CHAPTER 78

Dawson spied Geoffrey sitting on a hard bench in the main reception beneath a Last Supper tapestry.

His backpack rested at his feet, an exercise book balanced on his knees and a textbook open on the bench beside him.

'Hey, you wouldn't be more comfortable in your room?' Dawson asked, sitting down.

Geoffrey smiled and then shook his head. 'I don't spend too much time in there,' he said. 'Not unless I have to.'

'The Library?' Dawson asked, as Geoffrey just caught the exercise book before it slipped from his knees.

He shook his head. 'I like it here,' he said.

Dawson thought he could understand why. Students and teachers were moving back and forth through the space, all going somewhere else, all focused on what they were heading towards. No one even glanced in their direction.

Dawson smiled. 'Jeez, you remind me of me,' he said.

Geoffrey looked at him disbelievingly. 'No, I don't think…'

'I was in my fourth year of high school, fifteen, and I weighed sixteen stone,' he said, recalling the day he'd seen the scales hit that particular marker.

Geoffrey guffawed and for the first time looked like the twelve-year-old boy he was. 'No way.'

'Honest,' he admitted. 'I liked my food. A lot. My mum wasn't one for healthy cooking, and I didn't much like exercise.'

'How'd you get like this?' Geoffrey asked.

'I realised I wasn't happy with me. Some rougher kids befriended me, and I was grateful, but they only did it because they were planning on doing something bad and knew I'd be the one that got caught. I couldn't run as fast as they could.'

'And did you get caught?'

'Oh yeah,' Dawson said. But his memories were not of the police or even his parents. They were still of the poor old woman that fell to the ground when the rest of the group ran off with her handbag.

'So, what did you do, stop eating?' Geoffrey asked, dolefully.

Dawson smiled. Food had been his best friend too. 'No, I started going to the gym. I decided I wanted to change my body for me. Not because of other people but because I wanted to get fitter. I wanted to be able to do more before getting out of breath or starting to sweat. But I did it for me, Geoffrey. Not for some idiots who thought it was funny to call me names.'

'What were the teachers like at your school?' Geoffrey asked.

Not like Havers, he almost said. 'Some were okay, some were crap.'

'Did they make fun of you, too?'

The question hit him somewhere in the gut.

'Not intentionally,' he said, honestly. 'But they sometimes left me out of stuff, assumed I couldn't do it because of my size. That hurt a bit.'

'I wish Havers would leave me out,' Geoffrey said.

He didn't like the guy but he had a job to do. 'He has to involve you in the lessons, mate,' Dawson said, surprised to find himself defending the man.

Geoffrey shook his head. 'Not the lessons. I get that. He's chosen me to ring the bell on Saturday night.'

'Ring the bell?' Dawson asked.

'At the gala that's now a memorial service. The bell rings three times to signal the opening of the show.'

'And Havers has asked you to do it?' Dawson asked. Seemed like a bit of an honour to be asked, and he'd thought Havers didn't like Geoffrey that much.

'Yes, he said the hundred-and-fifty-step climb will shed a few ounces.'

Dawson had to clench his fist. He should have known.

There was so much he wanted to say to this kid about the man being a total dick and not even worth his time but once this investigation was over he would leave and never see Havers again. Geoffrey would not.

'I don't cry, you know,' he said, quietly. 'Not any more.'

Dawson felt something cracking inside him. He said nothing.

'I used to but I'm twelve now. Almost grown up.'

'Hey,' Dawson said, clearing his throat. 'No need to be rushing these years away, and it's no sin to cry,' he advised.

'So, did they stop?' Geoffrey asked, looking up at him. 'The kids, did they stop bullying you when you lost weight?'

Dawson shrugged. 'Either they did, or I stopped hearing them. It didn't matter because I was happy with myself. I felt I was achieving something, so I didn't care anymore.'

Dawson could see he had the kid's interest.

'Listen, I go to Pump Gym in Brierley Hill. They've got a cracking swimming pool too. I'll be there Sunday morning about ten. It's open hour for new members. Come and have a look and see if you like it.'

'I got a card,' Geoffrey said, quietly, staring down at his exercise book.

'A card?' he asked, confused.

'Ace of spades,' Geoffrey clarified. 'Shaun's death left a space,' Geoffrey continued. 'And they want me to join.'

'Do you want to?' Dawson asked.

Being part of an elite group of powerful kids had to be appealing to the child who seemed to get shit from most pupils and even some of the teachers.

Being a Spade would offer Geoffrey protection from the bullying and the taunting. It would certainly make his life at Heathcrest easier. It was not unlike his own situation. He had joined that group thinking it would improve his life.

'So, why?'

'It's because of my mum,' he said, flatly. 'She won an important case this week. She was on the news.'

Dawson could hear the pride in his voice.

'But that's why they want me,' he said. 'Nothing to do with me. It's because of my mum.'

Dawson tried to put himself in Geoffrey's position. Away from home, on his own, being bullied and taunted.

'Maybe it's not such a bad—'

'I told them no,' he said, as a bell sounded along the hallway.

'Why's that?' Dawson asked, feeling his admiration for this kid grow.

'It's not the kind of club I want to join,' he said, collecting his books together. 'Anyway, I've got to head off…'

'No problem,' Dawson said, watching him amble away.

Dawson silently applauded the boy's strength of character in not taking the easy way out of a difficult situation.

He only hoped the kid didn't live to regret it.

# CHAPTER 79

Bryant indicated to turn at the first cordon into the road that led to Lye railway station.

Evening traffic began to build up behind them as the two officers stared and shook their heads to say no access. Kim smashed her warrant card against the window as they both scrambled to move the orange cones out of the way. The female officer held up her hand in apology as they passed through, ignoring the horns of the disgruntled commuters behind.

Bryant pulled up at the second cordon at the entrance to the old station building.

Three officers were busy questioning pale-faced witnesses who were either leaning against or sitting on the wall. Kim heard a bespectacled young man in his late teens mention "phone" as they passed by.

She spied the train driver in the waiting room sipping a glass of water. A rail official was leaning over him, a hand resting on his shoulder. The driver was pretending to listen, nodding occasionally while staring at the wall opposite. There was only one film playing through his head right now, and it was a film that would stay with him for the rest of his life.

Kim continued walking. She had no words that would make him feel better.

The train was perfectly parked against the platform. Kim realised that the driver would have been slowing to ease into the station. Monty Johnson had gone and stood at the furthest point from the station building so that the train would hit him on its way in.

The train hadn't been moved since and wouldn't be until the pathologist said so.

She headed to the end of the platform.

'What we got, Keats?'

Two crime scene techs were down on the line with him, and Kim couldn't help feeling relieved that she couldn't see the state of the body.

Keats heaved himself up onto the platform. 'What's this guy to you?' he asked, removing the latex gloves. 'Definitely a suicide, according to eleven eye witnesses and I'm guessing that camera up there, so what's your interest?'

'He's the driver of the car that hit Joanna Wade.'

'Aah, I see. Well, there's no wallet or phone on him,' Keats said. 'Just driving licence in his front pocket, which we used for identification.'

'Injuries?' Kim asked.

'Too many to count just yet,' he answered with a sigh.

'Okay, thanks Keats,' she said, heading back towards the station.

'Going so soon?' Bryant asked.

'Nothing to gain,' she answered. 'We know he killed Joanna, and we know he killed himself. Getting a road map of his injuries isn't going to tell us why he did either.'

Bryant began to speak but she'd already changed direction.

She stood in front of the train driver. Maybe there was something she could say to help after all.

'Listen, you're never going to get that picture out your head,' she said, honestly. 'And it wasn't your fault. There was nothing you could have done and right now that's gonna mean absolutely nothing; but one thing you should know is that guy under the wheels of your train was no saint. He deliberately mowed down and killed a young woman last night, which is something else you should try to remember,' she said.

He raised his head and looked at her. Nothing would mean anything to him right now. No truth would penetrate the shock shield around him. Right now he wasn't looking to excuse himself. At this very minute he was happy to absorb all the blame, but once the shock wore off and he was looking to get clear of the misplaced responsibility, he might just remember her words.

'One second he was messing on his phone and the next...' He shook his head 'It was the sound of his body hitting—'

'His phone?' Kim interrupted.

The man nodded and lowered his head.

As they'd entered the station she'd heard a witness mention a mobile phone too.

'Could have just been looking down, guv,' Bryant said, quietly. 'These days we all assume—'

Kim stepped away from the driver. 'But he's the second person to mention Monty Johnson paying attention to a phone. But why right at that moment, Bryant?' Kim asked, heading back through the waiting room towards the platform. 'He's about to end his life and he's messing around on a phone. Who gives a shit if you've not replied to a message? You're gonna be dead in a minute.'

'But Keats said there was no phone.'

'And I'm saying there is,' she said, stubbornly.

She walked the platform until she was roughly where Monty Johnson had been standing.

If he was messing with his phone in his final few minutes, then he wanted to communicate something to someone.

They had been sitting in the man's living room with his partner at the time of death and nothing had been communicated to him. If he wanted to let someone know something he wouldn't jump with his phone. He would leave it behind.

'On the ground, Bryant,' she said, dropping to her knees.

He groaned but followed suit.

'It's around here somewhere,' she said, as they both rested on their stomachs and lowered their heads to the ground.

'I'll take the benches over there,' he said, nodding to the right.

'Thanks for nothing, buddy,' she said, realising she'd been left the two vending machines. She would need to get her hand right under there amongst God knows what. But she knew it had to be around somewhere. Either he had thrown it before falling onto the tracks or someone had kicked it out of sight during the initial chaos.

She crawled closer to the drinks machine on the left. The plastic skirt around the bottom was slightly higher, offering more room for her hand.

She closed her, eyes and slid her hand beneath the skirt. Immediately her fingers met some kind of wrapper that she flicked out of the way. She placed her hand palm down and began to pat the floor in a grid-like formation, careful not to miss an area. Her thumb landed in a pile of sticky liquid that she didn't even want to identify.

She rearranged her arm and turned her head. Bryant was trying to hide a satisfied grin.

She frowned. 'You've got it, haven't you?' she asked.

He nodded. 'You did say I should let you get your hands dirty now and again.'

She growled at him and pushed herself to a standing position.

'Here, it's clean,' he said, passing her a handkerchief from his pocket.

She gave her hand a good wipe before giving it back to him. She took the smartphone from her colleague and touched the home button. Surprisingly it spurred into life as all Monty's icons and apps appeared on the screen.

'No password?' Bryant queried.

Kim shook her head as she sat down on the bench.

'He wanted us to find this,' she said, scrolling through his call register.

'You think he took his own life out of guilt?' Bryant asked.

Yes, that was exactly what she thought.

'But why not just come to us and tell us the truth?' Bryant asked.

'Because of that bloody oath he made years ago,' she said with disgust.

Having scrolled back to the day before Sadie's death, Kim found no call made to or received by any name she recognised.

She pressed on his text message icon and her eyes widened as she saw the header for the top message in the box.

The stream held seventeen messages and was entitled

'*Welcome back.*'

# CHAPTER 80

Stacey replaced the receiver and leaned back in the chair, stretching her neck.

The boss had sounded a bit miffed that she would struggle to identify the person who had sent the messages to Monty Johnson's phone with a pay-and-go handset. With frustration, the boss had explained that it was all there. A message stream that detailed the instruction to kill Joanna Wade along with a promise that the club would welcome him back with open arms. The sender had even told Monty where Joanna would be and at what time.

Stacey had understood but the sender could have admitted to kidnapping the Lindbergh baby while riding Shergar and she still wouldn't have been able to find out who sent it. And the boss's final sentence telling her to go home had sounded like an order instead of a suggestion.

Stacey checked her watch. Yes, she had been at her desk for thirteen hours. Yes, she was also mindful of the boss's words during her appraisal. And yes, she really should think about going home. And she would have done if she hadn't hit on an old student record, hidden in the Heathcrest archives.

She reached into her bag and took out her mobile phone. Her call was answered on the second ring.

'Hey babe, just ordered Chinese and am filling two wine glasses with—'

'I'm gonna be late, D,' she said, using her pet name for Devon.

Stacey still couldn't believe how easily they had fallen into a relationship once she had found the courage to trust the woman whose dark skin and short blonde curls turned heads wherever she went. Devon was the first thing she thought about in the morning, last thing at night and plenty of times in between.

'Is this a keep my dinner warm late or feel free to eat it all late?' Devon asked with a smile in her voice.

Stacey's own lips reflected that smile. Being an immigration officer meant Devon could completely understand the pressures of work. Only last week Devon had been called in from a day off as they'd wandered hand in hand around Dudley Zoo.

'Probably the latter,' Stacey admitted looking at the computer screen.

'Tomorrow night?' Devon asked.

'For sure, D. And I'm sorry, okay?'

'All right, love you, babe,' Devon said, ending the call.

Stacey held the phone in her hand, stunned. Devon had said the L word. It was the first time the word had surfaced in their budding romance. Stacey automatically stilled the warmth spreading around her body and told herself that she'd just said it casually, like one would to a good friend or family member.

*But she's never done it before*, a small voice said.

She wanted to go straight round to Devon's place and ask her exactly what she had meant by that comment and if it was what she hoped for because she was pretty sure she was falling in love with Devon too.

She wanted to but she couldn't.

Because the file she'd found had a dated encryption code. She'd broken through the first layer to discover that it was for a fifteen-year-old girl named Lorraine Peters.

# CHAPTER 81

The Spades filed silently into the candle room. The dancing flames distorted their shapes into grotesque silhouettes creeping along the wall.

Once seated, the Joker looked directly at the empty chair.

'The card was left in Piggott's bed,' he said.

An air of expectation travelled around the room. A new card breathed fresh life into the group. The cards were already mentally preparing ideas for his initiation.

'And it was refused,' the Joker added.

Stunned silence filled the room as cards turned to each other in confusion.

'Sir?' asked the King breaking protocol.

The Joker let it pass. On this occasion it was understandable. To his knowledge it had only ever happened twice before.

Each card was wondering the exact same thing.

Why would anyone refuse the opportunity to become part of an elite, exclusive club that sheltered you for life? An invitation into the Spades offered access to every member of the club either past, present or future. Hundreds of influential, powerful men located in every sector: medicine, education, sports, business, politics and law.

The Joker allowed the information to sink in.

Refusal to join was an affront to everything they believed in, the values they honoured for the rest of their lives, an allegiance to a brotherhood that mattered above all else.

'You all understand what the punishment will be?'

A murmur travelled around the table.

'Take out your pins. It's time to vote.'

The Joker nodded towards the King for the first vote. The King pushed his pin to the centre of the table.

One by one every Spade pin travelled to the centre of the table.

The cards had voted.

Geoffrey Piggott had refused the Ace, and there was only one possible consequence.

The Joker knew what he had to do.

# CHAPTER 82

Kim glanced at her watch as Stacey bustled through the office, removing her satchel as she moved.

'Sorry I'm late, boss,' she said. 'Missed my bus.'

Kim crossed her arms. 'What time did you get off last night, Stace?' she asked.

'Around eight… ish,' she answered vaguely.

'CCTV says nine thirty,' Kim corrected, giving her a hard stare. 'A full hour and a half after I told you to leave.'

'I know, boss, I just…'

'You know, guys,' Kim said, opening up her words to them all. 'I've done all your appraisals this week, and I could stand here and talk to you about my duty of care surrounding physical and mental health. I could explain the rate at which your effectiveness drops as the day wears on. I could even bore you to death with figures of police burnout and breakdowns if I wanted to, but how about when I tell you to go home you just do it?'

She heard three mumbled responses in the affirmative.

She was the first to admit that staff welfare was not one of her strong points. Yeah, running into a burning building after any one of them was a no-brainer but making sure they got enough R&R between shifts was another story.

'Okay, we know that Sadie Winters was being fed antidepressants by her parents. We're not sure exactly what dosage she was taking but they were definitely in her system. We established that there may have been a girl at Heathcrest who had an illegal abortion possibly carried out by Doctor Cordell. We know the name Lorraine Peters means something to—'

'Boss, about Lorraine—'

'Hang on, Stacey,' Kim said, as Dawson stood and began noting the bullet points on the board.

'We also know that Monty Johnson was instructed to kill Joanna Wade by members of his old club in return for re-entry back into the group. We have the whole message stream on text but can't find out from whom.' She paused to demonstrate her frustration at that fact. Having the whole conversation but no name was driving her mad.

'And now Monty Johnson is dead, so we can't get any more information from him. Rupert knows nothing and thought Monty's messaging was due to an affair. So, we still have a lot of names, a lot of secrecy, private elite clubs, privilege, wealth, illegal abortions. And yet there's only one question that matters as much today as it did on Monday.'

'Why is Sadie Winters dead?' Dawson said.

'Exactly,' Kim agreed, looking at the board.

Shaun Coffee-Todd had been murdered by having nuts forced into his mouth. Joanna Wade had been killed by someone under instruction, and Christian Fellows had almost joined them. But it had all started with Sadie Winters. Her death was the key to the whole thing.

'There's not one thing there we can tie her to,' Kim said. 'She wasn't in the groups, she wasn't pregnant and seemed to have no enemies at all.'

'Shaun was in the Spade group, but Christian Fellows wasn't. It makes no sense,' Bryant said.

Dawson turned. 'It has to be linked to this illegal abortion,' he said. 'It's the only thing that adds up. Perhaps all of this is just smoke,' he said, pointing to the boards. 'Maybe these kids just heard the wrong thing at the wrong time.'

Kim shook her head. 'I get that for Joanna. Someone definitely wanted to shut her up but not the others. It's not proportionate,' she said.

'Huh?' Bryant asked.

'Murder begets murder,' she explained. 'If someone steals your bike you don't stab them multiple times. It's too much,' she explained. 'The death of two children, and a third attempt, in addition to Joanna's death to cover a seedy secret, is just not proportional. There's far more to lose from the subsequent acts than the original crime.'

'But we're dealing with people who value image above all else,' Dawson argued. 'These folks will do almost anything to protect their precious reputations.'

'I agree, Kev, but you don't use a hammer to crack open an egg. Don't get me wrong. I also think our good Doctor Cordell is involved in this somewhere. For some reason that abortion is intrinsic to this case. If it was someone named Lorraine—'

'It wasn't,' Stacey said, quietly but definitely.

'Wasn't what?' Kim asked.

Every gaze was on Stacey.

'Go on,' Kim instructed.

'Lorraine Peters enrolled at Heathcrest in 1990, when she was twelve years old. She was one of the two annual scholarships because of her swimming abilities. Olympic material, apparently.'

Kim sat back and listened. Maybe she should have let Stacey speak sooner.

'All was well for three years. She studied hard and began improving her swim times. She'd been entered for the junior world championships, except she started turning up late for practice. Started back-answering the sports coach. Talented girl by all accounts but the training is brutal. Six mornings a week and five evenings.

'Two days after her fifteenth birthday she dived into the swimming pool from the ten feet high diving board.'

'And?' Kim asked, confused. She'd probably done that a million times.

'The pool was empty.'

'Jesus Christ,' Bryant said, as Dawson visibly winced and rubbed his neck.

'It had been emptied earlier that day due to a high legionella reading. Lorraine didn't know that because she'd skipped training that morning.'

'She was in the pool in the dark?' Kim asked.

Stacey nodded. 'Her death was marked accidental.'

A moment of silence fell before Kim turned to Stacey. 'And this is what you were doing last night?'

Stacey nodded, and Kim recalled her earlier words.

'Stace, remember when I said about losing effectiveness in your job as the hours go on?'

'Yeah, boss.'

'Doesn't apply to you,' Kim said. 'These two maybe, but definitely not you.'

'Thanks, boss, but there's one more thing you really need to know.'

'Go on.'

'Lorraine Peters was pregnant.'

'What makes you think he'll be there?' Bryant asked, parking up at Russells Hall Hospital. It wasn't quite yet 8 o'clock.

'You didn't watch the news last night?' she asked.

'Not last night, no,' he said.

'Aah, ballroom night,' she realised. 'You and your good lady giving *Strictly* a run for its money?'

'Guv, I really wish I'd never told you.'

Yeah, she bet he did.

'Body of an elderly male found along the canal. Been missing for two weeks. Keats'll be in,' she said, definitely, as they strolled along the corridor.

Although reception wasn't manned, the hospital was coming alive for another day. Patients and visitors milled around the café area. Porters pushed out patients towards appointments, and red tee shirted volunteers stepped forward to offer direction. Not one person they passed wanted to go where they were heading.

As expected Keats was already preparing for his first job of the day when they entered.

'Did you get it?' she asked.

Keats frowned at her. 'You know, Inspector, I get more common courtesy from my customers than I do from you,' he said, looking towards the sheet covering the dead body.

She didn't doubt it.

'So, did you?' she repeated.

'An email may have arrived from your detective constable,' he said, taking out his Dictaphone. 'And I shall have a look once I've completed—'

'No problem. I'll wait,' she said, hopping onto the work surface. Her legs dangled in mid-air. 'I'm a patient person.'

He narrowed his eyes as he pulled back the sheet and switched on his recorder.

'Ooh, he's in a bad way, isn't he?' she asked loudly.

He switched it off. The ghostly white flesh bore the scars of the insects that had feasted all over him. Keats switched on the machine and opened his mouth to start again.

'Bloody hell, he fed a few communities, didn't he?' she asked, loudly.

He offered her a warning glance and tried again.

'Missing two weeks, eh?' she asked.

'Stone, quiet,' he snapped, pressing the pause button.

She nodded her understanding as he began again.

'Conducting the post-mortem of—'

'Just look at that lividity down his right side, Bryant,' she called out.

Keats switched off the Dictaphone. 'An email you said?' he asked, conceding defeat.

'It'll be better on the computer,' she said, jumping down, as he pulled the cover back over his customer.

'And what exactly am I looking for?' he asked, taking a seat at his desk in the corner.

Kim stood behind him.

He pointed to the chair opposite and turned his screen so she could see it.

'Post-mortem report of a fifteen-year-old girl,' Kim answered.

He squinted at the date.

'From the mid-nineties?' he asked.

'Hey, Keats, it wasn't that long ago,' Bryant said.

'What am I looking for?' he asked.

'Anything,' Kim answered.

He scrolled through the document that had been scanned on to the computer.

'She was pregnant,' he said, more to himself. 'Approximately nine weeks, which clearly you already knew.'

He reached the end and shrugged. 'On first inspection, it all looks fine. What were you hoping I would find?'

'Not sure,' she said, deflated.

'Tragic accident, clearly,' he said, scrolling back to the top. 'Multiple internal injuries from the impact and yet surprisingly little injury to the head.'

'Would she have tucked it under?' Bryant asked.

Kim imagined an experienced diver would have done so.

'Hard to say,' he said, frowning and then reading again.

'What is it?' Kim asked.

'It's no smoking gun but there are two pieces of evidence that tend to cancel each other out.'

'Go on,' Kim urged.

'Well, the theory of her head being tucked when she hit the ground explains the lack of head trauma but there are flesh marks to the neck that are not consistent with the head being tucked. It's either one or the other but it can't be both,' he said.

'So, why was this never investigated?' Kim asked, outraged.

'It was,' Keats said, pointing to the bottom of the screen where a few initials were scrawled together.

'That's the signature of Burrows. DCI Larry Burrows, the officer in charge of the case.'

# CHAPTER 84

It took only a few calls to locate DCI Larry Burrows.

'Never understood golf,' Bryant said, as they headed down the fairway to the ninth hole of the Staffordshire Golf Course near Wombourne.

Recently renamed, the course claimed to be the most picturesque golf course in the Midlands. Even the avenues of pines, rhododendrons, and sixty-foot fir trees wouldn't persuade her to part with over eight hundred quid to join, despite the fact it was popular with at least three local police forces.

'Hit a ball and then follow it. Hit a ball then follow it,' he said, shaking his head.

Kim reckoned most sports could be reduced to a similarly basic description, but with golf she certainly had to agree with her colleague.

'There he is,' she said, spotting the exceptionally tall male among a group of average-sized men. She recalled being introduced to him, briefly, when she had first joined the force. He had looked her up and down and dismissed her and then continued to talk to her male colleague.

That one simple action had told her all she'd needed to know.

'DCI Burrows,' she said, pushing herself into the middle of the group. 'DI Stone and DS Bryant, may we have a word?'

He looked from one to the other and frowned. Although retired he clearly didn't appreciate his golf game being interrupted.

'One of your old cases, sir,' she said, affording him the respect his position deserved.

'Can't it wait?'

'Not really, sir,' she answered, shortly.

He looked to his friends and sighed heavily as they moved away.

'Really, my dear, couldn't you have called and arranged—'

'Chief Inspector Burrows, it's regarding a fifteen-year-old girl named Lorraine Peters,' she interrupted. She would allow his endearment to pass. Just once.

His tanned face remained blank.

'She dived into an empty pool at Heathcrest Academy. It was your case in the mid-nineties.'

'Yes, I know the one you mean. You'll have to excuse an old man's memory, love.'

'Inspector,' she said.

'Yes?' he answered.

'Not *love*,' she corrected. 'Inspector or Stone. Either is fine.'

His face coloured slightly at the rebuke, but she didn't care. She would remain respectful, but she would not tolerate blatant sexism to her face. Prejudice in the force was not yet completely behind them, but the era of resigned silence and acceptance was.

'One of my officers is requesting the case files as we speak but we'd also appreciate your insight,' she said.

He shook his head. 'I can still see her now,' he said, placing his golf club back into the bag. 'Such a tiny thing lying at the bottom of that bloody pool.'

'It was ruled an accident,' Kim said, falling into step as he began to walk behind the others. 'Did you agree?'

'Not at first,' he said.

'Why not?'

'You'll see in my reports,' he said, bristling.

'Could you tell us now?' she pressed.

'It's nothing,' he said.

Kim stopped walking. 'Sir, there's clearly something about this case that still bothers you,' she observed.

'It's my *Midnight Express*, Inspector,' he said.

'Sorry?' she asked. It wasn't a term she'd heard.

'Haven't you seen the film?'

Kim shook her head.

'It's about a guy imprisoned in Turkey for drug smuggling. To cut a long story short he's eventually placed with the crazies who walk endlessly around a pole in the middle of the room. Our guy joins them but he's walking the opposite way.'

Kim got the analogy. 'You thought there was more to it and other people did not?'

'I did indeed, and my boss agreed with me, initially, and allowed me to run with an investigation, but eventually I got shut down. Costing too much money with no clear motive never mind a suspect.'

'The baby?' Kim asked.

He smiled ruefully, realising they weren't quite as different as he thought.

'Yeah, that was my logic too. I wanted to find the father but the funds…' he shrugged as his words trailed away.

'How far did you get?'

'DNA samples from the kids, well, the ones that were old enough, anyway.'

'Teachers?' she asked.

He shook his head. 'Not before the money ran out.'

'Then what?' she asked.

'That was it. Couldn't go any further. I was assigned new cases, and by the time the inquest was done I almost agreed that I'd been mistaken in the first place.'

'About what?' she asked, wondering what had caused his doubts.

'The placement of the body,' he admitted, reaching for another club.

Kim recalled her own feeling on the placement of Sadie's body and realised that this man would be far more disturbed than he realised if he understood just how similar they were.

There was an instinct that he possessed that was similar to her own. It was something that could not be taught. Except there was one small difference. She believed in her gut and had learned to argue on its behalf. He had not.

'What about the placement?' she pushed.

'It didn't look right. Too far away from the diving board.'

'You're saying she didn't dive from the board like the accident the inquest ruled?' Kim asked.

He shook his head. 'Not even close and there was nothing accidental about it.'

'Are you kidding me?' Stacey asked as Dawson entered the office with one box. 'That's the total investigation into the death of Lorraine Peters?'

Dawson nodded as he slid the box onto the spare desk.

'Looks like DCI Burrows wasn't all that keen on paperwork,' he said, taking the lid off the box.

He removed three brown Manila folders and an inch-thick computer printout.

Stacey came to stand beside him.

'Hardly a major investigation,' she observed, opening one of the files.

'The boss said he was cut short, but I've had shoplifting cases that have generated more paperwork than this.'

'Reckon it's all here?' Stacey asked.

Dawson shrugged. 'We'll never know. Paper trail and arse covering wasn't like it is now.'

Stacey closed the folder and touched the computer printout.

'What is it?' Dawson asked.

'I'm guessing DNA results,' she answered.

'All I can see is a whole lot of numbers. That's not gonna help us.'

He opened another folder and slid it towards her.

She could see that the first few documents were witness statements. She opened the last folder which contained the photographs. Stacey spaced out the photos, and they both viewed them silently for a minute. Lorraine Peters's body captured in time from every angle. Her long, athletic limbs splayed around her; once so efficient and powerful at moving her through the water, now limp and lifeless, smashed against the tiled floor.

She looked back at the witness statements. They would be no use to her. Any witness to the events that had led to the body in the pool was not going to be telling the truth.

'So, which folder do you want to—'

'Neither,' Stacey said, reaching for the computer printout. 'I'll take this one.'

Dawson pulled a face at her. 'But that's just a bunch of numbers. You're not gonna get anything from that.'

Stacey shrugged. 'Maybe, Kev. Yes they'm just numbers but, unlike your witness statements there, numbers don't lie.'

'That's the one,' Kim said, pointing to a small bungalow at the end of a row of identical properties that had housed Lorraine Peters's mum for almost six years. The small front garden was overgrown with weeds that came up to her knee. Kim saw recycling bags shoved into the corner by the front door, which opened as they approached.

Kim guessed the woman to be early- to mid-fifties, reed thin, with bobbed purple hair. She wore a blue overall and held the keys to the property in her hand.

'Maggie Peters?' Bryant asked.

'Inside,' the woman said, blocking the door. 'She don't need no windows, a new drive or boiler and she's got a bible.'

'Good to know,' Kim said. 'But we're not selling anything. We're police officers.'

'Oh, okay then,' she said, but still didn't move.

'Is Mrs Peters at home?' Bryant asked.

'ID,' the woman demanded.

They both obliged as Kim noticed the stickers on the front window about cold callers and unsolicited visitors.

'Can't be too careful,' the woman said. 'Only last week she had two nice ladies come to tell her she needed to go to the bank and transfer her money cos staff at the bank were stealing it from her.'

Kim ground her teeth. Yet another scam that played on the fears of the elderly.

'Luckily, she phoned me before agreeing to anything,' she said. 'And by the time I got here they were gone.'

'And you are?'

'Maggie's home help, carer, whatever they call us these days, and I live just over the field.'

Kim followed her through a small hallway into a lounge that looked out onto the road.

A thin frail woman smiled at them from the single armchair that faced both the window and the small television in the corner. A small-two seater sofa lined the back wall. Part of the sofa was occupied by a few books and a knitting bag.

'Mrs Peters?' Kim asked, offering her hand.

The woman took it and nodded as she looked around them.

'Shelly?'

'It's okay, Mags, they're the police.'

Maggie looked less than convinced it was all in order.

Kim took a seat in the vacant spot as Bryant began to move the woman's possessions to the side.

Shelly stood in the doorway.

'We're fine now, thanks,' Kim said, aware that the woman had been on her way out.

'Yeah, so am I,' Shelly said, folding her arms. She wasn't going anywhere.

Maggie smiled fondly. 'She's a Godsend. Takes care of me every day. I don't move so well any more,' she said.

Kim calculated that she was only mid seventies but appeared around ten years older.

'Arthritis,' she said. 'Rheumatoid arthritis in the joints, probably from the swimming.'

'You were a swimmer too?' Bryant asked.

'She was indeed,' Shelly said, reaching for a photograph from the windowsill. 'Competed in the Commonwealth Games, you know. Came fourth,' she said, proudly.

But Maggie Peters wasn't listening. Her eyes were on Bryant. Her body might be failing her, but her mind was wide awake.

'You said "too", officer,' she breathed. 'Are you here about Lorraine?'

Kim could hear both fear and hope in her voice. Maybe it was the fear to hope. She nodded at Bryant for him to continue.

'Mrs Peters, we're—'

'Maggie, please,' she said, quietly.

Bryant nodded. 'We're here because of certain incidents at Heathcrest. The name of your daughter came up,' he explained. 'We understand she was on a full scholarship at Heathcrest,' he said, guiding her gently back into the past.

Shelly sat on the arm of Maggie's chair and took her hand.

'Yes, she was approached at a regional championship gala. She was so excited and so was I. Her father, God rest his soul, was not as keen. And neither was Lorraine after we visited.

'We were shown around Heathcrest, and the more excited I got the quieter she became. Visiting the place had highlighted the possibilities for me but had brought home the reality of leaving all her friends and everything that was familiar for Lorraine.

'Her father told her to make the right choice for herself and that we would be fine with whatever she wanted to do.'

'And you?' Bryant probed for the words she wanted to say.

Maggie shook her head. 'It's what I wanted to say. It's what I should have said but I honestly thought that Heathcrest would be a fantastic opportunity for her. She would have access to better facilities, one-on-one coaching, focused training and a top-notch education to boot. I knew that with her talent and their expertise my girl would be swimming in the Olympics. And she would have been…'

'Was she happy there?' Bryant asked.

Maggie smiled. 'I tried to convince myself that she was. She'd lost some of her sparkle, but I told myself that she'd be fine once she made some new friends. Her training was going well. She'd shaved almost three seconds off her personal best. Her coach was entering her into higher pressure meets to acclimatise her to the world of competitive swimming.'

'So, what happened?' Bryant asked.

'She met a boy,' Maggie said, simply. 'Her attention moved from her training and also from her studies. She started missing sessions and questioning her coach.'

'I got a call asking if I'd speak to her. Attempt to refocus her attention. And I did so, earlier that day.'

'The day she died?' Bryant asked.

Maggie nodded. 'That's when she told me she was pregnant.'

'And did she tell you who the father was?' Bryant asked.

Kim held her breath. One name. All they needed was one name.

Maggie shook her head.

'She said it was a secret but that he was as happy about the baby as she was and that they were meeting later that night to discuss their future.'

'So, you're saying that the father of the child definitely knew about the pregnancy?' Kim asked.

'Oh yes, officer. He definitely knew.'

'You do know you're wasting your time?' Dawson said across the desk. 'Those numbers aren't going to tell you anything.'

'Found your smoking gun in the witness statements yet?' Stacey retorted.

He grumbled something incomprehensible as he reached for the next.

Stacey was working her way through the printout the old-fashioned way, how she'd been taught at school. She placed a ruler on the printout and travelled down the page one row at a time. Numbers were beginning to merge together and dance across the page.

She sat back and rubbed her eyes for a minute.

'You know, Stace, sometimes you gotta listen to experience…'

'Yeah, yeah, Kev,' she said, glancing back at the ruler lying idle across the page.

'It may surprise you but just now and again I know what I'm talking about.'

'Hmm,' she said, looking at the last two records she'd checked. She frowned.

'Your time would be better spent putting that down and helping me read through these…'

'Shush, Kev,' she said sitting forward.

'I swear to God, Stace. You're as stubborn as…'

She moved the ruler back to the previous record and checked each individual number.

'Kev, write this down…' she said, no longer trusting her own number-weary eyes.

He huffed but picked up a pen.

'… seven, one, three, three, six, two, nine, two, six, nine, one.'

'Yep,' he said.

She lowered the ruler and did the same again.

'Now, write this down underneath: seven, one, three, three, six, two, nine, two, six, nine, one.'

He frowned at her. 'Why have you just given me the same number twice?'

'Kev, stop what you're doing and tap into the Heathcrest website. I think I've finally got something.'

# CHAPTER 88

'I'm just not sure that means as much as you'd like it to,' Bryant said, once they were back in the car.

'Bryant, if the father of the child knew about the baby and was happy about it, why the hell didn't he come forward and say something when both his girlfriend and baby died?'

'Frightened, I'd imagine,' Bryant said. 'We're talking kids. Lorraine was barely fifteen…'

'And the fact she was meeting him that night doesn't make you think the father of the child could be involved in her untimely accident, and if you say "they're just kids" once more, I'll punch you where the bruises won't show.'

He stared silently out of the window.

'Look, Bryant, I've tried to protect you from this fact but kids do bad shit too. Not as much as adults, admittedly, but we do have to consider the possibility that—'

'Just not feeling it, guv,' he said, tightly.

'Bryant, did you retire and not bother to let me know? Cos right now your gut instinct is out shopping with your missus.'

'There is the possibility the father of the child wasn't a kid. Strange how the funding for the DNA ran out before they got round to testing the adults. Lorraine spent a lot of time with her coach. There were other teachers who could have taken advantage of a young girl out of her depth who was just trying to fit in. Sickening, guv, but we know it happens.'

Kim opened her mouth to concede the point, but the ring of her phone made her close it again.

Bryant returned his gaze to the window as Kim put her phone on to speaker.

'Go ahead, Stace,' she said.

'Boss, I think we've got something interesting in this DNA list. I mean, it may be nothing but…'

'Go on, Stace,' Kim said. She'd learned to listen carefully to the constable's nothings.

'I was going through the DNA profiles of all the boys tested against Lorraine's unborn baby, and one of the records was duplicated. Now, if your chief inspector is to be believed about who they tested, there should be seventy-seven records.'

'And how many are there?' Kim asked, frowning.

'There are seventy-seven, just like he said,' Stacey answered. 'So, with the duplicated test taken into account, it looks like one boy got tested twice.'

Kim got it.

'Which means that one boy wasn't tested at all.'

Kim watched as another expensive car passed them and eased to the front of the building to deliver another well-dressed couple bedecked in evening gowns, tuxedos, fur and jewels.

She couldn't help wondering if the alteration from concert to memorial service had changed the outfit of choice for any of them. Kim guessed that the press pack at the gates was having a field day taking photos of the local society elite. With the precision of a military operation each car crept towards the entrance, where a line of smart boys waited to step forward and open the car door. Another appeared at the driver's window and offered parking directions. The guests then walked the red carpet between ornamental decorative lights illuminating the path into the school.

How much of tonight's event would be given to the death of two young children and one adult? How much had events been adapted to accommodate the inconvenience? She couldn't help but wonder.

'Look, Tom Cruise,' Bryant said, pointing to the next impossibly long car in the line.

She could see his point. She'd seen Hollywood film premieres with less pomp than this. The external lights placed around the building shone patterns and a yellow romantic glow onto the brickwork. Four separate uplighters shone onto the bell tower to the right of the main building, emphasising its height.

'I think this is him,' Bryant said, looking in the rear-view mirror. The wing mirror showed her Dawson's small Renault nestled in between two limousines as though it were being escorted in.

Dawson left the car line and parked beside them.

'What is this, the bloody Oscars?' he asked as he got into the car.

Both Kim and Bryant turned in their seats as the cars continued to stream past them.

'Boss, these folks do know that two pupils and a teacher died this week, don't they?' he asked.

'Yeah, but why miss an opportunity to dress up, eh?' she said wryly.

Dawson offered her the computer printout, but Kim shook her head. She wouldn't be able to make it out in the dim light of the car, and she trusted Stacey's judgement completely.

'Of course, we can't tell who is who because they're just numbers here, no names,' Dawson explained.

'But someone would have a record of the corresponding names, surely?' Kim asked.

Bryant nodded towards the building. 'I'm betting it's in there somewhere.'

'Agreed,' said Kim.

She thought for a moment. 'Okay, Bryant and I can't deal with the past case and the present at the same time. We'll go and speak to Thorpe, while you try Sadie's friends again. We need to know if there are rumours about someone having an illegal abortion. Sadie's poem confirms she knew something and we have to nail that down.'

They all stepped out of the car, and three doors banged shut at the same time. Dawson headed off at speed as she paused to glance up and take in the imposing height of the bell tower.

# CHAPTER 90

Stacey tried to pretend she wasn't pissed off.

She'd never been one to sulk but being kept away from the questioning at this stage when it was her own efforts that had spotted the duplication in the DNA records had left a definite sour taste in her mouth.

'Bloody Dawson,' she said, kicking at the leg of the desk.

He'd taken the printout as well as her glory. She knew deep down that the boss always knew who had done what, but that logic did not sit well with her current mood.

She had already spent half an hour searching the Heathcrest archives for the list of students pertaining to the registration numbers on the DNA printout, entering all kinds of keywords and search criteria, but with more than 300,000 documents on the mainframe, she couldn't even get a list of results below five figures.

The boss had asked her to start looking for any scandal surrounding any of the male teachers around the time Lorraine had been a student. Stacey could understand why she was asking. It stood to reason that if someone in authority had been having a relationship with Lorraine there was a good chance they'd done it again.

And this was why she was no good at stropping, she realised. Her brain was always ready to offer her a balanced alternative view.

She sat back in her chair and pictured Devon getting in from work, kicking off her shoes and making a pot of tea. Only she could find a girlfriend with an addiction to a cup of tea.

She reached for the phone to give her a quick call. It was bound to sweeten her mood. The phone began to ring before her hand got there.

'Wood,' she answered.

'Constable, I have a lady down here that's looking for Dawson,' Jack said.

'Good for you,' she said to the custody sergeant.

'Says she really needs to speak to him,' Jack persisted.

'He's not here, Jack,' she explained. 'I'm sure you saw him tear out of here about half an hour back.'

'Can't say as I did but this woman seems jumpy as hell and won't speak to anyone else. Said Dawson's been looking for her, about Heathcrest, and she won't say any more.'

Stacey frowned. 'What's her name?'

'Mrs Forbes is all I'm getting.'

The name registered somewhere in her brain.

'Okay, on my way,' she said, replacing the receiver. The call to Devon would just have to wait.

Stacey headed down the stairs and let herself into the reception. Jack nodded to the only person around.

Mrs Forbes was standing so close to the automatic doors Stacey could see that the sensor kept trying to kick in to open, detecting her presence. A full-length brown camel coat dropped from her shoulders to her ankles. A grey woolly hat covered her head with just an inch of red hair peeping out from beneath. She was either regretting walking through the door or was eager to get out and she hadn't even spoken yet.

'Mrs Forbes,' Stacey said, approaching with her hand outstretched. She still wasn't sure who she was, but the name had seemed familiar and Dawson had obviously been trying to speak to her.

'I'm afraid Sergeant Dawson isn't here right now. I'm his colleague, Detective Constable Wood. Do you want to come through?'

The woman hesitated and glanced outside before nodding. 'Just for a minute, my husband is waiting.'

Stacey smiled reassuringly as she keyed herself back into the corridor.

'This way,' she said, leading the woman along the hallway to interview room one. 'We can talk in here. Can I get you a coffee, tea, a cold—'

'Nothing, thank you, I'm fine.'

She looked anything but fine, Stacey thought, as she watched the movement of her hands clenching and unclenching in her jacket pockets.

Stacey sat down and invited the woman to do the same thing. She shook her head. 'Your colleague, he visited my old house looking for me, well, for Harrison, actually.'

Of course. Stacey remembered now. He'd called her to see if she had any other address for the Forbes family, and she'd been too busy with the boss's work to help. This was the third kid who had left Heathcrest during the middle of the year.

'My name is Katherine Forbes, Harrison's mother.'

'Thank you for coming in, Mrs Forbes. I don't know if you're aware that we've been investigating—'

'I'm aware,' she said, offering nothing more.

'My colleague has been rather interested in the secret clubs at Heathcrest and particularly in why some students just seemed to disappear mid-term. Harrison was one of those students, Mrs Forbes. Was there some kind of incident?'

'Incident,' she spat as her face suddenly spurred into life. 'Is that what you'd call it? My son's life in ruins is an incident?'

Stacey was instantly sorry to have caused offence but as she didn't know exactly what had happened she had no clue what they were talking about.

'Mrs Forbes, I don't have all the details of your—'

'Isn't that why your colleague called by the house?'

'All I know is that one term Harrison was at Heathcrest but the next he wasn't and that my colleague was keen to find out more about it. Can you tell me why, Mrs Forbes?'

'Because he was tackled, officer, on the hockey field. Both knees smashed by two of his classmates while playing a sport.'

Stacey balked. 'I'm so sorry to hear—'

'An accident, they called it,' she said, coming closer. Seeing the rage in her eyes Stacey found herself sitting back in her chair. 'The teachers and kids. A tragic incident of overzealous play. My child is sixteen years of age and will never walk unaided again.'

'But, still, he has—'

'Without distance running he has nothing. It was his passion. It was his life. The injury was intentional, officer,' she said.

'Was it jealousy?' Stacey asked. Perhaps someone had wanted him off the sports team.

The woman shook her head.

'And you moved house because of—'

'Of course not. We moved because of what happened later.'

Stacey sat forward. The kid had been permanently disabled and there was more?

'On the day that we collected Harrison from the hospital we had a car accident. We were a few miles away from home when a white transit van overtook us at speed and then slammed on his brakes right in front of us. We ploughed straight into the back of him. If my husband hadn't automatically slowed down, we would all be dead. And that was the intention. The driver and van were never found.'

Stacey tried to process what she'd heard.

The woman shuddered. 'My whole family was in that car.'

'So, are you saying all of this happened because someone was jealous of his athletic ability?'

'Of course not. It was punishment.'

'For what?' she asked.

'Refusing the card.'

'"Refusing the card"?' Stacey queried. Now she was lost.

'Turning down the groups,' she explained. 'An ace of spades was left in his bed. He gave it back and said no.'

'And?' she asked as dread began to form in her stomach.

'If you know anything about that damned place you should know by now that no one refuses the card.'

# CHAPTER 91

Kim knocked and entered the office of Principal Thorpe.

She was rewarded with the irritation that crossed his face before his stock smile, etched with tolerance, took its place.

'You're here for the memorial?' he asked, smoothing his hands over the breast of his tux as though bringing attention to his attire.

'Not exactly, Mr Thorpe,' Kim answered, sitting down.

He hesitated before taking a seat himself, but the glance at his watch was for her benefit.

'Unfortunately we still have three deaths and a traumatised little boy in hospital not yet explained at your school.' And her directness was for his benefit. 'So, what can you tell us about a young lady named Lorraine Peters?' she asked, placing the printout on his desk.

His face lost some of its colour as his eyebrows drew together.

'I don't... I mean... what...'

Clearly, not a question he'd been expecting.

'You remember her?' she asked.

He nodded but offered no more stuttering responses.

'And you know how she died?'

He nodded.

'Sorry. I'd like you to tell me how she died,' Kim clarified.

'She fell into the swimming pool, if I remember...'

'I'm not sure "fell" is correct but, yes, she definitely landed and died in the swimming pool. That we are sure of. Did you know she was pregnant?'

He nodded, shook his head and then nodded again.

'Sorry, Mr Thorpe, but which is it?' Kim asked, confused.

'I'm sorry. I didn't know at the time, but I found out afterwards.'

'Mr Thorpe, are you aware of any of your students having an illegal abortion?' she asked.

He appeared both horrified and flustered as his brain tried to keep up with the change in direction of her questions.

'It's okay, we'll come back to that.'

That had been a deliberate change of subject. He was working too hard on trying to pre-empt what she was going to say next about Lorraine Peters, and she didn't want him forearmed. His guardedness told her he was hiding something.

'Sir, you were here at the same time Lorraine Peters and her baby died. As were Laurence Winters, Anthony Coffee-Todd, Graham Steele, and Doctor Cordell. You were all Spades at the exact—'

'I was not a Spade,' he spat at her, his face screwed up with bitterness. 'I detest those groups.'

'But you know what went on, don't you?' she pushed.

'I don't know what—'

'Something happened to that girl that is somehow linked to the events of this week, and you're protecting someone,' she accused.

'I'm not, I swear,' he protested. 'I wouldn't do that. I don't know what really happened to Lorraine.'

'So, were you or one of the boys tested?' she asked, tapping the printout, 'to see if you were the father of her unborn child.'

'Of course,' he said. 'We all were.'

The colour that had left his face at the word 'abortion' now came back into his cheeks like a tidal wave.

'Mr Thorpe, just how well did you know Lorraine Peters?'

He hesitated before answering and all pretence fell from his face.

'Inspector, I knew her very well indeed.'

# CHAPTER 92

Dawson paused before knocking on the closed door.

A few seconds passed before it was opened by a girl he didn't recognise who glowered at him and then tipped her head and smiled.

'Is Tilly around?' he asked.

The girl shook her head as he heard a familiar voice.

'Jesus, you again?'

He turned to see Tilly heading towards them dressed in a towelling robe, carrying a toiletry bag and her clothes.

'I've already told you, I'm too young for you so—'

'Bloody hell, Tilly,' he said, looking around to see if anyone was listening. Even in joke, such a comment could ruin his career.

She laughed out loud. 'Trust me, in this place they're all so self-absorbed that if they don't hear their own name attached to the sentence it doesn't even register.'

Assessing her attire he held up his hand. 'It's fine, I can come back.'

Even with another girl in the room there was no way he was going to talk to a teenage girl who wasn't properly dressed.

'It's okay,' she said, untying her robe.

He protested but then saw that Tilly was fully dressed in a short black skirt with black tights and a floral shirt.

'Just didn't want to get anything on my clothes when I do my make-up,' she explained.

Of course. The girls were getting ready to go to the memorial service.

'Could I have a word?' he asked. 'I won't keep you long.'

'Sure,' she said, stepping into the room.

'In private,' he said, glancing at the two girls sitting on the bed.

Tilly glanced at them apologetically. They grumbled and left the room.

'Can you leave the door open, please?' he called after them. 'They're not going to the memorial?' he asked, noting their ripped jeans and tee shirts.

Tilly shook her head. 'Depressing enough when it was a concert but now it's a memorial.' She frowned. 'Shit, that was insensitive, wasn't it?'

'A bit,' he acknowledged, sitting at the end of Sadie's bed as Tilly sat at the desk and adjusted a small mirror to the correct position.

'So, why are you going?' he asked. Even she'd admitted that the two of them weren't particularly close.

'Thorpe asked me. He wanted one of Sadie's friends to say a few words, and I was the closest thing he could find.'

The sentiment saddened him for some reason. A thirteen-year-old girl had been so detached from her peers that it was a struggle to find anyone to mourn her death.

'Tilly, I need to ask you something,' he said seriously. 'It's confidential and sensitive, okay?'

She nodded, looking pensive.

'I've heard rumours of girls from this school having illegal abortions. Do you know anything about it?'

The shake of her head was immediate and definite, but he wasn't watching the head movement, he was watching her eyes for deceit. And he caught her unconscious glance at Sadie's bed.

'You're not saying Sadie...'

'No,' she said, emphatically.

'But you know something, Tilly. I know you do.'

Again, she shook her head.

'I don't. Honestly, I don't. I'm just shocked. I mean, where did that come from? What makes you think someone's had an abortion?'

'You're asking questions just a few seconds too late, Tilly,' he said, knowingly.

She shook her head and licked her bottom lip while trying to hold his gaze to prove her point.

Dawson thought for a moment. This was not the confident, assured girl he had spoken to earlier in the week. This girl looked thirteen. And frightened.

'Tilly, I know you're scared to talk out of turn, but I need you to be honest. Someone else might be in danger, so if you know something…'

'Cordell,' she said, quietly, looking at the door. 'He's a Spade from way back. It's common knowledge amongst the girls that he's the one you go to if you're in trouble; however late you are, he'll get rid of it.'

'Go on,' he urged, gently.

'Miss Wade pulled me aside one day and told me about a poem Sadie had written and asked me if I knew if she was in any kind of trouble.'

'Did you read the poem?' Dawson asked.

She shook her head. 'Miss Wade had given it to someone else to look at, but she told me it was all about abortion.'

Tilly began to colour as she chewed her bottom lip.

'Tell me everything, Tilly,' he prompted gently.

'I read Sadie's diary. I was just trying to help,' she said, guiltily. 'I was going to tell Miss Wade anything I found, I swear. I was just making sure Sadie was okay.'

'Have you still got her diary now?' Dawson asked, remembering it was still missing.

'No, I promise. I put it straight back in her backpack. I only looked once and nearly had a panic attack that she'd come in and catch me.'

'And what did you read in there, Tilly?' he asked.

'Enough to put two and two together.'

'Who had the illegal abortion?' he asked.

'I think you already know.'

# CHAPTER 93

'We were the same age and I was her study partner,' Thorpe said, standing up and moving to the window. 'We met in the library three evenings a week, at first.'

Kim felt a rumbling in her stomach that had nothing to do with hunger.

'I felt sorry for her when she first came to Heathcrest. A person thrust into this environment amongst peers whose futures at the school had been preordained from birth. Heathcrest didn't take too well to new things. Treated them as oddities, and a girl plucked from the local comprehensive was an oddity indeed.'

He took a deep breath.

'We were in the same maths group. A subject she struggled with and I did not. I offered to help her, and we met in the library to—'

'What was she like?' Kim asked.

He smiled but was ready to answer. 'Sad, lonely and eager to fit in. I always felt that the dream of competition in swimming at the highest level was more a dream of her mother's than her own. Don't get me wrong, she loved the sport. Only someone who truly loves what they're doing trains on the level of championship competitors, but I felt that the joy was being sucked out of it for her.

'At her old school swimming was just a part of who she was. She had friends, interests, familiarity, normality. I think all of that changed when she came here. Her whole life became about swimming. It was the only reason she was here.'

'The girls didn't like her?' Bryant asked.

Thorpe turned and sat down.

'I saw it back then, and I see it even more clearly now as each new year begins. The groups form, the girls size each other up, form into packs of leaders and followers, assess their competition. Lorraine started part way through the school year. The packs were formed and there was no space for anyone new. It's one of the reasons I've tried so hard to stamp out the wretched elite societies and clubs here at Heathcrest. They benefit the few and demean the many. Kids not chosen already feel inferior, which can stay with them for life.'

'Were you part of one of those societies?' Kim asked.

He shook his head.

*But you wanted to be*, Kim thought.

'Was Lorraine bullied?' Bryant asked.

'Ignored and isolated, I think would be a fairer assessment,' he said sadly.

*Not by everyone*, Kim thought. The girl had been pregnant, so someone had been paying her attention.

'Did she start to miss your study lessons like she did with swimming practice?' Kim asked.

'Now and again, but we both did. Sometimes it was clear that even when she was there, she wasn't. I'd look up from my books, and she'd be staring into space.'

'Did you ask her what was wrong?'

'A few times but she wouldn't tell me.'

Kim sighed heavily. Lorraine Peters had been thrust into a world that was totally alien to her. The same rules no longer applied. Here at Heathcrest it didn't matter how hard she'd worked or how promising an athlete she was, she would never have fitted in. She'd been miserable, lonely and frightened, and someone here had taken advantage of all those things, courted her, possibly manipulated her and ruined her future. All for the sake of having sex with her.

Kim couldn't help feeling that once they found the father they would also find the murderer.

She narrowed her gaze. 'Principal Thorpe, were you the father of Lorraine's baby?'

He shook his head without hesitation. 'No, officer, I was not.'

'But you were in love with her?' she pressed.

'Oh yes, and I probably still am.'

Dawson pushed himself through the backstage chaos of the memorial service. A boys' choir dressed in black were chattering loudly as two girls attempted to practise the violin.

A smartly dressed teenager barged past with a trombone. He stopped dead as a familiar figure came towards him, her satchel stretched diagonally across her body.

'Stace, what the bloody hell are you—'

'I need to talk to you,' she said, guiding him to the edge of the room.

He took out his phone. 'That's what these are for, Stace,' he said, sarcastically.

'Yeah if they're switched on, you moron,' she replied.

He checked. Damn, he'd run out of charge, again.

'You sure this is a memorial service?' Stacey asked.

Dawson saw her point. The level of excitement was palpable, kids running round, eager to perform, take their moment in the spotlight, impress their teachers, peers and parents.

He shook his head. As yet he'd heard no mention of any of the names of their victims.

'Mrs Forbes came to the station to see you,' Stacey said.

The name sounded familiar.

'Harrison Forbes, the third kid who left term part way through.'

'Got it,' he said and then opened his eyes wide. 'She came in to the station?'

'Oh yeah, and she hasn't signed any non-disclosure agreement, she's just terrified that they'll try and get her son again,' Stacey said. 'Apparently it doesn't end if a kid refuses the—'

'Whoa, back up, Stace. What do you mean, go after him again?' Dawson asked.

So far, he'd found a girl who had almost died from a severe asthma attack, a teenager on life support after trying to drink himself to death, and now it looked like his instinct had been right about Harrison Forbes. For a bunch of clubs that weren't supposed to exist any more they sure were leaving a lot of casualties behind.

'Hockey accident that ended his career as a long distance runner. He's in a wheelchair for life. And then a white transit van tries to run the entire family off the road the day they pick him up from hospital. She's terrified that the Spades will find out where he lives. It's all about this bloody honour code. If you refuse to join it's a lifelong stain which—'

'Oh shit,' Dawson said, as the events of the week caught up with the words that were coming out of his colleague's mouth.

'What?' Stacey asked.

'Geoffrey,' he said, looking around, urgently. 'Geoffrey Piggott refused the card.'

# CHAPTER 95

'So, you're thinking Thorpe could have murdered Lorraine in a jealous rage?' Kim clarified with Bryant as they headed towards the concert hall.

'Don't you?'

Kim shook her head. 'Did you detect any rage when he was talking?'

'To be fair he's had a few years to calm down.'

Kim shook her head. 'I see your point, but he was too open about his feelings,' she said, passing the door to the backstage area.

'Reverse psychology?' Bryant suggested.

Kim shrugged. It was possible, but she wasn't really listening.

'Did you hear that?' she asked her colleague as she stopped walking.

'Err… no, because I was talking to…' he paused as the call sounded again. 'But I heard it that time.'

They were right outside the door to the concert preparation area and someone had called for Saffie Winters. Twice.

She strode into the room and headed for the nearest adult. It was Thorpe's assistant, Nancy, carrying a clipboard and wearing a set of headphones.

'Excuse me, did you just call out for Saffie Winters?'

'I did. Have you seen her?'

She shook her head as her stomach instantly lurched. Saffie was the star of the show, the headline act. She should be preparing to perform.

Kim grabbed Nancy's arm. 'Has she been here at all?'

The woman frowned at Kim's hand on her arm.

'Maybe a little while ago. I thought I saw her.'

'Well did you see her or…'

Her words trailed away as she looked questioningly at Dawson and Stacey heading towards them. The woman took the opportunity to snatch her arm back and mutter something inaudible as she strode away. Kim could see the anxiety on their faces.

'What are you doing here, Stace?' Kim asked. Recalling Alex's words, she'd instructed the constable to mine for any acts of violence carried out by the older kids at Heathcrest.

'I needed to tell Kev something about the Forbes family.'

Kim had no idea who that was or how that pertained to their current investigation but her current priority was a missing sixteen-year-old girl.

'Have you seen Saffie?' she asked, as the wall of unease continued to grow in her stomach.

Dawson shook his head. 'No, boss, but I think we need to find her. I'm pretty sure she's the girl who had the abortion. I reckon Sadie knew about it and was angry with her and wrote the poem.'

Kim nodded. It's what they had all begun to suspect. Somehow Kim had always felt that the girl had been at the centre of this entire investigation, and now she was nowhere to be found.

'Okay, we need—'

'Boss, there's something else. I think we might have a kid in danger.'

'Another?'

Kim listened as he explained what Stacey had already told him.

'And you think this kid, Geoffrey, is in danger because he refused to join the Spades?'

He didn't hesitate. 'After what I've learned this week, I'm absolutely sure of it.'

There were times when Kim trusted Dawson's instinct almost as well as her own.

'Okay, Dawson, you go and find this kid. Bryant, see if Saffie is with any of her friends, and Stacey stay here in case she turns up. I'm going to see if her parents have seen her.'

She turned to watch as her team moved slowly away in different directions.

'Hey, guys,' she called. 'Stay safe.'

But none of them appeared to hear.

# CHAPTER 96

Kim stepped into the ballroom, her eyes searching the room, amongst the tuxedos and ballgowns.

A couple swept past her, took a seat and began to peruse the programme handed to them at the door. The chairs had been arranged in two squares either side of a carpeted aisle that Kim's boots sank into. She guessed the place was approximately half full of splendidly regaled observers, eager for the show to begin. Which was due to happen in half an hour.

Kim looked to the left and then to the right as she headed up the aisle.

The Winters were front row left, seated beside the Coffee-Todd family. Of course, these parents would have pride of place. The memorial was for their children. Kim glanced around, wondering who would be here for Joanna.

She nodded to both families before speaking.

'Mr Winters, have you seen Saffron?' she asked.

He smiled tolerantly. 'She's getting ready to perform, officer. She has a solo.'

'I understand that,' Kim said respectfully. 'But have you seen her back there?' she asked.

. He shook his head. 'We wouldn't disturb her before such an important performance. She needs time to collect her—'

'Not even to wish her good luck?' Kim asked, as she tried to still the panic growing inside her.

He frowned. 'I sent her a text, telling her to break a leg.'

'And did she reply?' Kim asked, impatiently.

Winters reached into his pocket as alarm began to register on all of their faces. His hand trembled slightly as he scrolled down. He shook his head and held the screen towards her. 'In fact, I don't think it's even been read.'

Kim looked and saw only the tick to say the message had been delivered but no read receipt.

He put his phone away. 'What's going on, officer?' he asked, as his wife clutched his arm.

How the hell was she going to do this to a couple who had already suffered the loss of one daughter?

'Sir, it appears that your daughter Saffron has gone missing. And no one has seen her for hours.'

# CHAPTER 97

Dawson knocked once and then entered.

'Hey, what the—'

'Where's Geoffrey?' he asked, without preamble, glancing at the tidily made bed in the corner.

'Geoffrey who?' said the kid on the bed without looking up from his iPad.

The other two boys on the bed near the door guffawed and nudged each other.

'Geoffrey Piggott, your room-mate,' Dawson snapped.

The kid on the iPad shrugged. 'Who cares?'

Dawson felt the rage ignite in his body at the superior dismissiveness of his tone.

'I bloody care,' he said, advancing towards him.

The kid finally looked up from whatever game he was playing. His young face set in a sneer.

'Good for you, you're the only one.'

Dawson wondered at what stage common decency entered the school curriculum, and yet even he knew that cruelty in kids was not limited to the privileged.

'Hey, mister,' said one of the kids from behind. 'You care that much buy him some diet pills.'

The others laughed, and Dawson had a sudden vision of life for Geoffrey in this dorm room. No wonder he studied on a seat in the great hall. At least when he had been at school he'd been able to escape it at 3 o'clock every day. This kid had no escape.

He got tortured in lessons, sometimes by the teachers, at break time if he couldn't find anywhere to hide and then when he came back to his room.

'You think it's funny to make his life a misery?'

'Yeah,' they all said together.

Dawson detected not one ounce of regret amongst them. To them it was a staple of school life, go to lessons, go to lunch, bully the fat kid.

'Listen here, you bunch of little shits,' Dawson said, turning on them all. 'Dismiss him all you like right now while he's the fat kid and the butt of your jokes, but some day that kid is going to do something amazing with his life and boy will you wish you'd given him a chance. You poke fun at him to take attention away from yourselves in your pathetic little clan. Oh, and just so you know, this week he got the ace of spades, so someone else thinks he's pretty special too.'

He now had the boys' full attention, speaking a language they could understand. If nothing else, they knew how influential a club member could be. He chose not to add that the kid had refused. The shock on their faces was enough reward as they all wondered what his new-found power could mean for them.

'So, where is he?'

'Sports hall,' the iPad kid spluttered. 'He said something about the sports hall.'

Dawson turned and headed out of the room. A sense of urgency in his step.

# CHAPTER 98

'Should I come too?' asked Mr Coffee-Todd as Mr and Mrs Winters got to their feet.

Kim opened her mouth to advise him when Winters's shake of the head and warning glance told him no.

The three of them headed down the aisle together. Kim slowed to accommodate Mrs Winters's four-inch heels.

Thorpe appeared in the doorway, resplendent in his tuxedo.

Seeing her face, he frowned. 'Inspector, is everything—?'

'Saffron Winters has gone missing,' she said. 'No one has seen her for hours.'

His face relaxed. 'Officer, amongst the chaos of a big production it's understandable that people get mislaid for a short while. She's probably off somewhere composing herself.'

'Thank you,' Kim said, stepping around him. He really had nothing useful to offer.

'Should we try her room first?' Mrs Winters asked, holding her gown a few inches from the floor to keep up.

Kim stopped walking and shook her head. It was the first place Bryant would go. There was no point them all looking in the same place.

'Try her phone again,' Kim said, moving aside for more couples to enter the room.

Mr Winters did so and put the phone to his ear.

'Continually ringing out,' he said, after about fifteen seconds.

'Damn it,' Kim said, trying to think above the noise.

Although Lorraine Peters died before Saffron was even born, Kim knew that something about the girl was connected to the death of her own sister, Shaun, and probably Joanna Wade.

Kim toyed for a minute with the ethics of sharing what they'd learned, but the situation warranted it. She turned to the parents of the missing girl. 'I'm sorry but I have to ask, are you aware that Saffron recently had a termination, an illegal one?'

The initial shock on their faces was not at the information. It was at *her* having the information.

'We know, Inspector. She asked us to arrange it; but how is that connected to—'

'Sadie knew,' Kim said. 'She was angry; she wrote poems about it and tried to confront her sister.'

'But we kept it away from her,' Hannah said as her hand rose to her mouth.

'I'm afraid you didn't,' Kim said.

Right now, she had no clue how it all related to the death of a pregnant girl twenty-five years ago, but somehow she knew it did.

Kim had a sudden thought as she looked from one stricken parent to another.

'I know where we have to go,' she said, suddenly.

As she turned and started sprinting she hoped to God that for once she was wrong.

# CHAPTER 99

The gymnasium was situated right below the boys' dorm rooms and took Dawson less than five minutes to get there. He thanked God he had already spent hours navigating his way around the sprawling building.

He arrived just as Philip Havers was locking the door.

'Where's Geoffrey?' he asked.

Havers appeared to look puzzled.

'Piggott,' he clarified. 'The fat kid you pick on,' Dawson said, making no attempt to hide his dislike of the teacher. He didn't have the time.

'Why would I know where he is?' he asked, ignoring Dawson's comment.

'Because he was headed down here, to get a key or something,'

Havers shook his head. 'Not a clue what you're talking about. Now if you'll excuse me I have to—'

'No, I won't excuse you,' Dawson said, blocking his path. 'Not until you tell me where Geoffrey is.'

Havers didn't take too kindly to the physical barrier before him. His nostrils flared in response.

'What's the particular interest you've got in this kid anyway? You into young—'

Dawson pushed him up against the wall and held him there.

'I dare you to finish that fucking sentence, Havers,' he spat. 'Cos unlike you I'm not into bullying poor kids who can't fight back just because they're not as you'd like them to be; but getting them to turn on each other to...' His words trailed away as a sudden realisation hit him. 'It's you that's keeping the bloody Spades going, isn't it? You're the fucking Joker? Your speech about belonging and connections and lifelong bonds. Thorpe really has tried to stamp them out and—'

'There's nothing wrong with healthy competition,' Havers spat. 'Thorpe only hates them because he was never invited to join. Fucking wimp. It's survival of the fittest. I was the Nine of Spades and it never hurt me.'

Dawson pinned him harder. 'You set these kids against each other, encourage them to hate and bully for your own sick selection process.' Everything he'd learned this week flew through his mind. 'The fucking damage you've caused to innocent kids in the name of healthy competition,' he cried. 'Now tell me where he is,' he said, shaking him.

Havers held fast and shook his head.

Dawson realised he was wasting his time. He could deal with Havers later.

'I will be back, you evil bastard, but I swear if anything happens to that boy I will make your life a living hell.'

Dawson unclenched his fists from the man's shirt and let him go.

Havers smoothed down his shirt and smiled. 'You can try, but I have powerful friends just a phone call away.'

'They won't get you out of this, you sick shit,' he said, reaching the door. He turned. 'And if being the Nine of Spades made you the man you are today, I can assure you it did you no favours.'

Dawson turned away and began to sprint, with the definite feeling that he was running out of time.

# CHAPTER 100

'But wh-why would she be here?' Mrs Winters asked fearfully, as they reached the swimming pool.

Kim no longer had the need to shout as they had travelled a quarter mile away from the focus of the evening's attention.

'You've tried her phone a dozen times now and there's been no answer. If my team had located her they would have called by now.'

'But why *here*?' Mrs Winters insisted.

'Because everything that's happened this week is linked to an event more than twenty years ago when a girl named Lorraine Peters was murdered right here.'

Mrs Winters covered her mouth with her hand.

'I remember her,' whispered Mr Winters. 'But wasn't it some kind of accident?'

Mrs Winters looked at them blankly with no recollection at all.

Kim shook her head. 'I don't think so. Now stay behind me,' she advised, as she placed her palm on the door handle.

Mr Winters tried to get in front of her. 'No, Inspector, if my daughter is in there, I want—'

Kim jostled and pushed him out of the way, forcefully.

Exactly her point. She had no idea what they might find beyond this door, and she didn't want either parent going in there first. She had chosen not to share with either of them the depth of her fears for Saffie's safety with each moment that passed with no phone call from her colleagues. As yet the girl had not been found.

'Mr Winters, you need to do what I say,' she hissed, turning the door handle.

Kim stood still as the scene before her illuminated.

Saffron Winters was bound and gagged at the opposite end of the swimming hall.

A figure stepped out of the shower room.

'What the hell are you doing here?' he asked.

Kim quickly realised that the figure wasn't looking at her.

# CHAPTER 101

'Any luck finding Geoffrey?' Bryant asked, meeting Dawson in the hallway back at the staging area of the show, hoping for a fifty per cent success rate at least.

Dawson shook his head. 'You find Saffron?'

'No.'

'And she's not been back here,' Stacey said, joining them in the doorway.

'Officers, where is she?' Principal Thorpe cried, thundering towards them.

'Sir, we're doing everything we can to find her,' Bryant answered.

'Well, I hope you do it soon,' he interrupted. 'She's supposed to be opening the show in ten minutes' time.'

'Not our highest priority,' Bryant snapped. 'When compared with her physical safety.'

'Of course, of course,' Thorpe said, checking himself. 'But I really do think that she's just having a moment somewhere and doesn't realise the time.'

'The boss is out looking for her, too,' Bryant offered.

He nodded. 'Yes, she has Mr and Mrs Winters with her right now. They all took off at speed,' he said before moving away.

'Well that answers that,' Bryant said.

'What?' Stacey asked.

'Wasn't sure whether to head off and look for the guv but if she's got the Winters with her...'

'Oh shit,' Dawson said, suddenly checking his watch.

'What?' Stacey asked.

'The bell tower—'

'Is right at the other end of the complex,' she said.

'And it's where Geoffrey Piggott is due to be at exactly eight o'clock to ring the bell that starts the concert.'

All three of them exchanged glances as they considered the repercussions if Dawson's gut was right.

'Oh shit,' they all said as they began to run.

# CHAPTER 102

Laurence Winters closed the door and stood in front of it.

'Graham, what the hell are you doing?' he asked.

Kim caught up with the pure hatred that travelled across the pool between the parent and the school counsellor. As she looked around at them all she realised she was the only one who looked shocked.

'I'm finishing it, Laurence,' Graham said, heaving Saffie to her feet. The girl cried out but most of the sound was absorbed by the material in her mouth. Terror shone from her eyes.

*What the hell was he finishing?*

Kim tried frantically to fit the pieces together. Graham and Laurence had been Spades at the same time twenty-five years ago, but what did that have to do with Lorraine Peters and the murders of Sadie and Shaun? Had Graham been the father of Lorraine's child? Had Laurence hurt her, and Graham was avenging her death by killing Laurence's child?

*But why do that twenty-five years later?* It didn't make sense.

Joanna had given Graham the abortion poem to decipher and explore with Sadie. He had pretended that he hadn't understood it. And then Joanna had asked for it back to show her at the pub the night she'd died.

She suddenly realised that Graham had been able to tell them a great deal about Sadie's inner feelings despite the fact she'd never opened up in her sessions.

Graham Steele had been in possession of the girl's diary.

Graham Steele and Thorpe had been told by Joanna that it was Christian Fellows she had sent to look for Shaun Coffee-Todd.

Suddenly, Graham took a knife from his pocket and flicked it open.

He placed it at Saffie's throat. The girl screamed.

Hannah gasped and reached out.

'No one come any closer or I'll slit her throat, I swear.'

'Graham, I'm sure we can sort all this out if you just let Saffie go,' Kim said.

He looked at her as though only just realising she was in the room. His eyes dismissed her as he turned back to Laurence Winters.

'You don't deserve any children, you bastard, after what you did.'

Again, Kim realised she was the only person in the room that had no clue what was going on. She knew that everything that had happened was linked to the death of Lorraine Peters right here in this pool twenty-five years ago.

'Look at you, you fucker. Look at the both of you,' he said, including Hannah in his sneer. 'Look at the life you've lead. The charmed, perfect, entitled life with your happy little family. The fucking golden couple. Not so fucking happy now, is it, Laurence?'

'You killed Sadie?' Kim asked, taking a step along the length of the pool. She realised that he only had eyes for the Winters.

'Of course I killed her,' he spat over Saffie's head. 'And I'm going to kill this one and then we can call it a hat trick.'

The pieces suddenly fell into place in her head like an explosion playing backwards. Lorraine hadn't been sleeping with Graham as she'd originally thought.

'*You* were the father of Lorraine's baby?' she said, turning to Laurence Winters.

Before his response, Kim saw the distaste on the face of his wife. Kim was right: Hannah had known. All along she had known about the two of them.

All four of them now stood around the swimming pool where Lorraine had met her death.

'But you pushed her?' she said, turning to Graham. 'You pushed her into an empty pool?'

He said nothing but continued to stare at Laurence. As did she.

'Laurence, you knew she was pregnant with your child and you convinced him to push her. She was meeting the father of the baby that night. She was going to start telling people who you were.'

Laurence remained stubbornly silent. But Graham did not.

Still he did not look her way as he spoke, only at Laurence Winters. 'It was my initiation into the Spades, wasn't it, you bastard? You wanted me to play a joke. That's what you said it was. You said there was a girl who was getting on your nerves, stalking you, bothering you. Teach her a lesson, make her feel stupid so she'd leave you alone.'

Kim looked at the emotion in the counsellor's face, the anguish. Despite what he'd done there was something he didn't know. Something Keats had picked up when looking at Lorraine's post-mortem notes and now clear in her mind when she remembered a conversation with Saffie's ex-boyfriend.

Kim knew she couldn't suddenly take a rush at him to save the girl. He was too far away. The blade would have sliced across Saffie's throat by the time she got there. A plan started to form in her mind. She knew that she held a surprise for all of them. If only she could get close enough to deliver it.

'You told me to hide behind the diving board,' he continued. 'You said that's where you always met. You told me to keep the lights off and then just push her into the water. I'd had a drink; I was nervous; I wanted to succeed. I was new and wanted to be a Spade. I should have realised there was no water in the pool. I should have seen that,' he raged.

She took a step forward.

'And you did it?' Kim asked.

'I didn't know the pool was empty, and I didn't know she was pregnant.'

Kim took another step forward as the blade hovered close to Saffie's throat.

'Every night I've dreamed of that baby. Of that innocent child I killed because of you. It's haunted my dreams, picturing that life I took.

'But you just lived your life happily, never once thinking of Lorraine or your child, just happy to be shot of them. You've lived guilt free while I've shouldered it all. My life ruined because you wanted to fuck the new—'

'Graham,' Hannah cried.

Kim took another step forward.

'Oh fuck off, Hannah. You knew all about it. You were the golden couple. King of Spades and Queen of Hearts. You were meant for each other. Both intelligent, gorgeous, blessed, wealthy. A real power couple with a rosy, bright future ahead of you. Except Laurence wanted a bit of rough, didn't he?'

'But why Shaun?' Kim asked taking another step towards her target. But she already knew. Shaun's dad was the kid whose DNA had been tested twice.

'Because that bastard covered for him. They somehow swapped samples so that Laurence would never be found out. It's what Spades do.'

'Why didn't you come forward, Graham?' Kim asked, taking another step.

'He threatened me. Said he'd swear I was jealous and had killed Lorraine in a rage, and Cordell and the others would back him up. Told me I was a Spade and that my life would be hell for me and my family if I told the truth. Said he could arrange for my dad to lose his job and worse. He was an assembly line worker at Rover. I was a scholarship kid. He told me that Spades were everywhere.'

Kim stared into Saffie's face. Their eyes met. Kim gave her a small nod.

Saffie looked confused.

'So, you killed his child too?' Kim asked.

'These people don't deserve children, and these two certainly didn't deserve poor Sadie,' he raged.

The point of the knife caught Saffie's neck. A bubble of blood appeared.

To the girl's credit she winced but didn't cry out. Kim tried to reassure her by maintaining eye contact as she stepped once more to the side.

'You know what they did, don't you?' Graham said, addressing her for the first time.

'Yes, I know that Saffie recently had an abortion,' Kim said.

'An *illegal* abortion,' he said. 'Another child dead at the hands of these people. And it was a child, make no mistake. They can't keep deciding which children get to live or die while their own remain unaffected.'

Kim saw the tears begin to flow over Saffie's cheeks. What she had initially misread for disinterested detachment and coldness was really grief and mourning for her dead child. Her boyfriend, Eric, must have found out what she'd done and finished with her. It explained the hurt and disgust she'd seen in his eyes.

'She's too young to be a mother,' Hannah cried.

'Then she should have thought about that before she opened her legs. But I don't blame her. I blame you two. It was you who arranged for her to go to Cordell for the termination. You think the law can't touch you. You're protected by the Spades. Justice can never punish you. But I can.'

The tears were running openly over Saffie's cheeks and falling from her chin, leaving Kim in no doubt that the termination had not been Saffie's choice. Kim now understood why the girl had refused to go home after Sadie's death. Right now, she could not stand to be around the people who had forced her to abort her child.

But Kim needed to keep Graham talking to continue her journey along the pool. She had one tool in her arsenal, and it had to be timed perfectly.

'It was you who sent the messages to Monty Johnson, you who welcomed him back to the group in exchange for the murder of Joanna Wade,' Kim said. 'You knew when she asked for the poem back that she was going to give it to me and I'd realise what had set these events in motion.'

'You two seemed awfully close,' he said, glancing her way.

'Christian saw you, didn't he?' Kim asked. 'He saw something when you were murdering Shaun in the locker room. You took him into the janitor's room and strung him up, thinking you'd killed him. He'd done nothing wrong, you bastard,' she growled.

'I'm not the bastard,' he said, looking at Laurence Winters, whose eyes were trained on his daughter. 'He's the cause of this. It all started with him.'

Kim knew she had to re-engage Saffie's attention. The girl had to be ready to act when she got the opportunity, and Kim could only provide it once.

She took another step to the side.

'And the guilt for killing that child all those years ago was the catalyst for the murders?' Kim asked.

He nodded. 'That event has shaped my whole life while they have cheerfully continued with theirs, ignorant of the torture. The guilt I've lived with for twenty-five years. That I took a life, two lives and—'

'Except you didn't,' Kim said, finally arriving at her target. 'Did he, Mrs Winters?'

# CHAPTER 103

'What are you talking about?' Hannah asked, looking Kim straight in the eye.

Kim remembered everything she'd learned from Keats about the death twenty-five years ago; the marks around Lorraine's neck that didn't fit with being pushed into the pool.

For the first time she saw shock on Laurence Winters's face and knew she was right.

She had realised that Laurence wouldn't have climbed down into the pool to finish Lorraine off. He hadn't had the courage to do it the first time, he'd tricked Graham, so he wouldn't have had the backbone to do it when that plan failed. It was Hannah who had warned Alistair Milton away from Saffie. He had called her the ruthless one.

'Graham didn't kill Lorraine. You did.'

Kim glanced towards Saffie, who moved away from the counsellor in the first few seconds of his confusion. She stumbled and fell but Graham was not looking her way anymore. She scrabbled across the tiled floor towards Kim.

'You pushed her into the empty pool, Graham, but she didn't die. Not until Hannah Winters climbed down there and finished the job just to be sure. Nothing was going to break up the power couple.'

Graham staggered forward. 'No... no... no...'

'Yes, Graham, she's allowed you to suffer for the last twenty-five years knowing you didn't kill her. Hannah finished her off with her bare hands around her neck.'

Laurence's gaze was fixed on his stricken wife, numbed by shock. 'Hannah?' he said, doubtfully.

Stung by the horror in his face, her eyes hardened.

'One of us had to make sure she was dead,' she spat. 'She would never have left us alone. She would have had that child and been tied to us for the rest of our…'

Her words trailed away as Graham began running towards the couple that had ruined his life.

Laurence Winters stepped into the path of the raging bull who could only see the woman that had allowed him to fester in his own guilt. His eyes locked on her, hatred radiating from his gaze.

Kim lurched towards them but knew she didn't have the time.

'Noooo…' screamed Hannah as the knife slid effortlessly into Laurence's torso.

Immediately the blood began to stain the pure white tuxedo.

Hannah stood motionless as her husband buckled to the ground.

Graham stood, rooted to the spot, holding the dripping knife.

Laurence falling to the ground offered Graham a clear path to the true object of his hatred. He took a step forward.

Kim grabbed his wrist as he turned the knife towards Hannah. She dodged out of its path as he held fast to the knife and waved it around.

'Give it to me, Graham,' she said urgently.

She locked the fingers of her free hand around his grip trying to loosen his hold.

The expression in his eyes was murderous as Hannah took a step towards her writhing husband.

'Graham, give me the knife,' she said, again.

He shook her off easily. He wasn't hearing or seeing anything, only the woman leaning down on the ground.

Kim knew that any rational logic had left him. Anyone that got between him and his target would be hurt.

Three more steps and he'd be on Hannah.

Kim thought quickly. There were two places men were equally vulnerable whatever their size. His front was heading away from her, which ruled out the first.

She raised her right leg in the air and kicked hard at the back of his knees.

He stumbled and fell forward; the sound of the blade clattered against the tile.

Kim pounced on his back at the waist as though riding a horse. She had to stop him doing any more damage. Kim felt herself being lifted as he tried to buck her off his back. She held on tight to his jacket. She had to get that knife, and her only chance was while he was on the ground.

She lurched forward and landed around his middle back. His hand was back on the knife. She leaned forward, covering him, her breasts pushed against the back of his head.

She balled her hand up into a fist and smashed it down onto his fingers.

He cried out as his fingers splayed open.

She pushed the knife out of his reach as he lifted himself onto his knees, which caused her to topple off his back onto the tile. He lifted his injured hand and towered above her, his legs splayed above her knee. She raised her leg and struck him full force in the groin.

He tumbled down on top of her.

The weight knocked the breath from her body, but she took the opportunity to wriggle from beneath him. She balled up her fist and punched him in the face as hard as she could. The pain shot from her knuckles right up to her wrist.

Blood spurted from his nose as his eyes rolled into unconsciousness.

Kim turned to see Saffie nodding towards his right hand.

It took Kim three seconds to catch up.

Hannah Winters had disappeared and so had the knife.

# CHAPTER 104

Kim bent over Laurence Winters who was holding onto his stomach. The initial blood stream had slowed and from the noise he was making it was not life-threatening. He'd live and so would Hannah Winters if she had anything to do with it.

'Saffie, are you okay?' she asked, removing the gag from her mouth.

'Y-yes… but my Dad…' she said, moving towards him.

'He'll be fine,' Kim said, grabbing Saffie's wrists and untying the bandage that had bound her.

Saffie dropped to the floor beside her father.

'Dad… dad… it's me…' she said, as the tears rolled over her cheeks.

'Get his phone and call for an ambulance,' Kim shouted as she tied Graham's feet together and his wrists to the metal handrail that led into the pool.

'He's secure,' she said, taking out her mobile phone. She could sure use a hand right now.

She groaned when she saw the cracked screen. Her thumb failed to light it up. It must have happened when Graham landed on top of her.

Damn it, she couldn't waste any more time.

Kim looked at the distraught girl cradling the head of her groaning father, but she had to get after the girl's mother.

She hit the fire alarm button as she raced out of the door. The siren rang out immediately, blasting her ears. But it was the fastest way to get help to Saffron and her father. Yes, she could wait for help from whoever responded to the fire alarm but every second that passed put space between her and an emotionally distraught woman with a four-inch blade.

She looked up and down the corridor and saw a flash of silver gown disappear around the corner.

And even though she was on her own she could see where Hannah Winters was heading.

# CHAPTER 105

Kim heard the sobbing as she opened the roof door.

'There's nowhere to go, Hannah,' Kim said, spotting the woman to the left of a roof light. The knife sat on the ledge beside her hand.

'Don't come any closer,' she said, without turning.

Kim ignored her and took a step as quietly as she could. In Hannah's twisted mind the roof was a link to Sadie.

'It's all gone,' she said quietly. 'Sadie is dead, Laurence is dead, Saffie hates me.'

Kim should have guessed that her only regret was for herself.

'Laurence isn't dead,' Kim said, using her voice to cover the fact she was taking another step.

Kim saw her nod her head. 'Good, not that it matters. You saw the look on his face. Doesn't matter that he was the one who planned it. And I was the one that made sure it happened. It's because I never told him. I let him suffer all the guilt for her death.'

'Was that his punishment for sleeping with her?' Kim asked, moving closer.

She shook her head. 'No, it was his punishment for loving her.'

She turned, and Kim saw the emotion in her eyes.

'You think I'd have done it had she been a quick, meaningless fuck?'

She turned back to the night sky, her fingers tapping on the blade.

'Was it really worth it?' Kim asked. 'All the secrets, lies. Was it worth the murder of a young girl and her unborn child?'

'As I care nothing for what you think, I will say yes. Laurence and I had twenty-five fantastic years together.'

'But your daughter is dead because of what you did.'

'My daughter is dead because of what my *husband* did. Graham didn't even know about me until you told him.'

'What about Saffie?' Kim asked. 'Isn't she worth living for?' she asked, taking another step. She was now only a few feet away.

'We will never be close again. Not after what she knows about what I did, especially after the abortion. She wanted to keep the child, and I forced her into it. She'll never forgive me for that alone.'

'Why did you force her?' Kim asked.

'Her career. World famous concert pianists don't travel the world with a young baby in tow.'

'But why the importance of her glittering career? Why not just for her to be happy. Why wasn't that enough?'

'Because I had to show him it was worth it,' she said, simply.

Kim suddenly understood. Hannah knew that Laurence had secretly loved Lorraine back then and had always been trying to compete with a dead woman. And that included children he could be proud of.

'It would have been easier to compete with her if she were still alive,' Kim observed.

The dead could do no wrong.

'You're probably right but I'll never know.'

She turned to face Kim who was now standing beside her. Their eyes met and locked.

'I told you to stay away,' she said, tonelessly. A woman whose every emotion had been wrung out of her.

She was flat, empty, devoid of feeling anything.

'I have nothing left,' she said, grabbing Kim around the shoulders. 'And it's all your fault.'

Kim had no time to react as Hannah launched herself over the side of the building taking her along too.

Kim tried to break free as they hurtled through the air, locked in some kind of sick embrace.

Hannah's silver gown billowed around them as they rushed towards the ground.

# CHAPTER 106

The ground hit them like a speeding train, but something had cushioned the impact of her chest. Kim was winded but still alive.

Beneath her lay the body of Hannah Winters.

Suddenly her senses came back to her. All of them.

She screamed out in pain as the agony travelled around her body. She felt as though every bone and muscle was screaming out in protest. She tried to move away from Hannah, take the weight off her chest. She had to try and get help for the woman even though she knew it was too late.

As she tried to move her left leg, blinding red hot pain flashes travelled around her body bringing stars to her eyes.

But she *had* to try and move. She placed her forearms on the ground and tried to use them to move along.

Every inch brought flashes of agony and waves of nausea.

She looked up to try and shout for help and that was when she saw them.

Her three colleagues entering the bell tower.

# CHAPTER 107

'Jesus, Dawson, slow down,' Bryant called around Stacey to the sergeant who was leading the single-file charge up the narrow, winding stone staircase.

Bryant was sure they'd been climbing for hours. If he looked down he could see the eighty metres they'd ascended, and when he looked up he could see they were almost there.

'Geoffrey,' Dawson called again now they were closer.

Bryant thought he heard some kind of whimper in response.

'He's up here,' Dawson called.

Bryant heard the relief in Dawson's voice. Thank God, the kid was probably frightened of the dark and was just finding his way back to the stairs. Secretly he'd thought his colleague had been overreacting to the danger the kid was in. It had all seemed a little far-fetched to him that the kid would be at risk of death for refusing to join some kind of school club. He couldn't wait to get back down and christen Dawson with his new nickname of drama queen. Wait until the guv knew he'd had them climb a million steps to save a boy from ringing a bell.

Oh, how he loved to tell this kid he was wrong.

He made the final few steps with a smile on his face that eased the lactic acid burning his thigh muscles.

'Hey drama—'

'Fuck,' Dawson said, shining his torch into the middle of the space.

Oh shit, Bryant thought, swallowing hard. His colleague hadn't been wrong after all.

# CHAPTER 108

Stacey joined her colleagues in shining her torch into the middle of the room.

Three beams converged on the figure of a young boy rooted to the spot.

'Don't step forward,' Dawson warned, aiming his beam down.

The floorboards had given way leaving the boy standing on a thin beam of wood at the very centre of the space. They'd been climbing for at least four minutes and nothing had sailed past them. Stacey had no idea how long he'd been balancing precariously on the single plank, but she guessed it wasn't going to continue to support him for long.

'Don't move, Geoffrey,' Dawson said.

'O-okay,' Geoffrey stuttered, hanging on to the lip of the bell.

Stacey knew that if the beam beneath him broke he would not be able to hang onto that lip. The boards beneath her own feet felt solid and stable around the outside but that was a good five feet from the gaping hole beneath Geoffrey's feet that dropped all the way to the bottom of the tower.

'H-help me,' he whispered.

The fear in his voice kicked her right in the stomach.

'You just stay still,' Dawson advised, calmly. 'We'll get you down, I promise.'

Stacey marvelled at her colleague's steady voice when even she could see there was no way they could reach him. Every step forward risked both his life and theirs.

Bryant was already on the phone to the fire service. Unless they were waiting right around the corner Stacey suspected there was little they could do in time.

'Look around,' Dawson said, shining his torch towards the wall. 'Look for something that can help.'

All three torch beams turned away from the trembling child, but Dawson continued to speak, to reassure the boy.

'It's all right, Geoffrey. We'll have you off there in a minute. Just stay still.'

Bryant ended the call to the fire service. 'I'll call down to the school and—'

'No,' Dawson said, forcefully. 'The last thing we need is more people stampeding up the stairs, and we sure don't need an audience.'

Bryant nodded his understanding and began to look around for something to help.

Without moving her feet Stacey shone the torch at each wall in turn. Two arches were cut into each side of the building allowing in the night-time breeze. Her torch found initials that had been scratched into some of the stones, but it found nothing that would be long enough to reach him. But even if there was they couldn't risk him trying to move off that beam.

'The rope,' Dawson said, suddenly. 'Geoffrey, if I can swing it towards you, do you think you can catch it?'

'I'll t-try,' Geoffrey whispered.

Dawson uncoiled the thick rope, pulled it back towards him and then pushed it forward. The momentum of the rope swing didn't reach the centre of the space and missed by a good two feet. Dawson grabbed the rope and tried again. Despite him putting all his strength behind it he was throwing something too light to gain motion. It was still a couple of feet shy before drifting back towards him.

'Shit,' Dawson said.

Stacey saw the fear growing in the kid's eyes.

'It's okay, Geoffrey,' Dawson reassured.

He glanced their way before he spoke. 'I've got another idea. I'll walk it over to you.'

'Kev, no,' Stacey cried.

'Dawson, don't be stupid,' Bryant said.

He raised a hand to quiet them.

'If I go slowly, walking the rope, I'll be able to feel the boards beneath me. If anything cracks, I'll jump back.'

'Kev, no,' Stacey protested again. He was going to purposely add weight to the fractured part of the floor. He had no way of knowing what beams had been weakened or how much weight they could take.

He met her gaze.

'I've gotta try it, Stace,' he said.

She shook her head even though she knew the kid was stressing the beam every second he stood there. It could snap at any second.

'Don't be a damn fool,' Bryant said.

'If you've got any other ideas, I'll give 'em a try,' Dawson said, removing his jacket and then his shoes.

Bryant said nothing but shook his head.

Dawson took a breath and grabbed the rope. He took a tentative step forward.

Nothing.

He took another.

Nothing.

A third and Stacey realised she was holding her breath.

He took a fourth step like someone heading towards the hole in the middle of the ice.

He took another.

A creak.

He was now a metre away. Two more steps.

'Kev…' she whispered.

He held up his hand to quiet her and concentrated as though walking a tightrope.

One more step.

A loud creak.

One more step.

The wood disintegrated beneath his feet.

Geoffrey grabbed the rope as the floorboards fell away beneath their feet.

Both she and Bryant reached forward.

'Stacey, back,' Bryant warned.

Dawson's actions had weakened the remaining floorboards even more. They were only safe if they stayed right on the edge. She couldn't reach him.

'Hold on, Geoffrey,' Dawson said, from above him as they both dangled from the bell rope. 'Do not let go,' he warned.

'O-okay,' Geoffrey stuttered.

'Right, I need your help to start swinging the rope, okay kid?' he said. 'Between the two of us we can get the rope swinging.'

'Okay,' Geoffrey said, bravely, even though Stacey could feel his terror.

'Right, I want us to aim for my colleague over there, and when we swing close enough he'll grab you, got it?'

Geoffrey nodded.

'And then on the next swing he'll grab me, all right?'

Dawson glanced towards Bryant to make sure he knew the plan.

Bryant met his gaze and nodded.

'Okay, Geoffrey, swing,' Dawson said.

They both started bucking on the rope at the same time, causing a slight back and forth motion.

'Okay, harder,' Dawson said.

Stacey followed the line of the rope to the roof with the beam of her torch.

Where the rope fed through the metal eye the fibres were worn and frayed.

Her heart jumped into her mouth.

'Kev, stop,' she breathed, glancing up.

He didn't follow her gaze because he already knew. He'd seen it.

'Swing, Geoffrey,' he repeated.

'Kev, no,'

She could see the fibres fraying before her eyes.

'Stop,' she said again.

Bryant followed her gaze. His face lost every drop of colour.

'Dawson, stop,' he cried, seeing the frayed rope.

'Swing, Geoffrey,' Dawson called out, building momentum.

He lifted his head and met Bryant's terrified gaze.

'Get ready to grab him.'

'Dawson, you gotta stop,' Bryant said, unable to keep the tremor from his voice.

'Get ready,' he repeated.

The next swing almost reached Bryant whose arms were stretched as far as he could reach.

Stacey's gaze returned to the rope. It was hanging by a few threads. The weight of both of them was weakening it by the second.

'This time,' Dawson said, giving one almighty swing.

The rope travelled further, and Bryant got hold of the kid's jacket and hauled him to safety.

The rope swung back to the other side of the space.

*Just one more, just one*, Stacey prayed as Dawson swung away from them. If the rope swung once more, they could grab him. Stacey stopped looking at the rope and looked only at her colleague and friend.

The rope slowed as it swayed at the other side.

Her eyes were locked on his.

He gave her one of his slow cocky smiles as he began to swing back towards her.

'Kev,' she said but the word was drowned out by the snapping of the rope as it finally gave way and he disappeared from view.

# CHAPTER 109

Kim sat in her office staring out at an empty squad room.

The service started in an hour, but she'd wanted to drop in at the station first. Had wanted to make sure that everything to do with the case had been squared away.

He deserved that.

Hannah Winters had been pronounced dead at the scene, as she had suspected. One act borne of jealousy twenty-five years earlier had ended and fractured countless lives in the present.

Graham Steele had been charged with the murder of Sadie Winters, Shaun Coffee-Todd, Joanna Wade, and the attempted murder of Christian Fellows. The charges for Lorraine's death were still being worked out, but further crimes would be added to the list that would keep the counsellor behind bars for the rest of his life.

Perversely, there was a sense of relief in Graham's understanding that he had not killed Lorraine Peters and her child. As yet he seemed not to have connected himself to the present murders, as though they were unimportant to him. His need for vengeance had eclipsed the irony that he was killing children purposely for being tricked into killing one accidentally. The hatred of Laurence had gnawed and festered over the years, spreading through him like a virus with each fresh nightmare or reminder of what he'd done. Sadie's poem had been the catalyst for it all. Her missing backpack had been found in the boot of his car and her diary in his bedside cabinet. Kim still struggled to picture the man lying in bed at night reading the most intimate and personal thoughts of the thirteen-year-old girl.

Laurence Winters left hospital and had been swiftly charged with the attempted murder of Lorraine Peters. He had retreated into silence and refused to answer any questions on the historic crime, even though Graham was telling the whole story. There would be DNA tests to prove or disprove Graham's account and Laurence's involvement, but Kim believed him.

Havers had been charged with the attempted murder of Geoffrey Piggott, after three students confirmed they had seen him exit the bell tower just an hour before sending Geoffrey up there with the key. It appeared that the Spades network operated on a risk versus reward basis. Contrary to his expectation, the Spades had not come rushing to his defence, either drawing the line at attempted murder or unwilling to risk their own reputations for a sports coach. Kim was reminded of the Russian dolls. It was the elite, within the elite, within the elite, and Havers was nowhere near the dolls at the centre.

Thorpe genuinely hadn't known that Havers had been keeping the Spades alive and had vowed to re-examine all suspicious accidents and ensure that any guilty parties were brought to justice. A lesser man would have run away from the place as quickly as possible, but Thorpe was determined to stand strong and rebuild the battered reputation of Heathcrest.

Once events had begun to sink in Saffie had refused to visit or speak to her father. Added to her own anger was the knowledge of his actions in the past, along with her mother's death. It would be some time before her life looked anything resembling normal again. Until it did she had chosen to remain at Heathcrest. Principal Thorpe had assured Kim that they would take good care of her, and she believed him.

The funeral of Joanna Wade had not been the sombre affair she had expected. Her colourful friends and younger brother had ensured that the service was a celebration of her life, not her death. Particularly poignant had been readings from students of both her old school and Heathcrest about what Joanna had meant to them. After the service Thorpe had revealed to her that Joanna had moved to Heathcrest for the substantial pay increase and benefits following her mother's move into a care home. Joanna's pension and death-in-service benefit would cover the bills there for quite a few years to come.

And so, she had read all the statements, filed all the papers, replied to all the emails.

And then she had sat and talked to an empty desk. A desk that still held his personal possessions because no one had yet found the courage to remove them.

She had pictured him sitting back in his chair, his tie loosened, his button opened and sporting a lazy smile. She imagined him rolling his eyes at Bryant when his older colleague was trying to give him some good advice.

She could visualise him winking at Stacey when needling her about her addiction to the *Warcraft* computer game. And her secret smile that told Kim she enjoyed it.

She pictured him tapping away on his computer with a fierce single-minded hunger in his eyes when he knew he was on to a lead.

She could see him walking the length of the office in high-heeled shoes on the back of a bet from Bryant. Which he'd won.

Hundreds of memories had played through her head as she'd stared at the space that had been his.

One memory had got hold of her and would not let her go. There was a time that they'd stood in the car park outside the station. She had laid into him verbally for disobeying a direct instruction not to use the press for a public appeal.

She had made no effort to hide the disappointment she had felt in him, and he had made no attempt to hide his regret and hurt at her disappointment. She knew her approval had been important to him. She'd known it then, and she'd known it in his recent appraisal.

The phone rang, startling her even though she'd been expecting the call.

'Car's ready, Marm,' Jack said, sombrely into her ear.

He couldn't see her nod as she replaced the receiver.

She pushed herself to a standing position and reached for the elbow crutches issued by the hospital.

She hopped her way through the office and paused at the desk nearest the door.

She placed a single sheet of paper in the centre. The recommendation for promotion, complete with her signature at the bottom.

'Yes, Kev,' she whispered. 'You were ready.'

Kim threw her crutches out of the car as the police officer jumped out to help her.

She waved him away.

Bryant had offered to pick her up from the station, but she'd refused. She hadn't wanted to be alone in the car with him. He would want to talk, and she did not.

She began the trek along the walkway she knew so well. Everyone she'd ever loved was here somewhere.

She stepped into the chapel and remained at the back. There was barely standing room left. The space was filled with family, friends and colleagues.

A constable she recognised stood and offered his seat. She shook her head and glanced around.

The minister was speaking of Dawson as though they'd been old friends, reliving anecdotes passed second-hand from family members. She tuned out. He hadn't known Dawson at all.

He didn't know the total contradiction that the man had been. How selfish he could be one minute and totally selfless the next. He had not known the sharp intelligence that had been evident to her. The instinct in him and his passion for sorting right from wrong.

He had not known Dawson's empathy for the disadvantaged or the passion with which he'd attacked his work. He had not known the protective instinct when anyone he cared about had been placed at risk.

He had not known the man that she had known.

The congregation stood to sing a hymn, obscuring his coffin from her view. She didn't want to picture him still and cold inside that box. It was bad enough that her last memory of him was his body broken and bloodied, smashed against the ground, his eyes staring up to the top of the bell tower. That picture would remain with her for ever.

She looked around the chapel as the mourners sang. Each person held a different part of the man in their hearts, all carried different memories from each stage of his life. His parents, school friends, colleagues.

Kim saw Dawson's fiancée at the front, supported by her mum and dad. His child, Charlotte, would now grow up without him by her side. Oh, how she wished she could gather up all these memories and give them to her, so she would one day know the man he had been. How he had matured from the selfish, pig-headed man she'd first met to the one who wanted promotion to give his family a better life.

She spied Woody sitting beside Bryant and Stacey.

She saw Stacey's back lift now and again with an uncontrollable sob.

She watched as Bryant's arm snaked around her shoulders.

She knew that the rest of her team needed her there, beside them. To share, to mourn. But there was a familiarity, a welcome affinity to the starkness inside her. She felt it and she knew it and it comforted her.

For as long as she could remember her mind had been formed of boxes. Every one contained something that had the power to hurt her, to reach the depths of her soul and break her apart.

There was a box building in her head, and her heart. She could feel its construction and she had to make a choice.

Go forward and join her team and share in their grief, help them understand the loss of their friend, feel their pain and share with them her own. It was what they needed her to do.

She took one last look at the photo of Detective Sergeant Kevin Dawson that stood on the coffin, before she turned and walked away.

Geoffrey Piggott wiped at his forehead with a handkerchief. The handkerchief of the man that had saved his life.

He still couldn't think of that night without the lump forming in his throat. At first, he hadn't been able to believe his eyes when the police officer had found him at the top of the tower. He had already convinced himself he was going to die, pictured himself falling and his bones smashing against the ground.

But Detective Sergeant Dawson had made him a promise and kept it.

He had cried for two days straight, wishing he could take it back, begging for the man who had been so nice to him not to die. And then he had started to focus only on the man's courage, his determination to get what he wanted.

The memory had driven him downstairs to his parents. He had told them that he wasn't academically gifted, no matter what they believed. He had told them he wanted a fresh start at his local school.

They had agreed.

Geoffrey knew the insults would be no different. The kids there would call him names too. But he now knew he was strong enough to take it.

If Detective Sergeant Kevin Dawson had managed to find the courage to make changes to his life and become the man *he* had, then Geoffrey owed it to him to do the exact same thing.

He no longer had sporting heroes, or athletic gods that he looked up to. He didn't fawn over rich, fickle reality stars or short-term pop stars. He had been lucky enough to know a real hero.

And that's what had brought him here, to make the first of many changes that would help him become the man he wanted to be.

'You coming in?' asked the female attendant, nodding towards the doors that led into the gym.

He took a breath, reached for his bag and followed her through.

# A LETTER FROM ANGELA

First of all, I want to say a huge thank you for choosing to read *Dying Truth*, the eighth instalment of the Kim Stone series.

For many years I've been intrigued by the idea of a cloistered environment at private schools along with the elite aspect of wealth, privilege, secret clubs and societies and how they can affect students chosen to join as well as those not chosen to join and how these bonds can affect club members in later life.

As I researched private schools I learned more about hazing (initiation) rites and pranks and the sinister turn they can take. I read widely of the documented deaths that have occurred from such traditions. The more I read the more I knew this needed to form part of the story I intended to write.

I also wanted the opportunity to bring Alexandra Thorne back, to explore the complicated subject of child sociopathy, and where better than a storyline built around a school.

I hope you enjoyed it.

If you did enjoy it, I would be for ever grateful if you'd write a review. I'd love to hear what you think, and it can also help other readers discover one of my books for the first time. Or maybe you can recommend it to your friends and family…

Thank you for joining me on this emotional journey.

I'd love to hear from you – so please get in touch on my Facebook or Goodreads page, twitter or through my website.

Thank you so much for your support, it is hugely appreciated.

Angela Marsons

      💻 www.angelamarsons-books.com

      f angelamarsonsauthor

      🐦 @WriteAngie

# ACKNOWLEDGEMENTS

As ever, my first acknowledgment must be to my partner, Julie, who lives most of her life wearing a pair of headphones. Yes, she could tell me to go to another room and leave her in peace, but she never does. She is ready to drop whatever she is doing the minute I exclaim, 'Jules, I need a meeting'. She understands my fears, insecurities, doubts, and lives it all right alongside me. I am thankful for her every single day.

Thank you to my mum and dad who continue to spread the word proudly to anyone who will listen. And to my sister Lyn, her husband Clive and my nephews Matthew and Christopher for their support too.

Thank you to Amanda and Steve Nicol who support us in so many ways and to Kyle Nicol for book spotting my books everywhere he goes.

I would like to thank the team at Bookouture for their continued enthusiasm for Kim Stone and her stories. In particular, the incredible Keshini Naidoo who never tires in her encouragement and passion for what we do. To Oliver Rhodes who gave Kim Stone an opportunity to exist. To Kim Nash (Mama Bear) who works tirelessly to promote our books and protect us from the world. To Noelle Holten who has limitless enthusiasm and passion for our work.

A massive thank you to Mr Shaun Coffee-Todd who won the bid to have his name in this book. Shaun, your generosity towards the Grenfell Victims Fund was amazing and truly appreciated.

Thank you to the fantastic Kim Slater who has been an incredible support and friend to me for many years now and to the fabulous Caroline Mitchell, Renita D'Silva and Sue Watson without whom this journey would be impossible. Huge thanks to the growing family of Bookouture authors who continue to amuse, encourage and inspire me on a daily basis.

My eternal gratitude goes to all the wonderful bloggers and reviewers who have taken the time to get to know Kim Stone and follow her story. These wonderful people shout loudly and share generously not because it is their job but because it is their passion. I will never tire of thanking this community for their support of both myself and my books. Thank you all so much.

Massive thanks to all my fabulous readers, especially the ones that have taken time out of their busy day to visit me on my website, Facebook page, Goodreads or Twitter.